KIRIN RISE

To Natalia,

Always B U.

To Natalia,

Rise like Kirin.

KIRIN RISE
THE CAST OF SHADOWS

ED CRUZ
ILLUSTRATED BY RON LANGTIW

authorHOUSE®

AuthorHouse™ LLC
1663 Liberty Drive
Bloomington, IN 47403
www.authorhouse.com
Phone: 1-800-839-8640

Published by AuthorHouse   08/13/2014

ISBN: 978-1-4969-2964-8 (sc)
ISBN: 978-1-4969-2966-2 (hc)
ISBN: 978-1-4969-2965-5 (e)

Library of Congress Control Number: 2014913572

PREFACE

Ego and greed have been man's shortcomings since the dawn of civilization. Rarely have these vices been more prevalent than in the United States. At the end of the twentieth century, this once-great country stood at the forefronts of industry and military might. Resilient through generations, it finally succumbed to its ills. Government corruption and corporate greed ran rampant while society had achieved the ultimate state of apathy. All of this overwhelmed the country, destroying it from within.

The economic collapse in the early twenty-first century created an embittering gap between the upper and lower classes. The middle class was all but eliminated as masses of society lived in dire circumstances. Those hardest hit sought ways to escape their world and ease their situations.

Rising from society's woes was the United Federation of Mixed Fighting (UFMF). It exploded in popularity and absorbed the fan bases of all major sports. In a mere twenty years, the UFMF dominated the entertainment scene in the United States. It franchised its way into every aspect of society and helped to bring the world of the Roman gladiators back into current times. Society had lost its humanity, but no one examined the chaos to ask, "How did we allow this to happen?"

Each season of the league runs for six months as brutality and carnage replace sportsmanship and teamwork. Each fighter fiercely tries to gain the attention of sponsors, peppering each match with added brutality to score extra points. At year's end, those who qualify are invited to the main event known as the DOME. It is the most popular and inhumane "sporting" event in the modern era. The DOME is the ultimate test of skill and endurance, a single round robin tournament of blood and destruction that will leave one standing as victor. Corporations invest heavily in their fighters, greedy men gamble their souls, and the masses gather religiously to watch this weekend event.

Martial arts are an afterthought as the laws governing the country force regulation upon the schools. Expensive franchise tags and unjust sanctions created by the government–and influenced by the deep pockets of the UFMF–have blanketed the country. The majority of martial arts schools have been eliminated, forcing a handful of schools to exist in secrecy. These few bastions of ancient arts ignore the laws and sanctions and defy the will of the UFMF.

In truth, all it takes is one: one person, one voice, one single action to rattle the cages around us. The strength of this dominating machine will soon be put to the test.

Our special thanks to all those who supported our project from the very start. Thanks to my parents for setting my foundation, my Sifu for teaching me to find my own way, my students for inspiring me to share my knowledge, and my family for dealing with my crap.

Colin Adair

Mario and Cora Afable

Vicky Akelian

Carol Ali

William L. Allen

Alphonse Arias

Ray Arias

Val Arias

Nicholas Aaron Van Asma

Christina

Ed Barksdale

Crystal Barnes

L.F. Bartley

Vincent Bonnot

Nathaniel Brengle

Daniel Browne

Lorrie Buenrostro

Ryan Carandang

Nancy Carlsen

Anthony Cedeno

Jason Chappell

Hyann Chin

Jessica Grace Coleman

Michael Coronado

Melvin Cragged

Lenora Cravens

J.R. Dadivas

Eric Dao

Audrey de la Cruz

Danny de la Cruz

Dina de la Cruz

Flor de la Cruz

Jay de la Cruz

Luming de la Cruz

Papa Win de la Cruz

Romeo Confessor Dizon

Neuret Eddy

Tyler Elston

Andrew Feaster

Dannette Ford

Matthew Fong

Tayssir John Gabbour

Ken Gagne

Cid Galicia

David Gans

Liza Garcia

Susan Garcia

Oscar & Lolit Gramata

Zach Gilmore

Luke Goddard

Galo Gutierrez

Guilermo Guzman

Danish Haque

Sarah Hayden

Bobby Hayes

Harlan Heiber

Jared T. Hooper

Jan Ignacio

Dominick Izzo

Mary Jack

Jessica Jarrett

Newton Kwan

Justin Lee

Robert Lee

Karen Lim

Henrik Lindhe

Enrico Luna

Christopolis Tiberius Markus

Jane Martinez

Tom McGovern

Tony A. Mendoza

Josiah Michaels

Emmanuel Moreno

Andrew Movsovich

Candy Mozqueda

Kristina Murdaug

Danny Negron

Virgilio & Rowena Nicolas

Francis Nguyen

Marc Noel

Michelle O'Connor

Don Olympics

Cory Osborn

Jenny Ostrowski

Snacky Pete

Rejane Pierre

Matt Pohl MSP Games, LLC

Dave Polkoszek

Renee Pollock

Phillip Pooler

Alan Prentice

Marian Proszowski

Michael Pryor

Natasha Rac

Serena Lessin Repsold

Calvin L Roberts Sr.

Trina Roberts

Melissa Garcia Robinson

Diana Rocuant

Margie Rodriguez

John Roiniotis

David Rosen

Michael De Ruyter

Jason Saladin

Luis R. Santiago Jr.

Jaeeun Shin

Medy Silva

Wayne Silverman

Dicko Mas Soebekti

David Thompson

Josh Tomilnson

Long Tran

Heather Jenelle Ulangca

Antonina Vasilishina

Kyle Voisine

Tj Wallace

Ken Weingart

April Welch

Dani White

Susanne Wolf

Robert Wong

Calvin Woo

George Woo

David L. Wood

Devin M. Wood

Philip Xavier

Wa-ie Younka

Zi Yuan

Khine Zin

Character Information

Name: Kirin Rise–Korean name (Park Soo-Jin/박수진)
Born: Nov 4, 2012 (Age 19) Pyongyang, North Korea
Family: Adopted parents - Kevin and Diane Rise, Step Brothers - Jim, Steven, Mark, and Kyle
Profession: Photographer
Pet: Bacon (Male Bulldog)
Interests: Wing Chun Gung Fu and doodling
Best Friends: Gwen and Sage
Tidbits: Allergic to carbonated drinks and is addicted to coffee. She never swears, and she definitely can't dance. She is electronically handicapped.

Name: Sifu (Mr. Kwan)
Born: May 16, 1970 (Age 62)
Family: Wife–Megumi, three kids: Hana, Akira, and Hideo
Profession: Wing Chun Teacher
Interests: Wing Chun Gung Fu
Best Friends: His wooden dummy
Tidbits: Hates driving, flying, and water. Dabbles with card tricks to amuse the kids. He learned how to speak Japanese from his wife. He is a huge anime fan. For some reason he always wears a fanny pack.

Name: Tobias Jackson
Born: June 10, 2005 (Age 26)
Family: Mother, Father, older brother
Profession: Custom motorcycle designer
Pet: Siamese Fighting Fish
Interests: Wing Chun Gung Fu and cooking
Tidbits: Loves to draw and cooks. Karma is the name of his motorcycle. He's never had a girlfriend longer then 6 months. Favorite snack is ice cream in between two slices of bread.

Name: Sage Parker
Family: Mother, Father, little brother–Cage
Profession: Full-time student, studying biochemistry
Interests: Movie buff
Best Friends: Gwen and Kirin
Pet: Scrambles (Hamster)
Tidbits: Speaks 7 languages (English, French, Japanese, Khmer, Chinese-Mandarin, Korean, German), plays the violin. Loves playing the video game King of the Kage. Secretly, he is a really good dancer. He's a late night person, who seems like he never sleeps.

Name: Gwen Albright
Family: Mother and Father, only child
Profession: Part-time Student and computer consultant
Interests: Fashion and computers
Best Friends: Kirin and Sage
Tidbits: Loves watching reality TV. She can hack anything as she finds the challenge mentally stimulating. She's a very picky eater. Gwen hates when her friends call her up for tech support.

Name: Hunter M. Young
Family: Father and little sister named Bella
Profession: Full-time college student
Interests: Photography and sports
Tidbits: Loves wrestling and is very athletic. He is a huge fan of pro wresting. A Mac N' Cheese fanatic as he tries to perfect the ultimate recipe for it. Only sings when in the shower or alone in the car. His crush on Kirin was at first sight.

Name: Jacob H. Thorne
Family: Mother, Father, 3 older sisters
Profession: President of the UFMF
Interests: Chess, history buff
Tidbits: He became a falconry enthusiast, due to his fear of heights. Everything he ever does is over the top. He is an avid book reader and knows how to speed read. He is a huge Sherlock Holmes fan. He speaks 6 languages (English, Chinese-Mandarin, Italian, Japanese, French, Russian). He also has a photographic memory.

Name: H.T. Fawn
Family: Mother unknown, raised by two fathers
Profession: Thorne's PR man
Interests: Loves classic kids nursery rhyme stories
Best Friends: Ms. Yum Yum (Female Cat)
Tidbits: Deaf in left ear from a school yard incident. He is a fashion diva. He's never beaten Thorne in a chess match, but on occasion he can get Thorne to play a game of Risk. He has a large collection of knives.

Name: Diesel 'The Wall' Williams
Family: Wife and three kids
Profession: #1 UFMF contender for 2032
Interests: Does God's work and preaches occasionally at his church
Tidbits: He's been on the street since he was a teenager. He's the only one of seven siblings that was able to make something of himself. He frequents strip clubs when he's away on fights.

CHAPTER 1
My Name Is...

Déjà vu. The third match of the night ended the way the crowd had expected: in a blood bath. The crowd remained unsettled, their uneasiness due to the anticipation of the unanswered question, "What was the final score?" It wasn't enough just to win a fight; you had to do it in style.

The last contestant did not fare well. He lay limp and covered with blood in the ring. A single medical staffer and his assistant were in the ring examining him, but little effort was placed on his overall well-being. The staffer's main concern was to evaluate the severity of damage and send it to the judges for final calculations. His assistant's job was to drag the fighter from the ring so they could continue on with the next match.

After several minutes of examining the fighter, the staffer entered some numbers on his tablet and motioned to his assistant. With little empathy, the single assistant dragged the fighter from the ring like a sack of potatoes. He seemed annoyed at his duties, appearing to lay blame on the fighter for his circumstance. At once, several attendants rushed in diligently to clean the ring for the next match. More care was given to the inanimate object than to the human life.

The crowd grew weary waiting for the final score to flash above. Many anticipated how many credits would be exchanged between their wins and losses. The public had grown accustomed to such brutality and lost sight of what was important. They were more concerned with their pockets and less so with the fighters' life.

The score flashed brightly above the ring, illuminating the eyes of the spectators like fireworks. A wave of reaction spread throughout the arena. High-fives were flying and crowds cheering, while others realized how much they had lost. Mixed emotions filled the stands within seconds.

Meanwhile, the fighter had served his purpose and was discarded on the street like trash. The action demonstrated to the masses that their worth was close to nothing. This kept them subdued and manageable, while remaining unaware of the meaning of such actions. Compassion for one's fellow citizen had disappeared over the past decades.

The first Saturday of every month, the uninitiated got a chance to fight the big boys. The locals appropriately named this event "Chum Night" because those foolish enough to sign the waiver ended up as shark bait. Once they were tossed into the ring against the professionals, they were eaten alive. The pros showed no mercy and were happy to collect their paycheck from their prey.

The local people cared little for the well-being of the uninitiated, entertained by the slaughter fest, drinking in excess, and gambling beyond their means—all perfect distractions from reality.

Chum Night had come a long way from its illegal past, no longer confined to the shadowy basements of rundown buildings and crime-run enterprises. With everyone hit by hard times, they saw their opportunity and became a legitimate, thriving event. People needed to be entertained, and the United Federation of Mixed Fighting (UFMF) season was still a good five months away. While this was looked upon as a preliminary event, that did not stop it from being standing-room only.

It was a typical night with a lineup card of six fighters. Each fighter had his own reason for getting into the ring. The romantic belief of hopes and dreams being fulfilled was an easier sell for the motivation behind the madness. The truth was, and had always been, that money was what fueled their fire, especially during these times.

The fighters knew the odds were heavily stacked against them, but foolish hope made everyone believe that he could be the one. Tough times harbor desperation, and there was never a shortage of fighters to fill those slots. If it was not for the money, why would anyone be foolish enough to risk everything?

The rules were simple: just survive three rounds, and you took home a year's worth of pay. It was an irresistible temptation. Since Chum Night began, there had been a handful that came close to achieving this dream, but all had fallen short of the goal. The ones who were put into the hospitals and

3

later walked away were considered lucky. The majority were left broken and scarred, their lives becoming far worse. Chum Night was designed for one thing: to suck in the foolish and spit out the remains.

The fourth match was about to begin. The ring was already stained with blood, sweat, and the remnants of dreams.

For Mr. Linkwater, working Chum Night was more of a punishment. He had been demoted to the ranks of local broadcasting and longed for the days when he had mattered. Even in the sewers of the network hierarchy, he had dodged enough bullets and survived long enough to have some seniority. The American Way had become winning by default. He stared at his watch and thought, *Three more matches to go.* His evening plans involved being alone at home with his bottle.

Linkwater turned to his partner and struggled to whisper in his deep, harsh voice, "I hope they end the next three jerks quickly."

Linkwater took a sip of his drink, disguised as water but laced heavily with liquor. Like most, he covered his pains well with alcohol.

When Connor, his sidekick commentator, didn't respond, Linkwater muttered, "Do you know what I enjoy most about Chum Night?"

Connor made a half-assed attempt, "Let me guess, is it the cheap-looking ring girls?"

Linkwater, with a devilish look, said, "Oh, no ... it's much better than that, my friend."

Connor, looking somewhat annoyed, leaned away slightly to get out of the range of Linkwater's breath.

"I love the look of hope in the eyes of the competitors," said Linkwater. He laughed and continued, "They're so stupid to believe they have a chance of winning."

Connor stared at Linkwater, letting him rant further. Several minutes of uneventful jabbering finally ended. Linkwater got what he wanted off his chest. He took another sip and emptied his drink, crushing his can afterwards much like his dreams.

Connor shook his head. "You are one bitter dude."

Linkwater added, "What's even more entertaining is watching the family pick up the pieces. Now it's not just one crushed dream, but an entire f–ing flock. You see, Connor, that's the beauty of entertainment." He raised his hands, looking for approval.

Connor had heard enough. "Who's next on the draw?" Connor asked, making it look like his focus was on the job at hand.

Adjusting his glasses, Linkwater squinted at the match list. Linkwater asked, "Connor, I can't quite make out the next contestant's name. What's it say?"

Meanwhile, inside the Arena

The fighter sat inside a dingy, dark, and questionably sanitary dressing room, listening as a knock pounded from the outside of the door. A hoarse voice pierced the silence, "Hey kid, you're up! You got five minutes."

The request was ignored, as the fighter stared down at both hands shaking uncontrollably. To stop the shaking, the challenger pressed both hands against the counter and gripped it firmly. Sweat formed, creating an outline on the table. The fighter then took a moment to close both eyes and slowly inhaled one large breath. The roar of the crowd chanting for the next match to begin caused the walls to vibrate vigorously–a constant reminder of what was at stake.

In and out. In and out. Nice and slow through the nose. Let every breath in and every breath out, the fighter thought. The words had been echoed so often during the years of training that it was almost haunting. *This is how to deal with the fear and to quiet the mind. Control your focus. The outcome isn't important; focus on the process.* The fighter stared endlessly at the table, recalling lessons of the past.

The fighter was fixated on the goal: *Focus on one thing; focus on a single thought.* Breathing was the focal point, and nothing else mattered. It had come to the most natural and basic instincts. The fighter was waiting for that moment of control. The sound of the crowd began to slowly fade away, and not a single noise penetrated the fighter's concentration.

The only sound disrupting the silence of the room was the fighter's even breathing. Minutes turned to seconds, and eventually time stood still.

Finally ... the mind was empty.

The fighter slowly looked up into the mirror, took one last breath, and whispered, "Target, center, own it!"

Minutes Later

The crowd's restlessness grew. They demanded more. The announcer checked the time and began his stroll to the ring. With every step, the excitement grew—it was time. He stood in the center of the ring and waved to the crowd to settle down, trying to create the calm before the storm. He raised a tablet to read his lines, but did not speak, heightening the anticipation. Suddenly his deep commanding voice broke the silence, capturing the attention of the masses as he shouted, "Our next contestant ... from parts unknown, weighing in at one hundred five pounds?" He paused, a single eyebrow lifted, as he stared closer at the screen. Dumbfounded by that number, he quickly turned to the side of the ring, silently asking if the information was correct or if there had been a technical error. A quick scramble from his side assistant, followed by an uneasy wait for confirmation, led to beads of sweat dripping down his face. Finally, the ring assistant signaled a thumbs up and that it was okay to continue.

He shook it off and got back into character. "Again, at one hundred five pounds, style unknown, the fighter known as ... BLINK!" An over-dramatic introduction followed by an accentuated finger point had everyone staring toward the entrance at the far side of the arena.

Everything about the introduction was awkward—from a comical name like Blink to announcing an unknown style. These days all martial arts were integrated to a mixed style. There was no such thing as being a specialist in one particular art. The years had proven that, to win in the ring, you had to be a jack of all trades.

The crowd laughed, snickered, and drank. Many were asking, "What the hell is a *Blink?*" as chatter continued to run throughout the arena. One particularly glass-eyed man muttered, "Blink ... that'll be how quick the fight's over," before downing the rest of his drink. Those nearby laughed uproariously, and the lame joke spread among the drunk patrons.

The spotlight beamed toward an entrance where no one stood. Everyone wondered if this was a case of the fighter having second thoughts and chickening out. It wasn't unusual for that to happen, and most draws had several fighters waiting in the wing if that occurred.

#

In the darkness just before the light, Blink stood alone and could see the commotion out in front. A focal point was needed to get things moving, and Blink decided to make the ring the goal. One final deep breath, followed by a slow exhale, and Blink took the first step toward the ring.

The crowd murmured as the slight figure appeared in the light. At first glance, one would think a child got lost and walked into the wrong area. Blink stood in the spotlight with a hooded robe, appearing lost, as the fighter's hands came up to form a shield against the light. It cast an eerie shadow from behind.

Normally at this moment, music would be pumping into the arena, but Blink chose otherwise. Not a single beat was played. The crowd did not appreciate this underwhelming introduction. Seasoned vets and even the uninitiated made it their duty to create an engaging entrance to entertain the crowd. It was an homage, a sign that they were there to entertain.

Boos and curses echoed throughout the arena. The crowd hurled small foreign objects in the fighter's direction, as they felt they were being robbed and disrespected. As Blink walked toward the ring, the oversized hood kept Blink's face hidden from the crowd. The fighter saw nothing but one foot going in front of the other.

The crowd was vicious as they began mocking the size of the fighter.

"Holy shit, it's a f—ing midget!"

"I can't wait to see you get your ass kicked."

"I betcha this dumb ass fights just like a girl."

Meanwhile Connor and Linkwater

To say the fighter was small in stature would be an understatement. Connor caught a glimpse from a distance and grimaced, "Oh crap, it's a GP." GPs were human guinea pigs that fight promoters hand selected. They were picked specifically because of their size and their lack of fighting skill. Selecting GPs was like tossing a mouse into a pen with an anaconda. It was cruel and malicious, but worthy of the current standard of solid entertainment.

Connor shook his head with a flash of human compassion.

Linkwater took a peek and showed a general lack of empathy as he decided to have another drink. He added with his speech slightly slurred, "Good, this should be over soon."

The fighter entered the ring unescorted, with no manager or even an assistant within sight. Everything Blink did was out of the norm. The crowd, puzzled by such actions, continued to boo even louder.

Linkwater tapped Connor on the shoulder and joked, "They better not ask me to carry this schmuck out of the ring. He's gonna get pulverized."

Most fighters danced around to calm the nerves before a match. Upon entering the ring and finding a spot, Blink stood there, feet shoulder-width apart, slightly pigeoned toed, and motionless. Still covered with the hood, Blink shrouded the moment in mystery.

Linkwater remarked, "Uh, is he awake?"

The announcer watched and then murmured, "Freak," shaking his head. The announcer clenched his fist and bellowed, "Our next contestant, known throughout the lands for his destruction, hailing from the Bronx, New York, weighing in at two hundred thirty-five pounds of solid muscle—he is ... DJ the Deeestroooyeeer!"

The crowd went wild at the announcement of a fan favorite. Almost hypnotized, they chanted his name as they waited for him to enter the arena.

Connor nudged Linkwater and said, "Normally, I couldn't care less who fights—but, man, this guy is gonna be massacred."

Connor paused and added, "I really hate it when they do this."

Linkwater was callous. "I don't give two shits about who fights! You'd think the network could supply us with some umbrellas, 'cause this is gonna be a blood bath."

Conner looked away, disgusted by Linkwater's last comments.

Unlike Blink, DJ knew how to work the crowd into a frenzy, pushing the limits to the brink of rioting. DJ strutted toward the ring with his entire entourage surrounding him. It looked like a circus had come to town, as midgets passed out beads, threw confetti in the air, and tumbled down the aisle. Several drop dead gorgeous women with healthy chests escorted DJ, and an oddly dressed gentleman walked on stilts, towering over everyone.

The blaring music was nearly deafening and combined with the cheers of the crowd to make the entire gym tremble. DJ grabbed onto the ropes of the ring and shook them violently. His eyes looked possessed, as he leaned back, flexed his muscles, and roared. It was a signal to the crowd to prepare for what came next. DJ jumped into the ring, soaring over the ropes. When he landed, the crowd jumped in unison, simulating an earthquake. Every cool fighter had his signature trademark entrance, and that was called the *DJ Stomp*. The crowd roared with enthusiasm, energized by his introduction.

DJ settled into the corner after several minutes of goofing around in the ring. Throughout it all, Blink remained oblivious to all the commotion. There the fighter stood in the same spot, in the same position, seemingly lifeless.

The referee gestured for both fighters to approach the center of the ring. As they stood face to face, the differential in stature was overwhelming. DJ towered over Blink, like a man about to fight a child. The referee explained the rules, which were kept to a minimum.

For the challenger, there was only one rule to remember: survive.

DJ was swaying his head back and forth like a crazed man, trying to draw a stare from his opponent, but Blink ignored him. As the referee was going over the final instructions, Blink grabbed hold of the robe and threw it to the corner, where it floated gently to the ground.

The crowd gasped, stunned to see the unexpected figure under the robe: an Asian girl, beautiful with her hair tied up in a ponytail. Her features were soft and gentle, the kind that any guy would want in a girlfriend.

Considering her appearance, she had no business being here. Blink looked even tinier without the robe. Did she realize this was a fighting tournament and not a ballerina contest? Everyone in the arena was thinking the same thing: this was going to be a massacre.

Linkwater leered and murmured, "Well, well, well, what have we here?"

It was not unusual to have female fighters attempt open tournaments. Some fared well due to the luck of the draw. Most of them endured the rude jeers of the crowd, but the truth was, size did matter in the UFMF. Of course, Chum Night did not discriminate based on shape, size, or sex. In the end, no challenger had ever won regardless of gender.

But something was different about Blink. It was one thing to be a small guy, but she was a petite girl. Normally, odds of slim-to-none were favorable, but considering the type of brawler she was going against, she had absolutely zero chance. On paper, she was at a massive handicap. DJ was a veteran of the ring with a resume of considerable carnage. Blink, on the other hand, appeared to be entering her first fight. This match seemed to be over before it even began.

Ignoring further instruction from the referee, DJ quipped, "You're a cute one. What do you say you and me get together after this? I'll take it easy on you. I don't want to ruin that pretty little face."

Blink lifted her eyes as DJ waited for a response. She slowly raised her hand with a gesture that did not symbolize a yes. The crowd saw her rude gesture and started laughing.

Embarrassed and angry, DJ pointed directly at her face. "Okay, bitch! You think you're funny? I'm gonna tear you apart like there's no tomorrow. You'll wish you'd taken my offer." He turned his back with an evil grin on his face and stomped back toward his corner.

This was David versus Goliath, but this underdog story would not have a happy ending.

Moments later, the bell rang and the referee shouted, "Fight!"

DJ waved to the crowd, seeking their approval. They cheered, and he pounded his chest with each fist and let out a roar.

Blink casually walked halfway to the center of the ring. Then she stood motionless with her head slightly tilted, almost as if she were sleepwalking. No guard. No stance. She stood there with her hands down, not reacting to the imminent danger that was at hand, but watching DJ's every move.

Linkwater turned to Connor and said, "Maybe someone should tell her the fight started."

DJ decided to show off, chaining a series of aerial kicks to demonstrate his physical skill. He was bobbing and weaving well out of her range, trying to absorb the energy of the crowd's cheers. They were loving every minute of it because this was what they paid for. This was entertainment.

He made it clear that it was by his will that she was still standing. He would quickly end this fight, when he decided it was time.

Finally, after showboating for over a minute to milk every ounce from the crowd, DJ shouted, "Time to die!"

DJ turned toward Blink and rushed like a wild bull. Some were glued to their seats to see the onslaught, while others looked away, unwilling to see the gory outcome. Then, with two quick steps, he finally moved into Blink's range.

Once he entered her area, everything changed! A stampede was about to occur, and Blink was on the receiving end of DJ's fury.

It was like a signal went off in her head saying, *Attack!* This tiny, docile little girl moved in against this hulking figure. Even with his mass moving at full steam, Blink met him without hesitation. She did not duck and cover. Instead, she did something the crowd never expected.

It was a sight to see, so unusual that the crowd was somewhat dumbfounded by her fighting style. There was no set guard. She was square to her opponent, and her center remained steady and even with each step. It looked as if she were floating in to close the gap.

"What is she doing?" was echoed by hundreds of people watching the match.

The sweet and innocent look was gone. Death was in her eyes. She showed no fear as DJ rushed her. Her focus was on his center; nothing else mattered. The distance between the two closed rapidly.

Wham!

Blink waited till the last second, leaving DJ no time to react. The timing was pure perfection. DJ planted his foot and stepped in as she launched a single punch. Two forces collided in perfect harmony: her fist, his face. With that blow, his eyes rolled back, his head snapped upon impact, and he crumpled to the ground.

Thud!

Watching a human body go limp and crash to the ground was a horrific sight. It meant total loss of control. DJ lay motionless, unconscious from the hit.

Silence fell upon the entire arena.

It was not the reaction one would expect for a Saturday night brawl. The local beer-guzzling patrons had just witnessed something they had never seen before. Everyone was stunned, doubting their own eyes. Had fantasy just become reality?

This was no ordinary knockout.

What had started off as a low-card draw became a viral event moments later. Those fortunate enough to record the match played it back on their phones and other recording devices, wondering what had just happened. Others immediately texted and uploaded the footage on various social networks, spreading proof that this was no dream.

Linkwater and Connor were both speechless, sitting dazed and confused by the event that had just transpired. They slowly turned to one another, realizing that dead silent commentary was bad for the ratings. Fumbling for the right words, they stuttered, adding further to the chaos.

Moments later, flashes exploded like fireworks throughout the arena. Then the murmuring started.

"What the hell just happened?"

"Holy shit, did you see that?"

"Anyone know the name of that fighter?"

"What style was that?"

"It looked like she barely hit him, but he's out cold!"

More questions than answers filled the room with tension, to the point where it was going to explode. The crowd chanted, demanding a replay on the big screen. Moments later, the screen at the top of the ring began replaying the knockout. People stared vacantly, still having a difficult time believing in the impossible.

Blink stood there emotionless at the outcome as DJ lay sprawled out in the ring. She did not celebrate like others do when they harm another human being; instead, she signaled to the medics that they were needed. Since he was a Pro, they rushed in to make sure of his health, in a stark contrast to their lack of concern for the uninitiated challengers.

Through the chaos, the ring announcer grabbed hold of Blink by the arm. The announcer was excited, feeding off the frenzy of the crowd as he asked, "Do you have any words to say to the crowd?" His voice crackled like a teenager's.

She held the mic and stared at it for a second. Finally, she looked up and scanned the arena, making general eye contact with the crowd. They were strangely quiet, waiting to see what she had to say. Taking a moment to gather her thoughts, she yelled, "My name is Kirin!" She paused, allowing everyone a moment to absorb it.

"This!" She pounded her fist to her chest. "Is Wing Chun Gung Fu!"

Kirin looked at DJ, who was still being cared for by the assistants. She threw the microphone toward him and uttered, "Initiated," before making her way out of the ring.

The announcer shouted to her, "Hey kid, you forgot your winnings!" Then he handed her a cool 25,000 credits.

Kirin took the credits and stared at them for several seconds. She held them in her hand and wondered, *So this is what every fighter dreams of, risking everything ... just for money.*

She looked at the announcer, who smiled, hoping she would reciprocate. Instead, Kirin turned away and walked to the edge of the ring. She paused for a moment, looking at the money. Then, as hard as she could, she threw all the credits into the crowd.

She made it rain.

It was pandemonium. People were still recovering from witnessing the fight, and now credits were flying everywhere, adding fuel to the fire. The crowd went crazy as people scrambled on their hands and knees, trying to pick up whatever credits they could. Those who were not distracted by the money started chanting in a hypnotic rhythm, "Kirin! Kirin! Kirin!"

Kirin started strolling back to the locker room. Things were going to be different now. Unlike her entrance, where she had been an unknown, the walk back was much more difficult. The commotion of the crowd was growing exponentially as security did their best to keep them from her. The sound was deafening, causing the entire arena to shake, as people were pushing and shoving just to get a better glimpse of her.

Throughout the mad frenzy, everything appeared to be moving in slow motion for Kirin. Even the noise of the crowd could not penetrate her focus, as she heard only her heart beating. Kirin was still in fight mode. Almost dazed by what had just transpired, she finally saw the sea of onlookers before her. As she stared into the crowd, for a brief moment, she thought she saw a familiar face. She shook her head, snapping her out of fight mode. *Am I dreaming?* she thought. She leaned forward and searched for that face, but could not find it amongst the masses. *What just happened?*

After that night, nothing would be the same. Kirin had known even before the match that this was her opportunity to throw a pebble in the water, her ripple within the giant ocean. In a single moment, with a single punch, she had changed the course of human history forever, and there was no going back.

> *"Don't fear trying, don't fear failing, but most of all, fear not living." –Sifu*

Short Stories #1–Kirin's P.O.V.

Eight Years Prior: March 23, 2024

<u>I'm In–Day 1</u>

I remember the first day of class as if it were yesterday. Back in those days, the school was still open to the public. It was small and quaint, nestled in a shaded corner, hidden amongst the larger commercial buildings located in Chicago.

One would never realize that right under one's nose was the finest martial arts establishment. The frills of the large belt factories, the pressed uniforms, the high tech equipment, and the logo apparel were not for sale here.

This was the essence of Gung Fu.

The art had remained pure and untainted, marketed mainly through the whisperings of those whose lives had been changed. That was how Sifu liked it; he preferred to be discreet, unnoticed by the masses. A handful of flyers in his early days was the most effort he ever put into attracting students. His doors were always open, giving everybody the opportunity to learn.

Sifu's skill was well-known and respected throughout the country. I later found out that, in his youth, he had created a resume of destruction.

With a Sifu of his reputation and skill, one would think the school would be overflowing with students. However, there were never more than a handful. It was not the physical demands that weeded people out, but their mental fortitude. Society had grown impatient and demanded instant results.

It was one thing to say, "I want to learn Gung Fu!"

It was another to pay the high price that comes with perfecting such a skill. That price has nothing to do with money.

We were fortunate that Sifu never sold out. I'm sure temptation was there, as the skill to fight had become a valuable commodity. Tough times forced humanity back to its natural instinct to survive. The poor who were the hardest hit were forced into underground fighting. It had become a lucrative business and a promise of a better life.

Humankind is good at exploitation. Around every corner, greedy used car salesmen disguised themselves as Masters. Belts and trophies lured students, with the promise of skill, but the main goal of these so-called "Masters" was to maximize profits. Those places were a dime a dozen as they constantly tried to make a buck and churn out their next black belt. In those days, they were more common than your local buzz bar. Looking back, it's hard to imagine that those were considered the good times.

I'm not sure what drew me to martial arts; maybe it was because all four of my stepbrothers did it. Then again, you always want what you can't have. Due to my past, my stepmom felt it was best that I stayed away from anything that involved violence. I would always hear her say, "You're my only daughter. Try to act like one." So, if I was going to learn martial arts, I needed to do it secretly.

In the early spring of 2024, I began my search. I spent several Saturdays looking for a school. I quickly found out that the flashier places had little to offer. Their main sell was the promise of being able to fight right away. Even with my lack of knowledge, I always thought there was so much more than just fighting. As I kept searching for the right school, every one I checked out seemed like carbon copies. Finding variety became a difficult task, since the UFMF began franchising. I wasn't quite sure what I was looking for, but I knew I hadn't found it.

In a way, I discovered Sifu's school by sheer dumb luck. One day when I was walking around the neighborhood, I found one of Sifu's aged flyers hanging on the wall. I found it odd that someone would use this archaic marketing method in this age of technology.

I read the flyer; it was simple and straight to the point, but most importantly it offered one free lesson. The address was only a few blocks from where I stood, and I still had a few hours to spare before heading home. I decided to take a chance, as I tore it from the wall.

Five minutes later, I finally found the school. Outside the door, I saw a sign that said, "Wing Chun Gung Fu." The name alone was different from everywhere else I had checked out. Gung Fu was foreign to me, since most places taught a mixed variety of martial arts. I thought for a second, *Shouldn't it be Kung Fu?*

I took a huge breath and decided to walk in. Looking around, I noticed there were no school uniforms, belts, or trophies. Four dingy walls created the rectangular school. A few Chinese writings, several large mirrors, and a handful of pictures made up the decor.

Inside the school, students of all shapes and sizes gathered, some in jeans, others in sweats, and a few looking like they'd just came from work.

The first thing I asked when I got in was whether I should remove my shoes. To this day, the guys still razz me for asking that, but my knowledge of martial arts was limited to the movies and the Internet. It could have been worse; I could have asked them if we were gonna break some boards. One of the students kindly explained that you train in your everyday clothes because the chances of you being attacked without shoes is pretty slim.

I noticed another guy, probably in his late high school years, waiting impatiently in the corner for the class to begin. He looked as lost as I felt. Surprisingly, I made the first attempt at sparking a conversation and did not allow my shyness to get the best of me.

I spoke in a quiet voice, "Hi, uh ... my name is Kirin. Is this your first day in class?"

He introduced himself as Joe and was quick to respond. "Yup!"

I was hoping that Joe would throw more of a bone into the conversation, but then I tried to dig in further. "So, have you taken anything before?"

Joe replied, "Yeah, I took some JKD several years ago, but took a break. It's pretty much the same thing as Wing Chun."

I had no idea what JKD was, but I said, "That's cool. You could probably help me out since you know what you're doing."

With a confident smirk on his face, Joe said, "Sure thing, Wing Chun is simple, and it's all the same."

Several minutes passed before one of the students clapped his hands and called everyone together. He seemed to be in charge as he said, "Let's begin class." He gave a few instructions to the students as they quickly dispersed around the room.

Joe and I stood there, unsure what to do, until the student approached us. He was tall, fit, and looked to be in his late teens. He was of mixed race and wore his hair in dreads that seemed hypnotic when they moved.

"Hey, my name is Tobias. Are you guys here for the free class?" he said.

Joe nodded, and I quickly searched my pocket and handed him a crumpled-up flyer.

Tobias gave me a weird look and said, "You know, it says here on the flyer in large, bold print, 'PLEASE DO NOT REMOVE FROM THE WALL.'"

I quickly apologized for overlooking that detail and said, "If you like, I could post it back."

Out of the blue, an older gentleman grabbed the flyer from my hand and said, "Wow, I can't believe you found one of these." He smiled and looked at me for a second before saying, "Hello." I was relieved that he wasn't upset. I couldn't quite put my finger on it, but having him there in my presence felt warm and comforting.

The gentleman patted Tobias on the back and said, "I'll take it from here."

With a curious look on his face, Tobias said, "Really...? You sure, Sifu?"

He nodded his head to confirm that he was sure.

My Sihings—my older brothers in the art—later told me that having Sifu take the time to teach beginners was not the norm. Strangely, I never asked him why. I guess it did not matter.

The first thing he said kinda caught me by surprise. He said, "Don't be so concerned about fighting right away. I want you to spend more time refining your heart."

He spoke out of the norm, as every school I had checked out made fighting their number one priority. Immediately, he had captured my attention.

As I stood there listening to Sifu, I tried my best to maintain a blank look on my face. I could tell Joe was not impressed.

From the looks of it, his main goal was to get into fights. Joe made no effort to hide his eyes rolling in a snobbish manner. There was no way Sifu missed that, but he ignored the rude gesture and continued to speak.

I raised my hand cautiously.

He acknowledged me with a slight nod and asked, "What's on your mind?"

I said with a crackly voice, "What ... should we call you? Is Sifu okay?"

He smiled and said, "You can call me anything you want; it's not necessary to call me Sifu." He did not reciprocate my question with a similar one, as he made no effort to learn either of our names.

I was taken aback. I had always thought that teachers were very strict in dictating their titles of Master, Sensei, or Sifu. However, he took a more humble approach and did not place his stamp of authority on a title.

Instead, he started teaching us. Sifu spent some time with us, explaining in detail how he wanted us to open the basic stance—Yee Gee Kim Yeung Ma or YGKYM. Once we opened it, he made a couple of minor adjustments and asked how it felt.

Sifu asked, "Do you feel your weight evenly, between the heel and the ball of the foot?"

I stuttered, "I think so?" as I tinkered around with my stance. I looked over at Joe to find that he was more than confident that he had gotten it.

Sifu then turned his head and leaned slightly forward. He looked at both of us and said, "Okay, go work on this." Then he walked away.

Joe and I spent the next ten minutes working on the stance. I tried my best to fidget around with all the steps, hoping my weight was evenly balanced. I could tell the lack of action was getting to Joe. He made a couple of sloppy attempts to open up the stance but was more concerned with what others were doing around him. He looked like a five-year-old struggling to pay attention at a movie theater, squirming with boredom.

I, on the other hand, was intrigued. Sifu taught us easy steps to open up the stance, but I was sure there was more to it. I found myself lost, unsure whether I was in center or not. Sifu had explained what we were doing, but unlike the instructors at other places, he was putting his focus on something other than fighting.

It was quiet between the two of us before I finally broke the silence. I asked Joe, "Hey, do you think I'm doing the stance correctly?"

Joe looked frustrated and said, "We better not be spending the entire class on just this stance!" He glanced over and looked at my stance and said, "Yeah, you got it. This is simple."

I tried keeping the conversation going. "Well, this is our first day of class. Maybe it's good to focus on the basics."

Joe sneered at my remarks and said, "I'm gonna walk out of here if we don't do anything else."

Just then Sifu strolled up to us and asked, "Do you have any questions?"

Joe immediately responded, "Nope, I got this!"

I was too afraid to say anything and held back from asking my question. He nodded his head, put both arms behind his back, and then walked away. Sifu went through this process several times, each time asking if there were questions—and each time Joe and I would repeat our previous responses and silent gestures.

It was like déjà vu in the span of an hour. With fifteen minutes left until the end of class, Sifu again came up to us and asked the same question. My response was no different, but this time Joe blurted in frustration, "When can we work on something else?"

Sifu smiled and did not respond and strolled away.

Joe whispered loudly, "Kirin, I'm outta here. No wonder the first class is free. This is a total waste of f–ing time; do yourself a favor and leave with me."

Something in me said to stay, so I did. He was dumbfounded by my reaction, but I quickly took a stand and said, "I think I'll just finish the class." I buffered my statement to avoid sounding foolish, "There's like only fifteen minutes left."

Joe gave me a look like I was a total fool to waste any more time; then he gathered his stuff and stormed out of class. Even with Joe's commotion, neither Sifu nor any of the regular students seemed to be aware or even care about the incident. They acted as if these were natural events occurring. That was the last time I ever saw Joe.

A few minutes later, Sifu came up. He made no inquiry as to Joe's whereabouts and asked, "Do you have any questions?"

Sifu waited patiently for a moment before he turned to walk away. I finally mustered, "Uh, Sifu? I, umm ...." Sifu waited but made no attempt to help me get the words out of my mouth. He was like a lifeguard watching a person drown in front of him.

I then blurted a barrage of questions, "I honestly don't know if I have my center or not?"

"Do you stand like this in a fight?"

"Why are my thigh muscles so tired after only a few minutes?"

"How long should I be holding this stance?"

I don't fully remember how many questions I threw at him, but afterwards, I immediately looked downward, almost hoping that he had not heard me. I waited nervously as I adjusted my hair.

He gave me a warm smile and said with a satisfied voice, "Good, good. Now you are ready to learn, Kirin."

My ears perked up, as I was surprised that Sifu even knew my name.

He spent the last remaining moments of class watching me open my stance several times. Sifu was precise in his adjustments of my body, and he looked almost pleased with my continuing to ask questions about the stance. He pushed against my chest to test my stance and said, "Always remember to go with the force."

He then said, "Think for a second about what it means not to fight the force."

His words of wisdom were beyond the grasp of my twelve-year-old ears. I nodded just to pretend that I knew what he was saying. Unable to come up with a smart reply, I asked him, "Uh ... is this better?"

A stretch here, a tuck there, and a slight shift of the weight. After all these meticulous and tiny adjustments, he pushed upon my chest. In that instance, I could feel the force of his push surge through my entire body connecting one bone to another and then finally reaching my feet and running into the ground. It was like a domino effect of epic proportions working in perfect harmony. I felt solid as a rock with no effort at all. The sensation was indescribable: a feeling of unity within myself. I was in complete awe the moment I felt it.

I looked to Sifu and said, "I've never felt anything like this." It was like power without effort, and I giggled in confusion.

He smiled at me, almost speaking without words, and then walked away. In that instant, I was sold.

I thought, *I'm in.*

How Do I Use This?–2 years 89 days

I was weaving in and out of traffic on my bike and was already fifteen minutes late to class. Shaking my head, I regretted stopping for a cup of coffee. As an addict to caffeine, I always found a way to justify it. "Dang it!" I said.

Technically, there was no rush to be at class on time. To Sifu, class started when you wanted it to, and only if you chose to come. He believed in self-discipline. Whether you showed up or not, it was all the same to him. In the end, you are there because you wanted to be.

I finally arrived in front of the school and made a halfhearted attempt to lock up my bike. As I entered, there was a strange commotion surrounding one of the students. Sifu was giving some instructions, but all the other students were hovering around, and I could not make out from that distance who it was. Curious, I rushed forward to see what was happening.

I blurted, "What's going on?" The majority of the crowd ignored my inquiry, but Tobias and Robert at least looked to acknowledge my presence.

There I was, hopping up and down and trying to get a glimpse of all the action, but all I could hear was Sifu's voice.

Sifu said, "Keep the egg on your eye for the next fifteen minutes. By tomorrow's time, the bruise on your eye should be gone."

I said loudly, "Pluck a duck!" This time everyone except Sifu turned around and looked at me questioningly. Silence awaited me as everyone stared.

Tobias gave me a look and said, "You know that's still considered swearing."

I ignored his comment and spoke, "Anyone else find it odd that Sifu can boil an egg in the gym?" A domino effect of eye-rolling occurred as they all ignored me again. I thought, *It's a legitimate question. We're in a gym; how exactly did he boil an egg?*

Finally, the crowd parted and revealed Danny at its center. He sat thin as a nail and twitched nervously, making these weird head motions similar to a chicken pecking for its food. Danny had been in class at least a year ahead of me and was often the first to give me tips with the quirkiest examples. He started explaining how he got into a fight but then stopped and asked Sifu, "I don't get it, Sifu. The stance failed me?"

Sifu, not too shocked, said, "Tell me exactly what you did."

Danny explained how he got into some heated argument at school and one thing led to another, as it always does amongst boys. "Finally he put up his guard, and I got in my guard and my stance."

At that moment, the crowd that had hovered over Danny immediately dispersed. Everyone shook their heads except me, unaware what Danny had said that was incorrect.

The rest of the seniors walked away, and I heard Tobias shout, "Dude ... seriously, seriously?" Just like that, the moment of drama was quickly forgotten, and everyone else went back to their regular drills. I, on the other hand, was standing there with Danny. Both of us were left alone wondering what he had done wrong.

Sifu was standing there working on Danny, no doubt waiting for us to ask. I had to know as the answer was killing me.

At the same time, we both said, "So, you don't stand in YGKYM when it's a fight?"

I blurted, "Jinx!"

Danny frowned and looked away.

I said, "Danny, Danny, Danny." I smiled and clapped in excitement because that was the first time I had ever won that game.

Sifu stared at me awkwardly.

"Sorry, Sifu. You were saying,"

Sifu cleared his throat and said, "Let me ask both of you: when you were little and first started learning to write letters, how did you go about that?"

Danny said, "Well, from what I recall, I had a set pattern that I traced the letter in, and I did my best to trace that pattern."

Sifu asked, "What was the purpose of that?"

Danny was quick to respond, "It was to learn how to write the letters correctly."

Sifu spoke as we both listened attentively, "Not exactly. All of that in the very beginning served one main purpose, and the most important thing was to develop your hand skills for control and coordination."

I thought about it for a second, still confused, and jumped in, "So, I don't get it with the stance?"

Sifu responded, "Development and application are a world apart. Let me ask you: do you write anything remotely like how you learned in the beginning?"

Danny responded, "No."

I immediately backed up his statement with my own, "No!"

Sifu said, "Of course not, because how you write is an expression of yourself, and not how you can write. To do it like you did back in elementary school would be to fight against the force. That would make you move unnaturally, like a robot. Once you fail to move naturally, you'll lose."

Danny responded, "Well, why didn't you tell me that before?"

Before Sifu's mouth opened to answer, everyone practicing stopped and yelled in harmony, "He says that all the time! Development and application are totally different!"

Sifu, with a bit of empathy, said, "I did tell you that before, but only now are you ready to listen." With that last comment, Sifu walked away to tend to the rest of the class.

Both Danny and I were looking at each other.

I said, "I think he purposely does that."

Danny asked, "Does what?"

I responded, "Makes me feel dumb."

Danny looked at me and said, "Agreed."

> *"Once the excitement fades, knowing the rhyme to the reason will lead to continued action." –Sifu*

Holy Sh....–3 years 4 days

It should be known that there's a certain amount of leeway afforded when one brings home straight As. Now most teens would take full advantage of it, but for the first several years, other than sneaking off to take martial arts, I was what you could label an "angel." Whether it was good or bad, the art was teaching me to grow and not function as a mere robot in society.

Because I was the only girl, you would think my stepmom would be super protective, but I built trust over time, by being responsible and well-behaved. The key is to know just how much one can take from it without getting too greedy; otherwise, you will get burned. That principle is called storage, taught to me by Sifu, but I'm not so sure he'd be happy with how I was putting it to use.

It was an early Saturday morning, a bright and cheerful start to the day, when I snuck out. Well, maybe "snuck" isn't the right word, but I gave the same excuse as always: a school project with Gwen. The school part was true, to a certain extent, but this was for the school of Wing Chun.

I was excited for class because I'd had a week's worth of good practice coupled with a good night's sleep, both of which were rare occurrences. I got to school almost an hour before class. Beaming with confidence, I thought I had finally figured out how to do the stance properly and wanted Sifu's opinion on it.

I wasn't sure if anyone would be there, but I opened the door and saw Sifu with his back toward me doing the Siu Lim Tao form alone. He was playing some 80s music in the background, which I immediately recognized. While the other students considered his taste in music archaic, I enjoyed the retro techno beat. From the looks of it, he had been here for quite a while as he stood concentrating on a single motion. I was sure he heard me, but he did not bother to stop what he was doing. Sifu was drenched in sweat, something I had never seen before, considering Siu Lim Tao is the biggest non-calorie-burning form on the entire planet.

I watched and wondered, *Why so much focus on the form? He always stresses it,* but I was not ready to grasp that lesson. My impatience grew as I watched; I'd been hoping to pick his brain since I came early.

Suddenly, Sifu shouted, "Kirin, what brings you to class so early?"

I jumped and popped out of the corner to reveal my whereabouts. "Nothing, Sifu, I just had some free time to kill."

In the back of my mind, I wondered, *How the heck did he know it was me? He wasn't facing the mirrors, and his back was toward me.*

I said aloud, "Sifu, uhm … can I ask you a question?"

"Sure, what's on your mind?" Sifu replied as he grabbed a towel to wipe his face. He then started tapping his arms and body while he waited to hear my question.

Instead of asking, I said, "Uh, Sifu, what are you doing?"

Sifu replied, "It's chi packing."

With a puzzled look on my face, I replied, "Uh, what's that?"

Sifu answered, "Any time you work out and create sweat and heat, that's energy. Most people simply towel that off and waste it. But, you can use that to your benefit."

"How so?"

"Well, heat is energy, so when you see me tapping all around my body, I'm sending the energy back to the bone. You see, you're still young, but when you get older like me, the bone hollows out and gets weaker with fatty deposits and other waste. That's why you see a lot of old people fall, break something, and they can't get up." He snickered at his own comment.

"Okay, I know what you mean," I replied.

"So, every time I work out, I should do it."

"Is there really a difference?" I asked.

Sifu smiled. "Of course, why else would I do this?"

"Sifu, let me see," I said. Sifu extended his arm toward me to check. When I touched his arm, it felt like a rock. I was perplexed. "Do you do any workouts other than Wing Chun, Sifu?"

Sifu smiled and replied, "Does eating count?"

I was even more curious as I touched his shoulder and poked his back. He was a walking, talking, breathing rock. I shook my head, as I usually did when hanging out with Sifu.

"Okay, I'll ask you more about that later, but I wanted you to check out my stance and tell me what you think?"

Sifu asked me to open up my YGKYM stance. I began standing in place and slowly went through the motions.

As Sifu waited, I did everything to make sure I had control of my center. Step by step, I paid attention to every detail I could muster up from past lessons, as I was sure I had it this time. With all the work and countless hours of practice, this had to be it. I thought, *Four basic steps, I should be able to do this by now. It's already been three years.*

I said, "Okay, Sifu. I'm ready. Can you see if my stance is all right?"

Sifu placed a single finger at the top of my chest and gently applied pressure to my stance. Upon feeling his force, I pushed against it while trying to maintain my center, but I still struggled. Hope quickly turned to disgust as I shook my head, and let my arms drop.

I yelled, "I give up! Seriously ... it's been three years working on this stance, and it feels no different from day one."

When Sifu didn't respond, I decided to let off more steam. "Everything I'm doing is exactly what you said, Sifu. I have notes upon notes about everything you have ever said about the stance ... but every time you push upon my stance, I just do not feel like I can hold it."

"Hmm, interesting you should say that. So you know what, how, and why you are doing these things, and you're positive you're doing the same things as me?"

With confidence, I said, "Yes, Sifu."

He asked me to open up my stance again and said, "Is your center okay?"

I responded right away, "Yes, it feels good."

He tested my stance, and I rocked to the back of my heels.

I shook my head and bit my lip. "I don't get it. I'm doing the stance just like you showed me."

"Allow me to make some adjustments," Sifu said in a soft voice.

Sifu micromanaged my stance, with a pinch here, a tuck there. He guided me to straighten up, twist slightly, and put my chin down. I lost count of the endless minor adjustments.

"Okay, now I'm gonna test your stance again," said Sifu. When he pressed upon my chest, I felt like a rock—just like day one when I first felt it. He was able to recreate the sensation.

"It feels so solid, Sifu," I said.

"Of course it does, because now you're doing it exactly how you should do it."

I frowned in embarrassment. "I guess I wasn't doing it exactly how you were doing it, was I, Sifu?"

Sifu didn't reply. Instead, he spent the next half hour before class grilling me on everything I thought I knew about the stance.

Each question I either answered incorrectly or didn't have the slightest clue how to answer.

"Doing it and knowing it isn't the same thing," said Sifu.

When I didn't respond, Sifu looked me in the eye and said, "It's more than just monkey see, monkey do, Kirin. In everything thing that you do, not just Wing Chun, you must know the what, how, and why. Then once you believe you have figured that out, you must revisit it all over again."

Embarrassment quickly turned to frustration.

"I swear, Sifu, I'm practicing really hard. Why can't I get it on my own?" I said.

Sifu said, "Patience, you will get it."

I was too upset and depressed to listen as I said, "You've been saying that to me forever, and I still don't have it. You know the worst part is I understand everything you are saying, but there's something ... just a small piece of the puzzle that I can't make fit."

Sifu stood silently. "Do you mind if I try by myself one last time?" I asked, hoping that the third time would be the charm.

A few minutes later, the same process occurred. Every attempt led to the same results, as I rocked back onto my heels again. I shook my head and thought, *Why can't I get this right on my own?*

To Sifu, I said, "It just doesn't feel right. I'm trying my best to hold the stance, and I just feel tension when the force comes in. With your single finger, it feels like I'm gonna topple over!"

Sifu smiled at me, almost as if he had heard a joke. I, on the other hand, was hoping for something more than a smile from my teacher. In fact, I was hoping for a little support in my time of struggle, but I knew that would not be Sifu's style. Instead, like he's always done, he resolved a question with a question.

Sifu asked, "What's the most basic idea I've taught you in Wing Chun?"

I was definitely not in the mood. "Sifu, why must all your answers be cryptic?"

Sifu stood there and waited for an answer.

I blew off the hair that was covering my face, frustrated even more. Looking down with my hands on my hips, I answered, "What do you mean, Sifu, basic idea?"

Ignoring my obvious frustration, Sifu patiently answered, "You know what I mean, the most basic idea in Wing Chun."

I thought for a split second and started rubbing my hands over my face as I said, "Well, it's gotta be to go with the force."

I added silently to myself, *That obviously doesn't help me one bit. Everyone knows not to go against the force.*

I repeated myself, saying, "Yeah, that's it. The first thing you mentioned on day one: Go with the force."

Sifu said, "That's correct. Now, answer me this: when I push against your chest, what's the first thing you're doing?"

I thought for a second and then responded, "Well, I'm holding my stance, and when I feel that pressure, I push against your finger."

Sifu asked, "You do what?" He tilted his head slightly, looking directly at me.

Unaware of his meaning, I said again, "I push against your finger, Sifu!"

Sifu said, "And what, pray tell, is the direction that my finger is going?"

I responded, "Your finger's going into my chest, and thus I'm pushing against that."

Sifu asked again, "You're doing what?"

I quickly answered, "Sifu, I already said before, I'm pushing against it."

"I'm sorry, Kirin, I'm getting older. Can you repeat what you just said? Against what?" He cupped his hand around his ear.

I said, "Against the force—against it, okay? When you push my chest, I push against it to hold my stance in place." Sifu stared at me silently, almost signaling me mentally that he was giving me a hint.

I uttered my last comment again, "When you push at my chest, I push against it." This time the words had more meaning than what I'd seen on the surface. They echoed repeatedly, and something had clicked.

I said it again, with a look of self-realization as my eyebrow crept up slightly, "Ah ... against it...."

Sifu looked at me with a huge smile on his face. With a dumbfounded look and speaking softly to myself, I said slowly, "Pushing against your finger is fighting the ... Holy sh...."

> *"Lessons heard aren't necessarily lessons learned. It takes time for one to digest its true meaning." –Sifu*

Sifu's Journey Entry #1–Just Go Forward

Three Years Prior, Early Summer 2029

It was just past midnight as Sifu stood and stared outside his window. Inside the building he had bought several months ago was a room filled with the unknown. He was at the beginning stages of something, but what that was supposed to be was still unclear to him.

Lost in a vacant stare, there wasn't much to see as the darkness of the night swallowed everything. He could make out only a few trees and the surrounding buildings. Finally, a lone car passed on the road as he slowly sipped and enjoyed his tea.

"Mmm," he hummed as he downed it, savoring the flavor of chai. He did not drink it all, but appreciated the small amount he had. Sifu had learned to take his time and value the little things in life.

Several minutes passed, and the tea quickly lost its warmth. He continued to gaze outside, lost in deep thought as he stared at the endless night. Sifu was oblivious to the clicks of each second passing on his ancient clock. The sound of emptiness filled the entire room.

He closed his eyes. *I miss the noise,* he thought but quickly shook that idea from his head.

Again, he had difficulty heading home to go to sleep. He hesitated, and took a huge deep breath, letting out a sigh. Several minutes passed as he turned around and looked all over at the mess at hand. Shaking his head, he finally decided to do some work instead.

He walked slowly past the main area and through the kitchen, as he found himself by the dusty pantry area. He paused for a brief moment and realized, *Hmm, I really didn't come in for this tonight.*

Sifu turned to the side and stared at the door that led to the basement. He stood there for a minute, drawn to venture down the stairs.

Once downstairs, his initial reaction was, *This place looks even worse than upstairs.* From the corner of his eye, he caught a glimpse of his table, and felt it calling him to come over. He hesitated briefly, but trusted his feelings and went with the force. There, Sifu sorted through the mess in search of something. He stumbled upon an old picture of himself with some familiar faces. He stared at it sadly for a second before fumbling further for his goal.

Ah, there it is, he thought, with a bit of relief as he spotted his writing journal along with a pen. He grabbed both items now with a clearer intent. *I think it's about time that I started working on this.* Sifu blew the dust off his journal and opened it up. The inside was pristine, waiting for someone to create a masterpiece.

Even with all the technology existing today, Sifu decided to start his efforts the old-fashioned way, with pen and paper.

Several minutes passed as he transformed his desk from a cluttered heap into an organized workstation. In the pitch dark corner, his desk was laid out with a journal, a *pen*, and a lamp shedding enough light for him to write.

Sifu turned to the first page of his journal and grabbed his pen.

"Uh," he muttered.

He quickly pulled from his shirt a pair of glasses and thought sadly, *I didn't need to wear these fifteen years ago,* as he shook his head.

There he was, comfortably positioned in his chair. He spent a moment staring at the blank page gathering his thoughts and then finally placed pen to paper.

> *"That pressing feeling is the need to seek balance. Do your best not to ignore it." –Sifu*

CHAPTER 2
Aftershock

The events that unfolded that night were unexpected by all, and those in the arena hosting were ill prepared; security was lax and media was usually kept to a minimum.

People smothered Kirin as she struggled to make her way back to the locker room. Her actions in the ring made a beastly statement, but seeing her with the crowd revealed her true size. Kirin felt overwhelmed as her insecurities kicked in. She brushed her hair to cover a side of her face.

The crowd represented society's status quo, consumed by quick and instant results. People wanted answers as they were starving for any information about her. Throughout it all, Kirin remained silent, the unknown fighter five minutes ago turned instant celebrity.

People were shouting at Kirin for answers:

"Kirin, what's your last name?"

"Where did you learn that style of fighting?"

"Any plans to enter the league?"

"Isn't it Kung Fu? Not Gung Fu?"

The crowd and the media continued to yell and push. Chaos reigned, and there were still two more fights remaining on the draw. As Kirin worked toward the locker room, one of the reporters fell down. Lacking empathy, the crowd continued to stampede over him so they could reach Kirin. Whatever it took, no matter the price, just as long as you got what you needed—that was what society had come to.

Kirin stopped and turned around. She went back, helped the man onto his feet, and dusted him off. He was very appreciative and said a quick, "Thank you."

With a kind smile, Kirin responded, "No need to thank me. It's what normal people should do, right?" He nodded back to her and just smiled. The act of kindness went unnoticed as people kept showering her with more questions.

"Come on, honey, can you look over here for a shot?"

"Kirin, Kirin, why'd you throw the money?"

Kirin ignored the questions and continued to walk back to the locker room. Getting back had become a greater struggle than her match against DJ.

While all eyes were focused on Kirin, one in particular had a greater intent. A stranger within the crowds was weaving his way through the frenzy as Kirin neared the locker room. Timing it perfectly as Kirin opened the door to enter, he firmly grabbed Kirin by the arm and pulled her into room. The door slammed immediately behind them with the crowd outside. For just a second, there was silence from the frenzied mob. Kirin was caught off guard and tried to figure out what had just happened.

Tobias shoved Kirin's back against the locker and shouted, "Are you f–ing crazy, Kirin? Do you have any idea what your stunt has done?"

Refusing to back down, Kirin looked up, coming face to face with Tobias. "I'm tired of it.... I'm tired of it all." Kirin shook her head in disgust and opened up her arms. "Look around us. Why should we hide in fear? Like we...." she paused and then pounded her chest, "like we're the ones at fault here! Sifu has always told us to know right from wrong."

Bang! Bang! Bang! The door rattled upon impact. "Open up in there, will yah!" yelled the crowd outside.

Tobias and Kirin ignored the demands. Tobias breathed in deeply, trying to calm down and be the voice of reason, "It's not a question of right or wrong, Kirin. Whatever your plan is, it's not going to f–ing work!"

Kirin responded quickly, "We're not the minority, Tobias. There are others who are thinking the same thing."

Frustrated by her stubborn response, Tobias said, "You know what a minority is, Kirin? A minority at least has a goddam percentage. We are on our own. We are a f–ing handful!"

He raised his voice and shouted, "How many times have I told you that we do not live in your mythical and magical Wing Chun world, in a gumdrop house on Lollipop Lane, that's filled with logic and common f–ing sense?"

Kirin tried to interrupt, but Tobias continued to rant. "If you want to change the damn world, Kirin, then be a goddamn politician because what you did tonight is gonna bring the goons out hunting."

The pounding on the door grew louder. It seemed to be alive with its own heartbeat as the mob demanded that it be opened.

Kirin shouted toward the door, "Everything's okay! I just need, uh, ah … a couple of minutes." Her comments did little to ease the tension of the crowd.

Tobias ignored the sounds around him. "Do you know the chain of events you've started with this? Are you prepared to deal with that?"

Tobias stared deeply into Kirin's eyes. "Are you? Look at me, Kirin. Are you?"

With conviction, Kirin shouted, "I am prepared to deal with this, Tobias! What makes you think I'm not?"

Tobias shook his head in doubt. "Really … hmm really, you're prepared? Your actions expose not only us, but the entire f–ing group. But most importantly, it exposes Sifu, God damn it!"

Tobias grew even more frustrated. "What have I always told you? Always protect the goddamn source. Did you include that in your master plan? Or, is this another case of do first and deal with the consequences later?"

Kirin yelled back, "How exactly does this expose Sifu? He hasn't taught in years. We haven't *seen* him in years!" Kirin's face showed some sadness with her comment.

"They're gonna dig, Kirin, dig and find out everything about you." Tobias slammed his fist into the locker, showing his disgust.

"Kirin, you are not alone. Your actions will always affect the people around you. Did it ever occur to you that maybe Sifu doesn't want to be found?"

Kirin showed the first glimmer of doubt. Turning her head slowly away and staring at the floor, she whispered, "I am prepared to deal with this." She felt alone and vulnerable, questioning her own actions.

Tobias saw this and felt an ounce of remorse. A pause between the two occurred as Tobias slowly and gently put his forehead against Kirin's in silence. The anger subsided to a sense of understanding as they closed their eyes, remembering how it once was or could have been. Then, Tobias walked away and was lost in the shadows.

Kirin watched as Tobias left without another word. A small tear rolled down her cheek as she let out a sigh.

Bang! Bang! Bang! Kirin contemplated her next action as the crowd continued to pound the door. She looked around the entire locker area, measuring her surroundings. She yelled, "I need one more minute!" The pounding continued, and with annoyance growing, Kirin yelled, "For the love of God, give me one more *fricking minute!*" Just like that, the pounding stopped and gave her the grace of silence that she requested.

She headed to her locker and gathered all her belongings: a backpack, her shoes, clothes, and ID. She quickly started packing it all. She scrambled to get all her stuff ready and held her robe. Kirin looked at it for a moment and then threw it on the floor. A minute later, she was back in her regular street clothes. She looked around one last time.

#

Outside, a mob had gathered. The head of Chum Night emerged from the impatient crowd of reporters, security, and whoever else wanted a piece of the action. Nolan looked at his watch and began talking to his assistant.

He said, "So, what information do you have on her?" His assistant was frantically looking through his pad to check his information. Finally, after scrolling for several minutes, he was able to pull up data on the fighter.

Roger the assistant answered, "Let me see here."

Nolan asked, "Well, come on. What's it say?" as he tapped his foot impatiently.

His assistant squinted at the information and adjusted his glasses. "Just the standard information, sir, nothing special—just what we normally request."

Nolan asked, "She signed the waiver and you verified her ID, right?"

His assistant replied, "Of course ... of course we did."

"What's her full name, Kirin what?"

"It doesn't say Kirin on her information," Roger said as he fumbled with his pad to check further.

Nolan stared at Roger's pad. "What?"

Roger stuttered fearfully, "Her ID that we copied reads ... Valerie Gina."

With a curious look on his face, Nolan said, "Valerie Gina, Valerie Gina ... Why does that name sound so familiar?" Nolan began rubbing his chin, pondering how he knew that name. Clueless, Roger waited like a pawn for his boss to come up with an answer.

Nolan suddenly smacked his assistant on his head.

Roger yelled, "Ouch, what was that for?"

Nolan shook his head. "You idiot, Valerie Gina...." He spoke slower, hoping that Roger could pick up on the obvious. "Valerie Gina ... V. Gina? That's vagina, you fool!"

His assistant cowered again, expecting to be hit a second time as he quickly responded, "But, boss, we scanned her ID. It went through, and she paid the entrance fee."

Nolan, still upset, said, "What the hell, Roger?"

Roger spoke, "I followed standard procedure, boss. You know as long as they sign the waiver, pay the fee, and their ID clears the computer, we don't really care who enters the ring."

Nolan was disgusted by the response but realized it was the truth.

"Regardless, you could have at least put more effort into looking at the stuff."

"I'll double-check her info and run it through the system a couple more times, but I'm pretty sure if she faked the ID, all this information is no good either."

Reporters overheard this and began pestering Nolan. "So, is it true you don't have any information on the fighter?" More pushing and shoving occurred as they got a whiff of this latest news.

Nolan reassured them, "No, no, no ... we will have all the information, just a slight glitch."

Someone yelled, "Come on! It's been more than a minute already." That statement was justified, and the pounding resumed. A couple minutes passed, but this time no response came from the other side of the door.

"Where's maintenance?" Nolan demanded. "Call up Charlie and get him to open up this locker room door."

A few minutes later, maintenance came running with the keys. "Excuse me, coming through, excuse me ... coming through." The crowd ignored the request, making it tough for him to navigate through.

Nolan yelled, "What took you so long?"

The maintenance guy replied, "It's chaos out there, sir. I can barely move with that crowd."

Looking for Roger, Nolan called, "Roger, get more security in the arena and see if we can get the last two matches completed." Like a good assistant, Roger nodded his head and scurried away.

Nolan confirmed the obvious. "Hurry up and open the door!"

The maintenance guy quickly unlocked the locker room door and was shoved aside as everyone surged forward.

Nolan turned to the crowd and said, "All right, time for some answers." He opened the door and walked into the locker room.

People tumbled into the locker room like dominos. It was an amusing sight to see. Everyone began looking around, but there was clearly no one to be found. Suddenly all eyes fell on one object: Kirin's robe lay on the ground, the only proof that tonight's event had not been a dream. The crowd's need for immediate answers was not going to be fulfilled tonight.

> *"The minute doing becomes trying is the moment you decide to quit." –Sifu*

Short Stories #2–Kirin's P.O.V.

Lunch Time–Day 217

The Saturday class ended, but little did I know that day was far from normal. Everything was wrapping up, and as usual a handful of the guys were headed to eat out. The last weekend of every month, they would hit one of their favorite restaurants in the city.

That day was special because they finally invited me to go with them to a place that specialized in chicken wings. I had overheard them talking about it for months, but this was my first invitation. It was my chance to see if the taste lived up to the hype.

Well, technically, they didn't invite me, but Sifu was kind enough to ask me to join. Regardless, I had my in. I thought it was cool that Sifu joined the students for these events and everyone got extra learning time just hanging with him. It was win-win for those who were there: good food, good company, and Wing Chun all wrapped into one.

I started packing up my gear while others did the same, preparing to head out. Suddenly the door slammed open as three muscular guys came marching into the school. They were dressed in traditional gi from head to toe. Heads immediately turned, but I was oblivious to what was going on. I didn't give it a second thought, because I first thought it was an over-dramatic entrance for someone interested in joining the school.

The mood quickly changed as tension filled the room. The lead guy was holding a rolled up piece of paper and had a serious look on his face. He spoke not a single word and just stood there. Sifu took notice and walked casually toward our new guest. The guy handed the paper to Sifu, who briefly looked it over.

Sifu showed no reaction as he read the document. Then he patted himself down and said, "Hmm, where'd I put my pen?" All eyes were on Sifu as the students wondered what was about to happen.

The lead guy pulled out a pen and made a motion to hand it over to Sifu. Just before the exchange occurred, he intentionally dropped the pen in front of Sifu.

I watched what happened next in amazement and thought, *Wow, only Sifu*, with a grin.

Now, if it had been anyone else, that pen would have been a slave to gravity and hit the floor. But as it was falling, somehow Sifu caught it with his shoe, and managed to kick it back up to his hand. He simply smiled at the gentlemen, as if that was no big deal, and proceeded to sign the paper. The three were definitely taken back by his actions.

Sifu turned around and made eye contact with Tobias. Tobias nodded his head as Sifu continued to the back room. He walked past everybody without saying a word. It seemed like both of them realized what was going on, but the rest of us were left to wonder.

Tobias was the eldest of Sifu's students of this current generation; he had been with Sifu for close to ten years. The handful of encounters I had with him were merely corrections within the classroom and nothing more than trivial chat. I didn't expect much more, considering he was seven years older than I was. He was known as "the guy" when it came to Wing Chun, and I was told he was somewhat of a ladies' man.

I needed some answers and looked around the room to see who might know what was going on. A quick scan led me to John, who was nearby. I was certain he would have some answers. I shifted toward him, hoping I was right.

John was tall with geeky glasses. He was the class clown of the school, and sometimes pushed the boundaries of what was proper. There were also times when he had the entire class bawling. I tapped him on the shoulder as I asked, "What's going on?"

John whispered just loud enough so I could hear him, "This is a challenge match."

With a look of bewilderment, I said, "That's cool." I followed that up with, "Uh, what's a challenge match?"

The look John gave me said I should know, but I didn't.

"Seriously?" he said.

I shrugged my shoulders, as if he were speaking a foreign language.

He said, "Hmm, come to think of it, you are only twelve."

I controlled my temper, knowing John was again unaware of his social faux pas.

John continued, "They just started this eight months ago, but it's a new law that allows schools to challenge one another. The loser has to shut down their school."

I responded, "That's a law?"

John shrugged his shoulders and said, "You know how it is; if you got the cash and the lobbyists, they pass a law, hide other stuff within it. They make it confusing enough that people don't bother to care, and that's just the way it is."

Looking back from where I came from, the government did whatever it wanted to. I was beginning to wonder if there was any difference at all, anymore.

Before I could ask anything else, John said, "Come on. Let's get a good seat and watch.

John waved me down to join him as I sat in anticipation for the events to unfold. Never having witnessed this before, I was hugging my legs and hiding behind them. I had no idea what to expect from the frenzy in front of me.

Behind me, Big T and Danny had some side dealings going on. Big T was the biggest guy in school. He was bulky in the gut, and one would wonder why someone his size would need

Wing Chun. The T was a mystery to me, as no one ever called him by his real name. Danny, on the other hand, was the exact opposite: thin and skinny like a nail. It was an odd friendship that consisted of constant gambling together.

Big T and Danny were sizing up the opponent and using their hands to calculate something.

I caught bits and pieces of their conversation.

Danny whispered, "What odds?"

Big T said, "Three-to-one that Tobias takes him out in one move."

Danny gazed at Tobias, studying him. "Hmm, I don't know. He looks like he doesn't have his game face on."

I sat quietly, thinking, *If he loses, the school shuts down. Why wouldn't he be up for this?*

Big T tried to sweeten the deal. "Okay, four-to-one Tobias takes him out in two moves?"

Danny pondered that for a minute and said, "How much we betting?"

"Twenty credits?"

"Thirty, and you got yourself a deal."

I turned around to see both of them smiling, each thinking he got the better of the deal.

Listening to all this, I shook my head, wondering why I was the only one who seemed worried about what was going to transpire.

Tobias and his challenger were standing in the center of the room. His opponent started warming up and pacing back and forth, likely to get some blood circulating and calm his nerves. He did several kinds of stretches in preparation for the fight. His two other companions stood at attention, like they were his bodyguards. It looked kind of amusing, like it was right out of a comic book.

I gazed over to Tobias, who was on his phone texting. I assumed it was one of his many girlfriends. He looked as if he didn't have a care in the world.

He was still busy texting as he ran up to me and handed me his phone.

Tobias said, "Hey, kid!"

I interjected, "It's Kirin."

"Yeah, yeah. Tell me if I get a text back."

Puzzled I asked, "When exactly would you like me to do that, during your fight?"

Tobias nonchalantly said, "As soon as you get a text, just wave to me, okay?"

I shouted back, "Don't you think you should warm up or something?" Fortunately my suggestion did not fall upon deaf ears.

Tobias nodded. "Robert, come here. Let's roll."

I breathed a sigh of relief as I thought, *Well, at least he's warming up.*

Tobias and Robert stood opposite one another and did chi sao–a unique hand to hand drill, exclusively found in Wing Chun. The main guy caught a glimpse of this, and patted one of his friends on the chest laughing. "Look at those idiots! They're playing patty cake," he said in a mocking feminine voice loud enough for everyone to hear. Tobias made a slight head gesture to the side, but continued to roll with Robert.

I looked around for Sifu and found him in the back room looking for something. I was surprised by how casual he seemed. He looked like he didn't care about the fight. A few more minutes passed, and the challenger gave a signal that he was ready to fight. Tobias pulled away from Robert and patted him on the back, saying, "Thanks, man." Robert wished him luck and sat back with the rest of us, waiting for the fight to unfold.

The fight was about to begin as both guys stood about ten feet from one another. The guy posed in a guard, moving slightly in and out. Tobias had no guard, nothing at all, almost as if he were waiting in line for them to let him into a movie. He was formless, something that I did not expect. I thought, *Shouldn't he be in his basic stance?*

Suddenly the guy closed the gap and lunged for his legs. Tobias moved in as well, disrupting his opponent's timing and balance. He bounced right back onto his butt like he had run into a wall. He looked a little embarrassed and landed in an awkward position. Tobias backed up and allowed him to stand. His opponent dusted himself off and got ready to move in.

Again, Tobias stood there like he was on his coffee break. He flashed a look at me for confirmation, and I quickly shook my head, indicating there was no darn text. He grimaced, seeming bothered that he hadn't received a text. I, on the other hand, was just bewildered by his behavior.

His opponent made a fake jab to Tobias's face, and shot for his legs again. Tobias bypassed the fake, recognizing it as nothing but fluff. When he went for his legs, Tobias moved in again. As his opponent tried to grab Tobias by the legs, he shoved his head straight down to the ground and then backed off.

I had to admit, if that was a photo opportunity, that would have been one kick-ass pose. The guy ate dirt and didn't take kindly to having his face planted. He got up from kissing the floor with his nose spilling blood. He went to the corner to be aided by his friends, who helped stop the blood from spreading.

I wasn't sure why he was trying to take Tobias down because our school did not have any mats and was just a solid wood floor.

Tobias looked at me again, while the other fighter was being aided. I held up my hand and signaled to him a zero. He shook his head in disgust and stared back at me with his one eyebrow raised as he mouthed, "Zero?" and matched my hand.

I nodded to confirm.

Sifu finally came back from the back room. He had grabbed a light jacket and possibly some credits.

Tobias quickly turned his head.

Sifu looked at him intensely, pointed at the clock, and then strangely grabbed his belly. I was befuddled. It looked like Sifu was more concerned about eating lunch than the possibility of losing the fight and shutting down the school.

When the match resumed, Tobias looked like a different person. He definitely had his game face on. The other fighter set up in guard again and was ready to go, but blood covered his uniform. Tobias didn't wait for him; he just decided to move in with such ferocity that his opponent literally looked in shock. He stumbled back, off balance, but went low for a third time for a grab. As his head went down, Tobias launched a fist to his head. It was just like how Sifu taught us: always move in and always dominate the center line. The hit seemed to be in slow motion as it rocked his foundation, but Tobias didn't stop there. He followed it up with a series of multiple hits, even though the poor fellow looked like he was already limp from the first.

Just like that, the fight was over.

I had to admit, I was impressed. It was like a masterpiece of destruction that Tobias composed in front of everyone.

The challenger's two friends grabbed him up to his feet to drag him out of the school. I saw Big T hand Danny the credits for his winnings. Danny smiled and gloated. Everyone around started gathering their stuff as if nothing had happened.

I was covered in sweat from what seemed like a lifetime of excitement.

As the guys dragged their companion out of the school, Tobias shouted, "Hey fellas, how's the patty cake taste now?"

Embarrassed and beaten, those guys had no reply and walked out in shame. Big T nudged Robert on the arm and said, "Is it me, or does Tobias give the coolest f– you face?" Robert looked at Big T, and both nodded in agreement.

Tobias came up to me and asked, "No one texted?"

I had forgotten and saw that someone did text him. "Oh, uhm, sorry. Someone did text. I kinda forgot with all the excitement."

Tobias rolled his eyes and snatched his phone from my hand. "Thanks a lot, Carmen!" he said sarcastically as he walked away, checking his text. I heard him mumble, "Hello, booty call."

I yelled, "It's Kirin! Kirin!" but was drowned out by the chatter amongst the other students.

I looked around and realized no one cared what I had just said. I grabbed Danny by the arm. "Danny, you know my name, right?"

Danny snickered and with a look of confidence said, "Yeah, of course I know your name, Karen." He walked away and started chatting with Tobias.

I shook my head and looked at Big T. If anyone would remember my name, it would be Big T. I ran over to him as he was grabbing his stuff and said, "Uh, Big T, you know my name, right?"

He looked up to the right side of his eyes and said, "Sure, little sista, your name is uh ... your name is uh ... Bianca, yeah Bianca?" Then he gave me a huge smile, as if he were proud that he remembered my name.

I just looked at him with my jaw dropping to the floor. *Bianca?* I thought. *At least the other two goofs were in the general ball park.*

In a span of less than five minutes, I was known as Carmen, Karen, and fricking Bianca. I stood there dejected as everyone celebrated around me.

I looked over as Tobias grabbed his stuff and looked at the rest of the gang. With a huge smile on his face, he roared and then shouted, "Who's hungry?"

Sifu waved the rest of us to move out of the class. "Hurry up! Otherwise, it'll be a long wait before we can get seats."

I shook my head and thought, *This is my school?*

<u>A Piece of the Triangle–2 years 330 days</u>

Like any teenager, there was no greater joy for me than hearing the bell ring at the end of the day. Everyday after 3:30, I would gather my stuff and meet up with my two closest friends, Gwen and Sage. Weather permitting, we made it our daily routine to walk home from school.

I said frustrated, "I can't believe how much homework they dumped after a three-day weekend!"

Gwen agreed, "You're telling me. It's like they're punishing us for having fun."

Sage said, "I don't know about you guys, but I was forced to watch my little brother's soccer tournament all weekend. Even for my nerd-self, it was not my definition of fun."

We all laughed.

Sage paused for a second and then said, "Wait, are we laughing at the fact that I had a bad weekend or that I confirmed I'm a nerd?"

Gwen and I looked at each other and chuckled quietly. Sage, on the other hand, shrugged and decided not to argue the point.

I had known Sage and Gwen since I was eight years old and first came to the States. We instantly hit it off from the first time we met. Even though I couldn't speak a lick of English, Sage made me feel comfortable because he could speak my language. Gwen felt like the sister I never had as we would spend countless hours playing at one another's house.

Glancing at her, I said, "Gwen, you have to check the GPS setting on my phone."

Gwen replied, "What's going on with it?"

I said, "My mom's kinda suspicious at the locations she's getting when she checks up on me. I think your hack might be off."

Gwen asked, "Let me take a look," and I handed over my phone. Gwen was like a computer on wheels. She had been wheelchair-bound from an early age, so before she broke out of her shell, she spent nearly every waking moment glued to a computer. The benefit of forming our little group and having a super smart computer geek was immeasurable.

Gwen said, "You know, Kirin, you wouldn't have this issue if you would upgrade your phone regularly like everyone else. This phone is ancient."

"I know, but it works perfectly fine," I said.

Sage looked at me funny and said, "That's your phone?"

"Yeah, what's wrong with it?" I asked.

"Uh, nothing. Nothing at all." He gave me a weird look, but I knew what he was thinking.

Sage added, "Hey Gwen, can I charge my phone on your wheels?" as he gave her a puppy dog look.

Gwen looked up. "Come on, Sage. How many times have I told you not to run continuous downloads on your phone?"

"I know. I know. I can't help it."

Changing the subject, I asked, "Sage, can you please help me with my French?"

Sage answered in French, "Je serais plus que ravi de vous aider avec votre françaises, ms paresseux?" I didn't know what he'd said. At the blank expression on my face, Sage said, "Seriously, Kirin, you could be the laziest straight A student I have ever known."

I thought about it for a second. "You could be right about that, Sage."

Even with Sage's social deficiencies, he was brilliant in his own way. By age 15, he could speak seven languages fluently, and he planned on learning more. The only person I could recall who had a similar resume was the Pope. Sage had a knack for picking up the specific commonalities of a particular language and putting it together. I mean, he spoke Korean as well as I did.

Several minutes later, our pleasant trip home was disrupted. Almost like it was right out of a comic book, three huge wrestlers on their way to practice decided to interrupt our conversation. I recognized them—they were sophomores like us, but definitely on a questionable steroid diet.

The lead guy spoke, "Looka here, fellas, if it isn't the trio of dorkness."

Quickly Sage and Gwen's faces turned sour; they'd spent their entire lives as outsiders. I ignored their comments as well and continued to walk at a faster pace to keep up with Gwen and Sage. Sage whispered to us, "We should follow the school's bullying guide."

I cringed the moment Sage mentioned that and said, "That stuff never works; the schools are clueless."

Unfortunately for us, silence did not do the trick this day. They blocked our path again and started harassing our group. The guy from the left spoke, "Hey, Byron, don't you think Gwen would be a lot hotter if she could walk?"

Sage caught me by surprised and jumped in, "Why don't you guys shut up."

They laughed, and Byron shoved Sage hard to the ground, knocking his glasses off. Even though Gwen had heard every mean comment you can imagine, it didn't mean they weren't still hurtful. Her eyes swelled with tears, but she was more concerned that Sage had gotten pushed.

I retorted, "Why don't you meatheads run along and pretend you don't enjoy rolling around with each other during practice?"

The guy on the right angrily shouted, "What did you say to me, Blink?"

Blink was the racial slur the local bullies called me in school. I looked him straight in the eye with both fists already clenched, and said, "Do I need to speak slower?"

Gwen grabbed my arm and whispered, "Kirin, no, don't do it!"

Gwen's voice fell on deaf ears, as I was ready to fight. This time I wouldn't run away, unlike before.

Just before everything was about to explode, a voice yelled out, "Hey!"

Everyone turned their heads to find the source. It was a stranger—one I'd seen before in the hallways of our school.

The three bullies turned around immediately as the stranger spoke, "Do you guys want to get kicked off the team?"

They all responded, "No, sir, we were just goofing off with them."

The stranger shouted, "Get to practice, before I tell the coach on you guys."

Just like a group of scared rats, they hurried along without a peep.

I turned around to help Sage back up. The stranger came in and began picking up Sage's things.

He said, "Sorry about those guys. They, uh ... can get a little bit energized at times."

I decided not to accept his apology and said, "You're trying to apologize for stupidity."

He was taken aback by my comment and replied, "Uh no, I–I mean–"

Gwen stepped in to rescue him from my remark, "She didn't mean anything by that. Thanks again for stepping in, uhh?"

The stranger smiled. "Hunter, my name is Hunter. I'm a junior at your school."

Suddenly I realized I had forgotten the lesson Sifu taught me about self-defense. He spoke of it constantly, knowing the "when," as I shook my head in disgust at myself. Sifu always said that when it came to self-defense, it was not always a case of whether you could, but whether you should. He always said that, even if you're right, it doesn't always mean it's justified to fight. I just couldn't let go of the fact that it felt like I was running away.

In the background, all I could hear was the muffled voice of the stranger slowly coming back into focus. I abruptly said, "You know I could've handled myself."

Hunter smiled and said, "I know you could've. I doubt anyone who couldn't would have the guts to talk back to those guys."

I was unimpressed with the response and looked away, dusting off Sage some more. Hunter picked up Sage's backpack and glasses and handed them over to Sage. Apparently hoping to ease the tension with a joke, Hunter said, "Look, I was just trying to meet my Boy Scout requirement of one good deed a day."

Gwen smiled at the comment and spoke for the rest of us, "Thanks again."

Hunter said, "Seriously, I didn't do anything."

He looked over to me and said, "I've seen you around the halls in school. Your name is Kirin, right?"

I was a little taken aback that he knew my name as I tried to brush it off. Again, Gwen answered for me, "Yeah, you're right. She's Kirin, that's Sage, and I'm Gwen."

Hunter said, "I'm running late for practice, but hopefully I'll see you around." Hunter took of in a sprint but quietly gave a quick glance back at us.

Gwen asked Sage, "Are you okay?"

Sage responded with humor, "Why do you ask questions you know the answers to?"

Gwen rolled her eyes. "You know, it's fortunate for you I'm knowledgable in movie quotes as well, but it sure would help if you quoted movies from this era."

Being a mega movie buff, Sage would often quote lines to deal with the stressful situations.

With a sly look on her face, Gwen asked me, "So, did you notice that, Kirin?"

I asked, "Notice what?"

Gwen said, "Don't tell me I'm the only one who heard him say he's seen you around school before."

I shook my head. "Gwen, it's school. We see a lot of people all the time that I don't even know."

Gwen smirked and said in a teasing manner, "That's true ... but he also happened to know your name as well."

I said, "Oh, will you be quiet!"

"Emotions blind us from seeing the truth." –Sifu

Movie Night–2 years 298 days

It was Friday night, movie night for us at the Rise household. Friends and family were gathered for our weekly event. Sage brought his little brother Cage, and Gwen was there planted on her favorite couch. My stepdad Kevin was with us, along with my stepbrother Mark and his friend. The rest of the Rises were either away to college, in the service, or busy dragging my stepmom to a soccer event. I missed the good old days when everyone was at home. I had so many good memories of just family fun hanging together.

Butterscotch, our pet Labrador, was already nestled by the lower part of my seat. She liked it when I would tuck my feet underneath her as a warmer.

My stepdad always handled the selection, and he was a movie buff. I guess that was why he could always get into useless conversations with Sage. He did have good taste–or maybe his taste rubbed off on me.

Dad said, "Let's watch a classic tonight." Everyone moaned at the suggestion.

My dad insisted, trying to convince everyone that they would enjoy it. "You guys will like this, trust me."

I was always appreciative of the stuff that we had. Coming from nothing in North Korea and moving to the States into my family's home, I knew they had what most people would call a good life. In the current social hierarchy, you had the poor, the filthy rich, and a handful of pockets that were spread throughout every city. A "pocket" was the nickname given to the remaining middle class that existed in the States. My stepdad told me that there was a time when things were so much better. He told me that, twenty years ago, Detroit was looked upon as an isolated example of how cities could go bankrupt, but the government's growing debt and collaboration with corporations created a domino effect from one state to another. I was grateful to have so much, as I looked at all my friends and family who were with me.

My daydream was suddenly interrupted as a popcorn hit my head. I turned around quickly and knew right away who threw it. "Hey, stop that!"

Mark was there with his buddy Pete, trying to maintain an honest face, but struggling to contain his laughter. My dad jokingly yelled, "Cut that out, Mark, and apologize to your sister."

Mark replied, "Sorry, Kirin," as he turned around to see if my dad was paying attention. He smirked, and I laughed, knowing his apology was in jest.

Sage asked my Dad, "Mr. Rise, is this age-appropriate for Cage?"

My dad thought for a second. "How old is Cage again?"

Sage said, "He's nine."

Dad said, "Well, there's definitely fighting, a pinch of killing, and—oh, yes, maybe an adult situation here and there."

Sage replied, "The killing and fighting is fine, considering my parents let him play all those shooter zombie games."

Dad shook his head. "Okay, sounds fair enough. I'll just fast forward the uh ... adult situation when it comes up."

Sage nodded. "Sounds good, Mr. Rise."

Dad waved to everyone to settle down and said, "Okay, okay, let's get into position. Settle down so I can get this started."

A simultaneous "Shhh" echoed throughout the room. The lights slowly dimmed, and the upper ceiling illuminated with a slight glow, making it look like stars at night. The film started rolling as a Shaolin Temple appeared on the screen and slowly faded away. The sounds of Chinese music accompanied a large group of monks sitting around a mat.

Sage shouted, "It's *Enter the Dragon!*"

Everyone got excited and yelled, "It's Bruce Lee!"

Cage turned to his big brother and asked innocently, "Whose Bruce Lee?"

Looking at Cage, Sage joked, "Sacrilege."

Gwen laughed and punched Sage in the arm. "The movie's fifty years old, and he's only nine."

"Shhh," I reminded everyone not to be so loud. My knowledge of Bruce Lee came from seeing several of his films. But, after thinking about it some more, I did recall Sifu mentioning his name during class.

I was watching Sage. You would think a movie that was way before his time would be beyond his level of knowledge, but he knew everything. I could see him mouth the dialogue word for word, "It is like a finger pointing to the moon." Hmm, I had to give him credit; he was quite impressive at times, and not just dorky.

Time flew by as we all enjoyed the movie. It was rare to see fighting movies of this quality. In more recent movies, the actors didn't really need any skill to fight on the big screen. It was edited to death, tossed in with tons of special effects. I really enjoyed the old school way of seeing real martial artists showcase their skill.

Confident of what everyone would say, Dad asked, "So what did everyone think?"

Mark said, "Yeah, that was awesome, Dad."

Gwen added, "I agree, that was really good and ... he was pretty cute."

Sage goofed around, showing off his pose and making some weird sounds that sounded nothing like the movie.

I yelled, "Sage, that sounds more like a cat being strangled."

Sage gave me a look that clearly said that was just my opinion.

Sage asked everyone, "Raise your hands if you think I sound like Bruce Lee." My dad was the only one who raised his hand.

Sage tried again, "Okay, raise your hand if I sound like a cat being strangled."

Everyone in the room raised their hands together. To make my point, I raised both my hands and giggled as I looked at Sage.

Sage responded, "Jerks!" as he continued practicing his pose, confident enough not to care if he looked foolish.

Mark's friend Pete said, "It was good, but that stuff is so fantasy. There's no way you can generate that much power. The fact is size matters when it comes to fighting." All the guys snickered and nodded when Pete said size matters.

I thought, *So immature.*

Gwen muttered, "Oh, will you guys grow up?" Then we exchanged a glance and laughed along with them.

Dad said, "Everyone behave, Cage is here."

Cage looked around in confusion, asking innocently, "I don't get it. What's so funny?"

Turning to Pete, I said, "That's not true. You guys are basing everything on speed, size, and muscle."

Pete pulled his sleeve up and showed off his biceps as he bragged, "Uh, Kirin, that's all that matters." Mark, being a goofball, showed off his muscle as well; their lemming mentality was quite evident.

"Both of you guys are complete idiots."

Sage pulled up his sleeve and frowned. I patted him on the back and said, "It's okay, your mental muscle is huge."

Sage smiled, appreciating the little gesture. He whispered to me, "If only I could move objects ... dammit!"

I smiled at Sage before turning back to the older guys, unable to let it go. "No, seriously, that's the entire point of martial arts. It makes it so that the smaller, less physically gifted, can use it on the much bigger person."

Pete said, "I think the UFMF has proven that's all theory-based. Let's face it, Kirin: evolution has spoken and has declared that a waste of time."

Before I could argue, Pete added, "Come on, Kirin. You're a smart girl; you have to be in great shape like a top athlete to make this stuff work." I shook my head in disgust.

Sage quickly stepped in and said, "Your lack of faith is disturbing." Dad caught the quote, and they both chuckled as he reached over for a high five.

Dad added, "Sorry, Kirin, I gotta agree. It's all nice in theory, but you never see what you described work. You need size to generate the power."

I replied, "No, you don't, and I can prove it." That caught everyone's attention.

I looked around, determined to quiet the crowd. "I'll need a volunteer."

No one responded until my Dad raised his hand and said, "I'll do it."

I immediately said, "You'll get hurt. Besides, I'd rather prove it on Pete."

Dad started to argue as he looked back at Pete. "Don't worry, I got this." Pete gave him a quick wink and a thumbs up.

I thought, *The male bound of stupid is unified in this moment.* I motioned to my dad to come over. Dad was no small guy, and he kept himself in shape even at his age. He was easily eighty or ninety pounds heavier than me.

I said, "I'm gonna do a no inch punch."

Peter began laughing. "A no inch punch? What's that?" My closest friends Sage and Gwen, along with my brother Mark, knew I had been sneaking off for the last several years to take Gung Fu with Sifu.

Dad said, "Sweety, make sure you don't hurt yourself, okay?" Pretty patronizing of my dad, but I knew he didn't know any better.

I said, "Dad, you need something to protect your chest.

Pete snickered but said, "Mark, go get your catcher's chest protection." Mark ran to his room and returned a few minutes later with the gear.

Mark said, "Here, Dad, put this on."

I helped Mark put it over Dad's chest and then said, "Get in any stance you want, Dad."

Pete said, "Mr. Rise, get into a karate stance."

My dad looked at me and said, "Is that okay?"

I said, "It doesn't matter." There he was, standing in his makeshift karate stance. I put my fist right next to his chest.

At the last second, Sage said, "Kirin, I don't think this is a good idea."

Gwen looked at me and quickly agreed, "Yeah, Kirin."

I was too focused to hear or see anything around me. I had a point to prove. All eyes were focused on me. Pete and Mark watched in a jovial manner.

Dad looked over to the boys and said, "Now Kirin, seriously, don't hurt your ... uhhh." At the end of his single breath before finishing his sentence, I released the punch. It launched him off his feet as he staggered backwards, hitting the wall. It was so surreal, as if I were watching in slow motion. Eyes flew wide open, everyone gasped, and little Cage broke the silence, saying, "Holy shit!"

Everyone immediately rushed around my dad to make sure he was okay. He lay sprawled on the ground out of breath. At first, I was excited that I had proved my point, but then it dawned on me that it was my dad. I ran toward him, "Dad ... Dad, are you okay?"

Dad was trying to catch his breath. "I'm okay," he said–as he held his chest.

In shock, Mark asked, "Seriously, Dad, are you okay?"

My dad struggled to sit up and grunted, "Yes, everyone, relax. I just got the wind knocked out of me."

I teared up and said, "Oh my god, Dad! I'm so, so sorry." I hugged him tightly.

I whispered again into his ear, "I'm sorry, Dad." He hugged me and tried to comfort me even though he was in pain.

Dad looked at me and wiped the tears from my face. "I'm okay, Kirin." He then looked up at everyone around him and said, "That's my little girl!"

Everyone turned to stare at me in a state of shock, as if I had performed some kind of act of God. I smiled, but this time I humbly said, "That's what martial arts is all about."

I glanced over to Mark and Pete. They looked at each other, shrugged their shoulders, and simultaneously said, "What the...?"

> *"When you truly believe in what you are doing, there is no need to show off." –Sifu*

Sifu's Journey Entry #2–The Path

End of Summer 2029

The summer night was extremely warm, but Sifu blasted his air conditioner to counter the heat. He liked the ice cold feeling surrounding his body. It was another restless night for Sifu; he'd been tossing and turning in bed for hours, trying to fall asleep. It had gotten worse the last several weeks, that nagging feeling of uneasiness.

He looked over to his side to see what time it was–the clock glowed brightly with the numbers 2:30. He sighed deeply and closed his eyes as he realized he'd wasted several hours fidgeting in the bed. He couldn't seem to get that anxious feeling out of his system. Both meditation and sleep had failed him.

"Might as well get up," he muttered as he tried to justify it.

Thought soon became action as he slowly sat up on the side of his bed. His feet pressed upon the cold hardwood floor as he took a moment to gather himself. He wasn't sure what he wanted to do as he could see only the outline of his room at night. Taking great care not to make a noise, he moved to the bedroom entrance.

"There's nothing for me to do here," he said and slowly headed in the direction of the kitchen. In the kitchen, he opened the fridge and spent the next several minutes staring into it. His choices were limited, with only a single yogurt and orange juice inside the fridge. Neither one looked appealing, so he decided to save on the calories. His thoughts were definitely elsewhere.

Still lost in random thought, he entered the living room area and sat by his desk. It was spotless like his entire place.

"Hmm, maybe I need to write something?" He headed over to grab a seat and opened the journals he'd been working on. He noticed that he'd made progress as he turned to chapter two.

The page was blank and in need of content.

Again, he stared into the pages, but nothing came out. Minutes passed as frustration hit. He slammed his hand on the desk, and suddenly something fell from the edge. "Crap," he said quietly, regretting the amount of noise he made. He looked around him to see if his noise had disturbed anyone.

From the corner of his eye, he could see what had fallen. He reached for it, lifted it from the ground, and stared at a lottery ticket that Simo had played. Sifu held it at the edges, balancing the ticket at the tip of his fingers. His emotions rose, as he was about to tear it and throw it all away.

Instead, Sifu pulled back and sank, regaining control, as he casually placed the ticket back where it belonged.

"Well, it's not the writing; nothing's coming to me," he said in frustration. His eyes skimmed through the living room area, as he saw a picture hanging on the wall. It was Sifu's favorite picture of Simo. She had given it to him on his birthday several years ago. For a brief moment, his anxiety turned to a smile as he moved briskly toward it.

Sifu admired the picture. Encased in a simple 8 x 10 black frame was a picture of Simo eating noodles. He'd never been sure why, but it had always been his favorite picture of her. He spent the next several minutes studying the picture, glancing over every detail of her face. He then realized that the picture captured that simple look that Simo always gave him. It was that look that reminded him how much she loved him.

Sifu turned around, wondering what time it was–4:43. Two hours had passed, and still nothing accomplished. His smile disappeared as his uneasiness returned.

He reached out to touch the picture, but before his hand touched it, it fell. His skills kicked into gear as he reacted quick enough and caught it before it hit the ground. He checked the hook but found it was solidly in the wall.

"How'd this fall?" he asked, taking it as some sign from the universe.

He looked at the picture and saw that it was crooked inside. He shook it several times, until it appeared to be back in place. He then took a moment to clean a little dust that was on it before gently hanging it back up on the wall.

Tilting his head back and forth, he could see it was still not quite right. Frustrated, he grabbed the picture again and this time removed it from the frame. Staring again at the picture of Simo, he decided to look at the back of it.

"What is this?" Sifu murmured, caught off guard.

On the back, Simo's writings encompassed the entire picture. He was definitely curious about what he had just discovered. He looked at a random passage written in Japanese and read it:

なべをふっとうさせて、ひょうめんにうかんでくるあくをとりのぞく。あくがなくなるまで、くりかえしつづけてください。３０ぷんぐらいかかるでしょう。

—*Bring pot to boil and skim off any chunks or foam that float to the surface. Repeat this process until it is free from foam or chunks. This will take about thirty minutes.*

Sifu just sat there for several minutes, reading Simo's work. Sifu always thought she had such beautiful handwriting. It was her recipe. All those years, he'd had this picture and he'd never realized she had jotted the recipe down here. A deep breath, followed by a big yawn, and for the first time all night, Sifu felt tired. He took the frame and aligned it back on the wall.

"I think it's time to go to sleep." He grabbed the picture, turned off the lights in the living room, and quietly made his way back to the bedroom.

CHAPTER 3
Peace and Quiet

Saturday January 3, 2032

Kirin slowly opened her eyes, taking several seconds to focus. She saw her ceiling fan cycling above and immediately forced her eyes shut.

What a night, she thought. Still glazed over by the events of the previous evening, she guessed this was what a hangover felt like. Kirin opened her eyes again. When everything was in clear sight, she grabbed a pillow by her side and covered her face.

I could just hide here and live underneath the pillow and everything will be back to normal, as Kirin laid down exhausted. Seconds passed and reality set back in as she wondered, *What time is it?* Then she heard the smothered sound of sniffing from the side of her bed.

Sniff. Sniff. Sniff.

With the pillow still on her head, she turned slightly and peeked through the narrow crevice where a huge black nose was sniffing. It was Bacon, waiting anxiously at her side with a leash in his mouth, sniffing and drooling all over her bed. Bacon was Kirin's four-year-old male bulldog, mostly black with patches of white and brindle.

Kirin said, "Okay, okay, I'm getting up."

Frizzled and dingy, she sat up, wearing only an oversized T-shirt as she scratched herself in an un-lady like manner and blew her hair out of her face. She glanced at the clock on her nightstand.

The green neon numbers read 12:45. At first she was puzzled and wondered, *12:45 am?* She slowly pieced two and two together and realized that it could not be morning but 12:45 pm. "Pluck a duck, it's afternoon." She stared down at Bacon and said, "Why didn't you wake me up sooner, boy?" Bacon dropped his leash and tilted his head.

"Hmm, there's no point, might as well get up." Seconds later, she finally made it to the edge of the bed and eventually plopped her feet to the side. Bacon was quick to smell them and began sniffing her toes.

She giggled. "Stop it, boy. Stop!" Bacon ignored her and continued to do what dogs do. Still not fully awake, she yawned one last time. "What a dream!"

Kirin brought her hands to scratch her face and noticed a cut on her knuckle. Last night's events flashed through her mind.

Whomp!

A quick flash of a punch and a figure falling to the ground.

"Dang! That was no dream."

Now fully awake, she realized that last night was reality. She called out loudly. "TV, on!" From five feet away, the TV turned on, broadcasting some travel channel. She heard some discussion about Mexico.

"TV, find latest news events," said Kirin.

The TV searched through the outer reaches of cyberspace and returned a list of the top five news events. She looked at the top of the headline news and it read: *Unknown fighter goes viral.* Kirin gritted her teeth, and plunked her head in between her legs.

"Well, this cannot be good."

In a muffled voice, she ordered, "TV play top news story."

The TV responded, "Command unknown, please say again, Kirin."

Kirin shouted louder, but still muffled, "TV, play top news story."

Again, the TV responded, "Command unknown, please say again, Kirin."

Finally Kirin looked up and spoke slowly, frustrated by technology, "TV, play top news story."

The TV began to broadcast the main news story. A reporter stated, "In last night's news, a video that has gone viral is the talk of town. An unknown female fighter captured the imagination of the crowd, shocking the world by knocking out a fighter and being the first ever amateur to win a bout at Chum Night."

Kirin faded back into her bed and tossed the pillow back over her head. In the background, she could hear the news report of her fight and caught bits of sound bites. Finally, she looked up as the reporter said, "Here is the picture of the unknown fighter. If anyone has any information or news regarding her, please contact the following number or email."

Just like that, a picture of her face was plastered on her TV in full glory.

"Change channel."

"On News 58 today, do you know this girl?"

"TV, change channel."

"Here we are interviewing people who attended Chum Night lucky enough to see—"

"Change channel."

"In a few moments, we will interview Mr. Linkwater who broadcasted last night's event ...."

"Oh, crap," she said in frustration.

"TV, sound off. Every fricking channel is talking about last night's fight."

Kirin stood and headed to the bathroom. She turned on the water and splashed it all over her face. The cold water woke her up. She looked into the mirror with water dripping from her face as she muttered, "So, genius, what exactly is plan A?"

Suddenly a thought came into her mind: *My phone!* She ran back to her bed, jumping on it and looking in the top drawer. "Ah, there's my phone." Kirin stumbled as she grabbed it, knocking the mounds of mess from her nightstand.

She tapped the phone, and it lit up, revealing over a hundred voicemail messages. Kirin barked a laugh. "Do I even know a hundred people?" Scrolling in a panic, she searched for the most important one.

"There it is: Mom ... and she's called several times."

Without much thought, she jumped to the quickest solution. "Best way to dodge Mom is to send her a text with some crappy excuse."

Kirin frantically began texting her mom: Mom, preparing 4 Foto wedding gig busy, busy, BY. Can't TLK. L%k 4ward 2 CN U NXT sun.. caL yah s%n ... luv yah, Kirin. She looked over her message briefly and admired the little touches. She thought, *This should do the trick.*

"Okay, now that's dealt with. What's next?" She looked at her messages.

Digging further, she saw a voicemail from Sage and played it. Sage's voice said excitedly, "Holy crap, Kirin ... I just caught your video online! Its's only been eight hours since some dude uploaded it, and your video's gone beyond viral. It's already at 20 million views. Call me right away."

Kirin stood still in her loft, trying to quiet the moment. The TV was silent but was constantly flashing pictures of her face. Her loft was a complete mess with clothes scattered everywhere, dishes piled up in the sink, and her phone was vibrating nonstop. She stared upwards to look at the ceiling fan spin, as she felt the entire room spiraling out of control.

"FRICK!" she shouted, the sound of her yell echoing throughout the loft.

Shaking her head and grabbing her hair, she grunted. "I can't deal with this right now." She glanced over and saw the sunlight hitting her window. "I need some fresh air."

Kirin looked around but didn't see Bacon by her bed anymore. She called him a couple of times, "Bacon, Bacon! Come on, Bacon. Let's go for a walk!" She checked the corner of her bed, where Bacon's bed lay. "Oh my god, Bacon, you're back in bed!" Bacon raised his eyes at her and looked even more exhausted.

"Come on, boy. We can use some air." She smiled at Bacon like a salesman. Kirin walked to the other end of her studio, picked up the leash, and strapped it on to Bacon. Bacon continued to lie in bed and refused to move an inch.

"What gives? A few minutes ago, you wanted to go for a walk, and now you want to go back to sleep." She tugged gently on the leash. "I'm sorry, boy, but you're walking.... I need some company of the variety that doesn't talk or text." Bacon refused to move, even after Kirin offered him a treat.

"Dang it, Bacon, you win. I'll get the wagon for you." She put her hands on her hips and shook her head.

"Bad dog!" Kirin stomped her foot, but Bacon remained indifferent.

Kirin grabbed her favorite red hoodie, found a pair of jeans which she slid into, and smelled some used socks. "This will do the trick," she murmured, feeling like she'd accomplished something. She headed downstairs with Bacon, and each step was accompanied by a vibration from her phone. Each shake began to feel like an earthquake.

"Ugh, seriously."

She motioned to Bacon to stay, and Bacon surprisingly followed her command. Shaking her head, she thought that this day couldn't possibly be any stranger.

She dashed upstairs, opened her door, and flicked her phone across the room, where it landed on the bed. "Finally silence," she said as she went back downstairs to reunite with Bacon, who hadn't moved from his spot.

Kirin pulled out a little old red wagon she kept in storage. It had a slight squeak when it was pulled and was in dire need of repair, but it would do the job for this moment. It was just the right size for a little kid, but this wagon was for lazy bulldogs who refused to walk. "Okay, boy." Kirin lifted Bacon onto the wagon. Wincing, Kirin looked down. "Did you gain some weight? You're heavier than I remembered." Bacon relaxed, enjoying the lift as Kirin wondered who was the real boss between the two.

"Let's walk."

The streets were extremely busy and bustling with activity. It wasn't unusual for a Saturday afternoon in Kirin's neighborhood, but definitely more energetic than what she was used to. It was a mixed culture of people, as this was one of the few remaining areas that was deemed middle class.

Three minutes into her walk, a stranger accidentally bumped into Kirin.

"I'm sorry," Kirin apologized quickly.

"No, no, it's my fault. I wasn't looking where I was going," he quickly said his apologies and then gave Kirin a second glance.

"Hey, you look familiar," he said as he continued to examine her face.

Kirin responded, "Sorry, I've never met you before." She then made sure not to make eye contact and immediately grabbed the wagon's handle and started walking away.

The stranger yelled, "Aren't you that girl who fought on the video?"

Kirin turned around halfway and was quick to deny, "No, I'm not. You have me confused with someone else."

Kirin ran and covered her head with her hoodie. "Let's get out of here, Bacon!" The simple stroll with her dog became a run. Everywhere she looked, even after getting rid of her communication lifeline, her face seemed plastered over any kind of electronic device. Her little ripple had turned into something greater than she could have imagined, and she was ill-prepared to deal with the consequences.

Kirin killed some time wandering the streets of Chicago. Minutes quickly turned into an hour as she was unable to enjoy the views of the city, staring only at strangers' feet. She stayed low and inconspicuous throughout her walk, trying to find a moment of peace.

Grumble. Grumble.

Her stomach gurgled. Bacon's ears perked up as he wondered where the noise had come from. Holding her belly, she said, "I guess I should eat something." Looking up, she recognized the street sign.

"Ah, I know a good place to chow down," she said, heading toward her destination. Several blocks away from her goal, she saw a homeless man waiting and killing time. As she neared him, she realized who it was.

She walked briskly to him and said, "Afternoon, Mr. Johnson." She quickly pulled out some credits and gave them to him.

He was more than appreciative and said, "God bless you, Kirin."

Mr. Johnson had been homeless for many, many years. Kirin had known him since she was a teenager; they had first meet through Sifu. Since then, he had been a good friend to both.

"I hate to run, but hopefully that'll help." As Kirin turned to walk away, Mr. Johnson grabbed her by the arm. He looked around and leaned forward, whispering, "Careful, Kirin, they're looking for you already."

With a concerned look on her face, Kirin asked, "Who?"

"Everyone," he said slowly in an eerie voice. Staring into her eyes, he added, "Your display last night caught the attention of the guys on top. Word on the street is they're looking for you fierce."

Surprised, Kirin said, "You know?"

"You know word spreads quickly, especially for this," confirmed Mr. Johnson.

Kirin looked around and saw a group of safety tactical defense combing the street in the distance. The sentries had been instated the moment guns were removed from the citizens' hands several years ago. The public was told they would assist police and create a safer environment for everyone. That was always the selling point: it was for our own good and protection.

"Crap." Kirin looked down briefly and then back into Mr. Johnson's face. "Thanks for looking out for me."

She hurried along, trying to get out of sight. A few blocks later, she heard her stomach grumble again. Fortunately, she had finally arrived at her destination, where she peeked through the glass. It was fairly busy for a very odd time during the day, but then again, this day had been nothing but strange since she woke up. She was standing outside a little small noodle shop that she frequented with her friends. The outside was all glass with the sign somewhat faded from the years in business. It read 美味面条 (Yummy Noodles).

It wasn't much for originality, but she had never been a stickler for aesthetics. The restaurant was dog-friendly; often times they would leave a bowl filled with water and some treats outside. She tied Bacon to the post and double-checked to make sure his collar was on. "Hmm, let me make sure this is working." She pulled out her little tracker and hit a button. She fidgeted with it for a moment and entered the number twenty-five. The tracker would signal immediately if Bacon ventured further than twenty-five feet from her.

"Yup, there you are. Just making sure the GPS is working on you, boy. I won't be long, I promise." She scratched him behind the ears. Bacon, distracted by the water and treats, ignored her gesture of care and continued to drink.

Inside, the tiny noodle shop was a mass of activity. A loud, boisterous crowd had gathered that late afternoon to enjoy food and each other's company. The mixture of sweet and sour fragrances floated throughout the air, enticing those from outside to come in.

From a distance, Kirin could see one of the cooks sweating in the kitchen as he hand-wove the noodles from scratch. This was why she came: Yummy was one of the few places remaining that still took the time to make things from scratch rather than processing the entire or portions of the meal. People had grown accustomed to instant gratification and had little patience to wait for a meal. To many, if it looked like food and tasted like it, that was good enough for them.

It was a self-seating place, and as luck would have it, Kirin found an empty seat in the far corner of the restaurant.

"Perfect," she said, smiling briefly, believing her luck may have changed.

She squirmed her way through the tight seating area and grabbed a seat. Appearing somewhat antisocial, for good reason, she positioned her back to everyone else. Kirin kept her hoodie on and grabbed a menu, forming a mini fort. Feeling somewhat secure in her little space, she scanned through the menu to decide what to eat.

Several minutes passed as a waitress finally walked up to Kirin and asked, "What you have?" in a very thick accent.

Kirin made no attempt to make eye contact or say a word. Instead, she pointed at a picture on the menu.

"Is that all?" asked the waitress.

Kirin nodded and handed the waitress her menu, hoping she would take the hint and leave. The waitress was too busy to worry about formalities and rushed back to the kitchen to place the order.

Time stood still for the next fifteen minutes as Kirin waited patiently for her meal. She had no phone to doodle on, and she was lost in her own thoughts. Enjoying the quiet, she double-checked her tracker to see if Bacon was safe and still within range.

"Here you go," said the waitress, as she laid down two orders of soup and began walking away.

Confused, Kirin wondered, *What's going on?* Kirin finally turned around to speak to the waitress, "I, uh ... only ordered one?" But her voice fell upon deaf ears, as the waitress was long gone and headed back to the kitchen. Kirin shrugged her shoulders, mentally justifying it as a screw up. She smiled and took it as another sign of good fortune coming her way.

"Oh, well, I'm hungry enough to eat for two," she said as her stomach grumbled at that exact moment.

Kirin placed both hands gently on the bowl, feeling the heat warm her. The noodle was piping hot, as the steam rose to cover her face. She hovered above it, blowing several times and finally grabbing a spoon to take a sip of the broth.

Slurp.

For that instant, all her troubles seemed so far away. The soup, which brought her a moment of joy, was quick to take it away. It was delicious, almost as good as soup she'd had back in her past. It brought back memories of her time with Sifu. With each taste, sadness filled Kirin's heart as she thought, *I miss him. If anyone could help me right now, it would be Sifu.* Deep down, she knew that was a fool's hope.

Kirin was about to take one more sip, when suddenly a voice she had not heard for a long time spoke, "You know the best way to not look suspicious is to not dress so suspicious." In shock, Kirin froze with the spoon close to her mouth. The stranger spoke again, "I thought you outgrew wearing hoodies?"

The voice was familiar and soothing, and tears quickly started rolling down her face. Kirin dropped her spoon which splattered in the soup, making a tiny mess. She turned her head to look and then stood up immediately, confirming who the voice belonged to.

"I don't believe it!" she said with a trembling voice. She hesitated just for a second, wondering if this was a dream, and then moved toward the stranger to give him a tight hug. The stranger was caught slightly off guard, but reciprocated with a gentle touch and a kiss on top of her head. Kirin, not wanting the moment to end, squeezed every second of that hug and said with some comfort, "Sifu."

Memories flashed back to the last time she had given Sifu a hug. It was a much sadder and darker time that she recalled, when she gave that hug of comfort for that moment.

Kirin's face was smothered against Sifu's chest, muffling her voice. "It's been so long since I last saw you. How long, Sifu, three or four years?" she asked, not caring for an answer, but just giving him a reason to speak, so she could hear his voice again.

To Kirin, it may have seemed like years, but Sifu kept a watchful eye over her even if she wasn't aware of it. Sifu replied, "Let's just say it's been awhile, hmm ... it seems like yesterday when I would yell at you about your lousy stance."

Kirin smiled, not breaking the embrace. She thought to herself, *I missed hearing Sifu's criticism.*

Sifu said, "I see you have two soups. Would you mind if I joined you?" Kirin finally let go, and they sat opposite from one another. Her smile beamed from her face, like an awestruck fan seeing a rock star. Kirin felt at peace again. All concerns and worries of the day for that moment were forgotten.

Sifu stared at Kirin; she had grown into a beautiful young woman. He looked straight at her and said, "I enjoy this soup, much different from the one I sell, but it encompasses what makes things good and delicious."

Kirin listened intently as Sifu continued to speak, "You know why everyone loves soup, Kirin?"

Kirin shook her head no, and then said, "I'm not sure, Sifu," in a gentle voice.

Sifu did not respond right away. Instead, he began stirring the bowl, making sure all the ingredients had time to blend. Sifu looked at Kirin as he brought the spoon close to his mouth, but he didn't sip from it. He smelled it and paused almost to create anticipation for himself. Finally, the broth entered his mouth as he savored the moment. "Ah."

A moment passed as Kirin stared at Sifu. He finally said, "A good soup has that comforting feeling. It reminds you of the good times and brings you back to a place you love. It's almost like being back at home."

Kirin looked away, almost understanding what Sifu was trying to say. She was humbled by the words and replied, "Yes, Sifu, it does." She wondered if he knew that the words had further meaning now to her. "Sifu," she asked gently, "are you okay?"

Sifu responded with a slight smile. "If I'm alive, then I'm okay."

Kirin didn't press any further. Although her skills at reading people were nowhere near Sifu's, it did not take much to know Sifu was still not one-hundred percent himself. Light reflected off his hand, and she stared at Sifu's wedding ring.

She smiled at him and said, "I'm so glad to see you." Kirin finally settled down from the excitement and just began to notice how different Sifu looked. His face was more defined, his hair thinner, but most significant was the amount of weight he had lost.

"I almost didn't recognize you, Sifu. You've lost a good amount of weight," Kirin said with some shock. "You look good physically," she said cautiously.

With a somber look on his face, Sifu said, "It was never my physical health that was in question, Kirin."

Sifu then perked up and confirmed, "Glad you noticed! I have lost some weight. You know eating out with the students all those years kept me festively plump."

Kirin suddenly snapped her fingers and pointed at Sifu, as she put two and two together. She accused, "Did you order the second soup?"

Sifu did not answer her but just grinned. "Too much talking, Kirin. You're gonna miss out on the peak of the soup. Have some now before it gets cold." She listened to Sifu and followed his routine for eating soup. It was like old times when she would mimic his motions when learning the form.

During the moments of silence while eating with Sifu, Kirin thought, *I don't know how he does it. I haven't seen in him in years, and he's got like a GPS on energy and can just track you down.*

She looked at Sifu curiously. "Try to amuse me for a moment, Sifu, and tell me how I run into you at this unlikely hour, at this particular place?"

"Kirin, for the most part, the universe works on a smooth flow of events. Every so often, though, it does throw a kink, or so we'd like to believe that." Sifu paused and pondered for a moment before continuing, "And, when it does, you have to find that flow again."

Kirin carefully asked, "Is ... the universe flowing for you again, Sifu?"

Sifu gave a humble smile. "Same old, same old." Kirin noticed that it was not; even Sifu could not mask his favorite comment. Regardless, it was good to hear that quote from Sifu.

Sifu interjected, "Besides," he started, and Kirin finished with him," this is one of the few places that still prepares meals fresh!

She inquired, "Seriously, Sifu, is this by random meeting, or is there a reason for you being here?"

Sifu took a sip of the soup and wiped his mouth before answering, "I did not know. I just went where the force took me, and it brought me here at this particular place, at this particular time."

Kirin sat silently and marveled at Sifu.

"What was the first lesson I ever taught you, Kirin?" Sifu asked.

Kirin responded, "Don't fight the force."

Sifu smiled and said somewhat sarcastically, "See, you did learn something."

Kirin again found comfort in hearing Sifu's voice. She wanted to milk the moment for as long as she could; she had learned at a very early age to never take moments with loved ones for granted. She remained silent again, hoping to hear Sifu's voice fill the room with anything. The restaurant was noisy, but she didn't miss a word Sifu said.

Kirin suddenly recalled something Sifu had said. With an inquisitive look on her face and her head tilted, Kirin asked, "Sifu, maybe I heard you wrong, but did you say the soup here is good, but quite different from the one you sell?"

Sifu answered, "Why, yes, I did say that, Kirin."

With a puzzled look on her face, Kirin left it at that. Seeing Sifu after so many years out of the blue was enough of a shock. Finding out more about a noodle shop was too much to handle. Instead, Kirin asked, "I'm assuming you're not here to advertise then for more business?"

Sifu replied, "No, I'm not. It's a funny thing, Kirin. The other night I decided to catch a fight, and low and behold, it was quite entertaining." Sifu started pulling something out of his pocket that looked like a handful of credits.

Kirin looked down, hiding, even though she knew where this was going. Sifu said, "Strange, I managed to pick up a hundred credits off the floor."

Kirin thought, *I was hoping he wouldn't say anything, but it was a foolish hope.*

"By the way, I'll pick up the tab for these soups, Kirin. But then again, I believe these are your credits that I picked up after you threw it all away, so technically you're paying for it."

Kirin laughed gingerly. Then she bit her lip bashfully and said, "So, you were there, Sifu?"

When the silence stretched, Kirin asked, "Are you mad?"

In a calm and reassuring voice, Sifu said, "No, why should I be mad?"

Kirin grimaced and thought, *Stupid Kirin. If this was a genie granting three wishes, I just wasted one of them. You know Sifu never gets mad.*

Kirin ignored his question and then asked, "I'm curious, Sifu, did you send Tobias to talk to me?"

Sifu spoke softly, "I have not seen Tobias since I shut down the school."

Kirin frowned. "Then how did Tobias know I was there?"

Sifu chuckled and said, "I taught Tobias for quite a while, Kirin. I would've hoped he learned a thing or two about going with the flow."

Kirin said, "So you're telling me, Sifu, that fate brought both of you to the fights randomly the same night I fought?"

Sifu said, "I guess that's why they call it fate. Don't you think, Kirin?"

Kirin toned it down and said, "Sorry about that. I'm not trying be disrespectful, Sifu."

"No need to apologize, Kirin. But I'm curious: was Tobias a wee bit ... oh, I don't know ... animated?"

"Tobias was Tobias ... but his heart was in the right place. He was mainly concerned about you."

A moment of silence passed before Kirin blurted out, "So, what did you think ... you know, about the fight?"

"Not bad, not bad," replied Sifu.

Kirin missed hearing Sifu say that. It felt like old times asking for a critique from him. Sifu surprisingly added, "You hit the center, but you didn't hit the root of the center ... you're quite fortunate timing was on your side."

"What do you mean? I hit him straight down the center," said Kirin.

"You still have much to learn, Kirin. You look at the center as a mere target, but it has to be looked upon as the source."

Kirin said, "I don't understand, Sifu."

Sifu said, "I'll explain that later."

Then he looked at Kirin and said, "Tossing the money in the air, a pinch over-dramatic?"

"You always said Wing Chun relates to everything. Knocking him out wasn't enough, Sifu. I had to make a statement. You said in combat, when dealing with your opponent, you have to create that shock in their system."

Sifu said, "That is true, so tossing the cash into the crowd was your shock to the system."

"Yes, Sifu."

Sifu sat passively, almost forcing Kirin to blurt out her true feelings.

"I'm tired of it, Sifu, sitting by the wayside letting the world change in front of me, and not doing a thing about it. Society's become nothing more than drones; the rich pass laws, and we simply take it. Corruption runs rampant, and no one does anything about it. No one ever thought we would see an America without guns, yet we've come to that point. Everything's been monopolized to the hilt, and the America we know now is transforming into the very country I escaped from."

Sifu asked, "So, you're gunning to take down the UFMF?"

Kirin was surprised by that statement. "My fight was to make a statement, to put a little doubt in the entire system. That's all."

Sifu asked, "And, that's pretty much as far as you planned, isn't it, Kirin?"

Kirin looked down with regret. "Yes, Sifu ... I thought I'd make an impact, at the very least create a kink in their armor."

"Oh, Kirin, you've done more than that," said Sifu.

"What do mean?" Kirin asked.

"Well, you made the first move, Kirin. I don't think you have to do much afterwards," he said, taking in the confused look on Kirin's face.

"What I mean is the natural balance of things: you went active, and now you're passive. Trust me, the world just realized it's their turn, and they will be quick to ask for a response back from you. That pressure you feel, the unease, is knowing that your response is needed soon."

"Sifu, I don't have a plan," Kirin said, with a quiver in her voice.

"I know, Kirin. That's why I'm here. What have I taught you about knowing your opponent?" He sat there waiting for a reply.

"Don't just make a move. You should always be one step ahead of your opponent," said Kirin.

"That's kinda close. It should be several steps, but I'll forgive you for forgetting it, since last night was a big day, and I'm sure you're a little tired," replied Sifu. He added, "Kirin, if you know yourself and know your opponent, you will win a hundred percent of the time. Fortunately for you, this enemy is easily predictable. Your journey will be about knowing yourself," he said.

Kirin pondered his wisdom for a moment. As usual, Sifu was right. Who exactly was she?

Noticing a blank stare, Sifu said, "Now for instance...." He changed his focus to someone else. "Don't look back, but there's a gentleman three tables down having soup and reading the pad. Turn around and look, Kirin, but don't look like you're looking back," said Sifu.

"How am I supposed to do that?" she replied.

"I don't know. Just look back casually," he said.

"How do I casually look back?"

Sifu did not utter another word and took another sip of his soup.

Kirin slowly turned around and looked at the man Sifu had pointed out.

Sifu said, "He's been watching both of us since he got here. They are already looking to figure out who you are and everything about you."

She asked, "Sifu, what do you mean?"

"Had you knocked that guy out, no one would care. But you created a ripple ... rattled cages and placed doubt on the entire system. You're attacking most importantly their livelihood, their belief—or, as some would say, their foundation. You can't spit on their faces and think there won't be some repercussion," answered Sifu.

"Sifu, I didn't mean to make trouble for you. I know you've gone through some tough times the last couple of years," said Kirin. She looked at him, hoping he would understand. "Are you upset with me?"

"Kirin, I'm always the same, and I'm always here to help you."

"What should I do?"

"I'm not here to pick your path, Kirin. That's for you to figure out. But, once you decide where you want to go, I will be there to help you along."

Kirin and Sifu enjoyed each other's company, eating soup and talking about nothing. The mere half hour with each other felt like a lifetime to Kirin, but eventually Sifu said, "I think it's about time for me to go. I have some work to do."

Kirin was not ready to say goodbye, and she was saddened by the fact.

Sifu got up and was about to leave as Kirin reached out to grab his hand. "Sifu, seriously, how did you know I would be fighting at the place that night?"

Sifu looked down into her eyes. He reached into his pocket and pulled out a crumpled piece of paper. He handed it to her and said, "Take a look at it."

Kirin grabbed the paper and began opening it. Sifu said, "Do you know what that is?"

Kirin looked at if for a second and suddenly said, "Yes ... yes, I do." She turned to Sifu, and he could see the truth on her face. "I do. It's your old flyer that you used for advertising back in the day."

Sifu shook his head and said, "Yes, you're correct. It is. Do you know that those flyers were the only form of advertising I have ever used for the school?"

Kirin was taken back by that. In a world of self-promotion, she wondered why Sifu would go that route. She said, "I knew you barely advertised, Sifu, but no ... I didn't know that."

"For all the years that I was open and the hundreds of flyers that I posted, only one was ever brought back to me."

Kirin shook her head. "I don't get it, Sifu?"

Sifu said, "Read the flyer, Kirin. What's the most noticeable thing on the flyer?"

Kirin tried smoothing out the flyer and began trying to make out the words, "Well ... come to think of it, I always found it strange that the focal point of the flyer was not to remove it from its place, instead of promoting the school or the art."

"Like I said, Kirin, not one step ahead of the game, but several."

Kirin was confused. "Huh?"

"Of all my students, you were the only one who was willing to break the rules. A simple act of disobedience. Even with my warning written for all to see, you still decided to rip it off and bring it to school. This is the same piece of paper you brought that very first day. Do you remember?"

Kirin remembered that day, that insignificant moment when she ripped out the flyer and decided to bring it back to Sifu's school.

"You see, this was not a mere oversight by a twelve-year-old, being careless and not reading. Deep down, there was something in you that wanted to challenge the status quo. Since I've known you, you've proven me right. You've been defying authority ever since," said Sifu.

"So, you knew I was going to eventually fight?"

Sifu nodded. "I knew it was just a matter of time. It was never a question of if but when!"

> *"A random encounter is your inability to understand the meaning of the moment." –Sifu*

Short Stories #3–Kirin's P.O.V.

Detention with a Twist–1 year 207 days

"Get up! Wake up, Kirin." I looked up slowly as those were the only words I could make out from Sage's mouth. He continued to speak, as I began to gather my senses.

"Kirin, you're going to be late for your history class," he said.

I finally put two and two together, and I realized that I had fallen asleep in the library.

"Crap, you're right, Sage." I was on the brink of being late for my next class.

Sage said, "Another bad night of dreams?"

I nodded, got on my feet, and took off in a flash. Dashing in and out, weaving through the traffic of a high school hall, I was a good fifty feet from my class. Suddenly, I heard a teacher shout, "There is no running in the hall!"

I turned around in my tracks and stopped. Mrs. Kildare looked at me and said, "Yes, Ms. Rise, I'm talking to you."

I said, "I'm sorry, Ms. Kildare."

I spun around and a huge object slammed into me, catching me off guard. I had no idea what hit me, but my stance quickly reacted as I slightly shifted to deal with the force and shook off the impact.

There on the floor was a student dressed in his football jersey. He was a large and bulky guy, easily twice my size, but upon collision he landed on the floor while I was left standing. It took a couple of seconds for me to realize it was Malcolm from the football team.

Mrs. Kildare yelled, "This is why there is no running in the hallway, Ms. Rise," as she made her way to help the student up.

"I wasn't running. I was standing still."

Mrs. Kildare didn't like the response and gave me an evil look.

Several of Malcolm's friends started laughing and said, "Dude, you got knocked over by a little girl. What the hell?"

Malcolm dusted himself off and refused help from Mrs. Kildare. He looked at his friends, embarrassed, and responded, "Shut up, I slipped on something." His face began to turn beet red from embarrassment.

He looked to me and asked, "Uh, are you okay?"

I wanted to help him save face and replied, "I'm okay, just shaken up a bit from the impact. I mean, you're a really big guy." I did some B-acting wobbling around and then said, "Thanks for asking."

Unfortunately, the bell rang, and I was late for history.

Frick, I thought, trying to find a glimpse of humor in the situation. Several seconds later, I finally walked into class, where I could feel Mr. Taylor's stare down the back of my spine. I did my best to make it look like it was no big deal, but eventually he spoke, "Kirin, thanks for joining us late. You can join us later this week for detention."

I wanted to say something back but didn't respond. Instead, I sat obediently down on my chair, unfazed by the fact that I got my first detention. Instead, I was curious at what happened in the hallway. I'd been struggling in Wing Chun classes working on my shift, but when I least expected it, my stance along with my shift worked.

Why? I wondered as I continued to gaze outside the window, searching for an answer.

I zoned out of our history class, instead thinking about the lessons Sifu had given me in the past about shifting.

What did I do differently to make it work? Why now? Why'd it work when I didn't even expect it?

I recalled something Sifu mentioned about controlling one's center. He said that martial artists stand and walk differently, since we work on our center of gravity all the time.

He said, "When you walk, your center of gravity is balanced naturally, so when an object runs into it, such as another person, and they don't have control over theirs, you continue doing what you're doing and they end up either falling or being pushed aside."

Holy crap, he was right, I thought. *But then again, he's always right.* I smiled when I realized that I had just experienced what he was describing.

But as Sifu always said, "The difference between skill and luck is consistency." Unfortunately, I had done something without even knowing what or how I did it.

Suddenly a voice startled me, breaking my focus.

"Ms. Rise, Ms. Rise—I asked you a question. Not only did you come late to my class, but you also didn't bother paying attention. Maybe you'd like to explain to the class what I just said about the fall of the Roman Empire," said Mr. Taylor as he stared at me, waiting for an answer.

I was upset that he distracted my train of thought, and I knew I was probably going to regret the next words that came out of my mouth. So, I gave him an answer—a thorough answer that included not only what the book stated, but went beyond that for the next several minutes.

Mr. Taylor stared at me blankly and then finally said, "Ms. Rise, I don't know what it is lately, but I'm not too fond of your recent behavior."

Then I said, "It's not too difficult to read out of the same book and parrot the same things."

Mr. Taylor's eyes squinted at me like a laser. "I think you should go see the principal now, Ms. Rise."

I don't know what got into me, but I snapped, "For what, giving a better answer than what you gave?"

The class gasped at my comment and stared at me.

Mr. Taylor just pointed his hand at the door and said, "Leave now, Ms. Rise."

I gathered my stuff and headed out the door, leaving the rest of the class shocked at what had transpired.

I began my slow walk to the principal's office, not so concerned at what had happened. I was thinking about how my own Wing Chun training was affecting how I began to look at things. Suddenly a thought occurred to me as I stood still in the middle of the hallway.

The more time I spent studying Wing Chun and learning its ways, the less sense school made to me. I wasn't particularly sure if that was a blessing or a curse. I had always been a good student since I came to the States, but Wing Chun taught me the key was understanding the main foundation of each class. Once you figured out what that was for each subject and every teacher, it was like unlocking the mysteries to a quick and easy A. Even being in all the advanced classes was not a challenge at all, as school almost felt like it was a waste of time.

Besides, all my classes seemed so easy now, when compared to figuring out how to make Wing Chun work.

At the same time, I was starting to realize that almost all my classes were nothing but copies of our books, being mimicked by my teachers. I wanted more. I needed more than that.

What is the point of all that? I can read the same book on my own. Why can't all my teachers be like Sifu? I thought.

I looked around and realized that the hallway was empty. I clenched my school bag tightly and ran down the halls to the principal's office.

Delicious Fried Rice—3 years 17 days

The crowd was loud that night, and chatter filled the air. The aroma of food surrounded good friends as they took their seats.

I said excitedly, "Okay, you guys remember my order?"

Gwen rolled her eyes. "Yes, Kirin, I got it," as she continued to text, making me wonder if she really did.

Sage looked puzzled and asked, "Not sure how you can be so thin, for a girl who eats as much as you do."

I made a slight sound. "Hmh … I'll be right back. I just have to use the bathroom."

A couple minutes passed, and in the distance I could see Gwen giving the waitress our order. I tried scurrying back in time, but the waitress was done and already halfway back to the kitchen. Excitedly I said, "This is my favorite Chinese restaurant! Did you guys place my order correctly?"

Gwen said, "Yes, exactly what you wanted."

I asked, "How about you guys?"

Sage and Gwen spoke at the same time, "Yup, we put in our order as well."

"I can't wait." I checked my phone, hoping the minutes would pass by faster. Ten minutes passed as chit chat, texting, and regular teenage garble was spoken. Finally, the waitress came back out and started placing our order on the table.

She said, "Who had the salt and pepper fish, the ox and tripe, and the–"

I interrupted her question, raising my hand in excitement. The waitress didn't share my enthusiasm as me and just lowered my food in front of me. My eyes popped open and my lips smacked as I began sliding both hands together, hoping something magical would appear, which it already had.

"Target, center, eat it," I said excitedly. I thought, *Hmm ... I like that phrase. I should use it more often.*

Just as I was about to take my first bite, the waitress said, "And finally two orders of fried rice."

Those two words of *fried* and *rice* caught my attention–not because I craved it, but because I wondered why someone would order it.

Sage spoke up. "That's mine." He showed the same excitement I had for my meal, but for rice. The waitress said, "And I'm guessing you got the other fried rice?"

Gwen smiled with pride. "Yes, ma'am." She finally put down her phone and focused on the food.

Before I could take a bite, I raised a single eyebrow, perplexed. I sat there bewildered as both Sage and Gwen started chowing down. "You're right, Kirin, the Chinese food is *derricious*," Sage said with his mouth full.

Gwen concurred, "Mmm," as she smiled at Sage and continued to eat the rice. With a blank expression, I stared at them.

"What? You haven't even had a bite. I thought you loved the food here?" said Gwen.

Dead silence fell upon me as Sage and Gwen continued to eat. Finally they both looked up with food still in their mouths and said, "What?"

I said, "Okay, two things? One more so than the other. One: basic fried rice is simply soy sauce with rice. You guys both know this, right?" Gwen and Sage shrugged their shoulders, oblivious to the magic of Asian cuisine.

"But, I'll give you the benefit of the doubt. I mean, sure, I can kinda understand why you at least ordered one."

"But the second thing is: why two? Seriously, why two fried rice?" as I held two fingers up inquisitively, waving them back and forth between them.

Sage and Gwen slowly turned to look at one another. They paused and then turned toward me, staring blankly.

"It makes no sense at all. Did you guys not hear each other's order?" I asked.

"Sure we did," they agreed.

Sage added, "Gwen ordered first, and I pretty much like the same food she does, so...."

"And you still ordered double of something you could've shared?" I asked. I knew I had to go on the offensive to make my point clear. "Basic fried rice is made with soy sauce and rice, and you can add other ingredients based on your liking."

Sage asked, "So, it's not made out of brown rice or from Uncle Ben?"

I just rolled my eyes in disbelief.

Then I said, "Family style?" as I looked intensely at Sage. "Sage, you're Asian. Don't you eat this all the time at home?"

Sage replied, "Well technically, Kirin, I'm half-white/half-Asian ... and my mom usually makes American food, so to answer your question, not really."

I looked away. "Regardless, again I ask: why two fried rice? It's not like a burger that I'm asking you to cut in half."

I could tell Gwen was amused by my antics until she said, "Don't look now, but isn't that Hunter?" I froze for a second as Sage casually peeked over my shoulder.

Sage said, "Yup, that's him, and either he's interested in what we're eating, or he's got his eye on you, Kirin."

I reached over and punched him in the arm. "Ouch, that really hurt," Sage said, rubbing his arm. I turned around to double-check if that was Hunter as we caught him a bit off guard. He awkwardly looked down for a second, then looked up and waved hi to everyone with a somewhat geeky smile. I wasn't really sure what to do next, so I waved back.

Gwen asked me, "What are you doing?"

I said, "He waved at us, so I waved back. Heck, I don't know what the etiquette is for waving."

Sage spoke to his phone, "Search *etiquette for waving*."

"Shut up, Sage," both Gwen and I responded one after the other.

"Well, don't look now; he's coming over," Gwen teased.

My stomach sank as I thought, *I waved hi to him. I didn't wave him to come over.*

Sage responded, "Maybe you should've done the Ms. Universe wave. It's more neutral."

Gwen asked, "What's that like?"

"It looks like this." Sage took his right hand and started showing the front of his palm and the back and alternating it. Gwen started giggling; she often found Sage's humor quite amusing.

I asked Sage, "How is it you know how to do the Ms. Universe wave?"

"I'm fifteen years old. They're gorgeous women in bathing suits. It doesn't take a profiler to figure out my next move."

Gwen and I looked at each other and nodded at the logic.

Hunter reached our table and said, "Hey, Gwen, Sage ... uh, Kirin." We all smiled and did a simultaneous hand raise.

"So, you guys come here a lot?" he asked.

Sage threw his hands up in the air and did a really cheesy Asian accent. "What is that supposed to mean? Kirin and I are regulars 'cause we're Asian?"

Sage turned to me and said, "Kirin, can you pass me my abacus so I can calculate the tip?"

In a panic, Hunter waved his hand and said, "No, no, that's not what I meant ... I, uh...."

Sage started laughing. "I'm kidding. I'm kidding." Our table started laughing out loud, while Hunter looked relieved that he hadn't stepped over any racial boundaries.

He chuckled nervously.

Gwen asked, "Who did you come with? Do you have a hot date?"

Hunter said, "No ... I'm here with my family. Besides, I'm single," as he looked directly at me. I immediately looked away and drank some water.

"Really good water here," I said as I lifted my glass. I thought, *Really good water? What did I just say? Stupid Kirin.*

All of a sudden, a little girl came by tugging on Hunter's T-shirt. Hunter looked down and dragged her gently to the front. "Hi, this is my baby sister, Bella."

Both Gwen and I looked at the little girl and said, "She's such a cutie."

"How old are you, Bella?" I asked.

Bella replied shyly, "I'm five," holding up only four fingers before hiding behind Hunter. Hunter then introduced Bella to everyone in a slow voice, "By the way, Bella, this is Sage, Gwen, and Kirin. Now don't be rude. Can you say hi?"

After hearing my name, Bella peeked from behind Hunter and smiled, "Kirin...."

I looked at her and said, "Mhm, that's my name."

Bella looked up to Hunter and said, "Oh, is that the girl you always talk about?"

Hunter put her head behind his entire body and nervously responded, "Ah, little kids say the craziest things. Now, Bella, I talk about a lot of people," Hunter said as he tried to neutralize her comment. He looked back toward his table and said, "Well, I uh ... better go back to my dad and finish our meal."

Our group snickered as Hunter said, "I'm sure I'll see you around school," as he waved goodbye and gave me half a smile. We made a slight gesture that we would see him as well. Hunter started walking back with his sister, but after several steps, he turned around and said, "Oh, by the way, you guys should definitely try the fried rice.... It's so good." He turned back with Bella and then sat down with his dad.

Gwen and Sage were about to erupt with laughter as they stared at me. I palmed my face and pretended to smash it on the table as they finally burst into laughter.

The Origin–3 years 25 days

The restaurant was noisy as we sat in our regular round table. We had just placed our order, and my attention was focused on reading the Chinese horoscope to see if the suggested personalities were correct. The rest of the guys were either texting or playing games on their phones before our food arrived. Sifu was sitting quietly in the center of our circle.

"Mhh," Sifu cleared his throat, putting his hand to his mouth.

"Everyone!" Sifu said out loud.

One by one, Sifu said our names, "Robert, Ryan, Danny, Big T, Ken, Doc, Tobias, and Kirin." It was like a role call in the Army as everyone looked up when called upon. This was the core of the school, the regulars who constantly trained.

Sifu then spoke, "Why are we all here?"

We all had puzzled expressions, wondering if this was some sort of trick question. Some of us stared up at the ceiling, pondering, while others met each other's eyes, trying to clue each other in on the question.

Danny raised his hand, ready to answer.

Sifu looked at him and said, "Danny, we are not in a classroom. Just speak."

Danny looked around and proudly said, "I thought we were all here to eat?"

Robert rebutted, "Thank you for that answer, Captain Obvious. They glared at each other, waiting for the first one to blink. Robert won as usual, as Danny looked away and muttered a little swear.

Sifu then stepped into the conversation, "Yes, Captain Danny, we are here to eat and hang out with each other. Now look around. We are busy texting, talking, or playing games. We ignore the very company we should be enjoying."

Everyone looked down in shame after Sifu's comment. He was right, as he always is.

Sifu said, "Turn around for a moment and see everyone else at the restaurant."

We all glanced throughout the restaurant and saw exactly what Sifu was describing. Couples sat together ignoring one another; kids were texting, watching movies, or playing games on their phones. Sure, everyone was with one another, but only in distance, not in substance.

Sifu said, "Focus on the moment and enjoy it. The now is the most important time of day."

The guys apologized to Sifu and to one another and began putting away their cell phones.

"Now that I have your attention, let me tell you the story of where you came from," said Sifu.

Danny said, "I thought I came from my mom and dad?"

Robert immediately commented, "I'm willing to bet that you came from a turkey baster, Danny."

"Uh, shut up, you dick!"

I listened to them bickering until Doc said, "Guys, watch your language; we have a girl in the group now."

I spoke up, "You're right, Doc. Let's not upset Robert." Robert looked at me in disbelief as he made a snide comment in Korean.

Big T ignored the exchange, focusing on the food. "We're ordering chicken, right? 'Cause the other stuff I don't even recognize."

Robert said, "I'm sure Ken is disappointed that he can't find a burger and fries on the menu."

Ken glared at Robert. "There's a reason you're king of the dicks!"

Danny spoke again. "Uh, is there anything in the menu that hasn't died?"

Ryan countered, "As long as what I eat didn't require chloroplast to grow, I'm fine."

Tobias finally spoke up, "Everyone, shut up. Sifu's talking." Tobias was definitely the ring leader of our group, next to Sifu. If he spoke, we listened and followed. A hush gathered over the group.

Sifu calmly waited for the commotion to die down and began speaking, "As I was saying, not where you came from, but your Wing Chun lineage."

We all looked at each other and nodded, thinking, *Ooohhh.*

Sifu continued, "Wing Chun's history has been passed down from generation to generation by word of mouth. That's how Yipman did it, that's how my Sifu did it, and it's worked out pretty well so far.

"Now Ng Mui was a nun who taught the founder of the art Yim Wing Chun."

Doc interrupted, "Sifu, I know there have been talks about it in the past, that Ng Mui could have been a man, disguising himself as a nun at the time. What do you think?"

Sifu replied, "Doc, I know of what you speak. Back in the early two thousands, a group from a Wing Chun lineage said they discovered some new information that proved that Ng Mui was a man."

Danny, "So is it, Sifu?"

Sifu smiled, shaking his head as he looked at Danny. "Look at the art itself, Danny. There is no way any man could be smart enough to put something as brilliant as this together."

I smiled broadly radiating for all to see. Robert shouted, "Don't be too proud, Kirin. I bet she still had to cook the meals at the end of the day." I gave him that look in return.

Sifu continued, "Ng Mui was the number one elder of the five at the Siu Lim Temple. Her martial arts skills were already top notch, but she continued to study under her Sifu Gum Fung Chi as well as her grandfather. I believe the other elders were named Gee, Fung, Bak, and Maau, but that isn't too important to remember."

Ryan asked, "When was this, Sifu?"

Sifu paused for a second and said, "This was during the end of the second Emperor of the Ching Dynasty, somewhere in the late 1600s to the early 1700s."

From the corner of my eye, I noticed Ken was writing on his napkin. He then suddenly interrupted everyone and asked, "Sifu, how do you spell uh New Moy?"

Sifu answered, "N-g, space, m-u-i."

Ken replied, "Thanks, Sifu," and continued writing on his paper napkin.

"Anyway, at the temple, Ng Mui started to refine the art. She developed a style called Plum Flower Eight step or Mui Fa Bak Bo. Afterwards, by merely observing a snake and a crane clash, she developed the Snake and Crane Eight Step or Se Haw Bak Bo. Finally, after seeing how a little mouse smoothly walked across a field, it became known as Mouse Step Plum Flower Fist or Shu Bo Mui Far Kuen. All these three styles played important roles in the creation of Wing Chun."

Sifu looked around to all of us. "What you will notice with the history of Wing Chun is the constant evolution of the art from one period to another. So, whenever I hear someone claim it to be authentic or traditional, it just makes me laugh."

I asked, "Why do you say that, Sifu?"

Sifu said, "The art's constantly evolving. You see, how my Sifu taught it to me is not the same way I'm teaching to you guys ... and, who knows, when you guys get older and decide to teach, it will also be differently."

Tobias stated, "Hmm, that makes sense. I have to say I'm impressed that she came up with all this, from just watching."

Sifu said, "What have I always told you about the learning process? See it, do it, and teach it leads to the digestion of the art." Everyone looked around at each other, nodding, confirming that statement.

Ken interrupted again, "Uh, Sifu, hate to interrupt, but how do you spell the Plum Flower Eight? I was wondering if you can repeat that as well."

Sifu looked at Ken and kindly said, "Ken, just write it down for now. After I tell the tale, I'll go over each and every name to make sure it's spelled correctly." Ken nodded and got back to working on whatever it was he was doing.

Sifu started again, "Anyway, as fate would have it, a Cantonese guy from Canton Fon Kin province named Yim Ye Gung had a fifteen-year-old daughter named Yim Wing Chun. They made their living making and selling bean cakes."

Ken said, "Sounds like the original Chinese Burger."

Sifu laughed and then said, "God, let's hope not, but you could say her bean cakes went viral as she got her own nickname as Queen of Bean Cakes or Dou Fu Sai See."

Tobias kicked in, "Robert, kinda like you being the King of Dicks." Robert squinted at Tobias, a touch more than usual.

"Uhm," Sifu paused as he also looked at Tobias, "with popularity usually comes trouble, and just like the movies, some landlord named Wong found out about the bean cakes as well as her beauty. Wong made his passes at her, but she rejected him, so he concocted a plot to take her."

Tobias interrupted, "In other words, he got friend-zoned." Everyone at the table chuckled, except me—I wasn't sure what exactly that meant.

Sifu chuckled. "Now this is how fate decided to interject, because these paths happened to cross and Ng Mui taught Yim Wing Chun how to defend herself in a relatively short time. Wong eventually came to take her and was seriously injured by Yim Wing Chun."

Tobias said, "I guess this time Tina didn't want no cake and fed it to Ike." Several of the guys started laughing, but again I was totally clueless to the reference.

I interrupted and said, "At least he wasn't dead wrong. Get it? Dead Wong?" The guys stared at me as if I had passed gas. I quickly grabbed my drink and took a sip.

"Now Yim Wing Chun continued to study under Ng Mui. Later, she decided to refine the art even more with significant improvements. That is why she gets more of the credit and has her name stamped onto the art. Yim Wing Chun also taught her husband Leung Bok Chau.

"Leung Bok Chau ended up teaching the art to a student named Leung Lan Guai, who later taught it to two people, Wong

Wah Bo and Leung Ye Tai. Known as the red boat era, the art was refined with the addition of the sword and the pole and passed onto Leung-Jan."

Doc stepped into the conversation, "So, the original art didn't have weapons in it? That was added, Sifu?"

Sifu answered, "Yes Doc, Wong's and Leung's main contribution in history was adding the weapons to the art."

Ryan asked, "Sifu, is the bo and sword's main function just to teach us how to fight with weapons?"

Sifu quickly answered, "No, no ... the staff and the sword both help further in body unity. The staff helps with power while the sword helps with footwork."

I was fascinated, particularly because I only knew two forms and had no idea what the weapons were for.

Sifu resumed his explanation, "Leung Jan was a famous herbal doctor. His role in history is very important because at a young age Leung Jan learned from Leung Ye Tai, and later learned from Wong Wah Bo. Thus, at that stage he was the one who learned the complete art of Wing Chun Kuen.

"So around 1870 or 80, Leung taught in his shop and began organizing and further refining the art. He planned to pass it down to younger generations. Thus, you could kind of say this was his first attempt to spread it to the public. His best student was Chan Wah Shun.

"Chan Wah Shun lived from 1849 to 1913, and he was known as the money exchanger. Personally, I'm not sure what that means, but from 1901 to 1907, he had sixteen students total, the most famous of which you know as Yipman."

"Do you think 'money exchanger' means 'pimp'?" said Danny.

I replied, "God, you guys are so immature."

Ryan said, "You always have to be cautious about a guy who exchanges money for a living. Danny has a point."

Robert jokingly said, "Yeah, Tobias, don't you normally give singles to the ladies?" Tobias looked up and whistled quietly.

Sifu started talking again, "Yipman first learned from Cha Wah Shun, as I mentioned. Unfortunately, he died at a young age, and Yip did not finish his instruction. Fortunately he trained with his Si-hing Ng Jong So. Yipman at the age of sixteen studied in Hong Kong, and he met Leung Bik through his roommate who happened to be Leung Jan's son. Remember, he's the herbal doctor I mentioned earlier. He was smaller and learned a softer style as compared to Chan Wah Shun. Thus, Yipman was able to learn both hard and soft elements of the art.

"After the second world war in 1949, he moved to Hong Kong and lost all his possessions. Yipman had a friend who was a Choy Lee Fut teacher who allowed him to teach at his other location to make his living. During this time, Leung Sheung challenged Yipman and was easily defeated and became Yipman's first student."

Sifu leaned over and stared at Tobias. "Sound familiar, Tobias?"

Tobias chucked and smiled at Sifu. I watched and wondered what the story was behind that.

"Yipman's students were divided into three generations. The first generation was taught how to use Wing Chun for fighting; this was Yipman's plan to establish the style, and the art was not emphasized. The second generation was about focusing on the art itself, and the third generation got the short end of the stick as Yipman was no longer teaching them directly. The third generation only got to work with the Sihings—names like Leung Sheung, Lor Eal, Yuen Gou Wui, Chu Shong Tin, Wong Shun Leung, Ho Kam Ming, Bruce Lee, Moy Yat, Yip Chun, and Yip Ching to name some of the better known."

Tobias asked, "Sifu, have you ever met any of them before?"

"Yes, I met Sigung Ho several times and got to touch hands with him on several occasions." Everyone was in awe.

Doc asked, "What was he like?"

Sifu waved him off. "I'll talk about Sigung Ho later, but yes he was exceptionally skilled."

The group asked Sifu just to give them a little bone. "Come on, Sifu … just a little? Don't leave us hanging," said Robert.

"Okay, okay … obviously I met him when he was much older, already in his eighties. I was in my late twenties, and my Wing Chun was horrible"

"Wow, I can't believe that," said Robert.

"Can't believe what? That my Wing Chun was horrible?" asked Sifu.

Robert said, "Yeah?"

Sifu said, "There's an old saying that you ride a cow until you find a horse. Back in those days, I was lost, but then I found Sifu. He was the real deal."

I noticed that Ken had been writing on a napkin the entire conversation. "What are you doodling?" I said.

Ken responded, "I couldn't keep track of all the names, so I wrote it down."

Doc took a look at his napkin and then just started bawling. We all looked at each other, wondering what was so funny.

He grabbed it from Ken. Ken, who tried to snatch it back, but Doc was holding him at bay with his other hand.

They tussled until Ken finally gave up. Doc was unusually rambunctious and uttered, "Single stick, Ken. Learn it!"

"Give it back!" Ken shouted.

I was used to this—all my brothers acted the same way. *Must be inherent amongst men to be just stupid,* I thought.

Doc said, "Ken, this is like the most racist drawing I've ever seen."

Ken looked surprised. "What do you mean?"

Doc started passing Ken's napkin around, and one by one we all started cracking up uncontrollably. Even Sifu started laughing really loud, when he saw the napkin.

Robert asked Ken, "Dude, you draw like you're in kindergarden! What gives?"

Danny finally agreed with Robert, "Yeah, man, it looks like chicken scratches."

Ken retorted, "You try drawing on a piece of napkin. I can't possibly create a *Mona Lisa* under these conditions!"

Three-quarters of the group looked around, wondering who Mona Lisa was. Big T asked, "Is she hot?"

I rolled my eyes and threw a pair of chopsticks at Big T.

Robert yelled, "Hey T, don't steal them, like last time."

Big T just smiled and giggled.

Doc asked Ken, "Why is Yipman throwing snowballs?"

Ken grabbed his napkin back and said, "That's not snowballs, Doc! He's chain punching." Laughter erupted around the table.

Danny grabbed the napkin and said, "Dude, what's in your hands and Yim Wing Chun's hands?"

Ken replied, "I got a burger in my hand, and the Wing Chun chick has that bean thingy that Sifu said."

Danny replied, "I see that, but why are her fingers so long?"

Ken looked again. "That's not her fingers; those are chopsticks."

I started giggling, thinking, *That is so wrong.*

Ryan asked, "Why do you have a burger in your hand?"

Ken replied, "So you can tell that that's me."

Ryan said, "You're the only one drawn there that doesn't have slanted eyes. Doesn't that automatically make that you?"

Ken asked for the napkin and looked at it. "Hmh, you might be right." Everyone threw their napkins at Ken, who did a pitiful job dodging them.

Everyone bawled again as a handful of the guys said laughingly, "That is so racist."

It was all in jest. Everyone knew we were joking around; the issue of color never came into our conversations. We were a big rainbow conglomerate of races from Blacks, Asians, Whites, Puerto Ricans, Middle Easterners, and a few others. Sifu always told us to judge people by their energy alone.

I asked Sifu, "So, how did you come about meeting Sigung?"

Sifu smiled at me and said, "Let's leave that story for another day."

Suddenly the waitress appeared with our meal. Sifu smiled and said, "Ah, perfect timing as usual."

> *"Time is your most valuable commodity, and the present should demand your greatest focus." —Sifu*

Ken's Drawing

SECTION 2

Sifu's Journey Entry #3–Hollow Walls

End of Fall 2029

It was early afternoon, and Sifu was cleaning up the shop. He found joy in the process of getting things organized and would spend his time finding ways to improve himself. The sense of satisfaction never remained long with Sifu, who constantly challenged himself to find a better way.

Normally he would be sleeping at this time, but today was a good day for him, and he wanted to take advantage of it. He was consumed by other pressing matters. He looked at it as a succession of small improvements, as his life was starting to take shape. Sifu always followed his own path, and his plan was to eventually run a noodle shop during the wee hours of evening. But his interest did not lie in preparation for the night's work, but in other things.

Sifu went to the front of his store to double-check that his door was securely locked. There, he grabbed the handle and shook it twice, then a third time just for good luck. He then looked outside briefly for any activity and scurried away to the back. He had spent the last several months cleaning the lower, unused area and was putting the finishing touches on his little project. Sifu was never handy with tools, but like all things, the desire was there to finally learn, and the will eventually took over. Always a rule-breaker, Sifu was an old dog that eventually learned a new trick.

"Hmm, where is that?" He muttered as he searched through his tool box.

"Ah, that's what I need, perfect." Grabbing his screw driver, he tightened the remaining screws which held the lever in place. "Well, in theory, this should work," he said aloud with a giggle, finding ways to amuse himself. Sifu stood there admiring his work and, in the back of his mind, hoping his efforts would bear the fruits of his labor.

"For what it's worth."

Sifu grabbed the lever and took a step back. A few seconds later, the shelf popped open slowly, revealing the staircase to the basement. His eyes lit up, and a smile covered his face as he clenched his fist tightly and shouted, "Yes!"

Sifu then grabbed the shelf and swung it back and forth to make sure it worked smoothly. "Looks good." He turned on the lights in the basement and took one step down. He'd installed a handle on the back of the shelf, and he pulled it toward him.

Click.

The door was now sealed. Sifu knocked on the door, listening to the sound of each hit. "Definitely feels solid and secure," he said loudly.

Sifu felt a second of smugness, marveling that he was able to construct all of this by himself. "Not bad, not bad." His smugness immediately disappeared, as he realized something.

Sifu grabbed the handle and tried pushing it open. The door shook but would not budge. He tried several more times to jar the door open. "Uh, oh!" He sighed and shook his head, "Mental note: next time, make sure you construct a door to open on both sides."

Several minutes passed as silence filled the room.

CRACK!

Parts of the shelf wall exploded as Sifu's fist punched through the upper part. It was a sight to see. Sifu fiddled around and then pulled the lever from the other side. The shelf door finally sprung open, and he was free again, only to see the mess that littered the floor.

"A slight delay in plans, no matter." Sifu grabbed his broom and garbage container and went back to work.

"The only thing stopping you from learning is the ego." –Sifu

CHAPTER 4
You Have Our Attention

Saturday January 3, 2032

High atop the tallest building overlooking the city of Chicago, an unknown figure gazed over the handful of people and cars roaming the streets. It was quiet and peaceful on the outside as the city prepared to wake up. The little specks of humanity moved around randomly; from a distance, they looked like ants going about their business. He hesitated for a second and then cautiously approached the edge of the glass. He tapped the window glass several times with his index finger, pretending to crush the human ants from a distance. He was lost in deep thought.

Dressed in an expensive custom-made suit that cost as much as most people wished they could make in their lifetime, Thorne's appearance and presence commanded attention. He was what most men wished they could be, but could never achieve.

In the background, the faint sound of several televisions were replaying last night's activity.

For most people, it would be considered an early Saturday morning, but not for Thorne. He was always the first one to the office, last one to leave—and he was always on top of the game. That was how he got to his position, and that was exactly how he planned to stay on top, by always being one step ahead of the competition. Thorne never gave an inch and surely never took anything for granted.

The only other person awake this early on a Saturday morning was his personal assistant, Linda. She was Thorne's shadow, who knew what he needed and when he wanted it 365 days a year. Thorne checked his Rolex watch but otherwise remained still. He took a deep breath and spoke out aloud, "Linda ... ETA when Fawn arrives, coffee, and notify me as soon as he calls."

Linda's voice responded from the thin air, "Yes, sir, Fawn's about thirty minutes away, and the coffee will be right up. I will notify you immediately when he calls." Everything Linda said, Thorne already knew. He simply wanted confirmation.

Words could not describe the look of his office, as no expense was spared in creating the right atmosphere. Every inch, every spec, every detail was to perfection. Thorne desired control like no other, understanding that power and money were just the means to control.

Thorne's office had a spectacular majestic view, both inside and out. Specialized glass that towered over seventy feet high served as the wall and created a three-hundred-sixty degree look no matter where you stood. The windows provided an unobstructed sight of the entire city of Chicago, stretching for miles in every direction. The office sat so high up that if you stared outside when conditions were perfect, it almost appeared like you were walking in the clouds. Inside was a technological marvel of state-of-the-art electronics and rare, expensive art collections. It was the perfect mixture of the future as well as the past. If it wasn't the latest or one of a kind, it had no business being there.

It would be difficult for the average person to believe that this immense, posh space was for a single individual. It was also difficult to rationalize how the few could have so much and the masses could struggle with so little. It was a pure demonstration of excess.

Staring outside his window, Thorne gathered his thoughts, observing everything within his sight on this early Saturday morning.

Thorne looked at a perch that was nestled next to his table; it was empty. From the inside of his drawer, he grabbed his protective glove and picked up some minced meat that he stored away in the refrigerated compartment. He raised his hands, and within seconds his pet peregrine falcon swooped down from above.

"Good morning, Lightning," said Thorne as he rewarded her with a morsel to eat. Lightning adjusted her stance upon Thorne's glove and stretched out her wings one final time.

"Don't worry, I'm gonna have Linda take you out, so you can spread your wings today." He stared at her, admiring her proudly.

Linda suddenly spoke, interrupting his conversation, "Sir, he's on." Urgency filled her voice.

Thorne said, "Mute." Suddenly the several televisions linking the glass wall that were broadcasting last night's fight turned quiet. He walked over to the perch and tied his pet falcon to it, before removing his glove.

A voice spoke, "Do you have anything?"

Thorne gathered his composure quickly and replied, "Nothing, sir. We're at the early stages of gathering intel."

"Throw everything at this," the stranger ordered in a stern voice.

Thorne responded, "I'll oversee everything myself ... and I will find anything and everything about her, sir!"

Silence. Not another sound was spoken from the other side, as Thorne stood waiting. He looked upon the vastness of his office and then activated the sounds to the televisions by waving his hand. The glow from the screens flickered as he said, "Replay."

The television screens started playing the fight again—the same fight he had been watching for the last thirty minutes. He had been analyzing every aspect of the fight.

On his other screens, the local and global news were reporting this event. Even with his influence and connections, the news could not be swayed in this situation. The knockout was being repeated infinitely on almost every channel. Reporters were interviewing the local yahoos on their thoughts about the fight. Thorne shifted his focus and listened to the reporter on the screen interviewing a member from the crowd, "Man, that was so awesome, the knockout ... but then she tossed all the credits in the air, and I'm like payday, man! By the way, I want to do a shout-out to my friend John. Woo, I'm on TV!"

Thorne thought, *Idiots.*

Then Thorne caught a glimpse of Linkwater and Connor being interviewed about their thoughts on the fight. Thorne immediately turned away looking annoyed.

"Linda!" shouted Thorne.

"Yes, sir," she answered.

"I thought we sent out notice to everyone not to make any further comments regarding the fight," said Thorne.

"I did, sir," Linda replied.

"Contact Nolan personally, Linda and tell him if I hear one more peep from anyone from Chum Night, he'll be cleaning the rings next week," said Thorne.

"Yes, sir," said Linda.

Finally, on the major sports network station, debates were going on between a panel of four regarding the legitimacy of the fight. Thorne stared at the fight footage while listening to the debate of the panel in the background.

The host shook his head in disbelief. "I don't see how it's possible, even if we factor in luck ... with a hundred-pound-plus gap between two fighters, I cannot explain how she knocked him out."

Another panel member responded, "Maybe she was on some kind of juice?"

The third panel member jumped into the discussion, smashing his hands together. "Those fighters are all heavily tested and—"

The fourth member interrupted with a laugh and said, "She could be on every juice possible, and there is still no way in kingdom come that she should have been able to knock out a seasoned fighter like DJ in that fight."

While all this media mayhem was occurring, something finally caught his eye within the fight.

Thorne said, "Replay 14:42 to 15:03."

He watched as Kirin dropped her microphone and stared at the money before suddenly throwing it into the crowd.

"Loop it."

He watched it several times and slowed a certain scene, checking out specific facial reactions on Kirin's face.

"Pause."

Thorne stared intently at the picture of Kirin holding the credits until her face became a blur.

"Clever girl," he whispered.

"Actions speak louder than words, hmm? This was definitely planned," he said decisively as he began piecing information together.

All this time, the number count on the first video posted of the fight continued to fly. Within the hour since he had gotten to work, more than five hundred thousand had viewed the video. The growth was enormous; with media being over-saturated with thousands of reality shows, virals were now rare, and something of this nature took on a life of its own. He was checking various social networks, and they were abuzz. Post after post, line after line, this definitely drew the attention of the masses. There was no denying it.

Thorne had already calculated that this was a ripple effect and that something had to be done. He already knew that this wouldn't go away on its own.

Moments passed, and Linda slowly ascended the escalator from the ground below. In her hand was Thorne's regular drink that she prepared specifically to his liking.

Everything that surrounded Thorne was perfection, and Linda was no exception to the rule. She was every man's fantasy—a rare mix of European and Asian fusion at its best that created a sight that would make you look twice. Her hair flowed constantly as if a breeze were always by her. Highly educated and exceptionally beautiful, one would wonder why someone with her skill sets would work simply as a personal assistant. But, Thorne knew everyone and everything had a price, and he made sure he always got what he wanted.

"Quad shot of espresso, sir." She waited for a response, but did not get one. She pulled out a coaster and placed his drink on the table and turned away.

Thorne let a moment pass and then finally acknowledged her actions. "Thank you, Linda."

"You're welcome, sir." Happy for the attention, Linda looked away.

"Linda ... Fawn?" Thorne inquired as he took a quick sip.

Linda pulled out her tablet and checked. "Roughly twenty minutes, sir."

"Linda, no interruptions for the next twenty minutes," commanded Thorne. She nodded to confirm and walked sexily away. Thorne was lost in thought and did not glance over for his usual peek.

Looking at the clear glass, he spoke. "Computer, open a 46-inch screen and replay scene 2:50 to 4:20, loop."

The clear glass that showed the background of Lake Michigan blackened so that a section of glass could replay the fight scene.

There was more to discover. Thorne was meticulous in detail, realizing that if a picture was worth a thousand words, then this fifteen-minute video of Kirin would reveal even more.

He stood there like a machine, not moving a muscle, but the internal parts of his brain were active.

"Mr. Thorne?" asked Linda.

"Yes, Linda, what is it?" replied Thorne.

"Fawn just entered the building, and Justice is with him," Linda responded.

"Send them both in once they get into the office," said Thorne.

"Yes, sir," Linda confirmed.

Several minutes passed as Thorne kept watching more footage of the fight.

"Finally...." He finally drew his attention away from the screen.

"Screens off." The room turned silent other than the faint sound of the escalator.

Fawn ascended into the room. He was definitely a sight to see with his neon yellow jacket, his sixties style scarf, over enlarged sunglasses, and a pimped-out walking cane. He could light up a room not only with his wardrobe but also with his flamboyant sycophant personality. One would wonder what Fawn's role was, but he was the necessary evil to bridge the gap between corporate and the underground. He played his role well and made sure he got his hands dirty so that Thorne would not be tied to it.

Several feet behind him was Justice. At first glance, one would not suspect him to be Thorne's enforcer, but he was hand-picked above anyone else to be his bodyguard. That meant one thing: he was the best at what he did. Generally quiet and soft spoken, he made sure Thorne's safety was top priority.

He was prepared to die for Thorne; that was the price paid for his service. And, he was paid exceptionally well.

Fawn spoke in his usual feminine voice. "Sorry, boss, I got here as soon as I could."

Thorne ignored his excuse and said, "What do you have for me?"

Fawn nervously asked, "Uh, boss, I'm assuming you have me here early this morning because you're aware of last night's fight."

Thorne looked Fawn straight in the eye.

Fawn looked down and away like a scared dog who offended his master. "Uh, my apologies, of course you know about the video."

Thorne asked, "Who is she?"

Pulling out his tablet, Fawn hurried in haste to answer Thorne. "I've contacted Nolan who managed Chum Night, and he's sending the ID she used as well as stuff she left in the locker room. We're at the early stages still, boss. It'll be a bit, but she did forge the information to get in. It'll only be a matter of time before we figure out who she is."

"So, what you're telling me is you have nothing."

"Um, we're literally starting from scratch. There's a huge database of information to sort through to figure out who she is, so yes I don't have much right now."

"Listen to me carefully, Fawn." He looked directly at him. "She's a street fighter. She wasn't taught how to fight in the ring, so I want you to get word through the vagabond network and use that. Someone should know something about her." Thorne paused, and added, "She's from around here. I believe Kirin is her real name, but more than likely it's an adopted name. So I want you to check the hall for any information you may find on that. Finally, she's also either well to do or in contact with money."

Fawn inquired, "How can you tell, sir?"

"Fawn, no one throws away twenty-five thousand credits if they don't have some linkage to money."

"What about the colleges around here? Should I check on them? They might have information," suggested Fawn.

"Check, just to be thorough, but I highly doubt she goes to school. If anything, she's doing some kind of work that allows for flexibility in time."

"How did you get all this information, boss?" said Fawn.

"Because I'm me!" Thorne leaned over and stared directly at Fawn. "It's called observing, Fawn. I've given you a starting point; now work with that and get me what I need to know ASAP," instructed Thorne.

"So you want everything on her, correct, boss?" asked Fawn.

Thorne looked at Fawn and said, "Move Heaven and Earth and get me everything about her!"

"And what do we do once we have that, sir?" inquired Fawn.

Thorne said, "We are gonna test her out and see if she's for real."

Fawn asked, "And if she is real, what then, boss?"

Thorne looked at Fawn intently. "If she's for real, then we give her an invitation."

Fawn looked at him with a confused look. "But why, boss? Why give her the opportunity?"

Thorne said, "Because we can't just sweep it under the rug. Something this huge, that's gone viral this quick, we can't deny its existence. We need to bring her in and destroy and humiliate her in our place to make the point. Otherwise, the masses will start to question the system. This is just the kind of buzz that will lead to our undoing if we don't deal with it properly."

Fawn shook his head and then tapped it. "Right, right, that makes sense, boss. You so smart."

Thorne looked at Fawn again. "I expect a certain amount of ass kissing, but don't overdo it."

Apologetically Fawn lowered his hand to indicate a level. "Right, boss, I'll dial it down a notch."

"Fawn, move fast on this. I don't like sitting in the dark," said Thorne.

"Of course, boss, like the wind." Fawn made a hand gesture of flying, and then turned away, sashaying. Thorne rolled his eyes.

"I'm on it, boss!" Fawn called as he started down the escalator. Thorne turned to Justice and spoke merely with eye contact. Justice nodded and followed Fawn down the escalator.

Thorne spoke, "Linda, summon the heads. I'm sending Fawn to speak to them."

Linda said, "Yes, Mr. Thorne, when should I arrange it?"

"Give them an hour and have all of them meet at our usual spot."

"Yes, sir," said Linda. "Anything else?"

Thorne turned around and looked again outside. "Linda, come up here after the call. I have some work for you."

Thorne spoke again, "Lights out." Suddenly all the windows started darkening one by one, covering the outer view of the city, as Thorne sat in his chair, waiting with a single light upon him.

Meanwhile

An hour passed before the limo carrying Fawn and Justice arrived at a secluded warehouse. From a distance, they saw that several cars were already lined up with people waiting on the outside. They were chatting amongst themselves, caught up in a heated discussion.

The warehouse was not only in a bad neighborhood, but it also looked like a graveyard. It was a sign of the times as it was a once-busy factory that had shut down due to bad economics.

As the driver got out to open the door, all eyes were waiting for their main guest to arrive. Fawn took more time, letting Justice come out first, so he would get the final attention. Upon setting his foot on solid ground, Fawn immediately pitched up a hissy fit. He was disgusted with the place, as he thought the inside area clashed with his outfit. He stood in front of his limo with Justice by his side, staring at his watch. He yelled back to the driver, "Leave the headlights on. It highlights my suit." Fawn was always concerned with his perception, which made him the perfect PR man for Thorne.

Several of the underground leaders had been outside their cars waiting. In an unmarked car was the commissioner along with the mayor of the city.

Jabbiano was head of the North side.

Ping headed up the East side.

Travis was the South side.

Marquez controlled the West.

Everyone was already annoyed by the long wait, and they didn't appreciate Fawn's lax attitude toward the situation. Still, no one was willing to step out of line and let him know how they felt.

"Gentlemen, I'm so glad you could make our last-minute meeting. For those unaware, we are searching for this girl who fought last night's fight. I want everything you can dig up about her brought to me."

Fawn held up a digital image of Kirin.

"Linda will send you what we have, but use whatever means is necessary to get me what I need. Are we clear?" inquired Fawn, one of the rare times he seemed dead serious about his request.

Mr. Jabbiano broke the silence and started walking toward Fawn. "This is why you interrupted my Saturday? Not only do you ask us to come here at your disposal, you show up almost an hour late. If this is so important, why isn't Thorne here himself?"

Fawn was disgusted by the question. "As I have always stated, in order for this to work, the guise of separation between corporations and the underground needs to exist. Thus, when I talk, I am talking as if Mr. Thorne is speaking to you directly. Is that clear?"

Mr. Jabbiano approached Fawn along with his three huge goons. "You know what I think? I think that we signed into this deal getting the short end of the stick," Mr. Jabbiano said.

As the goons approached Fawn forming a wall between him and Mr. Jabbiano, Justice moved in front of Fawn and stared at the three very large individuals dwarfing him.

Fawn pulled out his cell phone and began playing a word game on it, showing little concern about the threatening situation.

"Hey, Fawn, I'm talking to you," yelled Mr. Jabbiano.

"Please, no interruptions. You're going to ruin my score." Fawn was completely engrossed in his game.

That pissed off Mr. Jabbiano. "F— this, fellas. Take care of him." As Jabbiano finished his last word, Justice moved swiftly.

All three went down in an instant as Justice was merciless. After he did away with his several bodyguards, he immediately headed toward Jabbiano, who retreated as Justice grabbed him. He spun him around, grabbing what little hair he had and forcing him down toward his knees next to Fawn.

"Goodie, I got the new high score," screamed Fawn excitedly, completely ignoring what Justice was doing.

Justice grunted, informing Fawn that his attention was needed. Fawn put away his phone away and said, "Hmm ... a man on his knees. I've never seen that before." Fawn smiled.

The rest of the leaders either looked away, awkwardly whistled, or stared upwards toward the ceiling.

Mr. Jabbiano was groveling, "I'm sorry! I'm sorry."

"Yes, I bet you are," said Fawn. "What's that saying–never bite the hand that feeds you? From the looks of it, you have been eating well and are getting a bit greedy."

Fawn leaned forward and smiled at Jabbiano. "Justice is about to be served." Fawn made a quick gesture.

Justice saw the signal and arm-locked Mr. Jabbiano, raising his hand up into the air and forcing his face into the dirt. Jabbiano grunted in pain.

"If you will, Justice," said Fawn.

Fawn pointed to one of Mr. Jabbiano's fingers. "This little piggy went to market," Fawn taunted.

"Aaahh!" Jabbiano screamed as Justice broke his first finger.

"This little piggy stayed home."

"F–!"

"This little piggy had roast beef."

"Dear Jesus, please stop," Mr. Jabbiano cried, his screams lingering throughout the warehouse.

"This little piggy had none."

"Aaahhh, God, stop, stop!" he groveled in agony.

"And this little piggy went wee wee wee all the way home," Fawn finished the rhyme.

"Ugh ... not the thumb, not the thumb ... Sweet Jesus ... Aaahhh!" Mr. Jabbiano was sweating profusely, squirming on the ground as drool spilled from his mouth.

Jabbiano fell to the ground, cradling his broken fingers.

"Now, Justice, be the big bad wolf and blow down the house," Fawn requested.

"Uh, that's a totally different rhyme," said Justice.

"Hmm, you're correct, regardless ... break his arm." In a sinister voice, he gave his last command to Justice.

"Aaahhh!"

Justice snapped Mr. Jabbiano's arm like a twig, and the crime boss rolled around in pain and agony.

Fawn clapped his hands like a giddy child, "Oh, I love nursery rhymes. I truly love them." Fawn glanced around with a huge grin on his face, looking for confirmation from others.

"Look, Justice, he's crying like the little piggies in the story."

Fawn looked up and thought for a second. "Hmm ... he looks more like a hog than a piggy. Don't you think?"

Fawn stopped briefly, thinking about his own question.

"Justice, what's the difference between a hog and a piggy?" Fawn waited for a response, but Justice merely rolled his eyes.

"Oh, you're no fun, Justice." He flapped his hand toward Justice. Then he leaned over Mr. Jabbiano and placed his finger on the tip of his nose.

"Please squeal for me," Fawn whispered.

"Huh, huh ... I don't understand," said Jabbiano.

"Squeal for me so I can figure out if you're a hog or a pig."

"I don't want−" said Jabbiano.

Fawn motioned to Justice. "Break his other arm!"

"No, no, no ... I'll squeal! Please don't, please don't...!" Jabbiano cried uncontrollably on the ground.

"Fortunately for you, I am merciful. Let me hear," said Fawn.

"Wee ... wee ... wee," squealed Jabbiano.

Fawn listened and finally decided. "Definitely a piggy." He looked proudly at the others, as if he had figured out the answer to a perplexing riddle. Fawn turned to Justice. "Break it."

Jabbiano looked up in surprise. "I made the sound! I made the sound!" He begged profusely.

Fawn looked at him. "I know you did, but I prefer the oink, oink sound. Don't you agree?"

Without hesitation, Justice broke his other arm.

Crack.

"Aaahhh!" screamed Jabbiano. The noise sent shivers through everyone in the warehouse before it was replaced by Jabbiano's eerie cries of pain. The rest of the members looked away.

"Does anyone else think they are being unfairly treated?" As Fawn made eye contact with the others, each and everyone one of them lowered their heads.

In a crazed, high-pitched voice, Fawn shouted, "I can't hear you!" as he leaned over with his good ear to listen.

"No, sir. No, Mr. Fawn ... you're more than fair," each group leader finally responded in fear.

"I thought so," he said snootily.

Then Fawn stared at Mr. Jabbiano. "You, down there, little piggy, what say you?"

With extreme agony on his face, he managed to say, "No ... No, Mr. Fawn, more than just and fair."

"Hmm," Fawn hummed, looking away.

Fawn stared at Justice for a moment until the bodyguard asked, "What?"

Fawn replied, "Seeing you break Jabbiano over here has made me hungry for pizza." He glanced down at the pitiful man on the ground and asked, "Hey, Jabby. Do you still have your pizza joint around here?"

Jabbiano said, "Yes."

Fawn replied, "Hmm, that place is good ... by the way, do you validate for parking?"

Jabbiano answered, "Yes, yes ... anything for you."

Fawn looked at Justice. "Call me a genius; I figured out what's for lunch today."

Justice made a slight motion reminding Fawn that business was still at hand.

Fawn turned around, "Oh yes, silly me, back to business. Very well then, take no action other than to contact me first ... understood!"

"Yeah, Mr. Fawn."

"Yes, sir. Yes, sir."

"Understood, sir."

"Very well then, have a fabulous day, gentlemen." As Fawn snapped his fingers and headed back into the limo, his message was clear. He made sure his rule was absolute.

> *"The world would be a better place if you could control yourself, rather than focusing your efforts to control others." –Sifu*

Short Stories #4–Kirin's P.O.V.

Dodge This–3 years 62 days

"Oh, crap!" I prepared for the worst, realizing the inevitable. "Dodge this, Kirin!" several guys shouted in unison at me. Swoosh. Swoosh. Swoosh. Swoosh. Swoosh. Swoosh.

I cowered in the fetal position, trying to protect all the vital spots. I thought, *Brace for impact.*

Whack! Whack! Thud! Whack! Thud. Thud!

There I was, lying on the floor, a victim of the game dreaded by nerds across the country. Dodgeball.

"You can't dodge everything, Kirin," laughed a group of jocks as they walked away.

Lying on the floor, I wasn't mad, nor could I be angry at my team. They were trying the best they could. It was true they couldn't hit me, and I could catch everything thrown my way, but I had one major handicap: I threw like a girl.

Unfortunately for me, they got wise to my game. Even though they were jocks, united they were able to create one functioning brain that came up with a simple strategy. They picked off my teammates one by one and left me for last. When that happened, even I didn't stand a chance.

I stayed on the ground, listening to the voice of mockery and laughter. Staring up at the ceiling, I saw only the bright lights hanging above me. I whispered softly, "Go into the light, Kirin. Go into the light. There you will find peace." I was smiling as I pictured a happy place with rainbows, unicorns, and waterfalls–and most importantly where dodgeball did not exist.

"Laps!" Coach Smith yelled.

Shattered like glass by the sound of his voice, my fantasy dissipated. A figure hovered above me, blocking the light. Sage extended a hand to help me.

"Come on, Kirin. Welcome to life sucks," Sage said disgustedly.

He helped me up from the ground, and I reaped the reward for being in the weaker gene pool physically: more laps.

Coach Smith was a sadistic teacher. He was old and grumpy, a former jock trying to relive his glory days. He thought by torturing the nerds he would still be part of the next generation of jocks.

Come to think of it, that did work.

Every month and a half, we would get a new scheduled activity for gym, and he was always favorable toward the jocks. May was tough times for the physically handicapped because it brought dodgeball. At least with other sports like basketball or baseball, you just lost. The game of dodgeball was all about punishment.

Coach Smith would try different ways of pretending to make even teams, but we went through the routine like sheep and ended up with our respective cliche groups. Dorks and geeks versus jocks and princesses–evolution could not change this, no matter how much man had evolved. I'd later come to realize that, as long as the illusion of fairness and balance was maintained, people fell in line and did what was ordered.

I really hated the start of the week, not because of school, but because it was often referred to as beat down Monday. The teams were evenly split in number, not in skill. The losers had to run five laps after their team was eliminated. It was the salt on the open wound, adding further humiliation to the situation.

On our third lap around, I could see the jocks relaxing and laughing at us during our exhausting run. From the corner of my eye, I noticed Hunter entering the gym area. He was dressed up in gym clothes, and he had a sheet in his hand.

I wondered what that was all about.

He walked over to Coach Smith, who was glad to see him come. He shook his hand and took the sheet, reading it before he patted Hunter on the back. Then he signaled him to join the jocks' side.

This was our second set of laps, and there was a good fifteen minutes remaining till the end of the period. We were destined to do a third.

"Line 'em up!" Coach Smith bellowed.

"Great, the circle of life," I muttered, grimacing at the thought.

The fellowship of nerds, including Sage and I, were still catching our breath. Beaten and exhausted from a low O2 count, we were going to have to go through this entire process again. Tim, the last of our team members running, was nearing the end of his final lap when he suddenly crumpled to the floor. He grabbed his ankle in agony.

"Ahh!" he yelled in pain. He was rolling around holding his ankle. We all ran over to see if he was okay.

Coach Smith waddled toward Tim and yelled, "All right, what seems to be the problem?"

Sage answered sarcastically, "I'm no doctor, Coach Smith, but seeing he's grabbing his ankle, I don't think it's his appendix bursting."

I snickered at the comment.

Coach Smith stared at Sage. "Watch it."

Sage looked away and let Coach Smith do his work.

"Okay, Tim, go to the nurse's office and get yourself patched up." Tim took a few moments but managed to drag himself away.

Tragedy for Tim immediately turned to a realization of triumph on our side. Mike, our leading geek, voiced our thoughts, "Coach Smith, we have an uneven number. We can't possibly play dodgeball anymore, can we?"

Coach Smith not only had a T-Rex body, but also a mind to match. He tried to compute the fact that he was short one for an uneven number. The visuals of a T-Rex trying to do subtraction with those shortened digits made me giggle. Everyone was excited by the prospect of a decent excuse to get out of this hell hole game.

At the very least, we could hold our heads up high with dignity that we did not have to do a third set of laps. Winning by default had become the American way.

My team members looked at each other, and we were all thinking that we finally had an out and could avoid the last fifteen minutes. We did our best to try to control our excitement.

Mental high-fives were spread amongst us with a quick nod to one another. Suddenly, Hunter jumped in, "Hey, guys, if you don't mind, I'll join your side, and we'll have an even number again."

We all looked at Coach Smith, who was so ingrained in his ways, but somehow managed to realize that this was the only way for the games to continue. He reluctantly agreed to his suggestion.

Everyone turned their heads in disgust at Hunter's offer. He had good intentions, but that led us right back into the pit of hell. Hunter walked into the group all excited, as everyone turned their back to him.

"What? What?" Hunter asked in confusion, wondering what he'd just done.

"Come on, Sage. Pay attention!" I said angrily.

Sage yelled back as he pointed to his head, "I am, but I've been catching the ball with my face for the last half hour."

Hunter didn't recognize anyone and decided to stand by me and Sage. We'd reached the point of simple hellos, waves, and small chit chats as we would pass each other during classes.

"Hey, Kirin. What's up, Sage?" Sage waved back, still in somewhat of a daze.

He whispered to me, "Why's everyone upset, Kirin?"

"Hunter, I know you don't know the situation, but every week, for fifty minutes, we get pummeled by these jocks in dodgeball."

"Oh, sorry," Hunter said apologetically. "Seriously, I didn't know."

I felt bad. Hunter had good intentions, and he was taking the brunt of the anger from all of us.

The team was deflated–and ready for another pounding.

"All right, everybody get ready for the pain!" yelled one of the jocks, pointing to us from across the room.

"Come on, guys. Let's try." I did my best to pump up the team, clapping my hands as my rally cry.

"Do or do not, there is no try," Sage muttered in a hoarse voice.

"For someone who's been catching the ball with his face, I'd settle for just try right now." Sage gave me a dirty look.

Hunter snapped his fingers and strangely enough said, "That's from ... that space movie...." Sage and Hunter looked at each other, bonding in that dork moment.

I rolled my eyes and cut Hunter off, "Will you two fools concentrate, and stop quoting stupid movie lines?"

Coach Smith said, "All right, ladies, ready ... Go!"

The jocks were super confident, as they did not even bother running to the balls. Then again, we had never beaten them before, so there was no reason for any doubt. Our side had all the balls, and I grabbed one for myself. From there, our team made some lame attempts to try to get them out, but the balls floated in the air like snowflakes. The sad thing is, that was even better than how I could throw.

Hunter yelled, "Kirin, give me the ball."

"What? Why?" I looked at him in confusion.

"Trust me on this. Give me the ball," Hunter said confidently with his hands outstretched, waiting for it. I figured he couldn't possibly throw any worse than I did, so there was nothing to lose. I tossed him the ball. His was the last ball that remained on our side, as we were getting ready for the barrage back.

Suddenly all we saw was a flash of red, like a laser beam from Hunter's hand toward one of the jocks. Then a sound bellowed that we had never heard before on our side.

"You're out!" yelled Coach Smith.

We were all stunned. Hunter had an arm like a cannon. He just beaned the crap out of one of the jocks, and they themselves were shell-shocked from the throw. We all looked at each other like Hunter was our savior. Maybe we had a glimmer of hope.

"Everyone, move back," I shouted.

All the balls were on the other end, and now they were upset. They had never lost a guy before, and payback was on their mind. My strategy was simple: either dodge the balls or catch them. Because of Wing Chun, I could literally absorb the force of the throw and catch everything in my general direction. My hands were like fly paper; whatever I touched stuck to me.

Two balls were thrown in my direction. I felt my center and easily adjusted as one sailed by me and I caught the other one.

"Holy crap!" said Hunter.

"What?" I looked at him.

"You've got some moves," Hunter said with a look of surprise.

"Here, make yourself useful." I tossed him another ball. Hunter grabbed it and threw, parting the jocks like Moses parting the Red Sea.

Swooossh.

"Yir ... out!" Coach Smith roared, unleashing a tirade of one-liners.

"Out! Sit down, buttercup."

"Bookworm, back to the library."

"Don't cry, Poindexter! Out!"

"E=mc ouch!"

"Force=mass x your face! Out!"

"Your I.Q. didn't help you then, did it? Out!"

Coach Smith was calling the game furiously, as both sides had a few left.

Sage looked at me. "I hate Coach Smith. When do you think that cholesterol level will take effect?" I laughed and told him to pay attention.

It was down to three versus two: Sage, Hunter, and I against a duo of jocks.

Hunter and I had the edges as Sage sat in the middle. All the balls were on their side, and we needed some ammo back. I caught a slight gesture from the jocks, and I realized they were both gunning for Sage.

I yelled, "Sage!" Unfortunately, Sage had that deer in the headlights look.

He was caught off guard and curled into a duck and cover position as the balls started sailing. I managed to move quick enough to push Sage out of the first ball's path. The second ball, which was just a second behind, aimed much lower, but I caught it with a single hand.

As I lay on the floor, Hunter ran toward me and looked at me as if he knew my thoughts. I quickly tossed him the ball, and he spun around with full force, rifling the last ball onto the jock's face.

"You're out!" yelled Smith.

"We won!" I hoisted my hands into the air, with a look of shock.

Even if it was only for this one day, we did something that we thought was impossible. We won for the first time. We actually won!

Excitement buzzed as everyone congratulated each other on our team. Hunter came up to me, and without thought I hugged him hard. Then I realized it was Hunter. I kinda blushed afterwards and looked away and continued high-fiving other people around us.

Coach Smith yelled, "Laps!"

At that beautiful sound, we cheered even harder, as the jocks begrudgingly began doing their laps.

"Hey, Kirin?" asked Hunter. I looked toward him shyly, still feeling awkward about the hug.

"How do you do that?" asked Hunter.

"Do what?" I said.

"Move like you're floating on air. It's ... it's like you're hovering over on the ground," Hunter said with a perplexed look. "I've never seen anyone move like that."

Hunter's words about floating on the air reminded me of our past footwork classes, and I could hear Sifu drilling us to control our center.

"Kirin, did you hear me?" asked Hunter.

Shaking my head, I snapped out of my daze and said, "Oh, sorry about that ... I, uh, control my center of gravity and keep it balanced. So, regardless of how I step, I can move in any direction smoothly right away ... kinda like a pinball."

"But all athletes do that. I do wrestling, and I'm aware of my balance," said Hunter.

"Uhm, how can I explain this...?" I thought for a second. "Well, your balance is based off muscle, but my balance is based off the body alignment. Does that make sense?" I said.

Hunter looked confused. "I'm not really sure what you mean."

I looked at Hunter and then asked, "Right now, how you are standing, do you feel balance?"

Hunter thought for a second. "Yeah, I am balanced."

I examined him and said, "No, you're not." I could see that he was leaning slightly to the back of his heel.

I walked over to Hunter and lightly pushed his chest. He immediately rocked back. I thought, *His chest feels so solid.*

"See, you were leaning on the back of your heels. That's why the slightest touch rocked you back."

Hunter shook his head. "I see what you just did, but you can see all that?"

I smiled. "It takes practice, but once you can do it, you see it immediately."

Hunter looked at me. "I don't know what you know, but whatever it is, it's incredible."

Sage yelled at me, "Come on, Kirin! Hurry up, we're gonna be late for our next class."

I turned back to Hunter and gave a slight smile. "Uh ... anyway, we wouldn't have won it without you."

Hunter smiled. "I'm just glad I could help."

"Well, I uh ... you know ... I uh, better get going...." I was turning back and forth, trying to think of something clever to say. "Uh–by the way...." Then I tripped over my legs and fell spectacularly on my butt.

Totally embarrassing. I hung my head down. *Master of my center,* I thought to myself as I ate a slice of humble pie.

As I stared down at the ground, a hand came out in front of my face. Hunter said nothing but, with a kindness on his face that I'd never noticed before, extended his hand to help me up.

Kirin's Nightmares—78 days

It was pitch dark, and the cold night air was making me shiver uncontrollably. I could barely even see my own hand in front of my face, but clung to both my parents' hands tightly. We had been moving through the forest for hours. Watching every step, listening for every sound, we were alone, scared, and hungry.

But this was our one chance to escape from the nightmare that never ended.

"Shhhh, 조용히 내려 (quiet and get down)," my father said as he motioned both my mom and me downwards. My father whispered cautiously and looked me in the eye, "Soo Jin, you must remember to run. No matter what, you must run." My mom looked at my dad and then kissed me on the head. I knew they were scared like me.

"No, Dad, I don't want to run...." My eyes watered with the words coming out of my mouth. "Mom?" I looked at her for some comfort.

"Soo Jin, you must. At least one of us has to make it," ordered my mom as she held me tightly. I rubbed my forehead as something was irritating it. My mom looked at me and tried cleaning my head.

"Ouch," I said.

She gave a faint smile as she tried putting me at ease. She whispered, "Hopefully that won't scar, you have a little scratch on your forehead." I tried looking up as my mom said, "Silly, you won't be able to see it."

Suddenly my dad motioned to my mom. From a distance, we saw a little light flicker three times.

"That's him," said my father as he grabbed my hand. Fear turned to hope. We were approaching our goal, our chance for freedom. I saw my dad embrace my mom with a glimmer of a smile on his face. She gave him a kiss back.

As we neared the light, a gentleman appeared. He was dressed in raggedy clothes like us, and was nervously looking in every direction. He waved us to approach and hurry as my father shook his hand and thanked him. He whispered

something to my father, but I caught only a portion of it. "...
Thank me once we're out of here."

My father introduced both my mother and me, and we
exchanged quick nods.

"Quiet, we still have a little distance to go!" said the stranger.
We all started walking away, heading toward a new life, when
the sound of dogs barking and voices filled the air. The comfort
on my parents' faces drained and was replaced by terror. We all
started running as the sounds drew closer.

"Take her!" screamed my father. "Go, go, Soo Jin ... Go!"

The stranger grabbed my hand tightly as I struggled to keep
up. I ran in total fear as hard as I could, not knowing where I
was headed. Both my parents were right behind me, with my
dad trailing in the rear.

"Keep running! We're almost there," the stranger said,
struggling to get those words out.

BANG!

With all the noise, a single sound struck out against the rest.
I turned to face its source and stopped dead in my tracks. I had
no idea what had happened as I stared at my dad, who stood
still for a moment. I looked at him, confused, wondering why
he would stop all of a sudden. His eyes flickered to mine, and
then he placed his hand on his chest. After holding it there for a
second, he removed it, and I saw it was covered with blood. He
turned pale white as he collapsed to the ground and my mother
ran to pick him up.

I began moving back to help them both, but I could feel a
tight grip preventing me from stepping further. My mom was
crying as she looked at me and screamed, "RUN!" She held my
dad in her arms.

BANG! BANG!

Voices surrounded us from a distance, and the sound of
the dogs barking grew even stronger. The stranger picked me
and ran into the darkness. "We have to go," he instructed me.
I screamed for both my parents as they started to fade from
my sight.

"We can make it!" said the stranger.

I looked back for a second and saw a glimmer of them both lying on the ground. I saw nothing afterwards. Tears streamed uncontrollably down my face as that image was ingrained forever.

"Father! Mother! *NOOOO!*" I cried.

Suddenly I screamed, and I sat halfway up from my bed, covered in sweat. Looking around my room, I quickly pieced together that I was safe, in the comfort of my home. It had been awhile since I'd had that nightmare, but it was always the same thing. I sat there crying, wondering why I hadn't done more. Why didn't I take a stand? Why did I just run?

I regretted my decision and my lack of action. I checked the clock on my nightstand and saw it was 2:30. I hoped I hadn't woken anyone up as I sat there.

Suddenly a tiny hand appeared from the corner of my bedroom door as Kyle walked in with his blanket. He approached me slowly in his one-piece pajamas. I just looked at him, trying to wipe away the tears. He stood by my bedside and looked at me gently.

Kyle said, "Are you all right, Kirin?" I nodded to let him know that I was, but I did not say a word. He put his tiny hand on my shoulder and leaned his head on me. Kyle then spoke softly into my ear, "It'll be okay, Kirin."

I looked at his kind face. "I know it will, Kyle. I'm sorry I woke you up."

He smiled at me. "Don't worry about it, Kirin. I had to pee anyway." We both smiled. "Give me a second. I'll be right back." I nodded to say it was okay.

Kyle dropped his blanky and scurried to the bathroom. I listened to his little pitter-patter across the hall followed by a flush. Seconds later, Kyle came running across again, waiting by my bedside.

"Thanks for checking on me, Kyle."

Kyle did not respond but asked, "Was it the same dream?"

"Yes, Kyle, the same one always. I thought I was doing well for a while, since I hadn't had the nightmare in months, but lately it's come back again."

Kyle said, "When I have nightmares, I hold teddy really hard, and he protects me." I looked at my little stepbrother and brushed his hair, grateful that I had someone to talk to at this moment. Kyle was a kind soul that did not act like a typical six-year-old.

"Kirin, you can have my teddy to help you sleep," said Kyle. I was so touched by my little brother's act of kindness that I gave him a big kiss on the cheek. Afterwards, Kyle wiped away the kiss and said, "It's just to borrow, okay?"

I said, "Thanks, Kyle, I'll give him back," and gave him a hug.

"Kirin, why is the nightmare so bad?" he asked.

"Sometimes, nightmares are scary because they feel real. This nightmare really happened to me, so it's not so easy to pretend. Before I met you and your family, I had a mom and dad." The word *had* pained me so much.

Kyle looked at me and said, "Are you okay?"

I nodded and continued, "The place I lived in was very, very bad, Kyle, and we were trying to escape. The problem was that I ran. I ran and left them. I was too scared to stand and fight. I just ran, and now they're gone ... forever."

I started tearing up again. The memory was always so fresh that it stabbed every time.

"I think you are very brave, Kirin," said Kyle.

I looked at Kyle and saw the sincerity on his face.

"So, you were my age then?" asked Kyle.

"I was close to your age, Kyle. I was eight at the time. My heart felt the pain even more.

"I'm sorry, Kirin," said Kyle. "Where is this place that is so bad?"

"Do you know where North Korea is?" I said.

Kyle shook his head and shrugged his shoulders. "Is it close to Floriduh?" I was about to tell him no, when he got up and ran to his room. A few seconds later, he returned and handed over his favorite teddy bear.

"Here, Kirin, take teddy," said Kyle.

I held teddy in my hand and gave Kyle a hug. "Thank you, Kyle." Kyle walked away and headed back to his room, but he turned around to look at me. I was tense and knew I wouldn't be able to sleep. Kyle noticed that teddy was not offering the comfort that he thought it would. He returned to my bed and said, "Kirin, do you want to pretend that we are having a sleepover?"

I smiled as Kyle crawled into my bed and wrestled into position. "Are you comfy, Kyle?" He yawned with a glazed looked on his face. I helped tuck him in, and within minutes he fell asleep. His kindness was comforting, but not enough to prevent another sleepless night. I sat there, sobbing and watching Kyle the entire night.

Taking a Stand–238 days

Zipping down the sidewalks on my little red bike, I was in a rush to get to class early. I felt starved for information, as one Saturday to the next felt like an eternity. I just had so much to ask Sifu because I spent most of my time practicing stuff on my own.

My helmet felt off. It drooped over my eye after every hard bump, but it served its purpose as it covered my head. It was busier than normal with people hanging around the neighborhood interacting with one another. I waved to some of the regulars along the way. There was Mrs. Chin, a middle-aged Chinese woman who worked her food stand. I often grabbed snacks from her after class as she cooked delicious food that she sold to support her family.

After clearing the corner, I could see the school from about fifty yards away. I was early, and I doubted that even Sifu was there to open the school. Regardless, it did not matter; I was in the mood to train, and I pressed harder to make my bike move faster.

When I got to the school, which was nestled in a corner, I noticed four guys hanging out in front of it.

"Ugh, stupid helmet," I said out loud as I wrestled with removing it.

The laughter from the four guys was loud as I parked my bike on the side. I looked up to see what the commotion was all about and noticed they were spray painting something on the window and wall of the school.

I dropped my bike and did not bother locking it up. The main guy was busy spraying, "KUNG FU SUCKS" in bold black. His companions who surrounded him were laughing and giving suggestions on how to graffiti my school.

I shouted at the top of my lungs, "What do you think you're doing?" They all glanced over and laughed at me before continuing to deface the school.

I screamed again, "Listen, you jerks, stop doing that!"

One of the sidekicks decided to face me. He said, "Hey, just mind your business and walk away, kid."

The other guy said, "Dude, why don't you make a smiley face and slant the eyes?" They started giggling together and continued to make racial slurs in the process. "Me luv you long time," one said, adding, "Asso," as the laughter continued.

The main guy started making a circle and slanting the eyes inside. Now I was really pissed! I removed my helmet and looked around. I was certain I was not the only one seeing this, but no one else was willing to do anything about it.

"Listen, stop graffiting my school!" I gritted my teeth in anger. This time, my words caught their attention, and they all turned around.

"Oh shit, guys. It's just a f–ing girl," said one of the thugs.

Another said, "You take classes here, little girl?"

"Look, if anything, we're doing you a favor. This Kung Fu crap doesn't work," said the main thug.

I thought, *Dumb ass, it's Gung Fu, not Kung Fu.* My anger grew as I went to the main guy and tried to grab the spray can from his hand. "Give me that spray can," I shouted.

He teased me, keeping it just out of my range as I jumped each time to grab it. The group of guys were not impressed by my effort, and the main guy shoved me to the ground. After seeing me fall on my butt, the main guy turned to his group. He smacked one friend on the chest and said, "Wing Chun Kung Fu." They all laughed, snickering as I lay there watching. Then they turned around and continued to ruin the front of the school.

I was livid lying on the ground. I refused to be helpless ... not this time. I quickly grabbed my helmet and started shaking when I made a fist. They were continuing their destruction, oblivious to the consequence. I was nothing to them. They were distracted, so I took advantage of it.

I did not have much Wing Chun skill at the time, but I had crazy on my side. The main guy had to pay, so he was gonna get it the worst. He had to be made the example!

I darted up behind him and gave him an upper cut with every ounce of power I had—right to his balls. He howled and dropped his spray can, yelling, "Ah!" He fell to his knees as if to pray, holding his groin in pain. That drew the attention of the other three guys, two of whom were close to him.

When they turned toward me, I swung my bike helmet with my left hand like a hook catching both of them in the face and knocking them both back.

Whack!

I lost control as my helmet flew upon impact.

The thug to my furthest right went straight down in a splatter of blood, and the other thug flew back into the guy furthest away from me, staggering his movement to get to me. The swing was so harsh it spun me around as well, knocking me off balance as I tumbled to the ground. Finally the fourth guy managed to get around his companion and started charging toward me.

I was in a bad position, but I quickly looked around and saw the spray can to my side. One step more, and he was right on top of me, ready to take a full swing and make me pay the price for my action.

I reached for the spray can and brought it up just as he drew back to hit me. Before he could swing, I unloaded the contents onto his face.

"What the f ... Ah!" He screamed with full fury as the paint went into his eyes. I emptied the entire can into his face. He stood there staggered, blind and trying to clear his eyes.

I dropped the can as he stood helpless in front of me. I closed the gap just like in the drills we had done in class and punched him square down the center, knocking him back.

What happened in mere seconds had felt like an eternity, and the other guys were starting to recover.

As I stood there wondering what to do next, the effects of the ball hit was wearing off and the other guy who ate the helmet said, "Holy shit, that bitch broke my nose," as blood dripped from his face.

I was in trouble. I panicked as I started to run, leaving my helmet and the bike. I didn't look back as I was sure they were catching their breath, ready to get me. While I had been going to school for eight months now, I was very unfamiliar with the neighborhood. I always took the same path from my house to the school.

As I started zigging and zagging from one street to a corner, I heard from a distance, "There she is!"

I passed by Mrs. Chin who saw me running in a panic. She quickly yelled, "Run, Kirin, I'll get some help." I faintly heard what she said, but was too concerned with getting away. I did not know what to do or where to go, so I searched frantically for somewhere to hide. No one was around to help me.

I turned around again and saw Mrs. Chin trying to help by blocking the thugs, but they quickly shoved her to the ground.

I stopped, wanting to help her, but she looked up from the ground and shouted, "Go, go ... Kirin, go ...!" The flashback of my parents brought tears to my eyes as I turned and ran. I thought to myself as tears dripped down my face, *I shouldn't have left her.... I shouldn't have left them.*

"Over here, I see her! I see her!" said one of the thugs.

I ducked around the corner and ran further down an alley. I was hoping this was the right way to hide from them, but my luck ran out as the alley ended abruptly, leaving me cornered. "Oh crap," I said in panic, out of breath. I looked left then right, then all around. "This is not good."

I turned around to back track and look for another place to go, but then all four of the guys blocked my path. Their shadows grew the further they stepped into the alley, making them appear even bigger.

I stepped backwards and tried to climb the wall. I started screaming, "Help, Help! Somebody help me." No one came, not a single soul. I was in trouble as I turned around to face them. I had no escape. I was scared, and I shivered as I placed my guard hands up, trying to make my last stand. I could not stop shaking.

"Look at my face! It's all spray painted in black."

"What are you complaining about?"

"I'm gonna kick her f–ing ass. Look what she did to my nose."

"Now, now, boys, we're all gonna have a little revenge," said the main thug.

I did not know what to do, as they talked amongst themselves, forming a wall. While they were in mid-discussion, I decided to close the gap again and went for a punch. This time, he ducked out of the way, and I missed completely. The next thing I knew, something hit me in the stomach that brought me to the ground.

"Ugh," I said as I was on my knees, clutching my stomach. I could not breathe. I just stared up at all four of them. They began to laugh as they circled around me.

"What did I tell you, little girl? That shit don't work, and especially now that you didn't catch us off guard," said the main thug.

I could barely hear what they were saying as I struggled to breathe and I clenched my stomach in gut-wrenching pain.

"All right, guys, grab her and hold her down." They surrounded me and grabbed my arms and my legs. I didn't know what they were gonna do, but I started to cry and struggle.

"Help! Help me, someone!" I tried to scream but nothing came out. I could barely move from all of them pinning me down.

"Hold the bitch down while I teach her a lesson." Then the main guy got next to me as I could see the evil in his eye. I struggled earnestly, but it did little to alter the situation. In a flash, I felt his foot hit my ribs.

Thump! "Ugh...." I coughed, gasping for air as everything became a blur.

I heard the sound of laughter continue as I lay on the ground. I did not know what would happen next, but I feared for the worst. The main guy got on top of me as I could feel his weight pressing. He lifted his fist for another strike. Just as he began his punch, I looked away and closed my eyes. I waited to for the impact of the hit, but instead I felt the weight of his body disappear from me. I opened my eyes and saw him fly across the alley into the fence.

I was still unaware what was happening, but the motion of two figures creating a storm of action appeared before me. Now screams filled the air, and attacks were coming from all directions. "What's going on? What's happening?" I mumbled as I struggled to sit up.

My eyes widened when I saw Doc and Tobias in action. I pieced together what was happening. Curling like a baby grasping my stomach in pain, I watched them work.

It felt like a dream. Tobias and Doc were working in tandem. While they may have been outnumbered, their advantage was their undeniable skill. It was incredible to see, as they worked in perfect sync with one another, neither one saying a word. Each one knew what the other would do, and they'd spent years training, leading them to trust one another. Doc moved with precision and accuracy, catching his opponents off guard before they even had time to react. His opponent would have that surprised look on his face, wondering how was that possible. Tobias, who I had witnessed before in challenge matches, was even more relentless. He struck fear in the hearts of his opponents just by being in their presence. Once in their range, he suffocated them with attacks. They didn't stand a chance.

One last guy remained, as Doc tossed him toward Tobias. Tobias turned around just as he was in range and delivered the pain. After several blazing attacks, his opponent crumpled to the ground. To add further insult to injury, he did a front kick so hard his opponent's body flew and hit the fence. In a matter of seconds, they remained standing while the rest were lined up against the wall.

Tobias yelled, "Doc, check on her! Make sure she's okay."

Doc approached me, as I anguished in pain. Doc tried to comfort me and said, "It's okay. It's okay, Karen. You're safe now. Are you okay?"

Tobias looked at the beaten four, pointing with his finger as he said, "Do not move from that spot. I'll deal with you in a second." Tobias then turned around and came over to check on me. He said sternly, "What were you thinking?"

I quietly whispered in pieces, "I had to protect ... the school," as I made an effort to smile, through my pain.

For some reason Tobias smiled after my comment and then asked, "Which one, Karen? Which one was spray painting the school?" I looked at the blurry images of the four but was able to pick out the ringleader. I pointed, and Tobias looked at him.

He panicked and looked to his friends for support, but they were all too afraid to do anything. He stuttered and said, "I'm sorry ... I ... I'm sorry. We were just having fun, and we weren't gonna hurt her, just scare her. I swear, I swear we'll clean the graffiti from the wall."

Tobias looked at him and said, "Oh, I know you're gonna clean that up, 'cause if you don't, I'm gonna hunt every one of you down." Tobias took a moment to let that statement sink in. "Tell me!" he shouted at all of them. "You think you're a tough guy beating on a little girl?"

"No, no ... I meant nothing by that, seriously. It wasn't personal." He waved both his hands at Tobias begging forgiveness.

Tobias yelled, "Show me the hand you used to spray the wall."

The ringleader only stared at him dumbly.

"SHOW IT!" he shouted even louder, as spit flew from his mouth.

The ringleader cautiously extended his arm forward, shaking in fear. Tobias looked to Doc and said, "Cover her."

Doc immediately got in front and blocked my view. Doc said, "You don't need to see this. Everything's going to be okay." I had no idea what was about to happen as Doc held my hand.

I could hear Tobias talking. "I know it wasn't personal; neither is this," said Tobias.

Crack! "Ah!"

The cry of pain echoed throughout the alley into the streets, scaring all the pigeons on the rooftop, scattering them. "My arm, my arm ... What the f–...?" I heard a tussle on the ground as the screams continued. I was able to peek and saw that the other three thugs watched in horror. They could not do a thing to help out their companion.

"Now listen, pick this douche bag up and get the hell out of here. Now! And remember ... today, mercy was shown!"

They quickly grabbed their companion and disappeared like rats into the darkness.

Tobias came back and asked, "Doc, is she all right?"

Checking on me, Doc said, "I think she got the wind knocked out of her." I heard the pitter-patter of more footsteps come about, as I noticed Robert, Ken, Big T, Ryan, and Danny surround me.

Ryan said, "Is Karen okay?"

Doc assured them I was and helped me sit up.

Tobias shook his head. "You're totally crazy. You barely know any Wing Chun, and you took on four guys and managed to do some good damage." He exhaled.

As I sat up from the ground, I whispered, "It's Kirin, Kirin ... Kirin's my name."

Tobias said, "My apologies, Kirin. What you did today was extremely brave ... I promise I shall not forget your name."

The guys hovered around me, making sure everything was okay. Tobias looked at them and me and said, "Guys, make sure you remember—make sure you never forget—this is Kirin." All the guys looked at me differently, staring me in the eyes. At that moment, I was accepted by the core as I had earned their respect.

Big T felt embarrassed and nudged Robert. "Damn it, I've been calling her Bianca. Why the hell didn't anyone correct me?"

Robert looked at him, "What the frick? Where the heck did that name come from?" Big T simply shrugged his shoulders. They all looked at each other laughing as I smiled.

"The foundation of the greatest structure is to believe in yourself." –Sifu

Sifu's Journey Entry #4–Unopened Letters

Winter 2029

From the top of the staircase, a silhouette figure of Sifu stood. He reached into the darkness and flicked on the switch. His highlighted body was unveiled by the light. He looked down the rickety steps into the darkness, carrying only his journal and a pen.

"Enough procrastinating, more work needs to be done," he said in a horse voice as he struggled to clear it. Sifu had been suffering from a cold he recently caught, and he was tired of lying around.

He took one step and began his descent to the basement. The staircase was shabby and run-down, and in need of an overhaul. Strangely, with each step downwards, there was none of the usual creaking that one would expect. Mastery of one's center has added perks, and that was definitely one of them.

In his basement, he found another switch and turned it on. The halogen light filled the room, creating a light glaze throughout. It revealed what Sifu had dreaded to deal with for so long: a huge mess.

It was a simple basement, rectangular in shape, matching the upper level of Sifu's restaurant. But regardless of where he looked, nothing resembled anything that could be considered organized.

Sifu had recently completed the hidden door and spent the rest of the month lugging odds and ends to the basement unsorted. Searching for a glimmer of hope, he spotted it: his corner work table where he'd been spending his months writing. The roadmap was far from complete. Then again, it all depended on how you looked at it; from a certain point of view, he was done. Technically he had everything stored in his head. All that remained was putting it in some tangible format for someone to gaze upon.

Sifu stood with hands on his hips towering over the clutter. Black garbage bags, DVDs, hard drives, and tons of notebooks were scattered throughout.

He let out a huge sigh. "Well, let's put knowledge to use. We do things one thing at a time." And so, the sorting began.

Notes, tons of notes from years of studying with his teacher. "Let's put those over in this corner," he said as he grabbed a handful.

DVDs, hard drives, VHS tapes, all outdated formats of the past. Hours upon hours of lessons and privates. He wondered if they still worked. He spent several minutes hooking up an old VCR machine to a TV and then tested to see if everything still ran. He reached out and grabbed a random tape and placed it in. Moments later, an image of him and his Sifu popped up on the screen. "I was so young back then, but my god, my Wing Chun was so lousy."

Sifu debated for a second whether he would rather have his youth back or his current skill. The answer was immediate to him.

He glanced back at the blank wall and imagined exactly what he wanted. "Let's organize. I need to lay this system out for someone to figure it out. I'll create it step by step."

Hours passed, and the mess was still that—a mess. Effort had been expended, but there was little to show for it. The blank wall had a few pieces of paper crudely taped onto it. Sifu had also jotted down several notes in his journal from reading some of his old material.

Sorting through more mess, Sifu spotted a cardboard box. "What's this?"

He blew the dust off the top and opened the box. Suddenly he realized what he was holding. Sifu fell to his knees and just sat there silently for several minutes. Those minutes quickly turned into half an hour as he was frozen.

With a glazed look on his face, he finally got the courage to look inside. Inside the box were unopened letters and cards, probably numbering a hundred. He placed his hand inside, sorting through the pile. He wasn't sure what exactly he was feeling for, but eventually he pulled out one of the unopened letters. His hands trembled as his heart raced, and he closed his eyes and tried to calm himself.

It was addressed to him from Tobias. He then randomly grabbed another card and looked at the name—Ryan. He set both of the cards to the side, in a nicely uniformed manner. Finally he reached to the deepest depth of the box and grabbed a handful of letters. One from Phil, Dave, Donna, and Bill. All of which were unopened. Some of them were from friends and family, while the names of others stretched from different generations of students that he had taught throughout his forty years.

He found several letters from Kirin clumped together. She had the most. He felt bad for not returning or even acknowledging the letters and cards. He still couldn't open them, to relive it again. Not just yet. More time was needed to heal.

"Once a thought enters, it needs action; otherwise, it remains a dream." –Sifu.

CHAPTER 5
The Invitation

Three Days Later, Monday January 5

Click. Kirin looked into her camera to see how the picture came out. A quick glance told her something wasn't quite right. "Hmm, looks a little off...." She began tinkering with the settings. With a few presses and several adjustments, she was ready to take another picture.

It was almost ten o'clock at night. Several days had passed, and Kirin was still in hiding. She was trying to gather her thoughts and figure out what exactly she had gotten herself into. All she wanted to do was make an impact. Well, she'd done that, and now the entire world was demanding an encore. Her hopes of having only fifteen minutes of fame were dashed, as talks about her spread even more. Whether it was TV or the Internet, her fight had become a worldwide phenomenon, and she had been given the nickname, "The-One-Hit-Wonder." She found it comical, but deep down Kirin liked the label. Her action created a ripple effect and brought back into question how someone of her stature could possibly knock out someone twice her size with a single punch. The theories being spread around were even more humorous. *Occam's razor* would've led the answer to the simplest of path, but society was in disarray. Overcome with emotion, they were unable to see the obvious. It seemed that the more she hid, the greater their desire to find out more about her.

Kirin was by the planetarium, her favorite spot to take pictures for her work. She loved the peace and tranquility of hanging out there, be it day or night.

The city was radiating with lights as it was unusually warm for early January. Kirin paused to stare at the Chicago skyline, admiring its beauty. As often as she tried, she could not quite capture what her eyes saw on camera. Regardless, she was at peace for the moment, as the only sounds she heard were the waves from Lake Michigan crashing against the shore. She closed her eyes, letting her senses take over.

"Come on, Kirin, quiet the mind. As Sifu always said, the answers are right in front of you," she whispered to herself.

"Zzz." Bacon, her ever-faithful sidekick, was snoring by the side of her tripod.

"I'm sorry, boy. I know it's past your bed time, but I appreciate you keeping me company. I swear, just give me another fifteen minutes, and we'll head back home." Kirin reached down and gave Bacon a quick pat on the head.

"Zzz. Bacon continued to sleep, ignoring Kirin.

Several more minutes passed as Kirin continued taking more pictures.

Click. Click. Click.

The pictures were coming out great, but they were not to Kirin's satisfaction.

Kirin looked inside the view finder to make a visual adjustment, as she decided to move the camera's view to another part of the city lights. Suddenly, she felt a tap on her shoulder and heard a voice say, "So, how are the pictures coming out?"

Kirin was caught off guard and immediately grabbed the stranger's arm from behind, locking it in place.

"Ah," cried the stranger in immediate pain.

She swept his leg, pinning his body to the ground as she was prepared to throw out a punch, and then ask questions later.

Thud.

"Wait. Wait! It's me, Kirin. It's me." With a look of terror, the stranger waved his hand to catch her attention. Kirin's anger changed from shock to relief as she realized it was Hunter. She helped him to his feet, and he tried to gather himself. Hunter got up like an old man from the ground, but upon standing up, Kirin leaped off her feet and gave him a tight hug.

"Uh," Hunter moaned, trying to get some air through Kirin's tight grip. He appreciated the touch and returned the hug.

"You scared me," whispered Kirin into his ear.

"I scared you?" Hunter replied questioningly.

Kirin looked at Bacon, who had slept through the entire ordeal. "Some watch dog you are!" Kirin said sternly to Bacon.

Hunter replied, "If it helps, I almost tripped over him."

They both laughed, looking into each other's eyes and then awkwardly let go of one another and stared away.

"I thought I would find you here," Hunter said confidently.

Kirin glanced at Hunter. "Why were you looking for me?"

Hunter shifted his eyes away shyly. "I'm always looking for you, Kirin."

Kirin blushed and looked down, unsure what to say to Hunter. Then she quickly changed the subject. "What are you doing here? I thought you went back to college." Kirin couldn't conceal the happy smile on her face.

"Nah, I got like one week left of winter break then I am headed back," Hunter explained.

Kirin was saddened by that news.

Hunter said, "Look, I'm here for a week. Let's make the best of it. Besides, you're the one blowing me off."

Kirin turned away and said, "I wasn't blowing you off."

Hunter smirked. "Really? Why don't you show me your cell phone and how many voicemails and texts I've sent you? You know, in most states, they would consider that stalking."

Kirin replied, "I thought you always said it was only stalking if the other person knew about it." They shared a smirk at their long-time inside joke.

Kirin fumbled with her next words. "Besides ... I, uh, you know I have a lousy carrier."

"Kirin, you were always a bad liar." Hunter laughed, enjoying her company. Then he gave her a suspicious look. "Hmm, knowing you, I bet you don't even have your cell phone with you."

"Guilty as charged ... you know me with technology," Kirin said lightly, trying to justify it.

Hunter stared away briefly, took a deep breath, and then quickly looked Kirin in the eye.

Kirin then asked, "No, seriously, Hunter, why are you here?"

"I'm here, Kirin, because I thought you needed someone," said Hunter. Hunter did not press the matter any further. He knew Kirin well enough to know that she would talk when she was ready.

"I'm glad you're here. You've always been there for me when I need you," she said as she kindly looked at Hunter. "You're such a good friend."

There was that word *friend*–the f-word that no guy ever wants to hear from the girl of his dreams. Hearing it from Kirin's mouth crushed Hunter inside, wrapping around his heart and squeezing. It hurt like no other, for the possibility of hope turned into reality. Hunter didn't like hearing that word from Kirin; she knew how he felt about her. With slight disgust, he looked down and away. He did not utter a word.

Kirin winced at her poor choice of words and moved toward Hunter. She stammered apologetically, "I, uhm ... I'm sorry. I didn't mean it like that. You ... you know you mean more to me than just that."

Kirin extended her hand to touch Hunter's cheek, her soft touch gently easing the pain of her comments, as she slowly guided his face to look at her. He turned his face toward hers, but refused to look at her.

Kirin's gentle voice said, "Please look at me, Hunter."

Looking at him, she could feel his sadness. She leaned up toward him, and surprising them both, Kirin kissed Hunter for the first time.

They kissed for who knows how long, but the world seemed to spin around them as they were lost in the moment.

"You don't know how long I've waited to feel the touch of your lips," Hunter said softly as he stared into Kirin's eyes. Hunter's heart was racing, alive again.

"I'm sorry ... I don't know why I just did that," said Kirin, pulling away and looking down. Her insecurities kicked in as she made sure her hair covered a part of her face. She was trembling from the kiss, but she didn't know why.

Hunter grabbed her by the arms gently and said, "I'm not."

When Kirin didn't respond right away, Hunter thought, *Just come clean and say what you want to say. Tell her how you feel.* Hunter began to open his mouth and–

Ring. Ring.

The mood was interrupted as Hunter's phone rang.

Damn it, he thought as he closed his eyes in disgust.

Kirin looked back at Hunter, who was searching through his pocket to find his phone. After pulling it out, he rolled his eyes and exhaled a small sigh. "It's Gwen," he said.

"What's up, Gwen?" he said in disappointment, wondering why of all times she had to call now.

"Did you find her?" Gwen's voice over the phone was loud enough to be heard by Kirin.

"Yeah, Gwen, I found her. She's standing right next to me," replied Hunter.

"Stick to the plan, Hunter. Let's all meet up in a half hour in Chinatown. Persuade her to come. I'll call Sage," said Gwen.

Hunter pulled his ear away from the phone as the chatter continued. "Got it, yup, okay, got it, okay, Gwen ... Gwen, see you in a few."

Kirin laughed, watching Hunter's reaction to Gwen.

"Look, Kirin, Gwen and Sage want us all to meet up at Chinatown in a half hour. You have to come," asked Hunter.

"What is this, some kind of intervention?"

Hunter shook his head. "All I did was offer to help look for you. The rest is Gwen's idea. Besides, this is the first time we've gotten a chance to hang out with each other."

Kirin thought about it for a few seconds and then said, "All right, I'll come with you, but I gotta drop off my bike and Bacon's carrier first. Do you have enough room to give us a ride?"

"Yeah, there should be enough. Come on, let's head out," said Hunter.

"Let's go, Bacon." Kirin clapped her hands to wake him up, but he refused to move and continued to snore the night away.

Kirin smiled and made a motion to lift Bacon, but Hunter quickly stepped in.

"You spoil that dog way too much. Here, let me lift him," said Hunter.

"Oh my god, did he gain weight?" said Hunter with a strained look on his face.

"Actually, he's been walking more," replied Kirin.

"Walking more or riding around town in that silly red wagon?" asked Hunter.

Kirin looked up to the sky, feeling embarrassed.

As he lifted Bacon, a foul odor filled the night air. "Oh my god, what the hell!" Hunter said. "What the hell have you been feeding him, Kirin?"

"Same as always ... he's just been gassy lately," replied Kirin.

"What the...?" Hunter shook his head.

"What? What's wrong?" said Kirin.

"I'm carrying his fat ass, and he's continuing to fart while he's sound asleep," laughed Hunter. They looked at each other and chuckled.

As Hunter walked toward the car carrying Bacon, he suddenly stepped on something.

"Oh crap, tell me it's not crap that I stepped on," he said.

As Hunter lifted his foot and was ready to wipe it, Kirin said, "No, it's not what you think. It's a bunch of flowers."

Kirin looked around and said, "I wonder who would leave this.... It looks fresh." *Wow these are my favorite, yellow tulips,* she thought.

"Uh, Kirin, let's hurry up. Bacon weighs a ton, remember?" said Hunter. Hunter and Kirin hurried to the car, packed up, and dropped off Bacon.

30 minutes later

Hunter and Kirin finally arrived at their late night spot in Chinatown. Once parked, they headed to the restaurant to meet up with Gwen and Sage. Kirin was still somewhat reluctant to go because the crowds made her paranoid, but Hunter did his best to calm her nerves. A few minutes passed as they stood outside the front of the restaurant, and Kirin saw a little homeless boy wandering the street.

She approached him and said, "Here, take it," as she handed him several credits. He looked at her briefly, grabbed the credits, and quickly ran away.

"That was strange, not even a thank you," said Hunter.

"He was probably just scared and shy, no biggie," Kirin brushed it off.

"I gotta ask you, Kirin, what's up with the hoodie? I thought you outgrew those after high school," said Hunter.

"I guess you could say I'm a person of interest." Kirin left it at that. Hunter got to the front door and opened it for her like a gentleman. As she was walking in, Kirin finally realized which restaurant they were at.

"Good lord, Hunter," said Kirin with a look of concern on her face.

"What? What's wrong?" replied Hunter. "Is chivalry dead?"

"No, no ... it's not you holding the door. Of all the places you guys picked, it had to be gangster owned," replied Kirin.

"Hey, don't look at me. I told Gwen to pick somewhere else." As Hunter tried to plead his case, Kirin ignored her gut feeling and put on her hood.

"All right, let's go in," said Kirin.

Times had changed. The majority of restaurants were corporately owned and franchised, dispensing the fast food crap that fed the masses. The handful of affordable mom and pop joints that were allowed to stay open were all tied to the mob. In the end, it did not matter, really; someone's hand was dipped into somewhere to run the establishment.

Inside the restaurant, the noise was deafening. It was bustling with energy, a microcosm of chaotic activity all jam-packed within several thousand square feet. The smell of the food immediately hit Kirin as she entered the building. It was designed to intoxicate one's senses and then trap the victim within its walls.

Both Hunter and Kirin peeked past the host and spotted Gwen and Sage. They waved from afar after seeing Hunter and Kirin from their center stall. Inside, the old friends greeted each other with hugs and handshakes; it had been far too long.

The old gang was together; it had been awhile. As they sat down, they smiled and looked at each other. While they were all still so young, it felt like the past. A dome of silence stood for several seconds while the jibbering and jabbering of people around them continued.

Then Gwen blurted out, "Are you completely crazy?"

"Look, I rarely agree with Gwen, but I have to agree.... You could've gotten hurt!" said Hunter.

"I'm sorry, but that was the f–ing coolest thing I have ever seen," said Sage, beaming with excitement. "Okay, I know you.... You probably haven't been paying attention to what's going on, but some dude started designing an action figure that looks exactly like you, and he's got like a hundred thousand orders from people who are ready to buy. An action figure, Kirin!" said Sage with a crazed look of excitement that couldn't be contained.

"I'm sure Hunter would be interested," said Gwen. Hunter just gave Gwen a look.

"I didn't say it was life-sized," chuckled Sage.

Hunter then gave Sage a look.

All three of them were saying something to Kirin, but she stared at them, unable to hear a single sound coming from their mouths.

"Stop!" shouted Kirin. "There's no point in criticizing. What's done is done."

"You know, you could've at least told me why you needed the fake ID.... I thought we are best friends?" asked Gwen.

"We are best friends, Gwen, but I didn't tell anyone. I thought it was better for no one to know. And, there's no way anyone will know you made the fake ID," stated Kirin.

"Of course no one will know. That's why I'm the best damn hacker in the world, Kirin," bragged Gwen.

"Sage, when the waitress comes by, can you ask if they have any humble pie for Gwen?" said Hunter.

Gwen then gave Hunter the look.

Sage said, "Uh, we were all wondering ... the twenty-five thousand credits you threw in the air ... oh, I don't know, it would've been nice to give your poor college friends a little pocket change.... I'm just saying."

Kirin rolled her eyes.

"First, Mr. Big Brain Sage, don't you have a full scholarship all expenses paid to the University of Chicago? Second, while Gwen only goes part-time to college, she's also paid beaucoup bucks working as an outside consultant to prevent hacking for several major corporations. Finally, Hunter's college is fully paid for by his wrestling scholarship."

Everyone looked away for a second, and then Gwen said, "Regardless, twenty-five thousand split amongst your friends would've been a lot better than your Merry Christmas self-cards." Gwen reached into her purse and pulled out Kirin's Christmas cards that she gave everyone.

Everyone laughed as Kirin stared at herself and then giggled.

The waitress came to the table and, with a heavy Chinese accent, asked, "You prepared to order?"

Sage stepped in and started speaking Mandarin to the waitress, ordering from the menu. He looked at Kirin and asked, "Can we order at least one fried rice?"

Kirin sighed dramatically as everyone waited for her answer. "Fine, yes ... order a fried rice."

Time passed as the group enjoyed their meal and continued to yack the night away. They were lost in the enjoyment of merely being together.

"Oh my god, I'm stuffed," said Hunter.

Sage said, "Maybe we didn't need to order the fried rice. I'm full as hell."

Just then Gwen said, "Why are you guys yelling?"

They looked around and realized it was dead quiet. No one was in the restaurant. "Uh ... Kirin, what time is it?" asked Hunter.

"It's only 11:30. What time does this place close at?" said Kirin.

"Not till 3:00 am," replied Sage.

"Is today a holiday or something 'cause the place is usually packed at this time, even during a weekday," said Gwen.

"What do you think is going on?" Hunter asked, looking around.

"I have no idea," said Kirin, but inside she knew something was about to happen.

"I have a bad feeling about this," said Sage.

"Not now, Sage," all three of them responded to his movie quote.

The main doors in the front of the restaurant swung open, breaking the uneasy silence. A dark figure stood outside and finally set foot into the establishment. He entered the restaurant in an eye-catching glow when the lights hit his suit. Fawn moved slowly, checking out the decor of the restaurant. He was followed by Justice, who stood to his side. Suddenly the local gang leader appeared on Fawn's other side.

The group just sat there, wondering if this was some reality show that was about to take place.

Sneaking through behind Fawn was the little boy Kirin gave cash to. He pointed directly to her, as he was handed some more credits and then shoved out of the door.

Just then, the noise of stampeding feet started rumbling into the room. Kirin looked at her glass, watching how it shook from the vibration being created. From the front, behind, and all the exit signs, at least thirty guys all sharing similar uniforms created a human wall around the entire restaurant.

"Oh, shit," whispered Kirin.

Sage looked at Gwen and Hunter and said, "This is bad.... Kirin never swears."

Tension started filling the room, as Kirin's heart was beating fast.

Fawn began speaking in his high-pitched, feminine voice, "Kirin Rise ... originally named Soo Jin Park, born in North Korea, escaped to China, and was adopted by Mr. and Mrs. Rise at the age of eight. Kirin has four stepbrothers, three older ones, one in the military special forces, two in college, and the youngest one still in high school. Graduated from Forest Sky High School in the top ten of her class. Offered a full-time scholarship to Stanford University which she turned down ... a mind is a terrible thing to waste ... and then she decided to open Kirin's Photo Design."

Fawn paused for a second, "Not too original with names, are we, Kirin? I would've gone with something catchy like KPD; you know what I mean?" He waved his limp wrist at her.

"Anyway, you are sitting with your closest friends: Gwen, Sage, and Hunter. I won't bore you with their details, but merely ask, and I'll tell you everything you need to know about them."

Fawn suddenly was interrupted by his own thoughts.

"Oh, by the way, Hunter, a C+ in psychology last semester...? Good lord, child, psychology is like studying finger painting ... tsk, tsk."

Hunter looked surprised as he watched what was unfolding. As Fawn approached closer to the table, a handful of the henchman slowly creeped up, surrounding them.

Sage turned to Kirin and said, "That's a dude, right?"

Kirin looked again to confirm, "Yeah, that is."

Fawn caught word of Sage's comment with his good ear. He snapped his fingers and pointed to Sage. Immediately one of the henchmen walked up to Sage and slapped him on the face before walking back and standing at attention.

"What the...?" reacted Sage, rubbing his cheek.

Kirin was about to stand up, but Hunter grabbed her by the arm. She turned toward him, and he quickly motioned by shaking his head.

"Of course, I'm a man. Don't hate me just because I'm beautiful," said Fawn.

Fawn suddenly slammed his hands on the table and looked at Sage. "Two plus two, Sage, equals ... what?"

Sage was caught off guard and simply uttered, "Huh?"

"It's four, Sage, four ... and I thought you were the intelligent one of the group, hmh...." Fawn sneered and looked down his nose at Sage.

He then stood silently and stared at Kirin.

"Let me begin by congratulating you on your fight several nights ago. It was ... how do you say ... impressive, to say the least." Fawn looked like he was directing an orchestra with the massive amounts of hand gestures he made while he talked.

Kirin spoke, "I think you have me mistaken for someone else."

Fawn looked away, insulted by her comment. "Clearly I don't, child. Come, come ... you can do better than that."

Fawn giggled to himself. He was amused by Kirin's childlike attempt.

"Where was I? Ah, yes, I know everyone there was impressed with your win, but then again that crowd is a bunch of Neanderthal meatheads," he paused, sighing, "but ... they do pay the bills."

He stared at Kirin and whispered loud enough for all to hear, "But I thought the theatrics of making it rain twenty-five thousand was the cherry on top. If only a rainbow had magically appeared behind you, it would have been utter perfection."

Fawn straightened and pointed to his chest. "That's me, of course."

Fawn paused to allow everyone a moment to absorb his comments.

"Now, my boss, on the other hand ... he is very much interested to know if the knockout on DJ was an act of skill or possibly beginner's luck."

Kirin remained silent and still.

"If you would be so kind as to honor us with another demonstration," said Fawn.

Hunter had heard enough. "You're out of your mind. Let's get out of here, guys." He stood up, but two henchman grabbed him and slammed his face to the table.

"You jerks, get off me!" screamed Hunter.

Kirin jumped up from of her chair, ready to attack. Fawn merely held his hand up as he circled the table like a shark. Gwen turned toward Fawn and said, "I can contact the police with a push of a button."

Fawn clapped and was extremely happy, "Oh, Gwen, I love your spunk. It's so charming. But let me let you in on a little secret...." Fawn pointed to a gentleman standing at the far entrance.

"Lieutenant James, Gwen here wants to contact the police. Can you do us both a big favor and have your men block off this area, so we don't get disturbed for the next ... oh, let's say ... twenty minutes or so?"

Lieutenant James grabbed his phone and did as Fawn had ordered.

"By the way, Gwen, Lieutenant James has those bumper stickers that say, 'To serve and protect.' Would you want him to get one of those from his squad car and place it on your wheelchair? The aesthetics would do wonders."

Gwen trembled in her chair, realizing the gravity of the situation.

Fawn rounded the table and touched Gwen's hair. "I like your hair, very colorful," he added as he sniffed it. Gwen's skin tingled in fear, she sat motionless not knowing what to do.

Sage got up and said, "Don't you dare lay a finger on her." A henchman then grabbed Sage from behind and pinned him to the table as well.

"Ah," said Sage. Gwen cringed, concerned about Sage.

Fawn ignored Sage's action and asked, "Do you like my jacket, Gwen?" With a scared look on her face, Gwen stared at Kirin, who made a slight motion.

"Yes, yes, I like your jacket," Gwen said in a shaky voice.

"Oh, do tell! You have such good taste. We could totally be BFF ... Uh." He broke off as he touched the fabric of Sage's shirt. With a disgusted look on is face, he said, "Good lord, did the Salvation Army have a sale this weekend?"

Not waiting for a response, Fawn waved his hand and giggled. "You guys are throwing me off the subject."

"Now back to our little demonstration ... we insist, if you would be so kind," said Fawn.

"If I demonstrate, will you let my friends go?" asked Kirin.

"But of course, Kirin," said Fawn with an innocent look.

"Let them go, and I'll agree to it," stated Kirin.

With his face still smashed against the table, Hunter said, "No, Kirin, don't."

Fawn motioned to the henchmen to clear out a section of the restaurant. Like good soldiers, they did as they were told, moving chairs and furniture as they left the center space open.

Kirin looked at the several henchmen who were holding down her friends. They let go of both Sage and Hunter, who shook themselves free. Gwen looked at Kirin in fear. Kirin gave a little smile of comfort, trying to assure her friend that everything would be all right.

"Please, my dear, center stage awaits you," said Fawn, who held his hand out to direct where the action would take place.

Kirin turned toward the center of the room and slowly started walking there. She was visually checking out the layout and positions of where everyone was. She removed her hood.

As she stood in the middle, she reached into her pocket and pulled out a simple rubber band. She slowly brought it up to her head as she combed her hair backwards and tied it into a ponytail.

She stood there steady and turned her head slightly to the side so that Fawn could see her eye.

"Let's make this interesting, shall we?" Fawn started circling the room as Kirin listened. "Enie meanie minie moe, catch a tiger...."

Fawn pointed to various henchman, all of whom stepped forward when called upon. As each one stepped forward, she watched how they stood, studying them, preparing for them. Fawn then pointed to the last henchman and touched him on the chest.

"Oh my ... you have muscles on muscles ... Bowflex?" he giggled. "Never mind. But yes ... definitely you! Yes, you six, that'll do. You six! Kirin needs someone to play with."

Hunter shouted. "What the f–? That's six guys–that's totally insane! No one can handle six guys." A pair of henchman held Hunter in place.

"Hush, child ... let's see how little Kirin will perform," Fawn said, looking at Hunter directly. Fawn strolled back toward the entrance where Justice stood. As Kirin stood in the center of the restaurant, the six men slowly started to surround her. Kirin could feel her heart racing from the tension.

Lub dub, lub dub, lub dub.

She worked to control her breathing–in and out, in and out–and focus on a single thought. She closed her eyes. *A single thought,* she thought, trying to quiet her mind. Suddenly she could not hear the beat of her heart, and all the sounds in the room were silent. At that moment, she opened her eyes again.

Target, center, own it, she thought.

SILENCE. TENSION. ANTICIPATION.

"WAIT!" a high-pitched shriek exiting the lungs of Fawn made everyone cringe. Fawn waved his hands down like a flapping bird to stop the action. All heads inside the room turned to him.

"You, join the party," shouted Fawn as one more of his henchmen surrounded Kirin.

"Now this is exactly perfect.... Think about it for a second, one sweet and innocent girl and seven guys." Fawn looked around, hoping everyone understood what he was thinking. "Don't you get it? Snow White and the Seven Dwarves. When is another opportunity like this ever gonna present itself?" said Fawn. The blank stares on everyone's faces made it clear that only Fawn appreciated the moment. He sneered.

"Okay, I've had my fun...." He made a motion of zipping his lips and then raised his hands, shouting, "Attack her!"

Unlike the movies, where the hero battled one opponent at a time, all the henchmen moved in on her immediately.

Perfect, she thought.

That is exactly what Kirin wanted, for everyone to come in, for everyone to enter her house.

As they all stepped in, Kirin waited a split second to make sure they committed their intentions. Then she immediately targeted the nearest warm body. Whoever it was, this unlucky soul, he would be the mark, the one she would make an example out of and unleash hell upon him.

She felt the squeeze of their intent and simply moved forward, punching a hole right through their circular human wall.

Whack!

The poor soul didn't stand a chance, as he collapsed right on the spot, crumpling to the ground. She quickly spun around him and used him as a shield, holding him briefly by the collar. They all stood in shock and Kirin used that second to her advantage, kicking him into the center.

This caught all of them off guard; she was no longer the one in the middle, but part of the circle.

Her game was as it always had been: dominate the center line, just like Sifu had taught her.

My game, my rules, my way.

These henchmen were no clowns, all initiated from the street to fight, but what they ran into was a force they had never seen. Doubt started creeping into their minds about how a tiny girl could bring fear into their hearts. They were in for a fight unlike any other.

Every attack on her was countered with pain, no hesitation on her part. No mercy. In fact, their reaction to her helped fuel the fire, as Kirin was being driven by rage. *My friends are my family. Protect them at all costs,* she thought.

Screams filled the restaurant as her switch was turned to on. She was relentless. The numbers clearly favored the henchmen, but Kirin appeared to be the one hunting the pack of seven. A punch from a henchman was immediately countered by a flurry of attacks. She didn't waste time. Guys were dropping like flies, and she unleashed the fury to make her point clear on each and every one of them.

"Ah!" screamed the one henchman as he was thrown in the air and crashed onto a table.

Crack!

Bones broke as fear spread throughout.

It was beautiful, like artwork, nothing fancy but everything extremely effective, as Kirin moved with the flow of the force. She did not plan her attacks in advance. Everything was direct and to the point, as bodies fell, bones snapped, and pounds of human flesh, thrown from every possible direction.

Justice watched silently, studying her moves. For once, even Fawn was at a loss for words. He stood silently, mesmerized by her motion.

Here friends were watching in awe. Kirin was making destruction an art form. They all looked at each other.

Sage shook his head, "Holy shit...."

"I know," said Hunter.

"Damn ... guys?" said Gwen.

"I know," repeated Hunter.

Sage turned to Hunter and said, "Hunter, if you and Kirin ever hook up, I'm pretty sure she's wearing the pants in that relationship."

"Agreed," replied Hunter.

The last henchman standing threw a roundhouse kick to her head. Kirin blocked it and kicked out his knee at the same time. The sound of human bone breaking accompanied by cries of pain was haunting. Kirin was fuming, almost as if she were insulted by the attempted kick. As he lay on the ground grabbing his leg in agony, she jumped up into the air screaming and landed in full force, delivering a punch to his face that put him out of his misery. She was on her knee with a clenched fist, breathing heavily—not from exhaustion, but from emotion.

Kirin immediately spun and charged toward Fawn. She was upset and looking for payback. She struggled to close the gap. Fawn, seeing her charge, did not react, other than to stare into her eyes as she drew nearer and smile.

She threw a punch at Fawn that was just about to hit when Justice stepped in, catching it. Kirin was surprised but decided automatically to continue her attack on Justice instead. For the first time, Kirin found an opponent who was capable of blocking her attacks. Kirin and Justice exchanged attacks and counters back and forth, but she was unable to get a hit in. Out of frustration, she forced an attack further than she should've, leaving her back exposed to Justice. He shoved her with his leg on her butt as she tumbled away from him. Kirin rolled with the force along the ground and sprang back up, ready to charge in again.

"Enough," said Fawn, holding up his hand.

Kirin looked up at Justice, staring him dead in the eye.

Our fight's not over, she thought.

Fawn made a sound that caused Justice to look back. The bodyguard nodded his head and stepped back to Fawn's side.

Fawn clapped in delight. "That was utterly fabulous!" He signaled to his henchmen to withdraw their positions.

Quickly they disappeared, gathering the injured off the floor and leaving Kirin's friends alone, until only Fawn and Justice remained.

"You have most definitely proven yourself worthy, Kirin Rise."

Fawn reached into his pocket and pulled out a scroll nicely wrapped with a bow. He tossed it into the air, and it landed just at Kirin's feet.

"What is this?" asked Kirin.

"It's a formal invitation from the UFMF to join the league, Kirin. If you happen to survive the season, there you will have a chance to enter the DOME."

He paused and then added, "Think of it as your opportunity to ... make your point!"

Kirin grabbed the scroll and stood up. She turned around to see if her friends were okay. When she turned back, both Justice and Fawn had walked away.

> *"When you see skill, take the time to admire it. It represent all that is incredible about the human spirit and it's willingness to sacrifice everything to be great at something." –Sifu*

Short Stories #5–Kirin's P.O.V.

No Pain, No Gain–1 year 80 days

It was a typical Wednesday afternoon as summer was approaching and the school year was nearing the end. I had arrived home from school and was alone in the house. I decided to break my normal trend of immediately finishing my homework. As I found myself out of my normal routine, I stared in the corner of our kitchen, where our TV stood silent most of the time.

Even when I first came to the States, I never found myself glued to it. I was motivated in the beginning just to learn how to speak English, but afterwards I soon realized that, with thousands of channels to choose from, everything had been saturated with either pro fighting or reality TV shows. It had gotten to the point where reality TV shows were now the norm. I guess the thought of an original idea had long died. Even my high school teacher and next door neighbor had their own shows.

So, I did what was normal for most teenagers, but unusual for me, and turned it on. A random show popped up.

Suddenly, something caught the corner of my eye as I took a quick peek outside. Mr. Ferguson was there with his wife holding the camera, filming his garden show. He waved at me, and I gracefully waved back, trying to be a good neighbor.

He continued waving, which was beyond the normal "hi how are you doing" length of time. I glanced over at the TV and then saw myself waving. After several looks between Mr. Ferguson and the TV, I quickly realized he was streaming the show live.

Oh good lord, I thought.

I walked away from the window, pretending I was busy. I was about to switch the channel as a commercial popped up for *A Hole in the Ground,* where, every weekday afternoon at 4:00 pm, you can learn everything you ever wanted to know about dirt. I closed my eyes and giggled at the universe's sick sense of humor. What were the chances that my neighbor's TV show would be first thing that popped up?

Riveting stuff, I laughed to myself. "TV off," I said.

Again, I was reminded why the TV was useless. I pulled out my phone and decided to listen to some music instead. *Tap.* I pressed my earrings, and the music transferred over to them, functioning as my headphones.

I put my feet up on a chair and sighed. *Ugh, hump day. Why can't Saturday come any sooner?* I looked forward to the weekend, but not for the same reason as most people. In reality, that was the only day I could go train with Sifu. Most of the time, I'd stay in my room and practice techniques on my own.

God, I wish I could train more, I thought, dreaming of that day. But, it was difficult enough to get Saturdays free without having my entire family wonder what I was up to.

As the moments passed, the munchies hit me. I scurried to the fridge to see what was there. Fortunately, my mom had a worldwide pallet, and she always made sure I never lost touch with my roots. Scanning through the fridge, I saw: leftover pizza, fruits, yogurt, a bottle of kimchi....

I was about to settle on kimchi on top of cold pizza when I got a text from Gwen.

Gwen: whats ^
Kirin: Gwen what does that arrow mean again?
Gwen: Kirin U promisD me you'd Lern how 2 txt properly

Kirin: I know, but can you just talk regular English for now? Not your text lingo.
Gwen: Fine. But next time, you have to learn.
Kirin: Okay, I promise.
Gwen: So, what I texted originally was, what's up.
Kirin: Oh, that's right. To answer you, nothing much I'm bored.
Gwen: Don't you mean most boredest? rotfl
Kirin: Funny, but the term is most bestest which I use in class. What does rotfl mean again?
Gwen: Rolling on the floor laughing. What are you doing now?
Kirin: Just sitting at home.
Gwen: Hey, have you been watching Bitchin'?
Kirin: No, you know I barely watch TV. What's that?
Gwen: It's that all-girl group of 6, where one of them is a guy?
Kirin: That's a show?
Gwen: Yeah, it's really popular. They have really good music, and each week they give you hints as to which one is the guy.
Kirin: Uh ... yeah, I'll make sure to record it next time.

It was just a typical conversation between teenagers. Unfortunately for me, I was still struggling to get a grasp on the social etiquette of texting.

Suddenly the door slammed open, catching me off guard. I shouted, "What's going on?"

Mark stormed through the door, clutching his shoulder in pain.

I immediately texted Gwen: I gotta run. Something's come up.

I asked Mark frantically, "What happened? What happened?"

In anguish, Mark replied, "I hurt myself during practice."

I was quick to scold him, "You're always injuring yourself with your Jiu Jitsu class."

Mark ignored the pain and spat angrily, "It's part of the training. You wouldn't understand."

It always frustrated me hearing those comments. But, I was annoyed even more that he was allowed to train and I could not. I knew my Mom's reasoning—because of my past. She wanted to shelter me from any kind of violence.

I said, "Can you move it, Mark?"

"Ouch," he whined. "It really hurts when I move it."

I shook my head. "Mark, Mom's gonna kill you. She said one more injury and you'd have to quit."

Coming to that realization, Mark said, "I know, I know. She can't find out about this, Kirin."

I said nothing. Mark looked up at me earnestly. "Kirin, you have to promise me you won't say a thing to Mom." I saw the sadness on his face, and I knew he really didn't want to quit.

I replied, "Mark, you have to go to the hospital. You might have badly injured your shoulder."

Mark replied, "I can't go. If I go, they'll know something happened, and I'm toast."

I said, "Well, you have to do something. Otherwise, your shoulder will get much worse." Mark was rubbing his shoulder, trying to comfort it somehow.

"Kirin, no hospital, period!"

"Okay!" I finally agreed to his stupid request.

We both sat there, trying to figure out what to do next. Suddenly I came up with something and said, "I know something we can do." Mark looked at me in pain, hoping that I had the answer.

I asked, "Can you ride your bike?"

He nodded his head and said, "I can still steer with my other arm, so yes I can."

"Good, I have an idea. Come with me. It's only 15 minutes away by bike."

Mark said, "Okay, I'm open to anything." I wrote a quick note and left it in the kitchen for Mom to see, just in case she got home early. I closed the house, and we both hurried to the garage to pick up our bikes.

I told Mark, "Follow me." Then I led the way, weaving through the streets and checking back every so often to make sure Mark was following me.

Finally we arrived at Sifu's school. Mark asked me, "Where are we?"

I didn't answer him back, instead saying, "Put your bike over there, and let's chain them together."

Mark listened, but once that was done, he asked me again, "Kirin, seriously, where the heck are we?"

I turned to Mark and said, "Look, you don't want Mom to find out you hurt yourself, right?"

Mark agreed with caution. "Yes...."

I took a deep breath and said, "I'll keep your secret if you keep my secret."

With a curious look on his face, Mark asked, "What's the secret?"

I answered, "I'm taking Gung Fu classes on Saturdays."

Mark asked, with a surprised look on his face, "What Kung Fu classes?"

I rolled my eyes. "No, Gung Fu."

"What's the difference?"

I shook my head. "Never mind. That's not important right now."

"Wait, they still have these places around?

I said, "There's not many, but this one has been around forever."

Mark said, "I knew it."

"Knew what?"

Mark replied, "I thought it was suspicious that you and Gwen would be out every Saturday for some school project."

I laughed. "School project, pfftt, please."

Mark grew serious and asked, "I don't get it. How is it that you're coming here every Saturday without Mom knowing?"

"I tell her I'm with Gwen."

"I know you tell her that, but she has a GPS on your phone," Mark replied.

I smiled. "God, Mark, one of the benefits of being best friends with a computer hacker is she can hack anything."

Mark thought about it for a second. "Oh my god, Gwen's hacked your signal!"

I grinned and said, "Yup. Whether Mom checks by call or cam, it doesn't matter. She thinks I'm somewhere I'm not."

Mark seemed impressed by my deviousness.

"So, do we have a deal or what?" I said.

Mark agreed, "Fine, we'll keep each other's secrets." I shook his right hand, and he screamed, "Oooww! The other arm, Kirin, the other arm."

"Sorry, sorry, totally forgot," I said, rubbing his arm gently.

I said, "Follow me," and I knocked on the door.

I crossed my fingers, hoping Sifu would be here already. Then I heard Sifu's voice calling, "I'm coming. I'm coming."

Sifu opened the door and said, "Kirin, what are you doing here?"

I said, "Sifu, can I come in?"

Sifu said, "Sure, sure, come in, Kirin." I turned around and told Mark to come in as well. Mark followed me into Sifu's school, said hi, and remained silent while I did the talking.

"Sifu, this is my brother Mark."

Sifu said, "Nice to meet you."

Mark smiled.

Before I could say another word, Sifu said, "Mind if I look at your shoulder?"

I looked at Sifu, wondering how he knew Mark hurt his shoulder.

Mark agreed, and Sifu started massaging a part of his shoulder as he said, "Relax, just relax."

Mark couldn't relax as Sifu was massaging his arm, so Sifu started asking him questions, "So, how'd you hurt your arm?"

Mark replied, "Jiu Jitsu class, sir, I rolled over it funny."

Sifu said, "Okay, I can see how that happens. Does this happen often?"

Mark thought about it for a second and nodded. "Yeah, it does, but it's part of the training, you know ... otherwise, how else will you learn?"

Sifu continued to massage part of his arm, waiting for him to relax. "Mark, do you happen to have a girlfriend?"

Mark turned his head quickly in surprise. "What? I don't–"

CRACK!

"Ah! Mark screamed, his face in agonizing pain, but seconds later he looked much better.

"Sorry about that," Sifu said. "I needed to get you to relax. Distraction can be a powerful ally." He laughed.

He worked further on his arm, massaging and tweaking before he again snapped his entire arm like a wet rag from the fingertips. Mark said, "Ouch!" and shivered like he felt a bolt of electricity run through him.

Then his face settled into relief. "Wow, that feels a hundred times better."

Sifu worked some more and then said, "Let me get some stuff from the back."

Mark sat down and relaxed, moving his shoulder with wonder in his eyes as he tried to figure out what exactly had just happened.

Sifu came walking back with several items in his hands, though he said, "I only need a couple of these." He started examining the area around Mark's shoulder, occasionally asking, "Does this hurt?"

Mark said, "A little."

"How about this area?"

"That hurts a little more."

"And now this?"

Mark squirmed in discomfort and said, "Yup, yup, that's it.... That hurts the most." I felt bad for my brother, but trusted that Sifu could work some of his magic. Sifu looked at the spot where he planned to put the needle in, as Mark began to cringe at the idea.

As big and tough as Mark was, he definitely wasn't so keen on the idea of getting pricked by a needle. He looked away. "Is it gonna hurt?"

Sifu said, "Is what gonna hurt?"

Mark said, "You know, the needle."

Sifu smiled. "You mean the needle that's already in your arm?"

Mark was surprised and looked down at the needle sticking out of his body. "Oh my gosh, I didn't even feel you put it in." Sifu smiled and continued to put several more needles at specific parts throughout Mark's body. Then he looked at his clock and said, "Let's give it about fifteen to thirty minutes." He gave a quick nod to Mark, who looked a lot better sitting on the chair.

I'd seen Sifu do this before, but it still amazed, how he used his skill in Wing Chun to heal people.

Thirty minutes passed, and Sifu removed the needles. Mark moved his shoulder around and said, "Wow, I feel absolutely great." Sifu placed a patch nice and tight on Mark's shoulder. Mark asked, "What's this for?"

Sifu replied, "There are herbs on this patch that should help the healing process." Sifu then started shaking his finger at Mark. "Now remember to remove this tomorrow. Don't leave it on past a day." He looked at me and added, "Kirin, make sure you remind your brother."

Mark nodded his head as he listened. Then Sifu said, "Most importantly, you need to rest it."

Mark protested, "But it feels back to normal already."

Sifu smiled and said, "If you use it right away, you'll injure it further. Give the body time to heal itself."

Mark said, "You know what they say: no pain, no gain."

Sifu shook his had and laughed. "*No pain, no gain* does not mean you hurt your body. Remember: hurt yourself today, and you'll pay the price later on. That's guaranteed."

Mark nodded and said, "Thank you so much, uh, Sifu." Sifu exchanged pleasantries with Mark as he began to walk us back outside. Mark looked at me and said, "Are you coming? Mom's gonna be home soon," as he started unchaining the bicycles.

I said, "Give me a second."

I looked at Sifu and said, "Thanks, Sifu, I really, really appreciate it."

"No problem, Kirin, any time," Sifu said humbly. Just before I went out the door, I spun around and said, "He's gonna hurt himself again, isn't he, Sifu?"

Sifu laughed, "Oh yeah, he's not gonna listen," and just patted me on the shoulder.

"The choices we make create our balance." –Sifu

A handful of us were headed out with Sifu. We just had a good time training, and it was time to eat. "Good" was a relative term, as everyone was leaving class wondering why they couldn't do what Sifu could.

Doc asked me, "Why are you so bummed, Kirin?"

"My god, my roll stinks," I said depressingly.

Robert said, "Yeah, it does."

I frowned. "Thanks, jerk."

Robert said, "Hey, I was paying you a compliment."

"How was that a compliment?"

"It's still way better then Danny's, and he's been here longer than you," said Robert. Danny leaped onto Robert's back and pretended to choke him. I giggled at them, thinking they reminded me of my brothers.

Danny said, "That's my plan."

Robert asked, "How is that a plan?"

Danny replied, "I have everything to gain by not being the best. Get it?" We all looked at Danny, wondering if he was dropped often as a child.

Ryan said, "Why can't I leave class feeling like I accomplished something? I always leave more depressed."

Ken replied, "Maybe you need some more homemade prozac!"

Ryan answered dryly, "Yes, after lunch, I'll stop by and get some more ice cream."

Sifu interjected, "If you leave class happy, that means you didn't learn anything."

Tobias said, "I must be learning a ton 'cause I feel suicidal." We all laughed, but at the same time we all knew that feeling.

Doc said, "Maybe you guys would prefer going to some UFMF school so you could school get a belt or trophy."

Ken then said, "I don't need a belt, but a word of encouragement from my Sifu every now and again would be nice."

Sifu looked at Ken. "Ken, is there a word in the dictionary that means worse than sucks?"

Ken replied, "I don't think so."

Sifu said, "Then that's good." Ken looked around, dazed and confused about whether that was a compliment or not.

As we continued walking to the restaurant, I started to notice something odd. I was side by side with Sifu, while the rest of the gang seemed intent on keeping a good distance from us. I looked around to confirm that it was not just my imagination.

Sifu said, "Kirin, give me a second. I'll catch up."

"Okay," I replied, as I ran up to the rest of the guys.

The guys were busy chatting, so I interrupted them, "Sifu's busy doing something."

They looked behind me and noticed that Sifu was engaged in a conversation with a man on the street.

I asked, "Can I ask you guys a question?"

Doc replied, "Sure, Kirin, what?"

I felt embarrassed to ask but said, "I may just be imagining this, but it seemed like you guys were purposely walking away from Sifu and me. Did I say something wrong?"

Everyone began laughing as Doc put his hand around my shoulder.

Doc said, "Kirin, it's not you. It's Sifu."

Confused, I admitted, "I don't get it."

Doc looked around, seeking approval from the group. Finally he said, "We're not in the best of neighborhoods, right?"

I shook my head in agreement. Then, he stared at me, as if the answer was obvious.

"Well, that's why we're not next to Sifu."

I cringed, thinking, *The safest thing would be next to Sifu.*

Doc smiled. "I know what you are thinking, that it would be the safest thing, to be next to him. Right?"

I nodded, and said, "Of course!"

Doc shook his head, and replied, "Kirin, Kirin ... you have to understand Wing Chun philosophy. Let's say you're walking next to Sifu, and suddenly a mugger comes. He then demands money. What do you think would happen next?"

I answered. "Sifu would spring into action and kick his butt."

Doc had a smirk on his face. "I believe you are one-hundred percent correct, that Sifu would do that. However...."

I stared at him, wondering, *What's the catch?*

Doc blurted out, "He would use you, as a shield!"

I looked at him in disbelief, and said, "Why would he do that?"

"Think about it, Kirin. It would create a moment of confusion. The mugger would be frozen, never ever expecting that that would happen. And, when it does, Sifu would use that to his advantage to finish him."

I stood there silently, and listened to the logic. In a way, one could argue that it made sense. I looked at the guys, and they all looked like they were being sincere. I just couldn't believe, that there was no way this could be true.

While I was busy contemplating that idea, the guys were all focused on Sifu. I turned around and saw Sifu speaking to a homeless person.

He went through his pocket and pulled out some credits.

As we approached, we heard say, "What's your name?"

"Lance."

"Lance, hopefully this helps a little," said Sifu.

Lance was appreciative. It looked like he hadn't eaten for a while. He was dressed up in old Army fatigues and had a backpack which he guarded by his side.

"What's your story, Lance?" asked Sifu.

"Well, sir, I'm a former Army special forces. My body's been torn up a bit, and I've had some bad luck on the way. One thing led to another, and I've been trying to get back on my feet," said Lance.

I looked at him as his last word seemed to bring the most pain.

Sifu gave him a pat on the shoulder. "I'm sure your luck will turn around."

They were merely words from Sifu's mouth, but they appeared to comfort Lance. Watching Sifu interact with people, it almost seemed he had the power of suggestion.

Afterwards, I pulled out some credits as well and said, "Hope this helps."

Lance smiled and said, "Thank you, ma'am. Hope one day I can return the favor."

I looked at him kindly and said, "Take care of yourself, and that'll be enough."

He was taken aback by my comment and then smiled. "By the way, the name is Lance, ma'am."

I giggled, as he called me ma'am. "It's Kirin," I said.

We waved our goodbyes and started walking closer to our restaurant.

Robert said, "Come on, Sifu, how do you know that guy wasn't faking? There are hundreds of guys out in the street, some of them just too lazy to work."

"I felt something, but whether he was or wasn't is not the point," replied Sifu.

"I don't understand, Sifu. What's the big deal?" asked Robert.

"I can only speak from my experience, but there are many points in a person's life when he or she feels lost and alone. While it may be natural to feel this, it's at those points where decisions are made that lead to one path or another. That's why I'm very cautious about being quick to judge. Personally, if I feel the need to judge, I judge from within," said Sifu.

I asked him, "So, do you see it as the universe balancing things out?"

"Actually, I believe the universe doesn't balance things out. The choices you make do. In the end, we are equal. I am no better than him, just because I have more in my bank account. When you start judging people aloud, that is the ego trying to put you in a higher place.

"Looking back at points in my life, I see I could've easily chosen another path that would have drastically altered the state where I am now. And while you all may be young and don't have much past to reference from, if you take some time to ponder, you will see what I mean."

I glanced around and saw that everyone was affected by Sifu's words.

"I don't believe in random encounters. Energies are drawn to each other for whatever reason, and along the way, if one pays attention to it, something as simple as a word of encouragement or a helping hand can get someone back on track."

I said nothing but listened to the words of Sifu. Every word he'd ever spoken always seemed to touch me. I started feeling ... emotional.

"What's up, Kirin? What's wrong?" inquired Doc.

"I know you guys don't know me too well, but as lousy as that guy may be doing, I came from a place even worse. I escaped from North Korea with my family.

"You are adopted, right, Kirin?" asked Ken.

"I am, Ken. My family tried to escape, but I...."

"Sorry, Kirin ... I didn't know. I didn't mean to bring it up," Ken apologized.

I was choked up and trying to hold back the tears.

I cleared my throat, and said, "That memory, no matter how long it's been, always feels fresh. I think it was sweet that Sifu showed a stranger an act of kindness," I said. "If not for the gentleman who helped me, I would not have made it. I guess Sifu was right: at that lowest point, the universe tried to give a helping hand to me."

The mood turned somber as my emotions were felt by all.

"Hey, Sifu, can you wait a minute?" said Robert.

Robert turned to everyone as they looked at him. He nodded his head.

All the guys started heading toward Lance, as Sifu and I just stood there watching.

I could see from a distance they stopped in front of Lance, and then each one fumbled in his pockets for some credits, before handing it to him.

He stood up in front of them, and saluted. The guys patted him on the back, thanked him for his service to the country, and then walked away.

Sifu whispered to me, "Lance was not lying. When he said he was trying to get back on his feet, he meant it literally."

I looked at Sifu and asked, "What do you mean?"

Sifu leaned over and said, "His right leg ... it was a prosthetic."

I stared at him in wonder and thought, *How does he see all this?*

The guys all came back huffing and puffing. Ryan commented, "Maybe Wing Chun should add some more cardio."

As they all huddled together, I gave every single one of them a hug.

> *"When you can control the ego, then you will see everything as equal." –Sifu*

Taken for Granted–1 year 223 days

It was a sunny Saturday morning, probably the last one we would have before winter came. Saturday was my favorite day of the week because it meant Wing Chun class with Sifu. It was roughly 9:30 am when I told my mom I was headed over to Gwen's.

Mom said, "Kirin, don't be gone too long, okay? We got someplace to go at around two, okay?" I gave Mom a quick kiss and promised her I wouldn't be late.

"Love you, Mom," I said.

I hated lying to my mom about class, but I knew she wouldn't understand. Her goal was to create a Disney-like environment and shield me from my past.

Fifteen minutes passed before I finally arrived at class. I opened the door and found that Tobias was already in the gym working with Sifu.

Dang it, I thought. *He beat me to Sifu.*

Sifu was standing next to him, checking out his twenty singleman technique.

As I walked in, I did my best to listen in.

"Again, Tobias," said Sifu.

There Tobias did it in perfect order: tan, bong, lop, pak, lan, bue, jam, wu, huen, jut, outside jut, gum, fak, pau, gan, ding, haan, low bong, jeong, kow.

Sifu said, "Way too much arm, Tobias. You have to use the body more. Remember: the body is what blocks, not the hands. The hands merely change position while staying on your center line. Do you understand?"

Tobias said, "I understand what you're saying, so the hands have to be passive always?"

"Yes, passive, but there is a balance. There also has to exist active within the passive, to make it fully work," said Sifu.

As I watched, they both turned to look at me.

I smiled and said, "I have no idea what the heck you're talking about." I shrugged my shoulders with a puzzled look on my face.

"Kirin, you're here," said Sifu.

"Hi, Sifu."

"Go warm up with punches," he replied.

"Sure thing, Sifu, I'm on it."

Our typical ritual the first thirty minutes of class was dedicated to basics. Sifu was constantly preaching to us that it wasn't how much you know, it was perfecting what you knew that created the solid foundation. He often said, "I just happen to do all the basic stuff better than everyone else."

Every so often, Sifu would come by and correct something he saw. He was meticulous in detail; he could see in an instant if you had it right or not.

Training wasn't what most people would expect. There was nothing physically exhausting about Wing Chun, but the best way to describe it was a constant test of one's mental endurance. People would quit classes because there was nothing to support their ego. No belt, no trophies, and Sifu did not care if you came or left.

I guess that was why the masses never filled up his school. In the modern world, everyone wanted something that multitasked. Specialization was a wasted talent. Society believed that a product that could kill four birds with one stone was superior.

But regardless of the direction society had taken, Sifu did not budge. He did it his way always as if to say, "I know what I'm doing and why, and that's all that matters."

Fifteen minutes had passed since the start of class, and only Tobias and I were there. Sifu said, "Well, I guess it's only you two today. Let's work on the singleman technique against one another."

Sifu gave us time to test out our stuff and then would come by to explain and demonstrate things we were both doing wrong.

"Tobias, do you want me to attack now and you do the blocks?" I said.

Tobias said, "Sure, I'll block for the next ten minutes."

I saw Sifu stare out the window as Tobias and I kept working on the drills.

"Tobias, do you think Sifu's upset that barely anyone showed up to class today?" I asked.

"You know, Kirin, it's hard to say. I honestly can't read Sifu."

"Where do you think the other guys are today?" I asked.

"Well, you know it's really nice today and the guys probably took advantage of it.... What can I say? The guys are probably bumming doing something else," said Tobias.

Sifu strolled back and asked us, "Do you have any questions?"

As usual, I did, and he quickly answered, explained, and demonstrated how to do it.

Time really moved fast for a two-hour class.

Sifu said, "Let's take a one-minute break, okay?" We both agreed and chilled out, grabbing some water and just hanging.

"Sifu, do you mind if I ask you a question?" I said.

"Sure, you can ask me anything."

"This may sound weird, Sifu, but why not market your class more? The stuff you teach compared to everything around here is like a thousand times better. I mean, you could have like hundreds of students, a big gym, and make a ton of cash," I said.

"Would you prefer I had more students?" asked Sifu.

"I like the smallness of the class, and I think I learn better this way," I responded.

Tobias said, "I know what you're saying, Sifu, but five blocks down there's that school that's franchised by the UFMF. The dude running it has like several awesome cars and drives a Porsche. He's rolling in some serious cash."

Sifu said softly, "Tobias, I know the gap between rich and poor is greater than ever, but being rich doesn't translate to being happy. Happiness comes from within, not from what you have or think you want. Anyway, the more you know yourself, the more you are at peace. The fact is, the rich simply have more toys to distract them from the truth. That's all."

Tobias looked at me, and we shared a moment without words. *Damn, Sifu is just so wise.*

"One of the things my Sifu told me was never make a living off teaching. Instead, share the art and teach the truth. That's exactly what he told me, if I wanted to develop my skill," said Sifu.

"I'm glad you listened to your Sifu," I said.

"He's much wiser than I am, so I always listen to him," said Sifu.

Tobias spoke up, "Sifu, do you think we sometimes take your teaching for granted? I mean, today, there's only me and Kirin in class."

"It's natural, I guess, for people to take things for granted, like that I'll always be around to teach," said Sifu.

I looked at Sifu, hoping the day would never come that he would stop teaching.

"Sifu, did you ever take your teacher for granted?" I asked.

"Maybe it's because of my path, but I never took him for granted," said Sifu.

Tobias said, "Do you mind telling us how you met your teacher?"

"I don't want to take too much away from your class," replied Sifu.

We both looked at each other, and I said, "We could spare ten, Sifu. Please tell us."

Sifu thought for a second and then began to talk.

"Masters aren't a dime a dozen, you know. You can't just find them in the yellow pages," said Sifu.

We exchanged a glance, and Tobias asked, "What are yellow pages?"

Sifu laughed and said, "Never mind, now I realize how old I am. Anyway, to make a long story short, I spent years trying to find one. I studied many different arts even before Wing Chun, and found many different Wing Chun teachers as well. But, it wasn't till the mid-90s that I found my teacher. He was different from many of the other teachers I had met. I'm not trying to say the others were bad, but it always felt that they had something to sell. Sifu, on the other hand, was just himself. He was concerned only about the art and nothing else."

"He sounds just like you now," I said.

"Sounding and being are two different things. He is a far better man than I will ever be, Kirin." Sifu smiled. "Anyway, he taught from a different state, so I only got to see him once or twice a year in the beginning."

"Weren't you concerned that learning from so far away would hinder your progress?" said Tobias.

"I wanted to learn. I wanted to be the best. The distance was merely an excuse," said Sifu. "What have I always told you? In the end, the will dictates everything, even beyond the skill."

"Yes, Sifu," both Tobias and I said.

Sifu continued to speak for several more minutes about his Sifu. He seemed to enjoy talking about him and the times he spent training.

"And that's why I never took him for granted. Every minute, every moment was precious. My Sifu has always meant the world to me. I am who I am because of him."

I looked at Sifu and saw that he was teary-eyed.

"I'll never take you for granted, Sifu," I said.

"Neither will I," said Tobias.

"Promise me you'll never stop teaching," I said, looking into his eyes.

Sifu smiled, but did not utter a word.

"People take things for granted because they are misguided by value. When you learn what really matters in life, you come to understand it's the simplest thing that carries the greatest weight." –Sifu.

Sifu's Journey Entry #5–Ten Thousand Punches

Early Spring 2030

For several months, Sifu had been training meticulously. He would get up at the crack of dawn and spend the first forty-five minutes of the morning working on Siu Lim Tao, the first form in Wing Chun.

He recalled a conversation with his own Sifu when he was much younger. His Sifu had told him that when you get older you don't sleep as much. He had finally gotten to that stage where he realized what he meant.

"Ah, older," he murmured as he scratched his head and looked into the mirror. He felt great and didn't have the same ills as most people his age, but he knew that he was different both inside and out.

Sifu woke up in his little apartment with no need for an alarm as his internal clock got him started. He did what people normally do in the morning and got dressed. He wasn't feeling hungry this morning and decided to start his routine.

"I feel like doing something different this morning," he said, and then paused for a moment searching for an answer.

Instead of Siu Lim Tao this morning, he decided to switch it up and do ten thousand punches. In his earlier days of training, doing ten thousand a day was the norm for him, but it had been awhile since he'd hit those numbers. He made another pit stop to the bathroom, mentally calculating how long ten thousand punches would take. Once done, he found the same spot where he normally did the first form and opened up his stance.

And so he began, slowly at first to get the blood flowing through his veins. "One, two, three ... fifty ... one hundred...," he counted and then glanced at the clock. He made a mental mark of the time when he started and then just continued punching.

Ten thousand punches would take roughly an hour and forty-five minutes to perform. Fifteen minutes passed as he continued punching, concentrating only on the target. Left side, then right side, over again. The punches were clean as the motions were flawless, each one capable of delivering a deadly blow.

Time passed as Sifu began losing himself in the process.

His focus trembled as he recalled a conversation he had with his teacher some twenty years ago.

My Sifu said, "The physical, mental, and spiritual are developed hand in hand. That is the balance necessary in all that we do."

"How so, Sifu?" I asked.

My Sifu explained, "Anything that requires motion or energy is the physical taking place, but knowing how, what, and why you're doing something evokes the spirit."

Frustrated, I decided to tell Sifu what I felt. "I can't figure it out. I believe I know what it is to fix it, yet I struggle to deal with it.... I just keep working and working on it, and it just won't come."

My Sifu said, "Remember this: all the answers are always right in front of you. But, your vision is often clouded and muddled with your thoughts—work, family, money, or it could be something as simple as want and desire. Thus, wisdom comes about with a steady mind.... Why do you think I did ten thousand punches back in the days?"

I replied, "To develop exploding power."

"That's only the physical side. What about the spiritual?"

"I have no idea, Sifu," I replied.

"Ten thousand punches takes some time to do. A single task leads to focus, and you do the punch repeatedly until that focus clears the mind, leading to stillness. Once the mind

is steady, the wisdom will come. That's why I did it, to calm the mind, gain the focus, and eventually you can see things others cannot."

Sifu snapped out of his thoughts and checked the time. He had been punching nonstop for almost two hours and was nearing the end as he began counting them aloud again.

Sifu was in a sweat. For months, he had been searching for an answer, which continued to escape him. He was about to chi pack, but suddenly it hit him. He grabbed a towel, dried himself off, and didn't bother to change his clothes. He ran out of his apartment and headed toward his store.

He swung open the door and quickly shut it behind him. Then he ran to the storage area and hit the lever. The door swung open, revealing the path to the basement.

He walked down the stairs and scanned the table where he was writing his book, creating the road map to Wing Chun. There it was: one of several unopened letters from Kirin. The first of many letters that had remained sitting in his basement since he first found them months ago.

He held it in his hand and slowly tore it open. He began reading Kirin's card:

Dear Sifu,
Words cannot describe how....

There Sifu spent the rest of the day going through each one.

"The answers are always simple, but the difficulty is facing the truth." –Sifu

CHAPTER 6
Sunday Night Dinner

The second Sunday of every month was a tradition at the Rise household. Since everyone was older, it was much more difficult to spend time with one another, so Mom made it a rule, unless it was the impossible, to be there for that Sunday night dinner. It had been a week since events had unfolded, and Kirin feared the worst. It was difficult enough to deal with the world's demands, but she would rather face that a hundred times over than confront her entire family.

The Rise house was considerably modest, but then again that could depend on whose point of view. Both of Kirin's adopted parents were doctors, and while they lived a comfortable life, they raised all the kids to appreciate what they had, and not take things for granted.

Kirin was sitting in her little red Volkswagen, parked outside her parents' home, where she had arrived early. She had been sitting there debating possible scenarios in her head for the last ten minutes. It was roughly 6:00 pm, and from the outside looking in, she could see the silhouette figures moving around her home.

Kirin thought it was strange that the shades were pulled down.

Winter finally arrived as the first snow fell that very day. The engine was off, and frost had started forming around the window. As she sat there, vapor began crystalizing with every breath. She was getting lost watching each snowflake hit the windshield of her car. Kirin was trying to gather up the nerve to go up to the front door.

Thousands of thoughts were running through her head. Every random scenario she conjured all played out to everything ending up terrible.

"They must know already. It's all over the news."

The sounds of whimpering came from her partner in crime sitting next to her. Kirin turned her head and looked at Bacon all snuggled in the front with his seatbelt wrapped around his special harness. Kirin had dressed him up in a little snow outfit, hoping the cute factor might be a good distraction. For once, he wanted to move as it was probably getting too cold for him inside the car.

"Give me a second, Bacon."

She closed her eyes, took a deep breath, and held it ... eventually letting the air escape through her nose. Snowflake after snowflake in the millions drifted down onto her car.

Knock. Knock.

The door swung open, and Dad smiled down at her. He rushed forward, grabbed Kirin, and gave her a huge bear hug. He quickly turned around and shouted, "Hun, Kirin's home! We're all here."

Mom strolled from the kitchen in her apron, smiling at Kirin as she opened up her arms to offer a hug. Kirin ran toward her and gave her a kiss on the cheek.

"Hey, Mom," said Kirin.

All of Kirin's brothers except Jim surged forward to surround her, sharing in the excitement of her arrival.

"This is a warmer welcome than I expected."

They all shouted, "I can't believe you kicked that guy's ass! That was unbelievable!" Everyone embraced her in the middle, as a celebration took place.

Dad said, "Okay, enough of the fun. Let's eat...."

Surrounded by the love and support of her family, Kirin smiled from ear to ear. She thought, *What more could anyone want?*

Whimper. Whimper. Bacon was growing impatient as his cry broke Kirin's daydream.

Kirin opened her eyes and looked at Bacon. "Well, there's no way in heck that's gonna happen."

"Let's get this over with, Bacon." Kirin realized it was time to face reality. She finally got the nerve to step out of her car, and came to the other side to let Bacon out. Unlike Kirin, Bacon was excited to go to her parents' house. Once Kirin undid his seatbelt, he vaulted out the car and headed toward the door.

Kirin shouted, "Wait, Bacon!"

As usual, Bacon ignored her and got to the front door. He started jumping on the door, scratching it, and Kirin broke into a run.

"Bad dog! No, boy, no!" Kirin shouted at Bacon.

Bacon looked up, heavily panting, waiting for the inevitable to happen. Kirin took a deep breath, slowly raised her finger, and rang the doorbell.

Ding Dong. Ding Dong.

She could hear footsteps slowly approach as she tried to put a fake smile on her face.

The door swung open to reveal Dad. He smiled as he said, "Hey, Princess," and gave her a quick kiss on the cheek. "Come on in. You're the last one here."

"Hey, Dad," Kirin replied as she looked around cautiously, thinking, *So far so good.* Bacon exchanged butt sniffs with his friend Butterscotch before they began to goof off and chase one another. She was the only thing, outside of food, that kept Bacon's attention.

Kirin shouted, "Wait, Bacon, I have to remove your outfit!" Again, Kirin's command fell upon deaf ears.

Inside to the left, she could see the living room, Steve was on the couch watching TV and waved at her. Kirin froze for a second, fearing the worst could be on TV. She exhaled in relief when she heard the sounds of football. Fortunately for her, it seemed that luck was on her side.

The Christmas tree was still decorated as her family was always the slowest to bring down decorations. Underneath, she could see presents still leftover for Jim, who missed Christmas this year, being overseas.

Cautious at the good reaction, Kirin was slightly startled as her dad grabbed her coat and said, "Hurry up, slow poke. Mom's waiting for you in the kitchen."

Kirin gulped, swallowing her own spit in fear.

Kirin stared down the hallway to the kitchen. It was a mere fifteen feet away, but she did her best to prolong seeing Mom. With each step toward the kitchen, it seemed to move further away, just like in the horror movies–only in this case, that was a good thing.

Eventually she got to the entrance of the kitchen and took another deep breath. Suddenly the smell of Korean cooking hit her nose: bulgogi, chap chae, deep fried mackerel, and of course kimchi. All her favorite aromas were dancing in the air.

Mom cooked an entire Korean dinner for tonight? A battle between her stomach and brain began.

Kirin's mom, like most moms, was the glue that held the family together. She bonded strongly with Kirin the moment they first met. She had done everything possible to make her feel at home when she first came to the States. Not only had she learned Korean cuisine, but she had also learned to speak Korean fairly well. Everything she ever did was for the love of her daughter.

Kirin peered around the corner to see Mom cooking by the stove. She did her best to act as natural as possible.

"Hey, Mom," Kirin said.

She seems pretty normal, Kirin thought, taking into account everyone's reaction so far.

"Kirin, go get washed up and get ready for dinner," said Mom.

Kirin nodded and said, "I will in a second, Mom."

Kyle was by the kitchen counter playing on his phone. "Hey, little one," Kirin said as she came around from behind and gave him a kiss.

"Little one? Kirin, I'm not sure you know this, but you're the shortest one in the entire family," said Kyle.

"I am not," she replied with conviction.

She looked around and saw Butterscotch chasing Bacon through the kitchen.

"What about Butterscotch?" She pointed.

"First, she's a dog and, second, if she stood on her hind legs, she's technically taller than you," replied Kyle.

"Hmm," Kirin hummed as she ignored his comments and drifted toward the kitchen table.

"Wow, Mom, you outdid yourself. An entire Korean dinner for tonight. What gives?" said Kirin.

Always thinking with her stomach, Kirin forgot her woes when she entered the house. She snatched a tiny piece of kimchi and started eating it. "This is so good and homemade," said Kirin.

Mom didn't respond, concentrating on the stove to make sure everything was prepared correctly.

Then Kirin saw in the center Mom's special Hawaiian ham.

"Mom, what's with the Hawaiian ham? That's Jim's favorite?"

"She made Jim's favorite because Jim's here." A voice echoed from behind.

Kirin spun around, surprised to see her oldest brother Jim standing by the kitchen entrance.

"Oh my god!" She smiled and leaped toward him to give him a hug.

"You're home! You're home! I thought it was another six more months before you'd be back," said Kirin excitedly.

"It was supposed to be, but I had a chance for a mini leave, so I decided to take it. So, how's my favorite little sister?" said Jim, finally letting go of Kirin.

"What do you mean favorite little sister? I'm your only little sister," she smiled. "Oh, hey, did you open your gift I got you for Christmas?"

Kyle snidely commented, "Jim, you're lucky you're family 'cause I heard Kirin gave away these crappy Christmas cards to her friends." Kyle held one of them up to demonstrate.

She ran to Kyle and tried to swipe it, but he hid it from her.

"Come on. Give it back, Kyle," she said.

"No," said Kyle. Kirin struggled to get the picture back from Kyle who kept taunting her with it. Kyle stood up, raising it far above her head as Kirin tried to reach for it.

"See, I told you were the shortest one," said Kyle.

Her instincts kicked in as Kirin punched him in the arm.

"Owe! Mom, Kirin punched me on the arm," said Kyle.

"That didn't hurt," she joked.

"No, seriously, that really hurt," said Kyle as he rubbed it to soothe the pain.

"Oops," Kirin said to Kyle, "sorry about that."

Mom responded, "Kirin, don't hit your brother. You know girls shouldn't be fighting."

Suddenly Kirin looked down, wondering if her mom's comments had extra meaning or not. A knot in her stomach began to form, the same one she'd felt earlier before entering the house.

Mom said, "Where's Mark? Someone tell him it's time for dinner."

Kyle, who was still rubbing his arm from Kirin's hit, said, "He's upstairs doing homework."

Kirin frowned. *Mark studying on a Sunday night?*

"I'll go get him, Mom." Kirin headed upstairs toward Mark's room. The door was closed, so she knocked on it.

Knock. Knock. Knock.

"Mark, it's Kirin. Time for dinner."

From behind the door, Mark replied, "Come in for a second. I'm almost done."

"I'm coming in. Make sure you're not looking at anything disgusting online," she teased.

Kirin walked in with her hands over her eyes.

"Kirin, quit goofing off." Mark got up from his desk and rushed to close the door behind her.

"What? I was just playing," she said.

Mark had a serious look on his face. "Kirin, everyone knows about the fight."

Kirin's stomach sank, and she sat on his bed. "Damn!" she swore as thoughts raced through her mind.

"Everyone?" asked Kirin.

Mark nodded. "Oh yeah, everyone."

"You sure? Everyone's acting so casual downstairs." Kirin clung to a faint glimmer of hope.

"It's the calm before the storm. Trust me, it's not gonna be a good dinner."

"But Mom made a complete Korean dinner with my favorite stuff," said Kirin.

"Uh, think about it for a second, Kirin. When they kill an inmate, they grant him his last meal. Consider this your last meal."

Kirin flopped backwards on Mark's bed.

"Anyway, why do you think Jim's here? They were hoping he could talk some sense into you and figure out what's going on in your head," said Mark.

"Is that why you were doing homework–to warn me?" asked Kirin.

"Yeah," said Mark. "Why the hell would I do homework during winter break?"

"I knew this was gonna be bad."

Mark looked at Kirin, shaking his head. "Kirin, you only know the half of it. Bad is gonna turn to worse."

"Why do you say that, Mark?" replied Kirin.

"It's bad. People have been calling the house nonstop, trying to figure out if you were the fighter. It's not just the house. Steve, Kyle, and I have just been denying to all our friends that it was you. They have even been bugging Jim about it, nonstop. If that wasn't bad enough, they're asking both Mom and Dad, and they've been saying no comment."

"I haven't heard the phone ring once," said Kirin.

"That's because Mom asked Dad to disconnect it."

Kirin laid on Mark's bed, rubbing her eyes and hoping for some kind of answer.

"Oh my god, so this entire meal is an intervention?" said Kirin.

"Yeah, pretty much," said Mark.

"Okay, if I sneak out of your window and jump out, everything will be back to normal," said Kirin.

"Kirin, I saw the fight. I know you didn't get punched in the head, but that's the dumbest idea yet," Mark said, unimpressed.

"Besides, I wouldn't open the window," said Mark.

"Why not?" replied Kirin.

"I'm willing to bet there are probably several cars lurking outside that spotted you coming here and are now watching the house," said Mark.

Kirin could not believe it and decided to peek through her brother's curtain. Lifting it slightly, she spotted her car. Then she noticed several other cars that were not there earlier when she had parked in the driveway. Studying one car closely, she saw the reflection of a lens through the car window. She quickly released the curtain and hid back in Mark's room.

"Oh, shit!"

Kirin looked at Mark as he stood silently. "So, what should I do, Mark?"

"You know that saying that Dad always says?" said Mark. Sadly, Kirin did know it, and she nodded in acknowledgement. "Yeah, you're pretty much gonna have to eat the cake."

Kirin closed her eyes and pictured herself in another part of the country. As she opened them, she found she was still in Mark's room. "Damn it, mental note: no super power to teleport self," Kirin said.

"Look at it this way, Kirin. What's done is done, right?" said Mark.

Mark, you don't know. It's only the beginning, she thought.

Minutes Later

Gathered at the dinner table, the family was all ready to dig into the meal. It had been awhile since it felt complete, since Jim was usually missing. Underneath the table, both Bacon and Butterscotch assumed the begging position, looking tuckered out from their earlier playful antics.

Kirin sat expecting the worst, knowing this was her last meal. A last-second change in emotion kicked in as she realized the inevitable was about to happen. She mumbled, "Screw it," and then said louder, "let's eat."

Mom interrupted her, "So, does anyone want to say grace?"

She looked around, waiting for a volunteer, "No one ... no one? Very well, I'll lead the prayers." She said it with a kind and tender voice that for a moment put Kirin at ease.

"Our Father, Who art in heaven, Hallowed be Thy Name; Thy kingdom come, Thy will be done, on earth as it is in heaven. Give us this day our daily bread, and forgive us our trespasses, as we forgive those who trespass against us; and lead us not into temptation, but deliver us from evil. Amen. Dear God, thank you for this meal we are about to receive and for having our entire family back home safe and sound. And ... what in God's name were you thinking about getting into that fight, KIRIN!" said Mom.

Kirin pinched the bridge of her nose as she closed her eyes and spoke, "Mom, this is gonna sound bad, but couldn't you at least have brought it up after we ate?"

"I agree with Kirin. Can we eat first?" asked Kyle as he grabbed a piece of the bulgogi with his fork.

Kirin's mom glared at Kyle and said, "Kyle, if you want to see your next birthday, I suggest you put that down immediately!"

Kyle dropped his utensils and quietly sank back into his chair.

Mom shouted to the rest of the family, "Anyone else hungry?" She scanned the room for a response as the entire male species bowed down before the matriarch and hung their heads.

"Oh, shit." This was gonna be bad; Kirin's swear count was already two for the day.

Kirin looked down at all the delicious food, almost teasing her, knowing that she might not ever get to taste it.

You know things are going really bad when you're having conversations with yourself while surrounded by a group of people, Kirin thought.

No one else spoke, but Kirin could feel their eyes boring into her. *Quick, Kirin. Come up with a home run answer.*

She blurted, "What's done is done," with a false sense of certainty.

Kirin's inner voice groaned, *Oh that's strike number three, as Kirin Rise just whiffed to end the game.*

She realized her flubbage and tried to bypass the seriousness of it by grabbing a piece of the bulgogi.

"Kirin Rise, I may not know Karate, or Ja Jitsu, or whatever it is you do, but right now I know crazy...." Kirin's mom didn't utter another word, as she sat there fuming.

Kyle looked at Kirin, and his advice was plain: *Do as she says.*

Kirin's mom spoke, "First, just to confirm, without a shadow of a doubt, that was you in the fight?"

Kirin hesitated for a second, looking down. Then she turned toward her mom and stared her in the eye. "Yes ... yes, that was me."

"Okay, we have that fully cleared," said her mom.

Mom suddenly looked at Mark as he quickly looked away, knowing all too well that he just got caught in a past lie.

Kirin's mom took a deep breath, and Kirin could see her seething with anger. Finally, she spoke, "Are you crazy? Are you trying to get yourself killed?"

"I wasn't gonna lose, Mom," said Kirin.

"'I wasn't gonna lose'? That's not the point! What were you doing there in the first place?" she yelled.

Kirin gathered her thoughts and said, "I wanted to make a point, take a stand, and I thought that was the place to make it."

"Okay, before you tell me of your quest or your reasoning behind this madness ... I'm confused; where did you learn to fight?" She stared at her husband.

Kirin's dad shrugged, looking around, as if confirming that he had nothing to do with this.

"Mom, it wasn't Dad. I learned Wing Chun on my own.... I started when I was eleven," said Kirin.

"What do you mean eleven? When? Where? How?" asked Kirin's mom, shaking her head in disbelief.

"Every Saturday for roughly five years, I've been studying, instead of hanging out with Gwen," said Kirin.

Mom rolled her eyes and said, "Oh my god, is there any other dark secret you've been keeping from this family? You sure you're doing photography? You're not some kind of exotic dancer on the weekends?"

Mark, Steve, and Kyle all giggled. Mom stared at them until they became quiet.

"Kirin, what was the number one rule I've always told you about this family? The very first day when we saw you at the airport," she said.

"To be honest with each other," said Kirin.

"All these years you hid this from me?"

"You wouldn't have understood, Mom. You're the one who always said girls shouldn't fight," said Kirin.

"You're my only daughter. I'm not asking for much. Why can't you act like one?" she said.

Kirin sat silently, as all eyes were on her.

"Kirin, I'm just so confused right now. I don't understand why you're doing this. First you turn down a full scholarship to Stanford, to do photography. Fine! Your dad and I accepted that. We figured we'd let you find your own path. But now you're making it extremely difficult for us to live with that decision when this is the path you're taking.... Why, Kirin? Why this? Explain to me so all this can make sense for both me and your father?"

Kirin stood up and didn't hesitate to answer. If there was one thing she knew, its why she did what she did.

"Don't you get it, Mom? What was I gonna do? Sure, I could've taken the scholarship to Stanford, graduated with a degree, and found a cushy job that made tons of money. Eventually start a family and live happily ever after. Then I thought, all for what? All for what? Life has to be more than just that. Even though life may be great for me in my little world that I created due to some random luck showered upon me by the universe, that doesn't help what's happening outside this very house. Just blocks away, the rest of the world is suffering. I can't pretend to live like that, Mom."

The words were said with such strong conviction that it caught everyone's attention.

Softly, Kirin added, "Please, please, Mom ... Dad, don't think of me as an ingrate. I am beyond thankful for everything ... everything you guys have given me. You've given me a great life. I know I would not be here standing in front of all of you if you had never adopted me. I'm positive I would've been dead."

Kirin pounded her chest.

"All of you know the hell I came from, the wrongs that exist, the evils of this world, and this is not to point a finger, but even though we're safe in our little bubble from what's happening out there, the reality is: it's all an illusion. It's only a matter of time before it pops.

"Mom ... Dad, you said it yourself. Right and wrong are no longer based on what's fair, but who has the most money. Since the corporations have taken over and bailed out the governments, this disguise of democracy that we still claim to live in is a joke. Rights continue to be lost; the people who live under it have become apathetic and fearful. People are sold the lie that the dream can still exist, but the fact is they can never achieve it anymore.

"For far too long, people have been willing to turn the other way, and now that all this has happened, they wonder: how did it come to be like this?

"The masses are fed the scraps of the rich and are expected to be thankful. They've forgotten what their God-given rights are.

"It's always about the money, and I wanted to remind people that it doesn't have to be that way," said Kirin. She looked down as tears rolled down her face.

Mom sat silently along with everyone else, as several minutes went by.

"Okay, I understand now. I understand why you did what you did, and while I wish you'd gone about it another way, your message is honorable, Kirin." And like you said, what's done is done. Hopefully, all this excitement will eventually blow over, with a little more time," said Kirin's mom.

Kirin felt guilty as her mom continued with her speech.

"Promise me, this is it?" Her mother was clearly hoping for a sense of relief.

Everyone relaxed as Mom set the tone.

"Perfect, let's eat now," said Kyle as he began to reach for the food. As everyone started passing around the dishes, Kirin stood there, shying away from looking at her mother.

"Kirin?" her mom asked with a look of concern.

She stood silently, her stomach cramping by what she was about to say. "I can't." Kirin reached in her pocket and pulled out her invitation. She hesitantly placed it on the center of the dinner table.

"Holy shit," said Mark, his eyes widening as he realized what Kirin had.

"Mark, what did I tell you about watching your mouth?" said Kirin's mom.

"Is that what I think it is, Kirin?" Mark asked in surprise.

The family looked around in confusion.

"What is it, Mark?" said Kirin's dad.

"It's a formal invitation to enter the UFMF league ... and I assume for this season," he said.

"So what? What does that mean?" Her mom sounded frantic.

"Only a select few get these invitations to enter the league to fight. The top thirty-two at the end of the year make it to the biggest event in the world, the DOME," Mark explained.

Kirin's mom looked at her, angered and confused. "I know that the UFMF is extremely popular, but I don't follow it. Is that what it is, Kirin?"

"It is ... and I plan to accept it," said Kirin.

Kirin's mom had heard enough. It was too much to take in. She walked away from the table, too upset to talk. As she left, Dad followed to make sure she was okay.

The brothers were all seated as Kirin stood still.

"Are we not gonna eat then?" asked Kyle.

Steve slapped Kyle on the head. "You dumb ass."

"What?" said Kyle.

"Kirin, walk with me," said Jim.

"Where you guys going?" asked Mark.

"I'm gonna talk to Kirin alone," said Jim.

"No, no ... I know you're the oldest, Jim, but she's our little sister, too. What happens to her affects all of us," said Mark sternly.

Jim hesitated but, finally agreed. "Fine, let's go down to the basement."

"So, we're not eating then?" said Kyle.

Everyone turned around and ignored Kyle. The three brothers and Kirin headed to the basement, trying to create stability from the current chaos. A minute later, Kyle joined them all.

"Kirin, you're gonna kill Mom. You're breaking her heart," said Jim.

"I know what you're saying. I love Mom with all my heart, and the last thing I want to do is hurt her," said Kirin. Then she stared Jim directly in the eyes, and said, "I have to do this. I have to take a stand. I have to fight back!"

"Explain to me, why are you fighting? I thought you made your point, already?" asked Jim.

"I'm gonna destroy them.... I'll be coming from the outside and destroying them from within. I planted the seed, but it still needs to grow. I'm gonna tear down their entire structure and shatter everything they stand for, by winning the entire thing," said Kirin.

"Kirin, one lucky punch doesn't make you a UFMF fighter. Those guys are trained professionals."

Full of confidence, Kirin said, "That wasn't luck; it was skill."

Jim interrupted, "Kirin, it's been proven that traditional martial arts does not work in the ring. That's why it's died down. That's why everything's been franchised."

"No ... no, what's been proven is that Americans lack the patience and attention span to develop true skill. Instead, what they've done is fast food the hell out of martial arts and everything that it was supposed to stand for," said Kirin.

"Kirin, you can't possibly think you're gonna win. This is complete madness. You're gonna get yourself killed," said Jim.

"I gotta agree, Kirin," Mark said hesitantly. "I know you can fight, but no rookie fighter has ever won, and the handful of women who have made it in the league have never completed a full season. Kirin, there's no way you're gonna defy the odds and win it all. I can't see it," said Mark.

"You knew Kirin could fight?" Jim looked at Mark. "I'll deal with you later."

Both Steve and Kyle shrugged their shoulders and posed as innocent bystanders.

"Kirin, I'm special forces. I've seen combat and used it, and even I won't fight those guys in the ring."

"I've always loved and respected you, Jim, but no offense, what you know is nothing compared to what I can do," said Kirin.

The brothers exchanged glances, and Kirin could see the anger on Jim's face.

"All right, enough of this. Let's make a deal. If you think you can really fight, beat me. If you can, that's the last you'll hear from me. But, when I beat you," he said smugly, "you're gonna apologize to Mom and put an end to this crusade."

Jim extended his hand and said, "Do we have a deal?"

Kirin shook Jim's hand confidently. "Deal!"

A Few Minutes Later

Jim lay on the floor, stunned by what had just happened. Kirin extended her hand and helped Jim back onto his feet. Steve, Mark, and Kyle just stood there in awe.

"I have no idea what you just did, but you kicked my ass without kicking it," said Jim.

"Holy shit, Kirin, you're bad ass," said Steve.

"Now that this is over, do you think we can go upstairs and eat?" said Kyle.

Mark hit Kyle on the head again. "Will you stop thinking with your stomach?"

"All right, Kirin, a deal's a deal. I just hope you know what you're getting yourself into," said Jim.

Kirin looked straight at Jim and said, "I'm gonna do what I should have always done, and that's to go forward. It's already started, Jim. I know that my actions have already created doubt. They know it, too. Why else offer me an invitation? I'd be the first non-UFMF member to be invited into the tournament."

"Let's say you're right; if that's the case, they're out to destroy you," said Jim.

"Let them try," said Kirin.

Jim sighed. "You're one person, going against a multibillion dollar industry that's tied into every facet of our society. You plan on threatening a way of life, trying to bring back something that people just don't care about anymore or possibly can't comprehend. This is people's livelihoods, their jobs, and you're gonna try to hit them were it hurts the most. You said it yourself: it's all about the money. If you hit them there, it's not just you anymore. It's anyone and everything you know and love that will be a target. I really hope you know what you're doing."

> *"Family is the starting point of our foundation from which we grow ... its value is immeasurable." –Sifu*

Short Stories #6–Kirin's P.O.V.

The Talk–2 years 187 days

"Hmh, where's your concentration tonight, Tobias? Focus on the target, not the attack," said Sifu. Tobias didn't say a word; he simply kept working on the drill.

"You're all over the place," said Sifu.

Tobias was the best, the leader of the school, but his concentration was waning tonight. Everyone could feel his frustration, and it was not just due to his Wing Chun being off.

Sifu asked everyone to pay attention. "What's the purpose of the block?" Everyone gathered around Sifu as we could tell that he had something important to point out.

Doc was unsure but said, "Logically, I would say to not get hit." A few nodded in agreement.

Sifu waited and then said, "No, absolutely not. If your focus is to block the attack, you are one step behind. If you fear getting hit, then you will get hit. Do not underestimate the mind's ability to make things come true."

I asked, "Then what should we focus on when doing the drill, Sifu?"

Sifu smiled. "Everything we do is to position ourselves so we can shoot. Once we end up focusing on the opponent's attack, instead of his center as the target, we fail to play our game. Does everybody understand?"

The students took a moment to let that information sink in.

"Okay, you got five minutes left. See if you can get it," said Sifu. The group dispersed and began practicing on getting the drill right.

Moments later, the door sprung open followed by a gust of wind. All heads immediately turned, expecting the usual ... another challenge match. Instead, what we got was a pleasant surprise. Two small figures simultaneously bolted through the entrance, flying in the air and striking a pose.

"I challenge you to my Snake style," said Akira with a hiss in his voice.

"Snake style is no match for the awesome power of Crane ... caw, caw," shouted Hideo.

Akira said in a cute voice, "Crane style is to *fauncy;* besides, you need to be more direct like a snake."

It was Sifu's twin five year-old little boys, each one posing in his respective style.

Sifu gave them the look as they reverted to Wing Chun poses and faced each other.

"I'm ready, Akira," said Hideo.

Akira nodded his head as his guard hands were up and ready. Hideo quickly closed the gap and did a pak punch—a simultaneous block and attack. Akira tried to block, but Hideo's punch got through and tapped his chest.

"Ow, you jerk, that hurt," said Akira.

"Sorry," said Hideo.

With tears in his eyes, Akira looked over to Sifu. "Dad, Hideo punched me in the chest."

With utter sincerity on his face, Sifu looked at Hideo. "Next time block better."

"Hmm," said Hideo, who wasn't happy with Sifu's answer.

Everyone turned to Sifu as he said, "This is why hamsters eat their young." The class laughed and continued practicing during the last moments of the drill.

Robert said to Ken, "Now I don't feel so bad when he rags on us."

Ken laughed. "Agreed, he's even more critical on his kids."

Sifu walked over to Ken and Robert and whispered. "I make them stand in Yee Gee Kim Yeung Ma as their time out punishment." He giggled and walked away.

Then a cute little girl came in. She was Sifu's eldest child, his nine-year-old daughter Hana. The twins stood at attention as she entered. She was the boss, and they listened to every word she said.

Hana looked at Akira. "Your pak punch was okay, but you over extended your arm, giving up your own structure for the hit and losing your control."

"Yes, Hana." Hideo stood at attention.

"As for you, Akira, you were chasing his hands. Aim to his center and cover yours, and the rest will take care of itself."

"Thanks, Hana." Akira leaned over to whisper, "You're much more helpful than Dad. He just told me to block better."

Hana smiled and patted him on the head. She was so mature for a nine-year-old. Then she ran up to Sifu and gave him a huge hug.

"Daddy," said Hana.

"Ah, my little pumpkin, did you practice your first form today?" asked Sifu.

"Of course, Daddy," said Hana.

Hana was definitely daddy's little girl. Sifu's expression changed when he held her.

Ryan looked to Danny and said, "Danny, she's definitely gonna leapfrog your ass."

"Shaddup," laughed Danny as he tried to punch Ryan.

Finally, Simo came in, closing the door behind her. Sifu said, "Okay, okay, let's end class for the night," as he approached his wife with a kiss on the lips.

"Hey, sweetie," said Sifu.

Simo would often pick up Sifu after class with the kids. For whatever reason, Sifu didn't like to drive.

Simo was so sweet. She was small in stature. She barely wore any kind of makeup, but had such a natural beauty about her. She moved so gracefully across the room, it made me wonder if she ever danced before. She was Japanese and at least a good twelve to fifteen years younger than Sifu. But the slight age difference did not matter, because seeing them together was the picture perfect image of what love was all about. The guys said that Sifu's first love was always Wing Chun, until the day he met Simo. It would have to take someone so special to trump the art Sifu held so close to his heart.

I noticed something, and inadvertently blurted out, "Sifu, how come you don't wear your wedding ring?" I quickly put my hand over my mouth after I realized that might not have been the most PC question.

Sifu just smiled. "We both have them, Kirin, but for me you don't need to see the ring on my hand to know that I'm married."

I nodded my head and agreed. Seeing them together made it obvious they were a couple who were meant for each other.

The rest of the class started gathering their stuff, while a few handful decided to goof off a bit. It would usually take fifteen to thirty minutes before we fully cleared class. Tobias was again busy on his phone texting. He was clearly upset, and I was willing to bet he was juggling a multitude of his honeys and one wasn't cooperating. I shook my head. Whatever it was, it was bad enough to distract him the entire class.

Sifu spoke to Simo for a split second and said, "Can you give me several minutes?" They smiled at each other as Sifu watched his two boys running around the school.

"Sure," said Simo and continued to exchange greetings with the rest of the class.

"Tobias, do you have a second?" said Sifu.

Frustrated with his phone, Tobias put it down and headed to the back room by Sifu's tiny office.

Hana saw me and came running. "Hey, Hana," I said, giving her a hug.

"Hey, Kirin, how's the training going?" said Hana.

"Same as always ... will you check out my stance?" I said.

"Sure thing." She smiled at me.

I looked over to see where Tobias was just as he rounded the corner to enter Sifu's office.

"Uh ... do you mind if we do it over there by the corner?" I said.

"Sure," said Hana.

I opened up my stance and held it in place.

"Go ahead. Check it."

Hana came by, looking around me. Then she pushed on my chest. She said, "Remember, when I push against your chest, don't fight the force."

I nodded, believing I understood what that meant. I thought, *I know not to fight the force.*

"Wow, Kirin, your stance has improved significantly since I last saw you. Dad was right; you are the hardest working student he has."

Sifu actually said that? I thought, as I asked, "Any critique?"

"Uh, just make sure you have alert energy in your stance. As Dad would say, the right amount of tension to spring into action," she said.

"Sifu has mentioned that, but I didn't realize that was for the stance as well," I said.

Hana's smile was just like Sifu's; they both radiated warmth. "Kirin, one principle applies to everything. Always remember that." She sounded so much like her father that I bit back a smile.

I followed her advice, and she checked my stance, and it did feel more solid.

"Yeah, that's it ... and you know what?" said Hana.

"Uh, what?" I was half-listening to her comments.

"It would be even more solid if you concentrated on your stance, instead of eavesdropping on the conversation," she said, giggling.

I whispered, "I'm not eavesdropping, Hana."

"You like him, don't you, Kirin?" said Hana.

"No, no ... he's too much of a player. I was just curious what Sifu was gonna say," I said.

Hana grew quiet, and I was able to overhear some of the conversation from the next room.

"Tobias, you're the head of the class, and everyone looks up to you," said Sifu.

"I know, Sifu. Sorry about tonight," said Tobias.

"I normally don't have this talk, Tobias, but since it clearly was disrupting you in class—" said Sifu.

"Uh, Sifu ... before you go any further, if you're gonna talk about the birds and the bees, I'm way past that."

Sifu chuckled.

"I was once young also, and I totally understand. Hmm, how do I phrase this? When you're at your age, it's natural to, how do I say ... want to sample all the ice cream that's out there."

Tobias laughed. "But you didn't go that route, did you, Sifu?"

"That's me," said Sifu as he paused. "No, I did not, nor am I passing judgement as to what's right or wrong," said Sifu. "Tobias, I'm not trying to force a path upon you. That's for you to decide. All I'm trying to share with you is the knowledge that there's more than one path. It is the balance which I speak of, in everything that we do."

"But Sifu, there's so much, uh ... tasty ice cream out there," said Tobias.

"You still have much to learn Tobias," said Sifu. "That's why you're having to deal with the constant headaches. You're merely looking at the outside cover, and once that's over, you have to deal with the real person. Think about it: if the cover was important, I would've done some fancier martial art instead of Wing Chun."

I heard Tobias laugh again.

"Besides, you're judging only by the looks alone; you need to dig deeper. You need to base your decision off a woman's F.E.," said Sifu.

Suddenly there was no sound. Something about what Sifu said must've caught his attention.

"What's F.E., Sifu?" asked Tobias.

"Hmm ... we will talk about that later, when you're ready," said Sifu. "The point I'm trying to make, Tobias, is that there's more than what you think. You know how I always say, in Wing Chun, concentrate mainly on yourself?"

"Yeah," said Tobias.

"The deeper meaning behind that is that respect for oneself comes first, so that respect for others follows. Love isn't selfish. You do things for that someone without expecting anything in return. Yet, that act of kindness is returned a hundred-fold. As more time passes with that special someone, instead of getting boring and stale, it grows to greater things, beyond what you can even imagine." That superficial level that everyone enjoys in the beginning is so minute to the bigger picture, it merely scratches the surface.

Tobias said, "Sifu ... you and Simo are one in a million. You just don't see that anymore." He paused and said, "Look, I always thought that, to find that, shouldn't I sample as much ice cream as possible? You know, sometimes I want vanilla or chocolate, and hopefully one day I'll get both," said Tobias.

"The problem is with your targeting. Your goal is about the sampling, and not trying to find your favorite flavor," said Sifu. "I don't know how. No one told me, but I quickly learned that, if I wanted to find great, I couldn't have my head in the gutter. They way you're approaching it right now is definitely in the gutter. You won't find that special someone when you're targeting the wrong things."

I leaned in further with Hana.

"Just remember, Tobias: more often than not, what you're looking for is usually right around the corner," said Sifu.

By that point, Hana and I were both leaning over the door, listening for more. She accidentally pushed me over, and I tumbled toward the entrance of Sifu's office. Both Tobias and Sifu looked at me.

I giggled and said, "Hana was showing me how to use structure. I, uh, guess I need more work."

Hana popped in and said, "Sorry, Dad, it's my fault." She quickly grabbed me up as we tried our best to escape gracefully. I was still within ear range of their conversation and continued to listen in.

"I hear what you're saying, Sifu, and that sounds all great, but I just need time to digest the meaning," said Tobias.

Sifu said, "Let me ask you this: would you do any art other than the Wing Chun I've taught you?"

Tobias responded immediately, "No, not at all, I love this art, your art, with all my heart. Nothing can compare to it."

Those words took on some meaning as Tobias paused to think of what he had just said.

Sifu patted him on the back. "That's what I'm talking about. That's what you should be looking for."

Tobias started grabbing his stuff and then quickly turned around. He looked at Sifu and then whispered, "So about this F.E? When can we talk more about this?"

Sifu laughed. "That's for another time. Absorb what I just told you for now."

> *"When you are ready to give yourself fully to another person, without expecting anything in return, that is the moment you'll understand what it means to love." –Sifu*

Pictures of You–3 years 44 days

I was halfway out of the parking lot, ready to leave school with Sage and Gwen, when I realized I had forgotten something. "Oh crap," I muttered as I searched through my school bag.

"What's wrong, Kirin?" asked Gwen.

"Hey, guys, go on without me. I'll catch up later," I said. Sage and Gwen waved goodbye as I quickly turned around. Walking back, I was fighting against the flow of students headed out of school. I laughed at the irony, considering I spent all my time training to go with the force. Most of them were headed home while others remained for after school activities.

I entered through the main entrance and decided to take a different route to my locker. After climbing several stairs to the second level, I was about to continue my walk to my locker when suddenly something caught my eye.

I turned to the right and saw a display of random photographs hanging along the school wall. It was different seeing something in print, since everything was always digitized through some kind of screen. They were beautifully taken shots of random subjects ranging from city landscape shots to close-ups of flowers. I spent a moment gazing at each one that captured my imagination.

As I continued to look, one picture stood out from all the rest. I stared at the image of a little boy on his knees holding a flower next to a grave. Besides him, a man put his hand on his shoulder. Unlike all the other pictures that dazzled with vibrant color, this was the only one that was in black and white. Yet, this image called to me more than others. I stared endlessly into the picture, which captured the essence of that moment. I kept looking deeper till it became lost in a blur of pixels.

"Do you like that pic?" The sound of the voice startled me as I turned around.

"I'm sorry, Kirin. I didn't mean to startle you," said Hunter.

"Oh, hi, Hunter."

I turned back toward the picture.

Hunter spoke, "I can't take credit for that pic, but the others are all mine."

"Who is it?" I asked.

"It's me.... My uncle took that picture of me, during the funeral," said Hunter softly.

"Who died?" I asked casually.

"My mom," said Hunter.

The answer caught me off guard as I said, "I'm sorry ... I, uh, I didn't know."

"It's okay. I know you didn't know ... But thanks for saying that." Hunter looked at me with kind eyes.

"You know, even though I was a little kid at the time, I appreciate the picture my uncle took. Every time I look at that picture, I feel that moment as if it were right now. And while it was a sad moment, it's my strongest memory of my mom. It was this picture that got me interested in photography, so I asked my uncle to teach me. Since then, I've been taking pictures—or, as I like to say it, freezing moments of time."

I said, "I like your other pictures as well, but this one definitely caught my eye."

Hunter looked at me. "They say pictures have different meanings for everyone. Why did this catch your eye, Kirin?"

I stood there for a second as my eyes watered and I felt choked up.

I struggled with each word as I said, "I have no pics of my parents or of myself when I was young. Only pieces of memories fragmented, and most of them I would rather forget. So, while this is a sad picture, that memory was at least captured, even if it was painful. As more time goes by, I lose more of the past."

I paused for a second. "I wish I had a pic, even if it was one like this," I said sadly.

"I'm sorry to hear that," said Hunter.

I stood there silently, feeling the weight of the moment lingering. Hunter's hand touched me on the shoulder, and I looked up.

"You know what? You should join the photography club. I could help you get started if you're interested."

I looked at Hunter and said, "When's the next meeting?"

"You're in luck. I'm headed there now," he said.

"I don't have a camera," I said.

"That's okay; you can share mine," he said, calmly hoisting his backpack as proof.

Hunter said, "Give it a try," as he spoke with his eyes.

He nudged his head to follow him and smiled.

His sincere voice and kind smile made me say, "Okay."

The next hour with Hunter went by in a flash. He had a way of making me laugh, and I discovered we had so much in common. Most of the photography discussions went over my head, but I didn't care. Hunter spent the time and kindly explained what I needed to know. The little things, and his attention to detail, were so appealing. For the first time, I was starting to see Hunter in a different light.

Hunter said, "So, what do you think? You want to join the class?"

I looked at him bashfully, and said, "Yeah, I'd like that."

Lazy Summer Day–1 year 137 days

We were in the tail end of our summer vacation, just weeks away from the new school year. Hanging out at either Gwen's, Sage's, or my house had become the routine. Gwen was the fortunate recipient to host us on this day, not that the change of scenery made much difference.

Being the only child, Gwen was the definition of a spoiled brat. Fortunately, her attitude never matched that label. Gwen's room was nothing you could ever imagine. Half of the room looked like a high-end shopping mall as Gwen seemed to have a dress for every day of the year. She was also highly skilled at sewing, so making her own clothes and costumes was another forte. That might sound like a typical girl who's just into fashion, but the other half of her room looked right out of a space station tower. It was an electronic nut's dream come true.

Her main computer was impressive, to say the least. It didn't have the usual flat screen, but a curved rectangular monitor spanning fifty inches across the desk as the main display. Sitting there, she could literally monitor the world from her fingertips. At any moment, I was expecting some superhero to contact her for directions to the nearest troubled spot.

"Guy's, I'm bored," I said.

"Oh, Kirin, can't you just chill for a bit?" said Sage.

"We've been chilling out for the last two months. Aren't you guys feeling antsy at all?" I asked.

Both Gwen and Sage made half-hearted responses.

I walked over to Gwen to see what she had cooking on her computer. "Tell me you got something exciting, Gwen."

"Oh, I definitely do.... I just downloaded the latest episodes of *Tubby Boo Boo*," Gwen said excitedly.

"*Tubby Boo Boo*? What the heck is that?"

"It's the best show ever, Kirin. She's like the great-granddaughter of the original reality show that started like twenty years ago. It's so funny."

I watched a short segment of the trailer Gwen showed me, of this little girl doing beauty pageants. One, I knew beauty was in the eye of the beholder, but I was just wondering which eye I should use. Two, she had no talent. And finally–an epiphany: that was two minutes of my life I could never get back.

"Gwen, you can't be serious?" I said with a disgusted voice.

"You gotta give it a chance, Kirin. It's fricking hilarious." She continued to watch the show and work on her computer at the same time.

"I can't believe someone with a brain so big can watch something this stupid."

"It's a guilty pleasure, Kirin. Lighten up," said Gwen.

"Eating chocolate in the middle of the night is a guilty pleasure. What you're doing is exactly what the masses are feeding into."

I waited for a response, but she was heavily engrossed watching and wasting time on this garbage. She continued to ignore me and laugh at the computer screen.

I turned around, hoping to get some support, and asked, "How about you, Sage?"

"Give me a few, Kirin. I'm gonna practice my virtual brawler *'King of the Kage.'*"

"What the heck is that?"

"That's the game that scans my motion so I can battle someone online," said Sage as he continued to fidget with his toy.

"So, you're gonna play fight for a while?" I asked.

"Yeah, it's the hottest game right now, and I plan on doing the tournament coming up at the Buzz Bar. You should definitely try it," said Sage.

"Sage, I know how to really fight. Why not invest in that? I can teach you, you know?" I said with hope he might bite.

"Nah, that seems like real work. Besides, I'm delicate," he said with a giggle as he placed a weird contraption onto his head.

I rolled my eyes in disgust. "So, you'd rather invest your time in virtual fighting?"

"What was that, Kirin?" replied Sage as he got into a lame fighting stance.

"Never mind," I said.

Sage said to Gwen, "Hey, Gwen, did you hear that Justin Badjer is back again with his ex?"

Gwen turned around. "No way, this is like the fifth time they've gotten back together. I can't believe that!"

Sage replied, "Yeah, I know. I'm shocked as well."

I responded, "Why do you guys pay attention to that?

Sage replied, "Kirin, you just don't understand. This is all part of American culture."

I replied, "You mean wasting time? Seriously, who cares who ... Justin Beaver is dating or doing?"

Both Sage and Gwen began laughing at me.

"What's so funny?" I asked.

Gwen replied, "It's Badjer, kinda like the animal badger but spelled different."

I pulled my hair. "Beaver, badger, gopher, I don't care! Stuff like that shouldn't have value in your lives." I was frustrated, but the guys were focused on wasting time.

"Oh my god, how long are you guys gonna do this?"

"Give or take half an hour," they both replied.

"Fine," I said. I decided to let them be and picked a spot in Gwen's room. I got in my stance and started working on the first form, figuring that I could lead by example.

45 Minutes Later

As I exhaled my last breath, I opened up my eyes again to see both Sage and Gwen staring at me.

"What?" I said.

Sage looked at me. "You're complaining that we were wasting time, but we saw you standing there for forty-five minutes doing nothing."

"What do you mean? I wasn't doing nothing," I said angrily.

"Yeah, I gotta agree with Sage; standing in place for forty-five minutes moving your hands around ranks right up there with watching Tubby Boo Boo and *King of the Kage*," said Gwen.

I bit my tongue and didn't say a word as I thought, *Even if I explained it, they would never understand.*

> *"One should learn the difference between leisure time and wasting time." –Sifu*

Sifu's Journey Entry #6—Playing Their Game

Summer 2030

Sifu sat patiently across the table as Mike glanced through more legal work on his tablet. They had been going through his stuff as well as his ideas for the last several hours. Mike was a past student of Sifu's whose forte was in detail. It came as no surprise to Sifu when Mike chose to become a lawyer. While many of Sifu's past students no longer trained with him, they still kept in close contact. Most realized in some shape or form that, even if they never came close to mastering the art, the lessons learned helped shape their path. The skills learned in Wing Chun were not limited to only fighting.

Mike removed his glasses and rubbed his eyes, just to give himself a break.

"Do you want something to drink?" asked Sifu.

"No ... it's all good, Sifu. I'm glad you gave me all this info in advance. From all the research I was able to gather, it appears you're safe," said Mike, who leaned back in his seat to relax even further.

"Well, that's good news," said Sifu.

"I'll have to double-check one or two more things just to be sure, but yeah, I think you somehow covered all the bases with this idea." Mike put his glasses back on and scanned over one final part.

Sifu smiled at Mike. "You think this idea is crazy, don't you?"

Mike replied with a smile, "I'm always impressed how well you can read a person, Sifu. But, to answer your question, I gotta admit: at first when you told me about your plan, I never would've thought this was possible. But, legally, you're not breaking any rules."

Sifu nodded. "I like the sound of that."

Mike laughed. "Sifu, I know you too well. Even if you were, you wouldn't care."

Sifu chuckled. "That is true."

Mike grew serious. "The only concern I do have is, what if no one gives you any credits for the meals? I mean, you're going on the pure goodness of people's hearts, aren't you, Sifu?"

"I'm banking on the fact that my soup's really good," he laughed.

"I get it, Sifu.... I agree. You sold me on the soup; it's incredible. But times are tough now, and preparing the soup is extremely time-consuming. You'll need to make a certain amount to really pull in some credits," said Mike.

Sifu was humbled by the compliment, yet still hesitant to accept the fact that the soup was incredible. He paused before answering Mike, "What have I told you about life?"

Mike responded, "Always go for it."

Sifu smiled. "You got it, I have to do at least what I teach, right? I figure it's worth a shot. While it may be difficult for you to comprehend, being a lawyer, it's not always about the money."

Mike countered, "It's reality, Sifu. Money has always made the world go round."

Sifu commented, "I know it has.... I know it has," as he looked away to the outside window.

Mike suddenly sat up straight. "You gotta remember something: you cannot advertise this in any shape or form. Otherwise, they can pin it against you."

"Mike, you're still young, but the Internet is nothing more than a technological extension of word of mouth. The root of all that is the human spirit and the energy it emits. I honestly believe, with all my heart, one's energy can draw out the followers," said Sifu.

Mike thought about what Sifu said and extended his hand for a shake. Sifu shook his hand and patted him on the back as they exchanged some final greetings.

"I'll get back to you shortly, but everything does look in order." Mike started packing up his stuff and was ready to head out.

Sifu said, "Thanks again, Mike. Remember to bill me."

Mike replied, "No. No, Sifu, that's not necessary. I'm glad to do this for you."

Sifu scurried along to the back of the kitchen and returned quickly. Then he handed Mike two bags wrapped up with his soup. "Okay, will you at least take this for payment?"

Mike's eyes lit up. "Definitely," he said as he smiled.

"I kept the noodles and broth separate; just combine it when you're ready to eat."

"The matching energy of people will draw them from across the globe and make strangers into friends for a lifetime." –Sifu

CHAPTER 7
Delivery

Two days later, Tuesday January 13

Strange only got stranger. That was definitely an understatement. Kirin shifted her car to park as she finally found an empty space. She paused for a moment, gripping the steering wheel of the car firmly, wondering where she was and what exactly she was doing here. Seconds passed as she sat silently in the car. The sounds of pedestrians and other vehicles breezing by went unnoticed.

It had been nearly three years since she'd seen Sifu before he magically popped out of nowhere to cross her path at a restaurant. Coincidence? Highly unlikely. She reflected for a second on their encounter and then reached into her pocket to pull out her phone. A quick click as she glanced over to double-check the text that Sifu sent her earlier. It was confirmed, but as she glanced over to the passenger seat where forty pounds of pork bones sat, she wondered, *Why the heck did he ask me to bring this?*

She muttered to herself, "Let's hope that this meeting will lead to some answers," as she pulled out the keys. Kirin put her hoodie and glasses on before stepping out of the car. She grabbed her stuff and started dragging it to the address. Outside, she took a quick peek through the window to see what was happening. She saw roughly fifteen people hanging out inside, mingling and relaxing.

She stepped back to get a better look at the outside, which looked like any other building along the street. "I'm at the right address, but there's no sign," she said, confused. "Weird just got weirder," she muttered as curiosity forced her to take a step inside.

As she entered the place, Kirin's eyes widened and her mouth popped open.

"What is this place?" she asked as she scanned the area, trying to piece together a reasonable guess.

Several circular seating areas were already occupied, with individuals talking. They appeared to be waiting for something, yet there was no food or menus in sight. In one corner was a fairly large L-shaped leather couch, which perfectly hugged the wall. On it sat a couple who were being a little too friendly in public, but no one seemed to care. The other corner was the complete opposite, as an individual sat with his back to everyone texting on his phone. In the center hung a huge television on the wall. As luck would have it, the television was blaring more UFMF news on the upcoming season. The news was interesting enough to gather several of the patrons' attention and keep their focus away from Kirin.

"Great," Kirin sighed and double-checked to make sure she was covered as best as she could.

Is this a house, a restaurant, a bar ... maybe uh...? What the heck is going on here?

Realizing that the answers would not magically come from standing there, Kirin decided to make her way through the room. She zigzagged a path to get to the other side. The more she tried to piece things together, the further away she got from anything that could possibly be plausible. Several steps later, she stood by a counter, much like you'd see at a diner. She looked on the wall overhead but still found no menu or pricing listed, nor was there a credit register or anyone to greet her. Her brow wrinkled in confusion, but that faded when she caught a whiff of a smell. "Mmmm, that smells really good," she said as her nose led her to stare into the kitchen. She paused for a moment and thought, *That smells familiar.*

A guy from one of the tables spoke, breaking her concentration, "Hey you, remember there's no cutting."

"Cutting, what are you talking about?" she said, puzzled as she turned around to see who had spoken.

"We've been here for two hours, and it'll be another hour before they start serving," the gentleman explained.

"No, no ... I'm here to deliver some pork bones." Kirin lifted her bag for proof.

"Oh, you're delivery ... my bad, cool, cool," he said excitedly as his tone changed. He then announced to everyone there, "Hey, peoples, delivery's here." All eyes turned toward her as Kirin lowered her head. She was uncomfortable receiving the unwanted attention. The group at hand was more concerned about the arrival of the food than who delivered it, as a round of applause filled the room. The same gentleman, who acted like he was a regular, shouted, "Lance, delivery!"

For a brief second, Kirin thought, *Lance?*

"Dammit, how many times have I told you delivery guys to come to the back entrance?" complained a voice from the kitchen. Kirin spun around again, trying to figure out who she was talking to now and what the heck was going on. Once she laid eyes upon the stranger, she slowly began to recognize a familiar face. "Oh my god, is that ... you Lance?" she said in surprise.

Lance smiled and said, "Holy crap, it is you–"

Lance stopped himself before he said Kirin's name and looked around to see if he had attracted attention. "Come into the kitchen," Lance said, waving her in to follow him. Kirin walked in his shadow and stood behind him at the kitchen.

"Sorry, sorry, I didn't know you were the one delivering the stuff." He grabbed the pork bones from her and set them on the counter. Kirin was thinking she needed to pinch herself because weird just became strange and there was a strong possibility it was going to turn to goofy.

"I can't believe what I'm seeing. It's you, Lance," said Kirin with a smile as she looked at him from head to toe. He opened his arms out as Kirin walked toward him and gave him a hug.

"I'm sure you're probably wondering what the hell is going on. I'll try to explain as much as I can," said Lance with a big grin covering his entire face. Lance pulled out a stool and offered it to her. "Here, have a seat," said Lance. "You're gonna need it."

"God, it's good to see you...." He smiled, seeming genuinely surprised to see her. He leaned over and proudly said, "Oh, by the way, you really kicked some ass in that fight."

Slightly embarrassed, Kirin smiled and bowed politely.

Lance pulled out some credits and handed them to Kirin. "This should cover the cost of the pork bones."

Kirin tried to refuse the credits, saying, "Oh, this is too much."

Lance waved her off and replied, "Nah, keep it for your troubles."

Kirin asked, "Lance, you didn't know I was coming?"

Lance replied, "I knew delivery was coming, but I didn't expect it to be you."

"Sifu didn't say anything?"

Lance laughed. "You know the old man; he's always mysterious." Both Lance and Kirin nodded their heads in agreement.

"Okay, so you've probably got a million questions running through your pretty little head, so ask away." Lance looked at her, waiting.

"Uh, okay ... well, I guess we can start with you? What are you doing here?"

"Well, I'm sure you have fond memories of me as the homeless special forces, but to make a long story short—and I'm cutting it way short—Sifu helped me get off the streets and trained me to be a cook. So, for the last year since we've opened, I've been helping him run this place," said Lance.

"Wow, that's really awesome," Kirin said with a smile.

As she looked around the kitchen filled with huge pots burning on multiple stoves, she asked, "So, this a restaurant?"

"That's not really that easy to answer. Technically, this is just a residential area, and the people outside waiting are kinda just hanging at Sifu's place. In a way, you could say they are his guests," said Lance.

"I don't get it. You're cooking food, and people are waiting on it; how can this not be a restaurant?" asked Kirin.

Lance explained, "Kirin, think of all the hoops you have to jump through to run a restaurant. Corporations run everything now, remember? The cities got a ton of red tape purposely forcing you to go through the corporations to be branded a franchise. If you don't go that route, then you're forced to deal with the mob." Lance seemed a little peeved talking about how the system was run.

While Kirin did not say a word, she knew exactly what Lance was speaking of. She took a deep breath to keep herself calm.

"You know Sifu; to choose between the lesser of two evils makes absolutely no sense to him. So, to avoid all that bullshit–sorry for my language, Kirin–legally speaking, this is Sifu's house. He can do whatever he wants in it."

"If that's the case, he can't charge for the soup, right?" she asked.

"You're correct. He doesn't charge people anything for the soup. He simply has a jar he leaves out on the counter."

"So, Sifu pays you?" she said hesitantly.

"Oh yeah, definitely ... he pays me quite well indeed. In fact, I'm looking at buying my own house soon," Lance said with a huge smile.

Kirin didn't respond, mulling over his answers. After a few seconds passed in silence, Lance said, "Kirin, look outside in the living room area. Those people sitting there have been here since six. An hour from now, there'll be a line," said Lance.

"I don't get it. How did it get so popular?" she asked.

Lance shouted to everyone out front, "The lady here would like to know what you guys and gals think of the soup?"

The crowd out front stopped everything they were doing and shouted, "The *most bestest* soup ever!"

Kirin laughed, "Most bestest? I used to say most bestest in class, as a joke."

Lance smiled. "I guess Sifu copied it and people have adopted the phrase."

Kirin could not help but laugh some more. That was why she'd always said it. It was funny and stupid and yet never got old.

Lance interrupted her laughter and said, "Kirin, you haven't tasted the soup. It's fricking incredible, so by word of mouth, it spread. Boy, did it spread! Second, it's a case of supply and demand; Sifu serves seventy-five bowls of soup on any given day. No more, no less. Once we hit the magic number of seventy-five, we're done for the day."

"Do you make just one kind of soup or...?" said Kirin.

Lance replied, "You know Sifu; he's a specialist. We make only Tankatsu ramen soup, and that's it. We serve it everyday, exactly how we want it, no exceptions. It's handmade noodles, the freshest products, and all from scratch. You know Sifu, he's a specialist."

Kirin asked, "When do you guys open?"

"We don't have a set time, but normally around 10-ish and by 3 to 4 we're pretty much done."

"I don't understand the economics of it," she admitted. "One: you don't charge for the soup. Two: you have a limited amount of soup, and three: you really don't cater to customization.... Am I missing something, Lance?" she said.

Lance said, "No, but you're missing the bigger picture, Kirin."

"So, I guess I'll ask it, if you don't mind ... do you guys make money?" said Kirin.

"Do we?" Lance laughed. "Oh man, we make a significant amount of money. At first, I didn't think this would work, but I guess kindness and the soup go hand in hand. People pay what they think the soup was worth, and most people think it's worth a lot. Let's face it: since everything's been franchised and processed food is king, this has become the perfect alternative."

Sitting up proudly, Lance added, "The way I see it, Kirin, it's either guilt or gratitude, because after they eat the soup, they just kinda leave money," said Lance.

"And you don't ask them to pay?"

"No, not a dime, never ... and yeah, there's always a few who just come and eat, but eventually they love the soup so much they end up giving as well. Maybe they realize if they don't give anything, we'll shut down."

Kirin looked around, trying to absorb everything seen and heard.

"Let me guess: this was all Sifu's idea?" asked Kirin.

"Yup. Sifu trained me from scratch," he replied.

"I didn't know he could cook?" she said, surprised even more.

"Like I said, Kirin, we just opened up a year ago. For the last several years, all Sifu and I have been working on is perfecting his wife's recipe," said Lance. "Did you know, he even went to Japan to perfect it?"

Kirin simply shook her head. "Well, I better let you get back to work."

Lance laughed. "Work? This is the furthest thing from work. There's no stress or demand on anything. We do things our way, and if they don't like it, they can leave. The regulars know the routine. For the most part, people just kinda hang out here throughout the night."

Lance looked at Kirin. "The old man's a genius, you know? Sifu, he's brilliant; he thought of everything."

Kirin just laughed and said, "So, where is Mr. Brilliant?"

"I'm glad you asked. If you would be so kind to follow me," said Lance.

Lance picked up the pork bones which he said would be used for tomorrow. "Here, let's go to the storage area." Kirin followed Lance as he entered inside.

"Kirin, close the door behind you."

Kirin shut the door behind her as she stood inside a long but somewhat small storage area. Lance set aside the bones and walked toward one of the shelves. There, he removed a jar and pulled a lever. Kirin watched as a secret panel opened from the wall.

"All right, Kirin, I'm gonna start prepping the soups for tonight. He's down there."

"Sifu, Kirin's here!" shouted Lance.

From the lighted basement, she heard Sifu's voice echo from below, "Come on down, Kirin."

Kirin shook her head in disbelief. "Things officially just got goofy."

As Kirin headed down the stairs to the basement, the rickety floors creaked with each step. Once down there, her eyes flew wide in wonder. She saw Sifu in the corner with his back turned to her, writing. To her right, she saw Sifu's old wooden dummy from their training facility. In another corner lay some poles and swords that he kept back in the days when he taught. While it wasn't her old school she knew and loved ... it felt like it.

She began walking toward Sifu, but something caught her eye. It was an entire wall with writings and postings connected to each other. At first glance, it looked like a random trail of mess, but upon examining it further, she began to realize it was more than just that.

Sifu did not say a word, but let her explore the small basement by herself.

She was looking feverishly over everything as the single wall spanned the entire length of the restaurant from below. Kirin looked at it as if she were staring up in the sky at all the stars being shown.

"Wow ... what is all this?" She touched the wall, making sure what she saw was real.

Sifu did not respond as she perused the postings on the wall. She read aloud, "The cutting-edge has many functions, but one of its function is to help link you to your opponent's center. Without that, your body will not have a natural reaction to the force.... I never knew that about the cutting-edge, Sifu?"

Sifu continued to write and said, "Is that right? Well, now you know."

Kirin asked, "Is that based off the principle of positioning?"

"Actually, it's based off the structure of the hand triangle," said Sifu.

As she continued to look at all the writings on the wall, she felt like a kid at a candy shop. She was in utter amazement.

She read another clip from the wall aloud, "In holding the tan sau in rolling position, since it is inside line, this is an active position, but with passive power."

She shook her head and said, "I have no idea what that means at all. This is all incredible, Sifu.... What ... what exactly are you doing?"

Concentrating on his work, Sifu said, "You like? I call it my road map."

"A road map to what?" she asked.

"Every detail you can imagine about the art of Wing Chun."

"How long have you been working on this, and how much have you completed?" asked Kirin.

"Oh, I would say over the last four years I've been working on this, and I'm maybe halfway done," he replied.

They fell into a comfortable silence as Kirin made her way along the wall and Sifu's pen scratched away over the paper.

"So, did you get an invitation from the UFMF?" Sifu paused his writing and waited for an answer.

Her concentration broken, Kirin spun to look at Sifu's back. "How did you know I got an invitation?" asked Kirin.

"Common sense, Kirin, that's what I would've done," Sifu replied. "Did I not tell you that it was only a matter of time, that they would make the move for you?"

"Hmm, you did say that." Kirin wondered where he kept his magic crystal ball. "So Sifu, why did you call me here? I don't think it was to bring you forty pounds of pork bone."

Sifu finally turned around.

"I called you here because you have less then five months to train for the league, and you are far from ready," said Sifu.

Kirin replied, "I agree I need more training, but ... you know, Sifu, I have learned a lot over the last several years."

Sifu nodded his head in agreement. "Hmm ... I think you should show me." Sifu got up from his seat and then walked to the center of the basement. There, he placed one hand behind his back and slightly extended his other hand out as a guard. He did not say another word and waited for Kirin to take her spot.

Kirin removed her hoodie and laid it on the floor. She stood several feet from Sifu. She wondering if this was really going to happen.

Sifu said, "Whenever you're ready."

The last thing she had thought she would be doing on this night was standing in a restaurant basement late in the evening, fighting her teacher.

Kirin and Sifu were standing opposite each other a mere five feet apart. This was unlike any fight Kirin had ever done before, since she never had the opportunity to spar with Sifu.

"Sifu, are you sure?"

"I need to know where you're at!" Sifu smiled at her and gestured her to begin.

They stood still for a minute, and Kirin sprang into action, closing the gap. She went to break Sifu's single guard with a pak and punch, but Sifu did not move an inch from his spot. He turned slightly to defuse the force and blocked it with a tan. Before Kirin could finish her initial punch motion, she felt the power of a chop come right at her neck as she flinched.

Sifu released the power, unlike anything she'd ever felt before, but stopped it an inch away from her neck.

Holy crap, he could've killed me on the spot.

Sifu smiled and allowed Kirin to gather herself again for another attack.

Kirin had gotten into many fights in her later teens after the school shut down—most with guys who were significantly bigger and stronger, but the force they generated was nothing in comparison.

Strange, Kirin thought, though Sifu's skill far outstripped any of those brutes. Kirin didn't get hit, but that chop made her question her skill. Kirin tried to shake it off and brought her guard hands back up.

"Let's do this ... target, center, own it," she uttered.

She moved in again as Sifu stood there. This time she went for a lop and punch toward Sifu's guard. He immediately blocked it with a bong sau. Kirin felt the change of the flow and paked and punched his bong sau out of the way. As she cleared his bong, she could feel her punch about to hit him. Suddenly, Sifu turned ever-so-slightly and lopped her punch, pulling her completely off balance. She had invested everything into that punch, believing it was going to hit, and now she was paying the price. As Kirin started toppling over, she could see that her face was about to hit the concrete floor. She closed her eyes, but at the last second, Sifu grabbed hold of her center, spinning her around. He caught her head with his foot just before she hit the ground.

Kirin looked up in surprise. "You see these things happen in old Gung Fu movies, but I never thought in my wildest dreams it would be happening to me."

The next several minutes were more of the same: everything Kirin tried, Sifu easily countered. *How could I suck this bad?* she thought.

All this time, Sifu was playing his game. He saw things differently from the typical fighter. Sifu's strategy was simple: he merely moved forward, always trusting in the flow of the force and never letting his ego block out what it was saying. He did not see the kicks, punches, or any strikes that a fighter normally throws, as he was locked into seeing only his opponent's center, which spoke volumes.

When dealing with a strike, a typical fighter would fade back or cover and calculate how to deal with the threat. But as Kirin threw another punch, Sifu adjusted his structure, merging it with hers so he could be in the optimal position to shoot back to her center. The target meant everything for him, as the fear of being hit was not his concern.

As Kirin moved, Sifu watched where her center was headed. It screamed her intent. He was always several steps ahead of her—no matter how fast she moved, she was always a step behind. Nothing she did could make up the difference. Kirin threw another attack, and Sifu welcomed it, as if daring her to hit him, but that invitation was merely a trap. She again over extended her structure, and he countered effortlessly.

Kirin realized she was getting her ass kicked without being hit. *Hmm*, she thought, *karma's a bitch. I guess this is how Jim must've felt.*

Kirin smacked the ground. "Why can't I make anything work?"

Sifu could feel Kirin's frustration, as emotion set in and her intents easily exposed her. When Sifu didn't respond, Kirin thought, *Why am I losing? He's got one hand behind his back, and I can't move him from that dang spot! Why can't I beat him."*

After several more exchanges, Kirin found herself on her back again. She lay there, panting, as Sifu extended his hand to help her up. Kirin looked up to Sifu with some humility, and she thought for a second before speaking. "You did this not to know where I was at, but to make sure that I knew ... where I was at."

Sifu smiled. "Don't be too hard on yourself. You have learned a lot since I last taught you. Just remember that learning is ongoing, and to this day I am still figuring things out."

"I'm sorry, Sifu," said Kirin.

"Nothing to be sorry about." He looked at her kindly and asked, "Are you now ready to train?"

Kirin smiled and looked somewhat surprised. "You're ... gonna train me?"

"Of course, didn't I say when you needed me I would be there?" said Sifu.

Reflecting on her last meeting at the restaurant with him, Kirin remembered him uttering those exact words.

"We have a lot to work on. You still fear being hit, and you're using emotion to win your fights. That attitude will not serve you well if you plan to win this entire thing," he said. "Besides, fighting will not be your main challenge."

"What do you mean, Sifu?" wondered Kirin.

"Remember: know yourself and your opponent," said Sifu.

"I remember," said Kirin.

"Hearing what I say, and knowing what it really means are two different things. Kirin, it's easy to be a hero when there's nothing on the line, but at some point when you have something to lose, then you'll find out your true character. I know right now you think it's about changing the world, but in the end, it will be about you ... and you better be prepared to deal with that," said Sifu.

"I don't understand, Sifu."

"It's one thing to go into a fight as an unknown, but it'll be a totally different experience when the lime light is on you, Kirin," Sifu said seriously.

It was too much for Kirin to take in, as the words simply passed by her. Realizing something, she said, "Wait a second, Sifu. What about the law? You closed down the school. I can't ask you to teach me."

"Even with the law, I couldn't care less," said Sifu. "Besides, laws nowadays are created to justify the evils of men."

"I don't know, Sifu. I can't risk it. You've gone through so much already; I don't want any trouble for you," said Kirin.

"Look, Kirin, I don't need a law to know right and wrong. History has shown that." Sifu smiled and gave a calm glance at Kirin. "Besides, I'm not breaking any law, Kirin. There's no school, I'm not charging you, and this is a residential place. As far as I know, all bases are covered."

Sifu glanced at Kirin still on the floor and chuckled.

Kirin said, "You do think of everything."

Sifu replied, "I'm merely playing the game for now."

"What do you mean, Sifu?"

"People in power use their intelligence not to make the world better, but to find loopholes to take advantage of. It's a shame, isn't it? If only they put their minds to good use," Sifu said with some disappointment.

Just then, the upstairs doors opened, and a stranger walked down the steps. With each step taken, the stairs creaked even louder. As Sifu helped Kirin get up from the floor, she looked to see the silhouetted figure.

"It's Tobias. What's he doing here?" she said, looking at Sifu.

"You need to train, and you need a partner as well," said Sifu. "So I got hold of Tobias and asked him if he would be interested in being your partner. He was kind enough to say ... yes."

Tobias looked around briefly and smiled. This was the first time he had laid eyes on Sifu in years. He walked over to Sifu, gave him a strong handshake, and then gave him a huge hug.

"It's good to see you, Sifu," said Tobias, looking somewhat teary-eyed.

Tobias glanced past Kirin and didn't say a word.

Kirin asked him, "Hey, you still upset at me?"

"I'm here, ain't I?" Instead of looking at Kirin, he stared at the wall that Sifu had been working on.

Kirin wondered what was eating him.

Tobias was no different from Kirin, awestruck at the work Sifu had compiled on the wall.

"Sifu, you've outdone yourself. This is most impressive," said Tobias.

"It's far from complete, and much more work still needs to be done," rattled Sifu.

Finally turning to look at Kirin, Tobias asked, "So, how badly did Sifu kick your ass?"

"It's not as bad as you think. Besides, if you think you're so good, why not see for yourself?" said Kirin.

Tobias laughed. "Because I'm not that dumb, Kirin. I know he can kick my ass."

Kirin had no response for that.

Short Stories #7–Kirin's P.O.V.

<u>Worth the Wait–2 years 254 days</u>

"How long has it been?" My words cracked through the thin, cold air.

Robert, who was hopping up and down to keep himself warm, replied, "It's been over forty-five minutes." I looked around, noticing that the rest of the group had their own methods of passing time as they tried to ignore the frigid Chicago weather. What would possess anyone to wait this long? For us, if it wasn't Wing Chun, the second best guess would be for food. Regardless, I was highly skeptical that no quality of food could be worth the amount of time we spent waiting, let alone in the cold.

"I'm freezing my butt off. How much longer, Ken?" I barked. Ken got the hint, rubbed his hands for either warmth or luck, and went back into the restaurant to check on our status.

Standing by the edge of the curb, both Danny and Big T found something to gamble on. I leaned over to catch a few words from their conversation.

"Big T, you in?" said Danny.

Big T looked undecided as he kept looking back and forth. Finally, he spoke, "Oh yeah, I say white guy comes back saying forty-five more minutes," Big T said confidently.

Danny thought about it for a second, staring blankly into space. "We betting on who's the closest to whatever number he gives?"

"Sure, let's do it straight out," said Big T.

"Okay, I'm saying twenty-five minutes then," said Danny.

"How much?" said Big T.

"Let's do the usual—a twenty," said Danny.

They both shook hands in an odd way, incorporating Gung Fu attacks. It was silly when I first saw them do it, but later on I appreciated their creativity.

Several minutes later, the door swung open, and Ken emerged, cloaked in the fragrant smell of BBQ from inside. Ken's face looked like he was the messenger of death as all eyes were upon him in anticipation. He grimaced and said, "Forty-five more minutes." We all gave a simultaneous sigh of frustration, as we began walking away from the entrance.

Tobias said, "The white guy, always the bearer of bad news."

Ken replied, "You can't hate on the messenger."

Tobias fired back, "Yeah, but I can hate the guy who recommended this joint."

That joke created a brief amount of heat before we realized time and the elements were our worst enemy again.

I saw Danny flustered, not so much over the wait, but losing to Big T. He pulled out 20 credits and handed it over. Big T was less than gracious after winning from Danny, and made sure he rubbed it in.

"Hey, can I ask you guys something?" I said, shivering.

The guys all circled around me, waiting for the question.

"How come you guys joke so much about each other's race?" I asked.

"That's simple, Kirin.... It's 'cause we don't care," replied Danny.

"Speak for yourself," exclaimed Ken.

I looked to him to say more.

"How come you guys pick on us pilgrims more?" Ken sounded serious.

"What do you mean...? Pilgrims?" I asked.

Ken shook his head. "These dumb asses came up with a code name for white people."

I thought, *Hmm wonder what they call Korean girls?*

Robert replied, "Can I get a show of hands if your race has ever been oppressed?"

The entire group raised their hands, and at the last second Ken joined in.

Robert stared at Ken and said, "You're white. How have you been oppressed?"

Ken made a goofy look like it was obvious. "Duh, how do you think America was formed? The colonists escaped from the oppressors of mother England."

Robert laughed. "That doesn't count.... That's white on white."

The group looked at each other and confirmed.

Danny replied, "Yeah, Ken, that's a no sell."

Ken began to laugh, and I realized he was kidding.

Doc stepped in. "Okay, enough with the joking ... Kirin, the world today still wastes its time and energy on the shape, sex, race, or anything else they can categorize someone. In reality, as Sifu has said in the past, we're energy, plain and simple. We see each other as human beings or equals."

"Yeah, Kirin, bottom line: all we care about is if you're a good person or not," said Ryan.

Robert then spoke, "Great, great, whatever ... can we now all hold hands and sing 'Kumbaya'?"

Ken interrupted, "I gotta disagree. Of the core, Robert's definitely racist."

Robert laughed and said, "How many times do I have to explain to you, Ken? When you go to a Korean restaurant, you get bad service not 'cause we hate you, but because we just suck at serving people. There's a total difference."

Ken laughed and punched Robert in the arm.

Robert said, "Okay, enough of this, can someone remind me again why we're waiting almost two fricking hours for a burger?"

Everyone pointed to Ken, who responded, "Trust me, it's a really good burger."

Robert rolled his eyes—and, for once, I agreed with him. I responded, "Eighty/twenty ground beef, salt, and pepper ... anyone else find this recipe too difficult to make at home?" The guys laughed.

"Can you repeat that again, Kirin?" said Ken.

I began to laugh as I stared at Ken. Then I realized.... "Oh, you're serious about that." I bit my lip, trying to keep it within.

Suddenly, Robert started talking, "Hey, any of you guys notice that Sifu never eats out with us when it's white food?" A hush fell over all of us, as we pondered on that question.

"Hmm, I think it's just coincidence," said Tobias.

"Wait a second, are you saying Sifu's racist?" said Doc.

"No, no, far from that ... clearly he's not, but what I am saying is that he's *food* racist. Think about it: every time we eat out, it's always somewhere Asian. But ... if we hit some classic American, he always has some excuse."

"Yeah ... oh wait, I think you're wrong. He did come with us to that fried chicken place, Ken," said Big T, snapping his fingers.

"How about that time when Ken recommended that mac 'n cheese place?" said Danny.

Robert nodded his head in agreement. "See, that's what I'm talking about." Robert was starting to gather some steam with his theory.

Tobias countered, "Hmm, your theory's flawed. Sifu does eat everything. I've seen it for myself."

"Did it occur to anybody he could just be racist toward Ken's palate?" I snickered.

Robert looked at me and said, "If that's the case, then I would be right." Both Robert and I nodded our heads.

Our group continued to pass time debating the possibilities.

Forty-five minutes passed as we finally got seats in the dark and loud burger bar. The waitress came by and took our orders.

I thought it was time to change the subject, since our discussion about Sifu was leading to nowhere.

Fortunately, Danny jumped in, interrupting our discussion. "I know I say this all the time, but dammit, can't I leave class one of these days not feeling so bummed out?"

"Join the club. Everyone gets depressed doing Wing Chun. It's just part of it," said Tobias.

"Even you, Tobias?" I asked.

"Oh yeah, almost every class, I'm wondering how I could stink so bad," he said.

"But, I've seen you kick so much ass, Tobias," I said.

"Dunking on midgets is nothing to be proud of, Kirin. When I work with Sifu, he treats me like a rag doll," he said with complete honesty.

"You know what makes our group different?" Said Doc.

"No, Doc, what?" I replied.

"We don't train like everyone else," he said.

Ryan said, "Yeah, yeah, I totally agree. It took me awhile to figure out why we train the way we do. And to the outsider, they would think that we're nuts."

Ken jumped in and said, "The art is really designed to kick ass. I know everyone says that, but when you look at how it was designed, everything we do is so simple, but getting yourself to do that is what makes it so difficult."

The guys all laughed and said as one, "Tell me about it."

When they stopped laughing, Tobias said, "It's like a total tease. Just do this, and you'll always win. But that simplicity is layered in an unlimited amount of detail and theory. Most people aren't willing to suffer through that. Most people would rather cheat and go the quick and easy route. It's a lot sexier to say fight first before the skill because when you focus on the skill first you don't need the reason to fight. Does that make sense?"

I said, "Yeah, that does. I think people always want the quick route, the easy route."

Tobias said, "That's true, but in the end, it almost seems like one has to be willing to endure the mental torture."

Danny then said, "Yeah, no one ever quit Sifu's school because it was physically exhausting, but the hundreds who left just couldn't handle it mentally."

"So, why do you guys stick to it?" I asked.

Robert said, "You've seen Tobias in action, right?"

"Yeah, of course," I said.

"Take that level of skill and multiply it by a million and then you have Sifu. Let's face it: it's the closest thing to having real super powers," he said.

Tobias said, "Couldn't you at least have said multiply it by a thousand?"

Robert said, "Do you think you're only a thousand away from Sifu's skill?"

"No, but it sure is less depressing than hearing a million," laughed Tobias.

The waitress finally came and took several minutes to sort out the orders. When she finally walked away, we each had a massive burger sitting in front of us.

"All right, guys and gal, let's eat it all at once and savor the moment," said Ken, who was genuinely excited for all of us.

As everyone grabbed their burgers, Robert pulled out a pair of chop sticks that he always carried around. Looking confused, Ken said, "Dude, it's a burger. What gives with the sticks?"

Robert replied, "You know I never leave home without these when I eat." Ken didn't even bother arguing with Robert and shook his head. Robert added, "Besides, it's not as bad as Ryan ... he brought his own cheese."

Ryan had a stack of cheese that he pulled out of his pocket. He looked at everyone and said, "What? It's seventy-five cents more to add cheese." The look on his face was priceless as it made me laugh.

We grabbed our burgers and simultaneously bit into them. For the next several seconds, everyone was quiet, savoring both the moment and the taste.

"Sooo...," Ken dragged his words, "so what do you guys think? Was I right ... huh?" He eagerly waited for our group's approval.

Robert made eye contact with me and then spoke in Korean, "Baegin-deul shiruh-hae."

I giggled and then looked at Ken and smiled. "Mmm delicious," I said as I realized I invested three hours of my life for a burger.

"It's great to believe in things, but not necessary to force others into believing it as well." –Sifu

232

The Substitute–1 year 181 days

Another challenge match was about to begin; this was the third one in the span of a month. More schools were being shut down around the neighborhood. As we continued to face every adversary and win, word spread, and it appeared that they were targeting us now.

We had all gotten accustomed to the ritual of these fights. Someone would come in to challenge, Tobias would kick ass, and everything would be back to normal shortly afterwards. The early stages were somewhat tense, but we all knew Tobias was a beast, and it was like watching a movie, short of getting the actual popcorn. The battle for most of us was figuring out how quickly the match would end. We left the gambling all to Danny and Big T.

Now as two guys entered, we knew this was gonna be a match. There was no question who was the fighter between the two, as one looked like he had tree stumps for legs. Robert whispered to me, "Holy shit, it's that Muay Thai school I've been hearing about."

Several of us gathered around Robert to listen to what he knew. "This guy is a beast from what I heard. The last challenge match he fought, he shattered the guy's femur with a single kick," he said intently.

Doc confirmed, "Oh crap, this is the guy you were talking about a week ago."

Robert nodded and said, "Yeah, that's him. I'm positive."

Ryan whispered, "Yeah, I'd hate to fight this guy. He just looks menacing."

Danny spoke up, "That's right. Word on the street is that they've shut down five schools in a row."

Big T countered, "Hey, you want to bet?"

Danny said, "I'm in." They fell into deep conversation, trying to figure out costs and odds together.

We all tried to keep our voices down so Tobias wouldn't overhear us. Regardless of how good Tobias was, we didn't want to jinx him in the process. Several minutes passed as the usual paperwork was drawn out before the actual fight.

Sifu was being Sifu and never made it appear he cared one way or another who entered the school. It was difficult to read if he was just confident or detached from all this. Either way, he always looked like things would work out for him in the end.

The energy before the fight was as light and festive as always. Everyone was waiting for Sifu to give the signal to Tobias. That was the ritual that we'd all gotten accustomed to. We watched and waited for that moment.

From across the room, Sifu suddenly pointed in Tobias's direction.

Tobias was on the phone, getting ready to hang up, and Sifu shook his head and pointed again. From my angle, it looked like he was pointing at Tobias, but Ken said to me, "Uh, why is Sifu pointing at Ryan?" Then several of us peeked to confirm who was behind Tobias. This caught everyone's attention as the room turned quiet, all of us trying to figure out what was going on.

Surprised by Sifu's gesture, Tobias looked behind him. Seeing Ryan, Tobias looked back at Sifu with one eyebrow raised in question.

Sifu nodded at Tobias to confirm. Tobias did not question Sifu's seemingly strange decision but merely tapped Ryan on the shoulder. Ryan was busy relaxing and chatting up with Doc, ready to enjoy the challenge match.

"Uh, what?" said Ryan.

"Sifu wants you," said Tobias.

"Wants me for what?" he said cautiously.

Tobias said sarcastically, "He wants you to take out the garbage."

"But isn't garbage day on Thursday?" said Ryan.

Tobias grabbed Ryan by the arm and then shoved him toward Sifu.

Ryan walked hesitantly toward Sifu as the rest of us watched him and exchanged glances with each other.

Robert was the first to find his voice. "Uh, what's Sifu doing?"

I responded, "I have no idea."

Ken said, "I could be wrong, but I think he wants Ryan for the fight." Some of the other students outside the core started feeling the stress of the moment.

"Uh, Sifu, why did you point to me?" said Ryan.

"I pointed to you because I think this is a good fight for you," said Sifu.

Ryan swallowed his own spit as he looked at his opponent. "Sifu, that guy is huge. He looks like he could bench press four hundred pounds, easily."

Sifu responded, "Hmh, I would've figured he could do at least five hundred." Ryan shook his head because those were not the words of encouragement he wanted to hear.

Ryan asked, "Sifu, what if I lose?"

Sifu joked, "If you lose, maybe I'll open up a noodle shop or something." Seeing that Ryan lacked the confidence, Sifu pointed to Robert.

"What do you see when I point to Robert?" said Sifu.

"An annoying Korean," said Ryan.

"Hmh, that's much more tasteful than what I was thinking, but in all seriousness, I see his center," said Sifu. "What do you see when I point to Ken?"

"A white guy with bad taste buds," said Ryan.

"True, but again, all I see is his center," said Sifu. "What do you see when I point to Big T?"

"One really big black guy," said Ryan.

"Guess what I see," said Sifu.

Ryan got the pattern and said, "His center."

"Actually, for whatever reason, I'm thinking of chicken, but you're right, probably his center." He said, "In the end, it's all the same: size, shape doesn't matter. I see only his center," said Sifu.

Ryan paused for a moment and said shakily, "I'm scared, Sifu."

Sifu calmly replied, "That's natural."

Ryan said, "But you're never scared."

Sifu replied, "That's not true. I just learned to control my focus."

Ryan said, "I don't know if I can win."

Sifu looked Ryan in the eye and simply said, "If I believe strong enough to select *you* to fight, why can't you?" And with that, Sifu patted Ryan on the back and walked away.

Everything changed as tension filled the air. This was unlike any challenge matches of the past because everything was riding on Ryan's shoulders. At first glance, one would never guess Ryan was a martial artist. He was somewhat big-boned and had a very gentle soul. Ryan's Wing Chun was really good, probably second only to Tobias, but he had never put it to the test in a fight. Everyone was starting to question why Sifu would choose this fight to find out.

But all that didn't matter because, if he lost, the school would shut down forever.

The opponent said, "What's with this? I'm looking forward to kicking Tobias' ass." He pointed to Tobias and tried to stare him down. Tobias looked back and definitely wanted that opportunity in return.

Ryan stood there. I could see he was nervous as he couldn't stand still and fiddled around.

"First fight, fat boy?" he said with full confidence. Ryan didn't respond. He stood there looking out of place. The room was dead silent as both fighters waited to start. I looked for Sifu and saw he was in his office dusting. I tapped Robert on the shoulder and pointed to Sifu.

Robert mouthed, "What the f–?"

Bam. Whack.

Apparently tired of waiting, the challenger landed a low kick to Ryan's leg, followed by a solid punch to his face. Ryan spun around and went down as the guys laughed. His opponent was dancing around, taunting him.

Tobias dropped to the ground beside Ryan and said, "Get the f– up, Ryan. Get up!"

Ryan wiggled around, trying to get a sense of where he was as he got into stance again.

"At least he's back up," I said to Robert.

Seconds later ... *Wham. Bang.*

I cringed at the sight. Another punch combination was delivered, and Ryan hit the ground again. We were all in panic, as we didn't know how much more Ryan could possibly take. The school was hanging by a thread, and it was all up to Ryan to pull off a miracle.

Sifu stepped out of the office and calmly started putting on a light jacket. He casually looked at Ryan, but did not react to his current state.

As Ryan lay on the floor, his opponents continued to mock him.

"I'm gonna enjoy being the one to close this piece of shit school down. But don't worry; when you lose, they'll probably tear this place down and replace it with a burger joint."

Ryan looked at Sifu and got up. He stood with his back to his opponent for several seconds, gathering himself.

He then turned around and screamed, "Aaahhh!"

I had never imagined Ryan could close the gap that fast. I could not watch as I covered my eyes with my hands and heard....

Wham!

Seconds later, I opened my eyes and saw Ryan standing over his opponent, huffing and puffing.

Breathing hard, he growled, "I ... Hate ... BURGERS!"

Just like that, the emotions teetered to pure jubilation, as we surrounded Ryan to celebrate.

I turned to Robert and asked, "What happened? What happened?"

"The guy tried to kick low, and Ryan just moved in and knocked him the f– out," said Robert in disbelief.

Ken said, "Holy shit, is he dead?"

As his partner was trying to wake him up, Sifu started walking toward him calmly and said, "Doc, go get an ice pack."

Straightening his jacket, Sifu kept walking, staring straight ahead as he said, "I hope he's not dead. You know how much work is involved in burying a body?" Everyone turned around at his comment.

As we stood there in stunned silence, Sifu turned around and said with a straight face, "Simo asked me to plant a tree once, a small tree at that, and that took several hours.... Imagine a body," he said with a straight face.

As the guy lay limp on the floor, Sifu hovered above him. He placed his index finger on the opponent's philtrum and started to massage it with his nail. Moments later, he woke up.

Doc came running back with an ice pack and gave it to Sifu. I thought he was gonna ice the guy on the floor, but instead he grabbed it from Doc and looked at Ryan.

"Here, put this on your face," said Sifu as he looked over Ryan.

"You knew I was gonna win, didn't you?" said Ryan.

"I did, but I didn't think you'd let yourself get hit that many times before you fought back," replied Sifu.

Ryan smiled. "Next time I promise not to block with my face."

Sifu said dryly, "Remind me next class to go over not blocking with one's face."

> "Your journey begins the moment you truly believe in who you are and what you are doing." –Sifu

Untouchable–2 years 68 days

It was a good hour into class, and people were struggling. Sifu had a specific chi sao drill called blockers. As the name indicated, your main goal was to simply ... block. Most people favored being on the attacking side, but Sifu was very strict, and wanted everyone to concentrate more on the blocking.

Clap. Clap.

"No, no, no ... you guys are missing the point. Anyone can attack; you can learn that quickly. The key is to focus on the blocking. It is through blocking that the lines of attack will come about cleaner," said Sifu.

Sifu motioned to Tobias. "If you will." Tobias approached Sifu, and they both began the sticky hand motions.

Sifu said to Tobias, "Just attack, anything you want."

Everyone knew that Tobias was the man, but when he worked with Sifu, it wasn't even close. Tobias was maxing at a hundred percent trying everything he could, but Sifu barely looked like he was putting in any effort. It didn't matter what

Tobias did or how fast, Sifu would neutralize the force and dodge every attack thrown at him.

I was at a loss for words, as I stood there wishing that one day I could do that. It seemed I wasn't the only one—the entire class was in awe. After several minutes of showcasing true skill, Tobias stopped.

"Damn, I just got bitched," said Tobias.

Sifu said humbly, "I didn't even attack you. How did you get bitched?"

Tobias shook his head, wondering what he could do to possibly get better. Suddenly Glen said, "Sifu, that looked good and everything, but Tobias didn't really try to hit you."

Tobias angrily answered, "What do you mean I didn't try to hit him?"

Glen had been around for almost a year. He had studied Wing Chun from different schools mixing and matching ideas, and he struggled with grasping the ideas that Sifu exposed to him.

"Now, now, Tobias, let Glen ask his questions," said Sifu.

I frankly found him annoying, but strangely Sifu was not bothered by his constant questioning. Sifu said, "Remember you are developing a skill when you chi sao. In its most basic form, both the attacker and blocker are trying to learn how to go with the force."

Glen said, "I understand that, but why doesn't Tobias continue to go through with his attack? It looks like if he followed through, he would've hit you."

Sifu said, "That's a good question because, as the attacker, you have to think. Going with the force means knowing when you no longer have the target. If Tobias continued with those attacks, he would never have landed them, nor would he be able to flow to the next attack."

Glen frowned and didn't appear to be satisfied with that answer. Sifu kindly asked Glen, "Come, let's chi sao." Glen approached Sifu, and they began to roll.

Sifu said, "Anything you want, hit me."

I don't know what it was, but I could feel that Glen wanted to make a point. Suddenly he did something that no one expected and tried kicking while during the roll motion. Sifu's expression never changed, but as Glen lifted his foot to kick, Sifu jerked his center downwards and brought Glen to the ground. Glen crumpled to the floor. Sifu smiled and offered his hand to help Glen up, but he ignored it and got back up on his own.

"Can we roll some more, Sifu?" said Glen.

"Sure," said Sifu nonchalantly. They began the chi sao roll motion again, and then Glen tried to force a punch through the roll. Sifu barely moved to block and brought Glen off balance. Again, he was down on the ground. Sifu extended his hand forward for Glen. He refused and got back up.

"One more try, Sifu," said Glen.

"Sure," said Sifu. They began rolling again, and I could feel that Glen was getting frustrated with his attempts.

"When you're ready," said Sifu.

Glen didn't need any more motivation. He wanted to prove his point and began rolling, this time with even more vigor. Suddenly Sifu stopped his rolling motion, and Glen stopped it as well. We were all looking at each other, wondering what was happening. I noticed Glen was twitching, trying to move his motion, but Sifu just held his position.

"How come you're not rolling?" said Sifu.

Confused, Glen said, "I am trying to roll," as he was clearly trying to muscle the movements even more.

"You sure? Here, let's roll," said Sifu. They began to roll again, and as Glen was about to initiate his attack, Sifu stopped his roll motion and just smiled.

"What are you doing?" said Glen.

"I'm not doing anything. I'm waiting for you to attack." They stood still for only a minute, but it seemed like a much longer time as Glen twitched but didn't move. We all wondered what exactly we were seeing.

Glen said, "I can't fricking move."

Sifu finally let go and said, "Not bad, not bad." Glen was confused and shook his head. He walked away in a daze, not knowing what exactly just happened. Sifu looked around the entire class and said, "All right, get a new partner and continue to practice. I'm gonna get some water."

I looked at Tobias and said, "What the hell was that?"

Tobias shook his head and shrugged his shoulders. "Don't ask me. I have no idea what the heck he just did."

Ryan stepped in, waving his hands. "Man, it's like magic." We all laughed—not just because Ryan was funny, but he was probably right.

Tobias looked at Glen and said, "Thanks, Glen."

Glen looked at Tobias. "Why?"

Tobias said, "'Cause that, my friend, is being truly bitched."

"Imagine what endless wonders one can achieve when one learns to control oneself." –Sifu

Sifu's Journey Entry #7–A Watchful Eye

Middle of Summer 2030

A stranger stood outside the front door. He looked around, confused, wondering if he was in the right place. He quickly pulled out his phone to confirm. It was. He found it strange: all that existed was an address, but no sign.

Well, I guess this is it, he thought. He approached the door and hesitated just for a second before knocking.

Knock. Knock. Knock.

He stepped back and waited to see what would happen. Suddenly a voice could be heard on the other side. "One minute, I'm coming," said Sifu, as the stranger listened to footsteps coming closer to the door.

Sifu hurried to the front door and unlocked it. On the other side stood Phil, Sifu's very first pupil from forty years ago, representing his first generation of students.

"Sifu." Phil smiled and quickly shook his hand before giving him a hug. "It's good to see you, Sifu."

"It's good to see you as well," said Sifu. "Come in, come in," he welcomed Phil inside.

Phil walked in and started admiring the inside of Sifu's establishment. After a quick glance, he said, "Wow, this is impressive. How long have you been open?"

"I haven't; it's still closed," said Sifu.

"Oh, sorry, Sifu, I just assumed you were open already. No wonder I never heard about this place. If I had, I would've checked this place out a long time ago," said Phil.

"Well, the truth is, only you and Mike know that I'm back," said Sifu.

Phil looked surprised. "Wow, I didn't know that. How's Mike doing, by the way?"

Sifu replied, "He's doing okay. He was here a couple of weeks ago helping me with this little project. Anyway, there are things that still need to be worked out, but it'll be awhile before I open," said Sifu.

"What's awhile?" inquired Phil.

"Oh, I'd say a good year or two before I'm ready to open," said Sifu.

"Okay." Phil left it at that, deciding not to press any further.

"Come, come ... grab a seat," said Sifu as he pointed. Phil sat, still curious about Sifu's last statement. He scanned the surroundings as he waited for Sifu to speak.

"How are things at the station?" Sifu asked.

"It's getting worse. Most of the cops are on the take, almost forced to do it. Their pensions are being held hostage," said Phil.

"So, in other words, worse than sucks," said Sifu.

"Yeah, as bad as you can imagine," said Phil, depressed at the truth, though he laughed just a bit at Sifu's comment.

"Anyway, I know you're running short on time, so I'll get right to the point," said Sifu reluctantly.

"What's up?" asked Phil.

"I hate to ask, Phil, but I need a favor from you," said Sifu.

"Sure, Sifu, you know me, anything," said Phil.

"I haven't been in direct contact with the young ones since I closed the school, but the eyes of the street say they've been active. Maybe a little too active," said Sifu.

"Yeah, we're aware of that activity, since most of the cops are gambling on their fights," Phil confirmed.

"I want you to keep an eye on them and see if they get in over their heads. It's only a matter of time before they run into the mobs," said Sifu.

"I promise, Sifu, I'll keep an eye out for them and let you know if anything major comes up," said Phil. He looked away slightly hoping that Sifu didn't notice. Phil thought, *Thank God he doesn't know.*

"Thanks, much appreciated, Phil." Sifu crossed his legs and smiled, but could feel something was weird in Phil's demeanor. Sifu did not try dig for more information and left it at that.

"Do you have to take off already? 'Cause I have some soup that I've been working on," said Sifu.

"I can spare a minute or two," said Phil as Sifu said the magic word: food.

Sifu quickly ran into the kitchen and poured a bowl of his ramen for Phil. "Here, try it," said Sifu.

Slurp.

"Oh my god, this is fantastic! I'm being serious; this is incredible. Is this what you're planning on selling?" asked Phil.

"It is, but I need more practice. It's still not as good as it should be," said Sifu.

"Please tell me I don't have to wait a couple of years before I can have this again," Phil said.

Sifu laughed and replied, "You can stop by anytime and be our test subject on the soup." Phil smiled and continued eating away.

CHAPTER 8
One Month and Counting

Five Months Later, June 1, 2032

Kirin started walking toward her window. It had been a challenging five months. She paused just a few feet away from it, fearful of taking another step closer. In the distance, she could see a billboard that had been erected just a week ago. It was a huge picture of her with the UFMF brand stamped in the corner reading, "WILL KIRIN RISE FALL?" It disgusted her, as she had refused to do the promotion. But signing the contract allowed them to have full control of her, and they merely used her face stamped on a model's body to do the ad.

The sun's warmth drew her closer. Kirin had been confined for far too long, driven into her loft by the droves that seemed to recognize her anywhere she went. She did not care anymore if they saw her and approached the window. Her hand touched the window glass as she closed her eyes.

Immediately she could hear the sounds from below as the windows began to vibrate from the crowds.

"Oh my god, it's Kirin!"

"We love you, Kirin!"

"Kirin rocks!"

She opened her eyes and looked down, as she gave a bashful smile and wave. The crowd below went wild, cheering and shouting in a frenzy. Everyday, it looked like there were more people as the season was a mere month away. People were holding up signs, cosplayers were dressed up as her, and photographers waited hours just to get a snapshot. Sifu had forewarned her of the possibility, but only now did she understand what he meant.

They muttered amongst themselves, discussing the slightest thing they could come up with about her. She knew that even a little appearance would immediately reach all over the net. Discussion about nothing was this generation's forte.

She walked over to the side and pulled down the shade, as her hands trembled. The sunlight slowly disappeared inch by inch; she felt trapped in her own loft. The muffled sounds of their chants could still be heard.

Bacon came over to her side, dragging his little red wagon. He released his bite as the handle fell to her feet. He sat down and looked up at her, begging.

"I'm sorry, boy. I know you want to go for your ride outside, but it's just too crazy." He whimpered at her comment, as if he fully understood what she had said.

Kirin suddenly had an idea. "Wait here, boy."

Kirin grabbed his wagon and placed Bacon on top of it. "I know it's not the same thing," she said as she tried desperately to cheer him up. Kirin spent the next several minutes pulling Bacon around her loft, pretending how it use to be. Maybe deep down Bacon did not care one way or another as he started panting during the ride. She needed something normal, and Bacon's simple act made her heart smile.

She started laughing and gave Bacon a hug. "I promise things will be back to normal. I promise." Again, another thought came into her head.

"Hey, boy, don't move from that spot."

She ran for her camera and started taking pictures of Bacon. *Click. Click.*

"Good boy! Look over here, Bacon ... good boy."

Kirin snapped picture after picture of Bacon, having fun with using her camera for the first time in a while. A few minutes passed, and Bacon figured out a way to get into position to sleep, even when it was the most uncomfortable place.

"Come on, Bacon—just a couple more shots, boy."

But it was to no avail as the snores started rumbling throughout the loft. Kirin put down her camera, upset that she could not do what she loved anymore. She had officially canceled all her outdoor gigs several months ago. It was impossible to do a job since an entourage of fans and photographers constantly followed her every move. Regardless of how nice she may have asked them, they needed even more from her. Whatever she had become to the masses—a symbol, a hero—she was not sure how to properly handle it.

Kirin began to wonder who was playing whom. Since she no longer had her steady income from her photography gigs, she had to live off the contract that she signed with the UFMF.

She'd had no choice once the money started running out from her photography business.

Bacon was sound asleep, and again Kirin felt alone and discouraged. She sighed and placed her camera on the ground.

With another deep sigh, she headed to her couch and spoke, "TV on." Kirin sat down and tuckered herself into the corner. Looking for some form of comfort, she hugged a pillow tightly.

"Channel surf," she commanded, and the channels began to change intermittently after several seconds, giving a glimpse of what each one was airing. She caught sight of her face and said, "Stay." Seconds later, Kirin was listening in on the broadcast:

Todd said, "Listen, Chris, I'm sick of hearing about Kirin Rise. She's become a self-promoted diva, and she hasn't even had her first fight in the UFMF."

Chris replied, "Todd, I totally have to agree with you! She's refused to do interviews and train at any of the sanctioned UFMF facilities. She's acting like she's somebody, when she's clearly proven nothing."

"Today's Vegas numbers have been posted on her chance to win the entire DOME event at 400 to 1," Todd said. "Your thoughts, Chris?"

"I'm surprised that Vegas even gave her those kind of numbers. You can quote me on this: the world will end before she wins, Todd. I can guarantee you this ... she won't finish the regular season, let alone make it to the DOME and win. Let's face it, she's just a girl."

"Switch," Kirin said in a depressed voice.

"CNN business news, good news continues as the UFMF stock is up over thirty percent in only the last several months. Analysts attribute the massive wide attention brought by the female fighter Kirin—"

"Switch." Kirin hung her head.

"Today in entertainment fashion, we're looking at worst dressed. Hi, I'm Davny Porter with VRAI Magazine, reporting live in New York. You voted for worst dressed, and a resounding eighty-five percent of you said Kirin Rise's 'Hoody Look' has got to go."

"Switch again," said Kirin.

There was no escape, even from her home; whether by television or Internet, she was the talk of the town. Everything about Kirin was being dissected, no matter how she approached it. Even when she kept publicity at a minimum, it did not matter. News was being generated about her out of thin air. Finally, one of the channels got her undivided attention as she watched and listened.

Announcer Connor said, "Here with us today is UFMF's top contender, Diesel 'The Wall' Williams. I'm so glad you can join us."

Diesel said, "I thank The Lord I'm here today to do this interview. Thanks for having me, Connor."

Connor said, "So many questions for you, Diesel.... As you know, the three-time defending champion, Dryden Rodriguez, is out for this season recovering from his injury, so Vegas has you ranked in top spot to win it all this year at 4 to 1. Your thoughts on that?"

"I'm very grateful that God has kept me healthy this year to fight, but at the same time I'm extremely disappointed that I will not have the opportunity to win the title against my arch rival and prove my overall supremacy."

As Kirin was watching all this, she thought, *Please don't ask about me, please don't ask about me, please don't ask about me.*

Almost as if he'd heard her, Connor said, "So, Diesel, I have to ask.... The talk of the new season has almost everything centered around the new rookie fighter entering the league, Kirin Rise. Your thoughts on her joining the league?"

Kirin buried her head behind a pillow, but peeked at the TV as she heard Diesel speak.

Diesel grabbed the mic from Connor and stared into the camera. "I'm glad you brought this up, Connor, because I believe as a messenger of God that this is what he would want me to share. If you look at the entire league, thirty-one of the thirty-two fighters selected have earned that spot through blood, sweat, and tears. I have personally trained with many of them. Some of them are finally getting their first shot in the league after years of trying. And yet, some little girl out of nowhere is given an invite by the UFMF, just because she's the flavor of the month."

Diesel paused, intensifying the moment. "You know what I think of that? `Bull****!" His final word was bleeped out as he pointed at the camera. "She has nothing but disrespect for the league. She doesn't train with us, she doesn't do what we do, and she's making a mockery of the UFMF with this B.S. Kung Fu, Gung Fu, whatever Fu crap.

"I can tell you this, Connor...." He trailed off, turning his intense gaze directly into the camera, "Kirin Rise, enjoy your fifteen minutes of fame because if I run into you in the ring, it'll be fifteen minutes of *pain!*"

Without giving Connor a chance to respond, Diesel quoted, "'Cursed be he who does the Lord's work remissly, cursed be he who holds back his sword from blood.' That's Jeremiah 48, verse 10. Believe you me, Connor, I will not fail God."

Diesel looked up and pointed to the sky. "This message brought to you by the man upstairs." Diesel was steaming from his speech and then tossed the microphone back to Connor.

Connor spoke into the camera, "Well, folks, I can definitely tell you this. I don't want to be Kirin Rise." He chuckled at the idea.

"Switch," said Kirin as she closed her eyes and tried to shut the world out.

"Now stay tuned, as we enter into the tenth season of everyone's favorite gardening show ... *A Hole in the Ground.*"

"Ugh ... kill me," shouted Kirin as she grabbed the couch pillow and placed it over her head. From underneath the pillow, Kirin heard muffled sounds of tips on how to prepare the lawn for summer weather.

She yelled, "TV off!"

Feeling lost and sad, Kirin threw the pillow across the room in frustration. Bacon opened his eyes briefly to see what all the ruckus was about and then quickly went back to sleep. She stared at the kitchen table and then hopped up, running toward it. She grabbed the phone and dialed a number, but she couldn't complete the last button to send it out.

It was her mom.

She so desperately wanted to talk to her, to hear her voice. Kirin had always been close to her mom, and to go this long without a single word from her was unbearable. She paused with her finger just barely touching the last button. Finally she pressed it and heard the sound of the digits dialing, but she canceled the call, hanging her head in sadness.

"Dammit!" She threw her phone across the room. She fell to her knees and started crying, feeling alone and isolated.

"I don't know if I can do this."

Several minutes passed, and nothing changed. Suddenly a gentle lick came across her face, several times. It was Bacon. She smiled in appreciation and gave him a big hug.

"You always know when I need you." She kissed Bacon on the face.

Ding Dong. Ding Dong.

She looked at Bacon and asked, "Who could that be, boy?"

Kirin walked toward her intercom and pressed the button. "Who is it?" she asked cautiously.

"Hey, Kirin. It's Hunter." His voice was muffled by the crowd.

Kirin said, "Uh, give me a minute. Make sure you don't let anyone else in." Kirin buzzed Hunter in, knowing it would take several minutes before he would make it upstairs to her loft. During that time, she ran to the bathroom to splash some cold water on her face to hide the tears.

She looked in the mirror and saw her eyes were puffy from crying.

"Oh, crap." She sighed and then her eyes flew wide. "Need some pants." She dashed into the bedroom to throw them on. Kirin was in a rush to clean up the mess, but then she looked over her entire loft.

Game over, she thought as she ran to the bathroom searching frantically for the air spray.

"God, this place smells like a dungeon." Kirin was spraying everywhere, trying her best to at least fool anyone entering her place from thinking it was a total dive.

Knock. Knock. Knock.

"One second, Hunter," she said in a panic.

Bacon titled his head as he watched Kirin spray his bed before she stashed the can behind it and stood. As she ran toward the door, she suddenly slowed down, trying to act normal. Kirin grabbed a scrunchy from her pocket and tied her hair in a ponytail.

She grabbed the door handle and swung it open. The shadowy shape in the hallway stepped forward, revealing the familiar face of Hunter. Kirin was happy to see her friend, but as she tried to smile, tears streamed down her face.

Hunter came in and hugged her without saying a word.

"I'm so sorry," she sobbed.

"Shh, shh, it's okay. You don't have to say anything," he spoke in a soothing voice. They stood there for several minutes as Hunter tried to comfort her with his touch.

Hunter asked, "What's wrong?"

"I don't know.... I think it's just a case of self-pity. I'm sorry you had to see that.... I'm so sorry, Hunter," she said, her voice trembling.

"No, no, don't be sorry," said Hunter.

Kirin said, "I'm glad you're here."

Uncertainly, Hunter said, "I'm not so sure about that after what I'm about to say.... I'm here to talk you out of fighting."

Kirin pulled away from Hunter's grip.

Hunter said, "I hate to be the one to say it, Kirin, but you shouldn't do this."

Kirin looked directly at Hunter. "I have to do this. You don't understand. I created a movement, and people are looking to me to lead them."

Hunter shook his head. "I admit, I don't quite understand what you're trying to do, but those people out there ... they don't care about you, Kirin."

Kirin looked down.

"I hate to be the bad guy. I hate to be the bearer of bad news, but I care for you, and I don't want to see you get hurt."

Kirin shouted, "Why can't you just believe in me?"

"I do believe in you. I've seen what you can do, but no one's bulletproof, not even you, Kirin."

Kirin turned her back to Hunter, but spoke loud enough for him to hear, "I can't just quit. It's not just me on the line. People are depending on me. They need this. The world needs this."

Hunter approached Kirin from behind and held her by the arms. Kirin trembled from the touch as all her senses came alive.

Hunter whispered in her ear, "Kirin, you're so much more to me than you think." He gently spun her around and placed his hand on her chin, so she would look up. "Kirin, whether you're ready or not to hear this, I have to get it off my chest." He stared into her eyes as she looked back. "Kirin ... I uh–"

Ding Dong. Ding Dong.

Hunter looked up to the sky and muttered nearly inaudibly, "I must have the worst timing."

Kirin looked at Hunter awkwardly and said, "I should ... uh, get that."

Kirin headed back toward the door and pressed the intercom. "Who is it?"

"It's Tobias." The voice echoed throughout her loft.

What's Tobias doing here? she wondered.

Hunter looked at Kirin, who wasn't quite sure how to handle this situation. "It's Tobias," she repeated as she looked upwards and started to whistle.

A few minutes passed as Kirin opened the door and waited for Tobias to come up the stairs.

"Come in. What are you doing here?" she asked curiously.

Walking in, Tobias said, "I got some free time this afternoon. I thought we could do some extra training."

Tobias then looked behind Kirin's shoulder, and there stood Hunter.

Kirin turned around and began to make introductions. "Hunter, you've met Tobias...."

Hunter aggressively moved forward, pointing a finger toward Tobias. "This is all your fault. You're the one who encouraged her to do this."

Tobias pushed Kirin aside and stepped toward Hunter. "Put your finger down. You have no idea what you're talking about."

Hunter spat angrily. "I don't? You're the one training with her. Should I do the math for you?"

Tobias protested, "This was Kirin's idea from the very start, so stop talking out of your ass. Listen, my friend, if you really knew Kirin, you would know there's no talking her out of this ... so either I leave her alone or help her."

Hunter responded, "I'm not your friend, and if you were any kind of friend, you wouldn't let her go through with this and get herself killed."

Tobias retorted, "Well, you should know all about being a friend, since you're in the friend zone." Hunter had enough of Tobias and rushed in after his last comment.

Fortunately, Kirin stepped between the two before some blows were exchanged. "Stop it! Just stop it, both of you."

They ignored her, staring each other down.

Ding Dong. Ding Dong.

She shook her head. "Who the heck could that be?"

She approached the intercom and asked, "Who's there?"

"Guess who?" a pair of goofy voices responded.

"Sage ... Gwen?" she said.

"Buzz us in," her friends requested.

A couple minutes passed before the freight elevator in Kirin's loft opened up to reveal Sage and Gwen. As the safety doors lifted, they noticed Hunter and Tobias standing on opposite sides as Kirin approached them. Gwen looked at Kirin and made a triangle symbol as Sage chuckled. Kirin made a face at both of them, but let it go, since she was glad to see them. She hugged them both quickly and said, "Come in."

Gwen said, "Were we interrupting something?"

Hunter said sarcastically, "No, it would be impossible for anyone else to come at a worse time." Hunter walked away, shaking his head.

Tobias waved at them, still peeved at the discussion he'd had with Hunter.

Kirin thought, *The universe must have a sick sense of humor and somehow brought all of you to my place at roughly the same time.*

Kirin said, "What are the odds you'd all be here?"

Sage replied, "Three-thousand-seven-hundred-twenty to one."

Gwen replied, "Never tell me the odds."

Kirin looked at them oddly, sensing something wasn't the norm. Gwen had never completed Sage's movie quotes before.

"What's going on here?" she said with a curious look.

Then Sage grabbed Gwen's hand as she lifted it.

"Oh my god ... when did this happen?" she said with sincere joy.

Gwen answered, "Roughly a week after your Gung Fu display at the restaurant."

Kirin rushed over and gave both of them a big hug.

"I'm so glad you guys finally got together," she said.

Hunter turned around and thought, *What the hell? That should have been me.*

Kirin was happy to have her closest friends with her when only moments before, she'd felt so alone. She thought, *The only thing that would make this better is if Sifu was–*

Knock. Knock. Knock.

All five of them looked at the door, wondering who that could be. No one had buzzed the intercom.

Kirin thought, *It can't be.*

"Did you hear a buzz?" asked Kirin.

Both Tobias and Hunter shook their heads.

Kirin asked, "Guys, you made sure you closed the door downstairs, right?"

Sage answered, "Yeah, it was only us two. No one else got in."

"Let me get that," Kirin said.

She walked to the door while the gang stood in anticipation, waiting to see who it was.

Kirin asked, "Uh, who is it?"

"It's me!"

"It's Sifu," she said, turning around to face them.

Kirin opened the door to see Sifu standing in the hallway with a bag.

"Sifu, how'd you get in?" Kirin asked.

"What do you mean, how'd I get in? I'm me." He laughed.

"Sifu, you shouldn't be here. You know what we agreed upon. I don't want you to have any exposure or association with me at all," she said.

Sifu smiled. "Don't worry. No one saw me enter. Besides, I brought a bag of Chinese food just in case I had to pretend I was the delivery guy."

Kirin couldn't help but roll her eyes.

Kirin waved him inside and shut the door, announcing again, "Guys, Sifu's here."

Sifu waved at Tobias, Hunter, Sage, and Gwen and said, "Good, I guess I brought enough to feed all of you guys."

Kirin closed the door as all five of them were talking amongst themselves.

Kirin shouted, "Okay, everyone, stop what you're doing. First, Sifu, why are you here?"

"I thought instead of you coming over tonight to train, you'd prefer if we train this afternoon."

Kirin just looked at them. "All five of you just randomly happened to show up at the same time today? Okay, you guys can't be here.... Actually, that's not what I mean; of course you can all stay here, but I have an important meeting in about an hour."

Tobias asked, "What meeting?"

Kirin replied, "The head of the UFMF arranged for me to meet with him face to face for lunch this afternoon."

Both Tobias and Hunter said, "What?"

Tobias added, "How come you didn't say anything about this to either me or Sifu?"

Kirin shrugged. "It's a meeting. What more do you want me to say?"

Sifu stepped in. "I agree with Tobias, Kirin. Do not try to do everything on your own. We are all here to help you."

Kirin waved her hands. "No, no, no ... it's just a meeting, that's all. I can handle this."

Sifu said, "I believe I should go with you to this meeting."

Kirin shook her head. "Sorry, Sifu. I'm putting my foot down on this. Remember what we agreed to?"

Sifu just looked at Kirin.

Kirin said sternly, "I said I would train with you, as long as we did everything possible to keep you in the shadows. The last thing I want is to have any tie-in with you, no matter how well you covered all the bases."

Sifu acted unsure. "Did I agree to that?"

"Tobias was there. He can confirm."

Sifu grunted, "Hmh."

Tobias said, "I don't think it's a good idea to go by yourself."

Sifu said, "This is not a casual lunch get-together. He's going to dissect you."

Kirin said, "I can handle this, Sifu. You have to trust me on this."

"Kirin...." Hunter began.

Kirin looked at Hunter. "I'll be okay. Now do you think you and Tobias can try not to kill each other when I'm gone?"

Sifu spoke, "It looks like it's just gonna be us five for lunch."

The five began to gather around Kirin's table and prepare for lunch. While her friends ate, Kirin showered and dressed for the meeting.

Thirty minutes passed as everyone hung out in Kirin's loft.

Hunter asked, "How are you gonna get out of here with that crowd outside?"

Kirin frowned as she had forgotten about all the ruckus outside.

"I'm not sure," replied Kirin.

Sifu was at the kitchen table still eating when he said, "Have Gwen put on a hoodie and simply look outside the window. That should give you enough time to duck out of here."

Kirin asked, "Gwen, are you up for that?"

Gwen smiled and said, "Sure, give me one of your hoodies. I'll give the princess wave for a couple of minutes."

Kirin said, "This meeting shouldn't be long. I'm ready to go. Wish me luck."

Hunter approached Kirin first and said, "Be careful, will you?" Kirin looked at Hunter, appreciating his concern.

"It's just a meeting; that's all." She tried to ease his concerns.

Hunter walked away, and Tobias approached her. "Seriously, I should go with you."

"Thanks, Tobias, but like I said, I can do this myself," she said.

Gwen shrugged into Kirin's hoodie and approached the window on her wheelchair, while Sage gave a wave, wishing her good luck.

Before Kirin stepped out, Sifu approached her and whispered in her ear, "Control your emotions, and be wary about revealing your hand." Kirin nodded and went on her way.

Kirin got into her car and giggled to herself. She thought, *I can't believe that worked.* She stuck the keys into ignition and said, "Let's get this over with."

Across Town

From a block away, she could see the front of the restaurant. A large crowd of fans and photographers were already there, as if someone had tipped them off to her location.

"Frick," she said. She had been hoping to avoid the attention of the masses. Kirin finally arrived at the front, where she pulled up to the valet. The barrage of paparazzi happened in an instant, even before she could put her hoodie and glasses on. The flashes were blinding, making it difficult for her to see. Her makeshift disguise did little to detract from the reaction of the crowd, as her name was chanted and pictures were taken feverishly. She felt claustrophobic, and her chest felt like it was tightening up. It was a frenzy outside as the doorman quickly ushered her into the restaurant.

Once inside, she took a moment to regain her breath and composure. The doorman asked genuinely, "Are you okay, Miss?"

Kirin began removing her hoodie and was about to answer him, when a glance at her surroundings left her stunned by the sight of the grand atrium. Marble floors paved the ground in intricate patterns, and the walls glistened and reflected every beam of light. Artwork along with a slew of pictures of celebrities helped make up the rest of the decor.

She thought in awe, *This is a restaurant?* as she removed her glasses.

The hostess was well-dressed and mannered. She quickly approached her and said, "Ms. Rise, I'm glad you can join us. Please follow me."

Kirin felt somewhat intimidated and said, "I didn't realize this place was so fancy. I think I'm under dressed." Kirin touched her forehead to make sure her hair was covering her scar, hoping no one would notice.

The hostess replied reassuringly, "You look perfectly fine, Ms. Rise. In fact, I think you look very beautiful in your simple outfit.

Kirin felt better after the kind compliment, but before she could respond, the hostess said, "There's no need to apologize.... Mr. Thorne is waiting for you."

As she walked further into the restaurant, a row of waiters stood in line on both sides, almost as if waiting to give her a military salute. They were dressed in the typical red jackets, well-polished black leather shoes, and bow ties. There they stood, motionless like frozen figurines, almost as if they themselves were practicing a stance.

Kirin saw people having their lunches and asked, "Are we eating here?"

The hostess replied, "While our restaurant has the most upscale of patrons dining here, Mr. Thorne is considered our most exceptional customer and has a private area for you to dine in."

People who were eating stopped in mid-conversation or chew and stared at Kirin. Deep down, she wasn't sure if they were staring because they knew who she was or if she was dressed inappropriately for the restaurant. Again, the attention was unsettling, so she hurried along, sticking close to the hostess.

Two waiters stood by the doorway. As the hostess nodded, they simultaneously swung it open, revealing the inside dining area. The hostess looked at Kirin with a kind, inviting smile and said, "Please ... you first, Ms. Rise."

Kirin walked in tentatively as both waiters bowed their heads. Briefly, Kirin thought of Sage. She wondered what he would say at this moment. *It's a trap*, she thought with a wry smile that quickly faded. The thought helped calm her nerves as she began walking into the room. Several steps inside, she saw a well-dressed gentleman sitting down surrounded by a group of people.

Quickly her view was blocked by two huge men dressed in suits and sunglasses. They dwarfed her in size and formed a wall in front of her. Kirin stood there and waited, unsure what was going to happen next.

"Gentlemen, that won't be necessary," said the man from the seat. When they glanced over their shoulders, he nodded. Kirin stood there waiting as they immediately stepped to the side and waited at attention. Then they stepped to the sides and stood at attention. Kirin thought, *Well-trained thugs.*

The man stood up, fixed his suit, and started approaching Kirin with a smile.

"Ms. Rise, can I call you Kirin?" said Thorne.

Kirin replied, "Uh ... yeah, sure."

Thorne extended his hand, and Kirin paused slightly before exchanging handshakes. His grip was firm and commanding, while Kirin merely matched the force of his grip with a gentle touch. For that split second, Kirin felt something was off, but continued toward the table. He offered for her to take a seat.

Thorne looked her over and said, "I love your outfit, the hoodie with the glasses. Our research shows that a singular outfit allows consumers to associate with you better. Almost like how a cartoon character never changes clothes."

Kirin awkwardly smiled, unsure how respond to Thorne's comment. She wondered why they needed to do research for that as it seemed pretty obvious to her.

A waiter was kind enough to guide the chair as she sat down.

"Thank you," said Kirin. The seat was extremely comfortable. Thorne unbuttoned his suit and sat down, his chair also guided by a waiter that he didn't seem to notice.

"I'm so glad we can finally meet face to face," said Thorne with a smile. Kirin made no response.

"Where are my manners? Let me introduce everyone standing behind me. To my left is my lovely assistant, Linda." Linda stepped forward upon command. Kirin couldn't help but notice how stunning Linda looked for an assistant. She looked like a model working out of place. They exchanged eye contact as Linda merely nodded to acknowledge Thorne's statement.

Thorne continued, "And I do believe you've met my charming PR man Fawn." Fawn was in a vibrant pink suit which only he could have pulled off. He made a slightly feminine hand wave at Kirin, as if he were greeting the crowd at a parade.

Thorne said, "Finally, I believe you've had the pleasure of ... meeting with my personal bodyguard, Justice."

Now Kirin had a name to the face, as she looked up directly to stare at Justice. He made no eye contact and merely stared ahead, almost ignoring the moment.

"Now over to my right are several of my legal team, who I asked to join us," said Thorne. Unlike his core, Thorne did not feel that individually identifying them was that important.

Kirin looked over to see three very well-dressed men in expensive suits, fancy watches, and thin-rimmed glasses. They simply stood at attention. They fit the billing for lawyers, as she thought how they would bend the rules merely for the money.

Kirin grew impatient and tired of the formalities. "Mr. Thorne, not to sound rude, but why am I here today?"

Thorne smiled. "You are so direct, like your style ... I like that." Thorne made a motion to the waiter. "I hope you don't mind that I ordered already for you," he said.

"It's fine. I'm not that hungry anyway," she replied.

Thorne responded with a slight command in his voice, "You should at least try some of the food here. It's some of the finest dining you can find in the entire country."

Kirin replied, "I believe the majority of the country would be happy to have three square meals a day."

"Hmm," said Thorne, unfazed by Kirin's snide remark. He stared directly at Kirin, but she was unable to return the eye contact.

"I wanted to personally thank you. UFMF stock is up over thirty percent, and most of it can be attributed to you joining the league," he said.

His statement pinched a nerve as Kirin finally looked up and met his gaze. "Analysts in the business news believe it would be up even more, if I ever agreed to any interviews."

Thorne chuckled at the comment, but knew she was right. Self-promotion was key in the business world, and while UFMF stock was undeniably doing well, it would do even better if Kirin did not refuse to be in the public spotlight.

Thorne tried to change the tone of the conversation. "Kirin, I think you and I may have gotten off on the wrong foot. I'm not a bad guy, you know."

Kirin grew tired of playing the game and replied, "No, you're not.... You are *the* bad guy."

The room turned silent as all eyes glanced over to Thorne to see how he would react. "Oh, Kirin, Kirin ... if I could give you a little advice, when you get older and learn more of the world around you ... don't be surprised how deep the cast of shadows spreads," said Thorne. He smiled and said, "Because often your worst enemy is the person you stare at ... directly in the mirror."

Thorne paused for a second and took a sip of his drink. He cleared his throat and said, "Now you can't possibly be upset at the little test we gave you?"

Kirin grew annoyed, "That's for starters ... you threaten me and my friends and have seven of your goons fight me."

Thorne shrugged his shoulders. "They weren't my goons. Besides, it's business, Kirin, nothing personal, but before we could offer you an invitation, we had to find out if you could or could not." Thorne sat smugly in his seat, satisfied if not justified for his actions.

Kirin said, "Typical, using other people to do your dirty work. I've seen people like you all my life. You never have the backbone to stand on your own." Kirin looked left to right at Thorne's team and said, "You always need an entourage to make yourself feel better?"

Thorne was not fazed by Kirin's attempt to unsettle him. He made no sound but simply glanced at the people around him. Within a minute, the entire room cleared out, leaving Thorne and Kirin alone.

"Is this better? It's just you and me, one on one. Hopefully now you'll be more comfortable speaking. Do you mind if I speak frankly?" Thorne asked in jest since he was going to do what he wanted, regardless.

Kirin responded in a spirited voice, "Go right ahead." She was daring Thorne to show his hand.

"I'm somewhat disappointed in you, Kirin Rise. Frankly I think a *thank you* is in order. Is this not what you wanted?" Thorne spread his arms open, suggesting that he was merely supplying her needs. He paused for a second, waiting for a response. Kirin gave no reply as she looked at him, trying to suppress the anger building up inside.

"No? You wanted your voice heard, and I have given you the opportunity to showcase yourself on the largest stage on the planet. A platform for you to shout in, so the entire world can hear you and your pathetic cause."

When Kirin remained silent, Thorne raged on, "I practically gift-wrapped and laid it upon your feet ... at your complete disposal."

Kirin looked at him, enthralled but was not quite sure how to respond.

"You wanted to play the game ... then play it!" Thorne smirked as he turned his back to her. Suddenly Thorne spun around and pointed his finger at her. "I've been more than generous and given you every opportunity ... yet, what have you done? Absolutely nothing ... nothing but hide, quiver, and cower like a scared little child." He said it in a patronizing voice.

All this time, Thorne was well aware of Kirin's plans. He had been challenged his entire life, knowing that when you're on top, everyone's always trying to figure out a way to knock you down.

Pushed over the edge, Kirin stood up and said sternly, "You're no different from the typical criminal standing outside. Only now you've figured out how to do it legally and wear a fancy suit in the process."

Thorne laughed. "Ah, right and wrong ... here you are, ready to point the finger and lecture me about right or wrong ... because in your mind, that's all you see. What you fail to see,

Kirin Rise, is the bigger picture. Right and wrong are merely labels, illusions hiding the truth that the world revolves around money and power! History has taught us that. It will always be the case, and nothing can ever change that.

"Call it what you want, but understand this, Kirin: there is no difference in how you and I look at things," Thorne said sternly.

"Don't you dare compare me to you," said Kirin as she clenched her fist, wanting to hit him so bad.

Thorne responded, "I agree. Comparing involves equal levels, and I'm clearly superior in every facet. I honestly thought this conversation would be more engaging. It feels like I'm talking to a child. Back in my day, when I graduated at the top of my class from Harvard, do you know what we called people from Stanford or people offered a chance to go there?"

Thorne waited and looked at Kirin. "Future employees."

Kirin gritted her teeth, taking in some deep breaths. The sight of him and the sound of his voice made her blood boil.

"You see, Kirin, again you're showing your true colors. When the opportunity arises, what do you do? You simply run. You've done it your entire life. And now that a few cameras get in your face, you freeze up like a deer in the headlights, too frightened to do a thing about it," he added.

That was the final straw. Kirin's heart was racing. She approached Thorne, only to be separated by a table. She said fiercely, "You want me to shout, I'll shout. You want me to fight, I'll fight. You think you covered all the bases? Only a self-delusional, egotistical fool would believe in perfection. You talk about history.... History's also on my side as all empires, regardless of how big and powerful, eventually collapse at some point. Mark this day, Mr. Thorne, as the beginning of the end."

It was Thorne's turn to wait mutely as Kirin pinned him in place with her glare. "Greed and corruption will be your undoing, Mr. Thorne."

Thorne recovered and said, "Your misguided faith in your abilities shall be yours, Kirin Rise."

They stood across from each other as Kirin's tension hung thick in the air. Thorne, on the other hand, remained unfazed by the entire situation.

Kirin spoke at last, "Fancy clothes, fine dining, and bad company do not make for a good meal." She turned her back and started walking out.

Thorne taunted, "Run along, little girl. Run along...."

Kirin turned around before she opened the door to leave. "Mr. Thorne, you are right about one thing ... I do owe you a thank you."

Thorne responded in a condescending voice, "I'm waiting."

"Thank you for giving me the opportunity to bring you and the entire UFMF down!" With those last words, Kirin turned around and left.

"You are never alone in your journey of life." –Sifu

Short Stories #8–Kirin's P.O.V.

Mom's Kimchi–1 year 118 days

The rays of sunlight greeted me early today, finding their way through my window. I stirred as the heat touched my face. It was a good night's sleep, not my usual struggles, as the frequency and intensity of my nightmares had lessened. My talks with Sifu along with my constant training helped me deal with my issues. The warmth felt so good hitting my skin, and I did not want to get up right away. I basked in it for a while. My body felt rested as I stretched. I could feel every part of myself.

Then I realized it was Saturday: training day. My eyes popped open, and drool began to form as I was salivating from excitement. I looked at the window and thought, *Class awaits me. Get up, Kirin.*

I looked around my room, realizing it was a mess. My mom would have a cow if she saw the inside. I leaned over to pick up my phone that was at the side of the dresser. "Holy crap, it's 9:30!" I said with some urgency. "Oh shoot, I'm gonna be late."

After a quick shower, brushing my teeth, and the normal morning hygienic necessities, I was ready to go. Unlike Gwen, the pitstop for makeup and hairstyling was not on my list. Since I was never a slave to fashion, I put on the first thing that caught my eye when I opened my drawers. *Not bad, Kirin, only fifteen minutes, and time to spare with a quick morning snack,* I thought.

Mom was in the kitchen busy preparing something. I opened the fridge and grabbed the first thing that caught my eye. "Ah, apple." Proud of my accomplishment and rewarding myself with a bite, I walked to Mom, and gave her a quick kiss, and said, "Bye, Mom, catch ya later."

I was halfway through the door when I heard Mom say, "Where do you think you're going?"

I turned around, cautious of her tone of voice, and said, "I'm headed out to see Gwen as usual."

"Nope, you can see her later. I got something to teach you," she said as if she had this planned for some time.

"Mom, we made plans, and I'm already running late. Can't we do it later?" I said.

"Young lady, I've got something important that you should learn," she insisted.

Shoot, I thought. *There's no winning this. She used "young lady" in the front of her sentence.* I was upset because I only got to go to class once a week, and she was ruining my plans. *Maybe if we hurry this up, I can miss only a portion of it,* I thought.

"All right, Mom, can we go through this quickly?" I asked. Mom didn't respond and continued to get her little project ready. Watching her, I would've sworn she was intentionally moving slower than normal.

"Kirin, I rarely get time to spend with you. Being a couple minutes late to Gwen's won't kill you," she said. "I'm gonna teach you how to cook kimchi today," said Mom as she tried to sell me on the fun with a huge smile.

I looked at her in disbelief. "Mom, can't we just go to the store like normal people and just buy it off the shelf?"

Mom responded, "No, Kirin, nothing can compare to something that's homemade. Don't ever sacrifice quality for convenience because there's always a price that's paid."

I didn't react with any enthusiasm at all. I knew this would take away from my plans. I then realized that the statement of quality meant this was gonna take some time.

Mom gave me instructions as I started working on the Napa cabbage. I half-heartedly paid attention to what she was saying and began preparing them nonchalantly. "No, no, Kirin, you're doing it wrong. Watch again how I'm doing it. There's a proper way to do everything, and you need to figure out right from wrong," she said.

I replied, "What's the big deal, Mom? Whether I do it one way or another?"

Mom said, "It's true you can do things many ways, but there's a reason why I'm showing you how to do it in this particular order. These steps weren't created randomly, Kirin. There's a reason why."

Mom gave more directions as I kept working reluctantly at making the kimchi. I would phase in and out from her words, wondering what I was possibly missing in class right now. Normally, I loved hanging out with my mom, but my Wing Chun class always took top priority for me.

"No, no, Kirin, you have to pay attention to details. That's what makes something go from good to great. Don't just do it; know it," she said sternly.

I replied, "Why do I have to know the details of making kimchi, Mom?"

Mom replied, somewhat flustered, "Kirin Rise, life is short. If you're gonna invest your time in anything, then whatever it is that's caught your attention, learn it ... and learn it really well."

I thought, *I know that lesson already, Mom. That's why I want to go to my Wing Chun class.*

She saw me mixing things and said, "No, no, Kirin, you have to taste it."

I responded in a whiny voice, "But why, Mom? I used the exact measurements you told me. It should taste okay."

"Kirin, every situation is always different, so think of tasting like ... oh, I don't know, like touching something. When my mom taught me recipes, she didn't tell me to memorize the amount, I would just go by the taste of things.... So, after you've tasted it enough times, it'll be like a memory." She then preceded to taste the kimchi sauce to see if it was just right.

Dad walked into the kitchen with a funny look on his face as his nose twitched, and he quickly turned around.

I laughed as Mom said, "Sorry, hun, I know the smell is bad."

She said, "Continue mixing it, Kirin," as she walked to the fridge to get something.

I sulked for several more minutes, not wanting to go through the process.

Mom was behind me watching and said sadly, "Okay, why don't you go? Your heart's not into learning this anyway."

"Thanks, Mom, I promise I'll work with you another day to learn it," I said as I quickly took off, hoping to catch whatever was left of class.

I ran to the garage to get my bike and started heading over to Sifu's. *I should still be able to get a full hour of class if I speed it up.*

I was focused on getting to class as soon as possible. There were so many things I wanted to work on. I had already missed the first thirty minutes, which was when Sifu usually focused on the basics. Sifu was meticulous in his explanations—he had a reason for everything he demonstrated, and he always emphasized the correct way to perform any move. The simplest motion carried weight, and it was up to the student to dissect it. He always said doing it wasn't enough. He believed knowing it was the balance necessary in order to make it work.

All these thoughts were racing through my mind as I biked to class. I figured by the time I got there I would have enough time to chi sao with the guys. Sifu usually left the last thirty minutes of class for us to play around. I loved to chi sao. The more I did it, the more I was addicted to it. It had the mental stimulation of chess, but the physical activity to match it. Everything was based off the feel and what came naturally.

All these thoughts were running through my head and then suddenly I stopped in my tracks, my bike screeching. I spent a minute just thinking about all the things I was looking forward to learning.

"Oh my god, everything that I wanted to go over in class, Mom was trying to teach me." I looked down to the ground, disgusted with myself.

Immediately, I turned the bike around. Within ten minutes, I tossed the bike into the garage and came running back into the kitchen entrance.

"Mom, I'm back!" I yelled as I opened the door.

She looked at me, confused. "I thought you and Gwen had something planned."

"Mom, I'm sorry I blew you off. I didn't realize what you were teaching me," I said.

Like a good Mom, she was quick to forgive and gave me a hug. "It's okay, sweetie," she said.

"I love you, mom," I answered, choked up.

Mom didn't say anything. She just squeezed harder and kissed me on my forehead.

"You want to help me finish the rest of the kimchi?" she asked.

"Of course, Mom." I smiled.

"Go wash your hands then, and let's finish this together."

"You can learn from everyone, only if you are willing to listen." –Sifu

The Chase–1 year 300 days

I thought it would be a good idea to bring Butterscotch to class, so I leashed her up and headed over to Sifu's. The weather was slightly chilled for the start of the new year, but the first snow hadn't hit. Butterscotch seemed more than excited to go for a walk.

It was the usual lie to my mom–well, kinda, since I eventually did get to Gwen's place after class. However, whether dealing with half-truths or not, it always bothered me that I lied to my parents. Regardless, to me the training came first, justified in my mind at the cost of a fib.

Ten minutes into the walk, the change of neighborhood became significant. Times were difficult for many. Most of the shops along the way were abandoned, with only a few remaining such as Sifu's, and in their place people opened up cart stands.

The carts felt more personal than the typical corporate franchised stores. I knew most of the cart owners by their first names. They were simple people trying to make an honest living in difficult times.

I would imagine my parents would have a heart attack if they knew where the school was located. I personally didn't find it that bad, considering where I came from.

Several feet away, I could see Mrs. Chin. I had to stop by and say hi to her. She had become a close friend in only a short time, as she sold fresh pot stickers along with several other Chinese hand foods from her cart.

As I approached, I said, "Hi, Mrs. Chin."

Mrs. Chin responded, "Morning, Kirin, you look hungry dis morning."

I lied to her and said, "Oh yes, starving."

Mom forced me to eat in the morning, but I knew every credit spent would help out Mrs. Chin, so I always ordered from her, regardless.

Mrs. Chin smiled and asked me, "You want usual?"

"Of course I do."

Mrs. Chin had a thick accent, but I could still make out what she said. She had such a good sense of humor, and her food was to die for. She was a victim of the times, once running a restaurant in the neighborhood, but being forced to choose between being mob-owned or corporate franchised. Unlike most of the other owners, she decided not to pick between the lesser of two evils and simply opened up shop right in front of her abandoned restaurant.

Bark. Bark.

"Shh, Butterscotch, you can't have any of this food," I said.

Mrs. Chin said, "Is that you dog, Kirin?"

I answered, "Yes, Mrs. Chin, her name is Butterscotch."

Mrs. Chin looked at me. "Looks delicious."

My eyes popped open as her comment surprised me; then Mrs. Chin started laughing.

Mrs. Chin said, "Just kidding, just kidding." I laughed afterwards, but made a mental note not to let Mrs. Chin watch Butterscotch, ever.

A few minutes later, we finally got to Sifu's school. Butterscotch was hopping around and wouldn't sit still.

Out of nowhere, an alley cat ran past us, and Butterscotch took off, as I lost my grip on her leash.

"No, girl, no!" I said in panic, as she chased after the cat. I ran after her, but she was so fast. It was hard to maneuver on a busy Saturday morning filled with tons of people and cars all jammed into the neighborhood.

"Butterscotch, stop, girl, stop!"

I was terrified that she would get lost or, worse yet, hit by a car. I continued to run and scream for someone to grab her leash, but all it did was make people wonder what that crazy Asian girl was screaming at. Suddenly, all I saw was a blur as a gust of wind blew by.

"I got her, Kirin," said a stranger.

I stopped for a second and realized it was Tobias. I started running again, chasing both of them. I'd seen Tobias in fights, but I never realized he moved like the wind.

He was darting from side to side, avoiding people and obstacles. As I tried to run faster, he seemed to switch to a different gear,–I could not keep up with him.

I yelled, "Butterscotch! Butterscotch, come back."

Tobias was a good thirty yards away when I saw him stop. I finally caught up to Tobias as he stopped at the corner, where he was busy looking for Butterscotch.

Tobias said, "I lost her." I looked around as well, but couldn't see any glimpse of her.

He pointed and then took off again. "There! A disturbance through the crowd, that has to be her."

"Where?" I said.

And just like that he was gone, weaving his way in and out of the crowd and moving his center with total control. It didn't matter if something got in his way. He just flowed with the force and not once did he run into a person. Tobias definitely had some moves, jumping over obstacles and scaling parts of the wall. As worried as I was for Butterscotch, I couldn't help but stare at him, amazed.

Tobias shouted, "I lost her again!" I watched from a distance as he looked left and right, trying to spot her.

I tore my eyes from Tobias, scanning the area for Butterscotch, and I spotted her at last. She had stopped running, but stood motionless in the middle of a busy street. She looked scared and confused, like a deer in the headlights.

"Oh no, girl," I whispered as I ran as fast as I could to her.

From a distance, I saw a car speeding in her direction. I was not going to get there in time.

"Nooo!" I shouted.

In another blur, Tobias scooped up Butterscotch, but the car didn't seem to react in time. They were both going to get hit.

I cringed. The driver finally realized what was about to happen and slammed on the brakes.

Screech!

It must have been Tobias's training, because even with a car headed in his direction, he managed to keep his cool.

With Butterscotch in hand, Tobias ran toward the car and hopped on top of the hood, walking across the roof and finally the trunk. He landed lightly on his feet with Butterscotch cradled in his arms.

I stood there with my jaw dropped in awe.

Holy shit, I thought. I imagined this was how the masses felt when they saw Jesus walk on water. Instead, I just saw Tobias carry a sixty-five pound dog, and walk over a speeding car.

Tobias saw me and started walking Butterscotch to me.

I gave a kiss to Butterscotch, scolding her with love, "Bad girl, don't you ever do that again." I was just so happy to see that she was all right as I hugged her tightly.

I looked up as Tobias smiled.

"Well, that made for an exciting morning," he said.

I didn't know what to do, so I just hugged Tobias. "Thank you so much! You saved her."

Tobias said, "It was no problem," as he patted me on the back.

"Come on," he said at last. "We're gonna be late for class."

The gang was gathered, hanging out after a good day of training. It seemed like training never ended; even when we ate, we were learning. Everyone looked forward to the sit downs with Sifu. It was always the best; it felt like we were listening to old campfire stories of his past.

We were all enjoying our meals when I asked Sifu, "The guys have told me you've put your Wing Chun to test quite often.... Can you tell us about some of your fights?"

Sifu looked at me humbly and said, "Kirin, I do have one in particular that I want to share with all of you, and hopefully you can all learn from my mistake."

Hearing Sifu say this caught everyone's attention, as it seemed like he had such regret in what he had done. The first thing I thought was that he had lost a fight.

I asked, "Why do you say that, Sifu?"

Sifu said, "I was young and stupid. I was hanging out with my friend, minding our own business, when suddenly four guys were looking for trouble."

I asked him, "What happened?"

"It was just like in the movies. Everyone wants to be the hero, and I did not have enough faith in my Wing Chun. I had to show off my skills. The truth is, I had such little skills, that I was trying to prove my worth to myself."

He looked around at us, but no one interrupted with a question, so he continued, "My friend was a tiny guy, and for whatever reason, he was like bully bait. Unfortunately for us, he attracted the four guys for trouble. In the beginning, it started off as being in the wrong place at the wrong time. They started picking on him, and I stood up to defend him."

I said, "That doesn't sound like a bad thing. You were there to help your friend."

Sifu said, "It was, Kirin ... because if I had real skill, I would not have had to fight."

"I honestly don't understand, Sifu. In that situation, you were forced to fight, so I don't see what was wrong with what you did," I replied.

Sifu said, "There's no such thing as being forced to fight. If you have real skill, Kirin, your energy can neutralize the situation and make everything peaceful. That is the true skill of fighting without fighting. Instead, I merely became part of the circle of violence. I was a fool; all I wanted to be was the hero. In the end, I became the bully."

Ryan entered the conversation and said, "How were you the bully?"

Sifu replied, "I kicked their butts and thought it would be cool to display my power. I wanted to show off in front of everyone. I sent all of them to the hospital and almost got in big trouble for that. I was no better than all of them combined. I abused my power."

Robert asked, "Kicking four guys' butts does not seem like a lack of skill to me, Sifu."

Sifu smiled. "It looks like that, but every action has a price to be paid. Always remember, Robert, just because you can doesn't mean you must." Sifu paused with a concerned look on his face.

Danny said, "Is that why you came up with the four rules in fighting?"

"Yes, and I'm sure everyone knows them by now?"

Several of us coughed, and a couple stared down at their plates, indicating that maybe Sifu should repeat them again.

Sifu asked, "Who knows the four?"

Doc fortunately answered since I never heard of them before. "Know the when, decide, don't fight the force, and match the intent."

Sifu said, "Can anyone explain what that means?"

I said, "Yeah, I'd like to know. I never heard of this before."

Doc said, "I'll do my best, Sifu."

Sifu said, "Your best or Danny's best?" We all laughed, except Danny.

Doc then started to speak, "The first rule, knowing the when, simply refers to a life or death situation. As you have said many times, don't use your Wing Chun for stupid things–only when it's life or death."

I said, "How will you know, Sifu?"

Sifu said, "Trust what you feel. That little voice you hear every so often is the truth. In the end, you will know ... you will know."

Doc continued, "The second rule involves decision, and with that you stated that you either run or fight."

Big T said, "So, which one is right or wrong, Sifu?"

Sifu said, "Either one. The main idea of self-defense is that you do not get hurt. If you run unharmed, that's good self-defense; don't you think?"

Robert added, "So, if running isn't an option," he coughed, "Ryan."

Ryan replied, "Hey, that's the whole point of studying Wing Chun, so I don't have to run. Is it my fault I'm allergic to running?"

Ken pointed out, "Kinda like Kirin not being able to drink carbonated drinks?"

Everyone stared at me. "What?"

I said, "Oh yeah, it's true. It like burns my throat if I drink that."

The group started laughing as they never had heard of such a thing before.

I tried to make my case. "Guys, seriously, it's true."

Robert said, "Someone order Kirin a cola."

I muttered, "You jerk."

Robert replied, "Just making sure I don't lose my jerk status."

"Don't worry," I retorted, "there's no one even close to second place."

Doc interrupted, "Okay, enough ... let me finish. The third thing kicks in if you decided to fight: never fight the force. The basic rule of thumb is, there is alway someone bigger than you, so do not try to out-muscle someone."

I said, "That makes sense."

Doc looked at everyone to make sure they were listening. "The final and last rule is match the intent. Sifu, maybe you want to talk about this in detail."

Sifu said, "That was very good, Doc—and yes, I'll take over and discuss the last part. No mercy in a life or death situation is understanding the mindset of what's taking place. If the bad guy is aimed at killing you and your thought process is simply to hurt him, you will be at a disadvantage."

Tobias whistled, "Damn, that's bad ass, Sifu. Man, you gotta snuff the guy out."

Sifu said, "No, no ... but you have to be willing to match intent at any given time; otherwise, you will already have been beaten."

I asked, "Can you give a real life example? I'm kinda confused by what you mean."

Sifu nodded and thought a moment, "Imagine I have a gun and I point it at your head."

I thought, *Since that law passed, we do have to imagine that we have a gun.*

"You also have a gun, but you aim at my leg. Two people willing to pull the trigger, but two people with completely opposite intent. Who do you think is gonna win that situation?"

I shook my head. "Hmm, now I see what you mean."

Ryan said, "That's pretty deep."

Sifu replied, "It's not deep. It's just common sense."

I said, "You really seem to regret what you did, Sifu."

Sifu said, "I do regret it with all my heart, but back when I was young, I didn't. Unfortunately, I will have to pay the price for my action."

Tobias said, "Wait a second, so I'm learning how to kick ass, without kicking?"

Sifu said, "No ... fighting is the lowest part of the art. You train for a single thing: to answer the question that needs to be answered...."

We all looked at Sifu, waiting for the answer.

"Ask yourself," said Sifu, "who am I?"

> *"Often times the greatest demonstration of power is restraint." –Sifu*

Sifu's Journey Entry #8–A Belly Full of Info

End of summer 2030

It was a warm and sunny Sunday afternoon. Sifu was running a tad late, so his routine walk ended up being more of a brisk jog. He was headed off to his regular place.

Can't be late, he thought as beads of sweat began to form around his forehead. Sifu was not much of a jogger, and even in his youth he frowned upon the thought of running. Fortunately, his jog was short, as his apartment was only several blocks away. He had moved there just a few years ago from his house after he decided he needed a change.

Every moment spent from a simple walk to a breath of fresh air was enjoyed. It had become his daily routine for the last year and a half to go help out at the local soup kitchen.

On his jog, he could see the streets had changed from the last several years; unfortunately, it was not for the better. An increasingly large amount of families continued to struggle to make ends meet. Thus, the streets were being overrun with more homeless. It had come to the point where the poor had even less and the rich had even more. Somehow this had become justified in the world, and the people had grown helpless to do anything about it.

From a distance, he could see a huge line forming with old men and women, families, and little kids on their own searching for their next meal. This was what the American dream had come to: not so much the land of opportunity, but lower expectations of getting three square meals a day.

Upon arriving at the location, he gave a quick glance to the group and waved to inform them that he had arrived. Willie, an elderly regular, turned around to the crowd behind him and said, "Hey, every one, Sifu's here." A chain reaction like every Sunday occurred when he got there, as the crowd all realized who was there. A synchronized, "Good morning, Sifu" harmonized throughout the streets of Chicago.

Sifu found it somewhat amusing that they referred to him as the teacher. The title was unusual since most did not know of Sifu's past teachings, but somehow word got around and it had stuck. Sifu unlocked the door and held it open once he entered.

Willie said, "I got the door, Sifu." Sifu patted him on the shoulder appreciatively and turned on the lights to set everything up.

He knew people were hungry, so he hurried along to make sure the meals would be prepared properly. He was always the first to open up every Sunday, but several other volunteers would arrive shortly to help dispense with the food and other necessities.

It would be a good thirty minutes before everything would be prepared and meals would be dispersed, but most of these people, while hungry, felt at home once there. Regardless of their situation and for this short time, this was the only place they could call a home.

There were many regulars who volunteered to help, but Sifu was the main person that everyone knew. He took the time to learn everyone's name. It was impressive that he would remember every person who stepped through those doors. John, Marsha, Rick, one by one, he would spend a moment and cultivate a relationship with total strangers. He made them feel like they mattered again and worked to recall facts that were minor but precious to that individual. At the same time, he made sure their bellies were full.

Not only did he spend his time feeding the needy, but he used his expertise skill in healing as well. After the meals, he would pull out his kit, helping ease the pain with a massage here and a needle there, or much needed medical herbs. Thanks seemed like a broken record, every one appreciative of his efforts and his work–all of which was done for free.

Such acts of kindness in these times were unheard of. He was bucking the trend, doing something that wasn't concerned about the bottom-line–something that had been lost over the years. He performed basic human acts of kindness without asking what was in it for him. He simply wanted to help out his fellow man get back on his feet.

The regulars would often say, "You could be rich, Sifu, if you opened up your own shop to the elites."

As the line chugged along, each one would see Sifu and greet him. To many, the chit chat that followed seemed like idle conversations, but Sifu's act of kindness unintentionally created an elaborate network of information:

"You know Sifu over by 57th Street? Word has it they're tearing down the building. They paid off the alderman to get zoning rights...."

"By the way, this is confirmed, Sifu: there's a gang controlling the district area over by Ravenswood."

"The two cops patrolling the beat at midnight by Irving Park have been bought off by the mob."

The eyes and ears of the city reported to Sifu.

Unfortunately, he was also the bearer of bad news. Budget was limited, and he could serve only so many people for food at a time. It was heartbreaking to turn away the many needy each week. He was saddened by that. The possibility of shutting down due to further budget cuts loomed, yet a mere several blocks away another luxury apartment was being placed. The city talked about not having enough money for the poor. In reality, there was always money, for the right people.

In a Wing Chun world, common sense existed, but he could not piece together exactly how things worked.

CHAPTER 9
First Fight

July 4, 2032

The atmosphere in the air was frenzied as the crowd in the sold-out stadium was ready to erupt. This was unlike any opening day for the UFMF league. The stars were perfectly aligned as the start of the season would coincide with the birth of the nation, on this Fourth of July. The hype and marketing of Kirin for the last several months had created such a stir that one had to wonder if the anticipation could equal or possibly surpass the expectations of the two hundred thousand fans in attendance.

Within twenty years, the domination of the sport had taken over the country. Key strategic moves had been laid out by the heads of the company, and Thorne was determined to see them play out. Things appeared to be falling perfectly in place for the UFMF.

Globalization was the goal, and the UFMF was on the verge of achieving it. This season was going to be the key stepping stone to bringing the sport to the entire world. All eyes—especially the investors'—wanted to see how the season would end up.

Currently, thirty-two fighters made up the league. Fighters worked their way up in ranking to make the league. Some strived for years to get a chance to join the UFMF. Being in the UFMF meant instant celebrity status and financial success. For many, this was the only ticket out of poverty, so being part of the UFMF was the ultimate status. In the current economy, being able to achieve the American dream was simply that: a dream.

The thirty-two fighters were further divided into four divisions. The divisions were based on regions—North, South, East, and West—to bring a great sense of regional unity. New York, Chicago, L.A., and Dallas were granted mega stadiums. Politics and, more importantly, money helped to land these stadiums, which kept these cities from being poverty-stricken like the rest of the country. When they were constructed, the four became the quad wonders of the world, considered by many to be some of the greatest man-made constructions of the century.

The stadiums became landmarks and instant attractions. They were immense, dwarfing any other facility and swallowing up thousands of acres when they were first built. The stadiums were all circular in design with three tiers surrounding the base. The outer surroundings were for shopping and eating, and families gathered there from early in the morning all the way to closing time just to hang out. Advertising dollars were spent drowning consumers in products they probably just did not need.

The inner tier of each stadium was even more impressive as it contained the casinos. State-of-the-art, no expense spared, they were the perfect magnet for hope. The casinos based within the stadiums were starting to rival numbers generated by Vegas. Gambling was a bigger draw now than ever. Since middle class America was almost extinct, the hope of advancing laid better odds at chance than in working hard.

This was the beginning of a six-month season. Each fighter would fight twice a month, totaling twelve fights by the end of the year. Wins were not enough, as points were also awarded based on style, but mainly brutality. These points played two vital roles for a fighter. First, they helped determine who would advance in case of a tie. Second, points were part of a reward system by sponsors of the match: the more damage, the more cash.

The top sixteen in points would then make it to the DOME. The two-day event became recognized as a holiday weekend.

The end goal was to win the DOME. Every fighter's dream was not only the prestige but the dollar amount tied to it. Winning the DOME meant being set for life, not only for you but for your family's future generations. Twenty-five million was only the start; the endorsement deals following such a win made the initial amount seem almost insignificant.

Linkwater and Connor had both been promoted to the big time, beneficiaries of the fight they announced between Kirin and DJ. For Linkwater, this was his second chance at the pro level, and Connor's good timing landed him the opportunity of a lifetime.

Linkwater started speaking, "We are here live at the opening day of the 2032 UFMF season."

Connor stated, "I wish everyone could be here today, Link. I just cannot describe to you the energy in the air. It is electrifying."

Linkwater nodded his head and agreed. "Connor, this honestly feels like the DOME atmosphere in July, and the funny thing is we haven't even had our first fight."

Connor said, "We'll be right back after these messages from our sponsors."

Somewhere in the Fighters' Area

There was a good hour before the first match kicked off the start of the season. Tobias was in Kirin's locker room, waiting uncomfortably. Tobias was watching the television hanging on the wall, previewing all the talks on the upcoming fight for the day. He was uneasy, unaccustomed to such huge events. As he watched the television, it shook consistently from the vibration of the stadium crowd.

Tobias sat anxiously in the corner, tapping his foot. "Man, I never knew so many people were into this."

Kirin calmly turned around and said, "You've never watched any UFMF fights before?"

Tobias shook his head. "I never bothered to; figured I always had something else better to do. Besides, two guys sweating all over each other for several rounds, isn't my idea of fighting or entertainment."

Kirin said, "You're definitely not the typical guy."

Tobias merely ignored Kirin's comments and said, "I know the first fight isn't for another hour, so I guess that means it'll be a good three hours before you're on?"

Kirin tied her hair in a knot as she answered, "Yeah, give or take an hour. I'm the third fight."

Tobias made a strangled sound, and Kirin turned to look at him. "You know, you don't look so good?"

Tobias stuttered, "I'm ... I'm okay."

Kirin walked toward him, "No seriously, you look kinda pale."

Tobias looked up at Kirin. "I'm Blasian. How can I look pale?"

Kirin laughed. "I don't know, but you don't look like your normal self.... By the way, you do realize I'm the one fighting, right?"

"Yeah, yeah, of course. I've just never been a fan of huge crowds ... and when you're in a stadium packed with two hundred thousand crazed fans along with the hundreds of millions tuned in on the Internet and TV ... it's a bit overwhelming."

Kirin smiled at Tobias.

Tobias hesitated for a moment and then said, "Okay ... the truth is I'm nervous for you. I know you can fight, but ... I just don't want anything to happen to you."

Kirin patted him on the shoulder. "I thought you were here to be my moral support."

Tobias answered, "I'm sorry. You're right ... but seriously, Kirin, you're stronger than you think you are. You always have been. You could have done this without me."

Kirin looked at Tobias with gentle eyes.

"Maybe I could or couldn't.... All I know for sure is that you were there when I needed you the most ... and for that, I'm eternally grateful."

Tobias sat silently, placed at ease by Kirin's words.

Kirin had never seen this side of Tobias before. He had always been the symbol of strength since she first laid eyes on him in school. This was the first time she had ever seen Tobias show his vulnerable side to her. He sat on a chair, looking up at her with kind eyes. She got on one knee and grabbed Tobias by the hand as she stared at him.

"I never got a chance to thank you," she said.

She leaned forward to give Tobias a kiss and then–

Knock. Knock. Knock.

Kirin stopped just an inch away from pressing her lips against Tobias's.

She looked to the door and said awkwardly, "I better get that."

Tobias smiled as Kirin walked to answer the door. Tobias closed his eyes and thought, *God, karma's a bitch!*

"Who's there?" she said.

No answer from the other side. Kirin decided to take a peek to see if someone was there. As she opened the door, she froze in her tracks.

"Mom!" she said with such happiness.

Kirin's mom didn't respond, but with a gentle smile on her face, she opened her arms for Kirin to fall into. Kirin didn't hesitate to hug her mom tightly.

"What are you doing here?" she said as tears filled her eyes.

"I'm here because I thought you needed me." Kirin's mom paused as she relished the touch of her child. "You ... do need me?" her mom asked, unsure.

Kirin hugged her mom tighter. "Of course, Mom, I'll always need you."

"What am I, chopped liver?" said her dad.

"Oh, Daddy!" Kirin wiped away her tears and leaped into her dad's arms.

"Hey, Princess," said her dad.

"I missed you, too," said Kirin.

"Well, I guess being second place to your mom isn't so bad," joked her father.

"Oh, Dad." Kirin continued to hug her father.

"Both of you, come in, come in...," said Kirin.

Kirin's parents entered as Tobias stood up and introduced himself. "Mr. and Mrs. Rise, I'm Tobias."

"Tobias, pleasure meeting you for the first time," said her mom, looking at her. Kirin looked away and whistled, hoping her mom would not press further.

Tobias exchanged handshakes with both her parents as they stood silently looking at one another.

Kirin looked at Tobias and whispered, "Did you do this?"

Tobias shook his head. Confused but happy, Kirin decided to ignore how her parents got there.

"Mom ... Dad ... I'm so glad you're both here, but I am surprised that you would be here," said Kirin.

Kirin's mom began to speak, "Don't misunderstand me, Kirin. I am still a hundred percent against you doing this ... but I would rather be here with you, instead of it lingering in the back of your mind."

She and her mom exchanged a smile before her mom added, "Promise me one thing...."

Kirin said, "Anything."

"Promise me you'll stay safe." Her mom started to cry and hugged Kirin.

"I promise, Mom ... I promise," Kirin whispered in her ear. Dad came over and hugged both his wife and Kirin. It had been months since they had spoken or seen one another, and Kirin felt a sense of peace finally being with her parents.

Back to Linkwater and Connor

Linkwater spoke to the camera, "The controversy keeps surrounding Kirin Rise, as there is no doubt she is the number one draw for today's event."

Connor replied, "Over the last month, she has definitely been more vocal. In fact, you can't do anything without seeing her on TV, commercials, and the Internet."

Linkwater replied, "She's definitely broken out of her shell speaking to the public and become the people's fighter. Let me add to this, Connor: there is no doubt that Kirin Rise has amassed an extremely loyal, almost cult following."

Connor said, "I believe it's a dangerous gamble on her part. This is a lot of pressure for a nineteen-year-old to handle. Normally, I would say that you can recover from a loss in the first fight of the year, but her first fight will definitely set the tone."

As the camera rolled, Linkwater turned to Connor. "She's been very vocal about the UFMF and its role in passing laws and its rise to the top."

Connor replied, "If that's not enough to spark a heated debate, her attitude and style of fighting have brought even more sparks to the entire league. Here's a short clip of an interview I had with her."

The screen changed to an image of Connor and Kirin.

Kirin said, "I have no animosity toward any of the fighters. I have nothing but the utmost respect for these incredible athletes, but I train on my own because what they're doing and what I'm doing are two different things."

Connor asked, "How so, Kirin?"

Kirin replied, "If my goal was to be bigger, faster, stronger, there's the law of diminishing returns.... I could max all my physical skills, but at one hundred and five pounds, I would lose. Let's face it: size does matter. So in the end, I have to play a different game. I'm not here to be the best athlete, but the most skilled fighter."

The screen returned to Linkwater. "Wow, no matter how she tries to sugar coat it, I can see why every fighter has disdain for her and her attitude."

Linkwater turned to Connor and said, "I've seen her workout footage, and so has the rest of the world, and I have to tell you ... *I don't get it!"*

Without giving Connor a chance to respond, Linkwater added, "Getting ready for a fight and spending that much time on this chi sao and forms to me is just an utter waste of time."

Connor added, "I agree. Over the last several decades, traditional martial arts has all but died. Everything has some kind of fusion to make things work well in the ring, yet she's done the complete opposite trying to bring it back to this era."

Linkwater added, "I agree. Here's a chi sao footage we're going to play for you.... See for yourself, folks."

The video started rolling and showed Kirin and Tobias chi saoing in the park with a huge crowd gathered to watch her train. Minimal movement was done as they worked on developing certain drills for several hours.

Connor shook his head. "It looks like patty cake to me. When I asked her if she sparred, she said she does it differently from how we define it and that there's definitely no hitting."

Linkwater laughed. "No hitting? That's like alien talk to me. You have to get hit to know how to fight."

Connor smiled and said, "Fortunately, we have an expert in Wing Chun Gung Fu. Joining us is Grandmaster Chang. Thanks for being here, sir."

The camera panned out, revealing an elderly Asian gentleman. He had a car-salesman smile, as he looked toward the camera. Grandmaster Chang said, "Thanks for having me."

Linkwater asked, "Grandmaster Chang, you've seen her single fight as well as her training. Can you give us a little insight on what she's doing or how this could possibly help her in today's fight?"

Grandmaster Chang said confidently, "First, let me say I am an expert in Wing Chun Gung Fu, but I am also a full member of the UFMF association school."

Connor stepped in. "For more information on joining Grandmaster Chang's UFMF school, see the info below."

Grandmaster Chang added, "It's simple, Connor, adapt or die. Wing Chun by itself cannot win in the ring. She has no answer if taken to the ground or if she ends up in kicking distance. She's trying to go traditional, but let's face it: that will never work. I can see from her movements she doesn't have the basic understanding of structure."

Connor replied, "I think that's part of her draw. People have never seen this kind of approach before, and it's creating a ton of controversy."

Grandmaster Chang added, "I don't know where she studied her Wing Chun, but I can tell you it's very amateurish."

Linkwater said, "I'm gonna play devil's advocate; how'd she get that knockout against DJ then, Grandmaster Chang?"

Grandmaster Chang smiled and said, "Link, I have a broken clock, and twice a day, it's right. She fought an aging veteran and got a lucky hit.... That's all." Linkwater and Chang chuckled in agreement.

Linkwater said, "I have to agree. Checking on the Vegas lines, they aren't quite sure where to place her. As of this morning, Vegas odds have her at a whopping four-hundred to one to win the entire thing. The next closest fighter is listed at eighty to one, and mind you, this is out of the thirty-two fighters listed."

Connor added, "Talk about a long shot."

Linkwater replied, "Let's face it. If you believe this is the season pigs can fly, betting on her will make you a rich man." Linkwater shook his head. "I can't imagine anyone—"

Connor said, "I have to be honest. I don't quite understand what she's doing. There's definitely many unanswered questions in a lot of people's minds: Can she hit? Was it simply luck? Does size matter? History in the UFMF has shown that it does. How will her approach to training translate to the ring? The list goes on and on."

Connor paused and said, "She's going against a ton of hurdles which look to be insurmountable, for a seasoned veteran, let alone for a female rookie. I just can't see it happening. I guess we'll find out if she can win or not."

Linkwater stared into the camera and said, "Is Kirin Rise a one-hit wonder? Our answer right after a word from our sponsors." Immediately a commercial cut in with Grandmaster Chang getting a fifteen-second advertising clip of his school.

Meanwhile

Thorne stood alone in his executive booth. For the last several minutes, he had been busy talking on the phone. Thorne said, "I'm aware of that, sir."

The voice on the other side said, "Make sure to keep me up to date."

Thorne replied, "As always, sir." Silence. He looked at his phone and then placed it back in his pocket. Thorne stood looking through the window of his suite, watching the crowd cheer in anticipation. In his hand, he held a pad where he had been looking at some bylaws of the UFMF. On any other opening, he would be at his tower doing more work, but he knew the gravity of this first day and wanted to see things with his own eyes.

Thorne spoke aloud, "Linda, bring everyone inside."

Linda responded from outside, "Yes, sir."

Moments later, an entourage of Thorne's lawyers entered the suite with Fawn, Linda, and Justice. They stood there at attention waiting for Thorne's next order. He had not spoken a word, but everyone could feel the tension within the room. Linda stood next to Fawn as she elbowed him to initiate some response. Fawn quickly waved her off and stepped forward.

Fawn said, "Umm, sir, we are all present, as you requested." Still no response from Thorne as Fawn cautiously stepped back within the formed line. He shrugged his shoulders at Linda.

Thorne kept staring out the window as he said, "Fawn, please grab the pad from my desk and read what I highlighted." Fawn broke formation and did as he was told. As he spent the next several minutes reading, his facial reaction changed from neutrality to disgust. When he finished, he looked toward Thorne, who kept his back to the group.

Fawn began to speak on behalf of Thorne, "Do you know why I love fairy tales? I love them because, in the story, you visit these magical places of make believe and fantasy ... places and things that can never possibly exist in the real world."

Everyone was looking at each other wondering where Fawn was going with this.

Fawn stared directly at all three lawyers and said, "Do you know why you were all asked to come?" Fawn raised his hand immediately, preventing an answer. "You are here today because somehow fantasy has become reality. Somehow a nineteen-year-old non-college-educated girl was able to find a loophole within our stated contracts and have a nonprofit organization as her major sponsor."

Several of the lawyers were looking at one another, jostling in position for an answer. One of the lawyers cleared his throat and answered, "Sir, as much as we hope to cover and foresee every possibility that could arise, I don't believe anyone of us had the, umm ... foresight to think that one of the fighters would not go with a major corporation as a form of sponsorship. When we drafted the rules, we left room so that any form of sponsorship could occur." The lawyer looked down and cleared his throat again as his voice was beginning to crack from the tension.

"Do you know how much your lack of vision has cost us? Instead of having Fortune 500 companies spend millions and millions of dollars advertising on this year's biggest fighter ...

do you have any idea who or what Kirin Rise is going to be prancing into the ring with?"

One of the lawyers answered, "The ... umm, Salvation Army."

Fawn was livid. "The Salvation f–ing Army!" He shouted it like a toddler throwing a tantrum. "Do we look like a charity!" screamed Fawn. "'Cause last time I checked, I recall every one of you assholes getting paid for your work and not being here out of the kindness of your heart."

"Umm, no, sir ... uh, we had thought or believed that no one would ever turn down the money involved with all the major companies," one of the lawyers said as he fidgeted and adjusted his glasses.

Fawn cleared his throat and smiled gently at the lawyer he had spoken. "Believed? Is that like believing that they could put Humpty Dumpty back together again?" He shouted, "I don't need you to f–ing believe! We pay you fools an insane amount of money to make sure nothing like this would occur, yet here we are, placed in this position."

One of the lawyers raised his hand and suggested, "At the end of this season, we could easily change the rules."

Fawn took the pad that he was carrying and threw it across the room as everyone ducked out of the way.

Crash.

Linda responded, "Uh, I'll have someone in maintenance clean that right away."

Fawn responded, "No, Linda, after I'm done talking, I'll have these fools who are called lawyers clean up this mess. Maybe at least they can do that right."

One of the lawyers said, "But, sir, UFMF stock is up over sixty percent for the year, and it has doubled since you spoke to Kirin. Everything from popularity and merchandising to franchising and TV revenue is at an all-time high. The projections over this year and the next are expected to be off the charts. All of which, I might add, is placing us in perfect position to expand the league globally by next year."

"Always look at the bigger picture," stated Fawn, a lesson he learned all too well from Thorne. "I agree that growth looks incredible, but let's face it, we could be making more."

The three lawyers exchanged glances.

"Do you know the moral of the story behind the three bears?" asked Fawn. The lawyers stood silently, fearful of answering incorrectly.

"I'll tell you what it is. It's not that Goldilocks was trying to find what was just right. It's that more is never enough!" he hissed as he approached all three of them. Fawn continued to speak as he began circling the lawyers, making them feel uncomfortable. "However, that's not the main issue."

"What is it then, sir?" replied one of the lawyers.

"It's a mere distraction, and she knows it," said Fawn.

"Richard, would you be so kind to fill the rest of your colleagues in on the details?" said Fawn.

Richard, who was the lead counsel, replied, "Since she's started talking, she's gotten the ball rolling on the debate of the elimination of guns as well as targeting our franchise law on martial arts."

Thorne was listening to the entire conversation. He knew the price tag of getting those bills passed was an unimaginable amount. He shook his head, recalling the work involved.

"She has a voice." Everyone turned around to see Thorne finally join in on the conversation. "A huge following, at that, and the average Joes outnumber the one percent when united. She's looked upon as some kind of saint, donating all her revenue from outside advertising to all the local charities. We look like the big, bad corporation that's only concerned about money."

"Uh, Mr. Thorne, we are the big bad corporation only concerned about money," said Richard.

"I know that, you fool, but image is everything. Next thing you know, there'll be an uprising from the local yahoos. She's already got a huge following of protestors looking to challenge the laws that we lobbied for and got passed."

One of the lawyers said, "She is in violation of the bylaws about speaking against the league. We could fine her or suspend her."

Thorne's eyes glistened as he said nothing and stared at Fawn.

Fawn looked at the lawyer and responded, "That's your answer?"

"Yes, sir, that's my answer," said the one lawyer confidently.

Fawn said, "Are you sure that's your final answer? You don't want to call or text someone to make sure?"

He approached the lawyer and began patting him on the face. "You f–ing genius," said Fawn in disgust, as the last pat was a hard slap to the face.

"You're fired. Get him out of my sight, Justice," said Fawn.

Justice grabbed the lawyer and quickly escorted him out of the office.

"Anyone else have any brilliant f–ing ideas?" said Fawn as he looked around. "That genius wants to suspend her. She's clearly tied into the current success of our company. We suspend her, and I can guarantee you our stock prices and revenues drop with it. She's like a goddamn parasite."

Fawn went over to Thorne's table and grabbed a Kirin Rise doll still sealed in the official UFMF box. "Does anyone know how many f–ing dolls we've manage to merchandise and sell?"

Richard answered, "Uh, no, sir."

"It's not even the start of the season, and we've managed to match this year's merchandise sale to all of last year. All of last year!" said Fawn.

"Uhm, sir," said Richard.

"Spit it out, Richard," said Fawn.

In a sheepish voice, Richard replied, "You did ask her to speak out." Immediately, Richard cowered and looked down, almost awaiting punishment for bringing up the obvious.

Fawn had no answer as he thought for a moment.

Thorne stepped in and replied, "We brought her in to control her, not to have her enter our organization and run it amuck."

Thorne paused as a thought entered his mind that required his full attention. He looked at Fawn and said, "Fawn, you need to dig deeper. There's no way she'd make these moves on her own. Someone's gotta be helping her out with these decisions."

"But, boss, I've done a thorough background check on everyone she knows, friends, family, acquaintances.... You name it, I've dug through everyone in her past."

Thorne looked at Fawn. "Double-check it, triple if you have to. Don't come back to me without a name for an answer. Use every damn resource that we have."

Fawn responded, "Of course, boss."

Thorne smiled, turned around, and looked out over the masses of fans, waiting for the fights to begin. Linda knew the meeting was over as she escorted everyone out of the suite so he could be alone.

A Few Hours Pass

Knock. Knock.

Kirin spoke softly, "Come in."

The door opened as a stage handler peered through the door. "Uh, Ms. Rise, you're up in five minutes." He held his hand up to confirm the time. Kirin nodded and began putting on her robe. It was a customized red hoodie that Gwen made for her that looked similar to the everyday one she wore on the street. Unlike Chum Night, she was relatively calm. She looked at both her parents and gave them one last hug. With confidence in her voice, she said, "Everything will be all right." Her mom felt the comfort and gave her a hug back. Her dad came by shortly afterwards and planted a kiss on her forehead.

She turned to Tobias and then said, "It's time. Let's do this."

Tobias and Kirin started heading down the long path, already surrounded by handlers to make sure they entered in the right way. From a distance, they could see the opening where both the sound and the light were stemming from.

Kirin turned toward Tobias and said, "I've seen these opening walk-ins."

Tobias glanced at her.

Kirin replied, "We don't have much of an entourage."

Tobias asked, "What's it normally like for a fighter?"

"They make it a big spectacle, anywhere from ten to twenty people surrounding the fighter. The champion from last year had an army of people come with him."

Tobias said, "I'll tell you what: win this first fight and don't get hurt, and I'll get you an entourage. Maybe you want one similar to DJ's with midgets and clowns?"

Kirin giggled at his comment as they both continued to walk to the entrance. Tobias then said, "I'm afraid to ask, but do you have an intro song when you go in?"

Kirin said, "Oh yeah, I selected something."

Tobias looked at Kirin with curiosity, wondering what she selected. Kirin said, "You know, you're supposed to be my ring manager. Do you have any idea what you're doing?"

Tobias laughed at Kirin. "I'm totally clueless. I figured I give you water, wipe the sweat off you, and hopefully I don't have to drag you out of the ring."

Kirin laughed and punched Tobias on the arm. "Well, that's comforting to know." Tobias rubbed his arm after the hit.

Suddenly the handler told them to stop, and they found themselves at the entrance of the stadium. Kirin watched as her handler was having a difficult time listening to the instructions in his ear piece. The sounds of the crowd were taxing to one's ears. While they waited, Kirin and Tobias looked around in awe at the size of the stadium. Although several people had described this experience, the magnitude could not be appreciated unless you were there. The long stretch getting to the entrance was nothing compared to the slim path they had to walk into the masses.

Kirin's jaw dropped, "Holy crap, this is like nothing I'd ever imagined it would be."

Tobias gaped like Kirin and added, "Tell me about it."

They looked like two little kids entering a toy store for the first time. The vastness of humanity was overwhelming. It was one thing to hear the number, but seeing two hundred thousand people screaming was indescribable.

Kirin asked breathlessly, "Are you seeing this?"

Tobias shook his head. "I'm seeing it, but my mind's having a difficult time believing it. Someone pinch me."

Kirin punched Tobias on the arm again.

Tobias spun to face her, "What the hell! It's just a figure of speech."

Kirin smiled. "Believe it!"

Tobias looked at Kirin, who turned her attention back to the crowd. "I said pinch me, pinch me ... not punch me."

Kirin replied, "I can't hear clearly. It's loud, you know." Then she inhaled deeply and said, "It's time."

"How do you know?"

Kirin replied, "I just saw our handler motion to his assistant." Tobias gave Kirin that look.

But she was right; the news rattled throughout the air as the ring announcer began introducing Kirin. The crowd went wild, and Kirin felt their motion and frenzy pound her like waves crashing against a wall.

Kirin said, "Wait for it.... Wait for it...." The first strains of music filled the air, and the crowd quieted, trying to determine what it was.

Tobias shook his head and closed his eyes. "That's your song selection," he said as he immediately recognized the beats.

Kirin was all smiles, proud of her choice. "Since Sifu can't be with us, I thought I'd pick a song he liked."

Tobias rubbed his forehead and replied, "You better win."

She raised her hands, enticing the crowd to join her, which didn't take long as the crowd started getting into it. Tobias shook his head and grinned. "This is so embarrassing."

Kirin began singing the song, "I try to discover a little something to make me sweeter. Oh baby, refrain from breaking my heart—"

"I can't believe they're singing it with you," said Tobias.

Kirin pointed up to the enormous monitor hanging above. "I asked the guy to make sure the words came out with the song so people could join in."

"Seriously?" He looked around and noticed that everyone was singing as well. "Seriously?" he said again and began laughing at Kirin.

Kirin looked at him. "What's so funny?"

Tobias pointed at a specific group. "Look at all those fans throwing fake credits and making it rain."

Kirin looked around as her signature rain maker throw was being mimicked throughout the stadium. Tobias pointed at the sea of middle finger foam hands that were sold throughout the stadium. He said, "Man, the UFMF has no shame; they'll sell anything they can about you."

Kirin frowned and said, "Tell me about it."

As Tobias and Kirin started walking, they met fans carrying posters and shouting.

"Make it rain! Make it rain!"

"Marry me, Kirin!"

"Target, center, own it!"

Kirin began to laugh as she stared at one of the signs. It read: *Hey, one-hit wonder, your gonna lose!*

Tobias looked at her and asked, "What's so funny?"

Kirin pointed to the sign and said, "He spelled *you're* wrong."

#

Connor yelled into the camera, "This crowd is going crazy, folks. You have no idea how loud it is in here."

Linkwater said, "I have to say that's an interesting song selection she chose."

Connor added, "Leave it to Kirin Rise to pick retro eighties and get the crowd in a frenzy."

Both fighters were announced as Linkwater began talking more about Kirin's challenger.

Connor asked, "Link, what can you tell us about Kirin's opponent?"

Linkwater smirked. "This will definitely be a true test for her. Santiago Gutierrez is in his third year of the league. Last year, he got to the quarter finals of the DOME, and he is a grappling specialist."

Connor added, "This is a tall order for Kirin Rise. She's taking on a fighter who is entering his peak." Several minutes passed as the formalities were exchanged and the hype was brought to the very limit.

Finally, Linkwater said, "All right, gentlemen, the fight's about to begin. Last thoughts ... who are you picking?"

Grandmaster Chang said, "I'd bet the house it's Santiago, hands down."

Connor nodded in agreement. "The clock's struck twelve in my book, and no magic is gonna help Cinderella Kirin for this match. Santiago easily!"

Finally Linkwater spoke, "In my twenty years of covering fighting, wisdom and knowledge says bank on it ... Santiago in one round."

Suddenly, the bell rang as all eyes from the stadium and around the world watched. Kirin wasted no time and charged in, catching Gutierrez off guard. He adjusted and went to shoot for her legs, but that delay, that hesitation on his part, was his undoing.

Moments Later

Again the impossible had occurred. The deafening roar of the thousands in the stadium turned to silence. The awestruck crowd recovered and in a blink the stadium shook violently from the frenzied reaction. Immediately the flood of data traveled through space, spreading the news amongst the masses.

Linkwater said, "Wow, Kirin Rise has answered that question: lightning can strike twice in the same location."

Connor shook his head. "I'm not sure I believe what I just saw, but that, my friends ... was domination."

The ring announcer came back inside and waited for the crowd to settle. He motioned for Kirin, who stepped forward to say a few words to the crowd. The announcer said, "In a new UFMF record, at 5.2 seconds, the quickest fight ever, your winner ... Kirin Rise!"

Turning to Kirin, he said, "Kirin, do you have any thoughts you'd like to share with the crowd?"

Kirin looked around and smiled. Speaking with confidence, she said, "The one-hit wonder ... now has two!" She held her two fingers up to the crowd, who responded in glee, happy that their hero had risen to the occasion. The crowd erupted, taking her words to heart. She energized the stadium, and the number of believers swelled.

The ring announcer waved the crowd down so he could speak. "I know this is your first official fight, and a lot of the experts don't believe you'll go far. Any thoughts?"

Kirin answered, "In the end, I know what I'm doing, and I believe in what I'm doing, and that's all that matters." Kirin looked around the ring and stared in the direction of Linkwater, Connor, and Grandmaster Chang.

Kirin said, "Grandmaster Chang, thank you for your expert opinion." She made a respectful bow toward him and then raised her middle finger. The crowd shouted with laughter as Grandmaster Chang looked down in embarrassment.

Just as her first fight had stunned the crowd, her second fight went instant viral. Within seconds, the headlines read: *Rise's to the Occasion!*

Three Months Later, First Week of October

Three months had passed and the light did not fade from Kirin's star. She had been breaking every rule and expectation and was one of only four fighters who remained undefeated. Female, rookie, underdog with a 6 - 0 record, not a single expert could've predicted what she had accomplished.

Kirin sat in her favorite coffee shop—Red Eye—with Gwen and Sage. A large crowd was blocked off from entering. Hoping for a glimpse of Kirin, they waited patiently.

Inside the coffee shop, Kirin did her best to enjoy her latte even with the craziness only a few feet away from her. With everything going Kirin's way, the noise of the crowd was still unsettling for her.

Gwen said, "I don't know how you do it, Kirin. The crowd is insane," as she stared outside at the fandom.

Kirin nodded her head. "It is ... but most people are good deep down." Despite her words, Kirin knew that she still did not have an answer to Gwen's question.

Sage was excited. "Kirin, do you want to know how many followers you have on all your social networks?"

Kirin laughed. "Well, that's your job, isn't it, Sage? You're the one who told me to start it up to promote the cause."

"It's so unbelievable. You could literally type that you just burped, and you'll have like a million likes in a couple of minutes," laughed Sage.

Kirin said, "Let's limit bodily functions, okay, Sage?" No matter how long Kirin had been in the States, she still could never understand the fascination that people had with others' lives. She always thought it was odd that one's main priority wasn't oneself.

Kirin caught Gwen's eye and laughed. It was good to take a break from training and hang out with her friends.

Suddenly the door swung open as a portly gentleman wearing a sling cast around one arm waddled through wearing a fine custom-made suit. He had several of his henchmen pave the way, as he struggled to stay in a straight line. One of the henchmen immediately spotted Kirin and pointed directly at her.

Kirin looked at him and said, "Oh crap." Then she looked down and did a karma check.

Gwen asked, "It's not another fight, is it, Kirin?" Sage looked concerned as well.

Kirin waved her hand down and said, "I don't believe so. There are too many people here."

The portly gentleman finally got to their table and said, "Ms. Rise, I'm sorry to disturb you, but I was wondering if I might have a moment of your time ... uh, privately."

His henchmen looked around as the inside of the coffee shop grew quiet.

Kirin quickly responded, "I'm actually busy with my friends right now."

"Well, you know what, Ms. Rise? I'm gonna insist on this meeting," said the gentleman as one of his henchmen pulled out a seat and helped his boss.

Kirin looked around with caution and motioned to her friends. "It's okay, Sage, Gwen.... Give me a few minutes." Kirin was unsure, but felt nothing would happen in such a public setting. Both Gwen and Sage got up and sat by the counter, watching to see what would transpire.

"Thank you so much. Ah, where are my manners? My name is Mr. Jabbiano." He labored to get his words out. He cringed for a second, showing a slight discomfort with his arm and finally sat down.

Kirin said reservedly, "Umm, okay. What is it that you want to talk to me about?"

"Ms. Rise, I've been very impressed with your fighting. Unfortunately, you've cost me a hefty sum of credits since I've bet against you every time," Mr. Jabbiano said, forcing out a laugh.

Kirin responded, "Maybe you shouldn't bet against me."

Mr. Jabbiano was not pleased with her snide remark. "You know, Kirin, if you don't mind me calling you that, my father long ago–God rest his soul–told me an old wise saying. When the game is over, the king and the pawn go into the same box," said Mr. Jabbiano.

He pointed at her. "Right now, you think you're untouchable because all the world loves you, but only a fool thinks that way. You see, everyone has a price, everyone has a weakness, and to believe you're above all this shows your lack of understanding."

Kirin did not say a word as she stared directly at him without backing down.

"Don't get me wrong ... I'd like to congratulate you on your success, but I believe your luck is going to run out," said Mr. Jabbiano.

"How so?" Kirin asked, as she leaned forward.

"Well, you see, your next opponent is a fighter who I've heavily invested in, and I believe if you know what's good for you, this is one match that you won't–how do you say?–Give it your all." Mr. Jabbiano was winded from his string of sentences.

Kirin responded, "Are you threatening me, Mr. Jabbiano?"

Mr. Jabbiano said, "No, Ms. Rise, I'm simply giving you a warning." He struggled to stand up from his seat as one of his henchmen helped him. He stood proudly adjusting his pants and then looked Kirin in the eyes. "Never underestimate the evils of men."

Short Stories #9–Kirin's P.O.V.

Comic Books–Day 197

Jim was by the stove frying up some eggs for breakfast for all my brothers and me.

Jim said, "Okay, who wants what again?"

I said, "Sunny side up."

Mark answered, "Over easy."

"Scrambled," was Steven's order.

Kyle responded, "Poached with a pinch of lemon and hollandaise sauce."

We all stared at Kyle.

"Just kidding, scrambled's fine," said Kyle.

Steven, Mark, and Kyle all had that late-night look, so I said, "You guys look terrible."

Yawns, stretches, and weird scratches did not make a pleasant view for the morning, but I wouldn't change it for the world. My brothers were great.

I asked, "Did Mom come home yet?"

Jim replied, "No, she should be home in a couple of hours, when her call is over. Dad told me she had a busy night."

I nodded. "How late did you guys stay up?"

Steven looked at Mark and said, "I don't know ... not too long. About midnight, I think."

Jim said, "Okay, no one tell Mom we let Kyle stay up that late, or we will all be grounded."

Glances were exchanged around the table in silent agreement. Sibling bonding confirmed.

I shook my head and said, "You guys know Kyle shouldn't be up so late. I bet all you guys were doing was gaming."

Jim turned around and looked at the guys, who nodded their heads to confirm.

Steven said, "You should've joined us, Kirin."

"What were you guys playing?"

Steven started saying, "It was that shoo—"

Mark interrupted, "Uh, it was nothing. You didn't miss anything. Just stupid video games as usual."

Jim stepped in, "All right, everybody's eggs are ready."

Kyle yawned and replied, "I changed my mind. I don't want any eggs."

Jim answered, staring at him, "Then Kyle can starve and not eat."

Kyle thought about his option and then said, "Fine, I'll have some eggs."

I asked, "Where's Dad, by the way?"

Mark answered with food in his mouth, "He's in the garage sorting stuff out."

Looks of fear spread around the table as Steven asked, "It's not fall clean up yet?"

Jim said, "No, no ... he told me he was looking for some old stuff of his."

I could see my brothers breathing sighs of relief. Household duties were not part of our weekend plans, and no one was in the mood for raking outdoors.

About fifteen minutes passed as everyone cleaned their plates and decided to find different ways to bum the weekend. I, on the other hand, was curious to see what Dad was doing in the garage.

I walked in to find him sitting on the floor with several stacks of boxes laid out.

"Hey, Dad," I said.

"What's up, Princess?" he asked absently, too engaged to turn around to look at me.

"Watcha doing?" I asked.

"Oh, looking at all my old comic books I used to collect when I was a boy. I accidentally stumbled upon them. I honestly thought your mom threw these away, but I guess she never did," he said.

"What are comic books, Dad?" I asked

He pause for a second and realized that I had no clue what he was talking about.

"Sit down with your dad, Princess," he said.

As I moved to sit down beside him, he said, "Well, you know everything you read is on digital pads? Back in my day, things were still written and drawn on paper." He went on to explain that some of the books, like the one he was holding, were told in drawings and words.

"Which one are you reading now, Dad?" I asked.

"It's my favorite. I love the ones with heroes in them," he said.

"How come you love those kinda comics so much?"

Dad paused for a moment in deep thought, trying to dig for an appropriate answer.

"I don't think I'm alone on this, Kirin. I think everyone loves a hero."

I gave him a curious look and waited for his explanation.

"To me, comic books are ageless and are representative of the times and struggles that we go through in society. Regardless of the period, they always have the same underlying theme. Kirin, if you look at the world and see the chaos, trouble, and suffering that exist, you pause for a second and think to yourself, why? It makes no sense. I believe deep down we know this to be true and wonder how such wrong can exist. We know that it can be better and the answer should be right there in front of us to fix ... but, for whatever reason, we just can't. So, when you read about a hero, he or she takes on the role of a person, but more often than not, he represents a symbol of how things should be. In our minds, we want someone to make it right."

"I like how you say that, Dad. I really wish they existed," I replied.

My dad smiled and put his arm around me. "They do exist."

I laughed a little and said, "Daddy, you're being silly."

"No, no, sweetie, not in the literal sense of being able to fly or super strength, but remember that one person can impact the world and change it forever," he said confidently.

"Really, Dad?" I said.

"Sure, history has shown great men and women who have changed the world around us," he answered.

I looked at him with doubt. "Name me one person?"

My dad didn't even hesitate. "Alexander Fleming."

I asked, "Who?"

"The name may not ring a bell right away, Kirin, but every one of us has been affected by his work at some time. He was the man who invented penicillin."

"Oh, he's the guy who made medicine," I said.

"No, Kirin, it's greater than that. Like many individuals, he discovered things, but unlike people today, he made a decision for the greater good. He could've patented his discovery and made millions of dollars, but he felt that the world could benefit so much more if it was produced on a large scale."

"Wow, that is impressive," I said.

We lapsed into silence, and I looked over Dad's shoulder as he turned the page in his comic book.

"It would be great to be one of those heroes, wouldn't it, Dad?" I said.

"Who knows, Kirin? I think maybe you can be a hero," he said.

I laughed. "Dad ... you're being silly. I'm just a little girl."

He looked at me with such seriousness on his face. "No, Kirin, I'm not. I don't believe that our paths crossed by chance. I don't believe that the hardship that you had to endure in the very beginning was for no reason. I don't know what it is, but the moment your mom and I laid eyes on you, we both knew right away you were different. I think you're a special little girl who can ... be that hero," my dad said.

I didn't say a word and looked at him earnestly.

He gave me a faint smile and said, "Just a little girl ... One day, Kirin, you're gonna make everyone want to be just like you. Just a little girl."

He then kissed me on the head.

"What is it that I would do?" I asked. My dad was so supportive of me, and I loved him so much for it.

He replied, "I don't know what it is, but it's your duty to find out what makes you so special. I don't want you to follow the same path that your mother and I did."

I asked, "Why would you say that? Both you and Mom are successful at what you do."

Dad said, "Kirin, success is doing what you love ... being you. If I could turn back time, I would've played baseball, and I know I could speak for your mom as she would've loved to have been a chef. Remember, you get one lifetime, so don't play it safe. Go for it ... always."

I looked at my dad and smiled. For a brief moment, he sounded just like Sifu. But, I could hear the regret in my dad's voice, the dream that never was fulfilled.

He stared at me directly and said, "Promise me, one day you'll find out what that is!"

I didn't know why I said it, but I answered without any doubt, "I will."

I looked at my dad, and stared into his eyes. Something that very moment set things in motion for me.

"Dad, do you mind if I read some of these comic books with you?" I asked.

He smiled and said, "Sure thing, Princess ... sure thing."

> *"Will you have the answer to that question, when your time ends on this planet?"* –Sifu

No Excuses–3 years 70 days

Gwen was chomping on the school lunch as I finally sat down and joined her.

"Where's Sage?" I asked.

"Mmm ..." Gwen answered in mid-chew, "he's running late."

I opened up my lunch and pulled out my meal.

Gwen wiped her face. "How come you never eat the meals here in school?"

I answered, "Have you seen our choices?"

Gwen replied, "Yeah, it's not so bad."

I started laughing. "Hotdog, nuggets, pizza, and burger ... that's not so bad?"

When she didn't respond, I said, "You know my mom only gets me fast food when she wants to punish me."

"That is so wrong." Gwen laughed. "What did you bring?"

Looking excited, I answered, "Mom packed me some prepackaged sushi."

"Ew, that fishy thing. Yuck," said Gwen.

"You know sticking to a Western style diet is gonna kill ya," I laughed.

"I'll take my chances. Besides, I don't like food that's still moving." Gwen smiled.

I chuckled. "You goof ball, sushi's raw, not alive. Besides, I'm not sure you can even call what you're eating nowadays food."

After eating and chatting for a few minutes, Gwen frowned and said, "What's wrong, Kirin? Your mind seems to be elsewhere lately."

"I can't help it. I can only go to Wing Chun class once a week. There's gotta be a way for me to attend more often," I said.

"I don't get it. Why are you so obsessed with it?" asked Gwen.

"I can't quite put my finger on it, but the moment I walked into the school, I just had to learn it," I replied.

Suddenly Sage came up and said, "How are my two favorite girls?"

Gwen laughed. "Sage, I think Kirin and I are the only two girls you hang out with, so that's by default."

Sage frowned. "I know. What's up with that? I figured if I hung out with cute girls, you would be a magnet for more." Sage grabbed a seat and sat down between us.

I smirked. "Well, Gwen's high maintenance, and I'm antisocial. You need more of a rah-rah cheerleading type."

"Dammit, why are the gods so cruel?" Sage shook his hand in the air, staring at the ceiling.

"Why were you late?" I asked.

"I forgot my violin, so I had my mom drop it off for me," said Sage.

"Well, that's your problem, Sage," said Gwen.

"What?" replied Sage.

"You're not gonna get any girls in band," said Gwen.

"Wait, I thought chicks dig guys in band," said Sage.

Gwen shook her head. "That's lead singers, guitarists, or drummers ... Sage."

"You forgot violin," said Sage.

Gwen and I looked at each other and laughed.

Then I suddenly came up with an idea.

"Sage, when do you go to band practice? How often?" I asked.

Sage replied, "Once we start, it's normally five days a week right after school."

"Five days a week," I said excitedly.

"Yup," confirmed Sage.

"Who can join? Can total beginners be in it?" I asked.

"Yeah, they have a beginner level," replied Sage.

"Oh my god, oh my god ... this is perfect." I was almost salivating at the thought.

Sage looked at Gwen and said, "I don't like the look of this. She's got that crazed 'I got an idea' look."

I smiled. "Think about it. I tell my parents that I joined band, and now I have the perfect excuse to go train daily. Depending on my homework schedule, I could technically go five days a week."

Gwen rolled her eyes and said, "Wait for it, wait for it."

I smiled at Gwen. "Now, I can't pull this off unless my incredible, beautiful, and smart hacker BFF helps me." I gave a sad puppy dog look to Gwen and waited.

Gwen replied, "All right, I'll help you out, but you owe me for this."

I ran around the table and hugged Gwen.

"Thank you, thank you, thank you!"

Sage frowned at me. "Hey, I'm the one who helped you come up with the idea."

I walked over to Sage and gave him a kiss on his cheek. "Thank you, Sage."

Sage blushed.

That's probably the first kiss he's ever gotten from a girl, I thought.

Gwen said, "You know, sooner or later, you're gonna get caught."

"Aren't you the greatest hacker ever?"

Gwen said, "Yes."

I replied, "Well, then there's nothing to worry about, is there?"

Sage interrupted, "Enough about this, time for lunch ... hello, hotdog."

I looked at both of them and rolled my eyes.

> *"When the desire, passion, and will combine, it makes for an unstoppable force that will find a way." –Sifu*

Second Best–1 year 132 days

Doc said, "Let me look at that." I handed Doc my phone, and we continued to wait in line. Several of the other guys had already received their orders and had grabbed a spot in the park. I enjoyed days like these, even if they were rare. The problems that existed in everyday life, for a brief moment, appeared to be normal.

"Seriously, Kirin, you're the youngest of the group, and I hate to say it, but you're electronically cursed," said Doc.

I shrugged my shoulders, not denying the truth. "Hey, it's not me. The stuff just goes bad once I use it. Besides, unlike you guys, I wasn't born with electronics."

Doc looked at me funny and said, "Make sure you never use my stuff."

Robert was in a good mood, unlike most days, and said, "I gotta admit, this is the one rare time Ken picked a decent spot."

Ken jumped in right behind Robert, grabbing him by the shoulders as he said, "Booyahh," and taunted the rest of our group.

With a weird look on his face, Tobias said, "Please don't do that again. They're gonna kick our ass in this neighborhood."

Ken confidently replied, "What's to worry about? We all know Wing Chun."

Tobias retorted, "Then I'm gonna kick your ass." Ken nodded his head and refrained from his whiteness.

We all got our lunches and hung outdoors in the park. It was a beautiful sunny Saturday afternoon. I swallowed a bite of my food and said, "I agree this is tasty for a hotdog."

"Yeah, this is delicious," said Danny, showing his lack of manners as he talked with his mouth full.

Ryan said, "How are you part of this conversation? Yours is a tofu dog."

"I know, but it's the best tofu dog I've tasted," said Danny.

With food in his mouth, he continued, "Guys, today's class was a bitch. If you guys want, I'm game to work out afterwards in the park. Seriously, who'd think working on closing the gap would be so difficult?"

Several of the guys confirmed they could, but I replied, "I can't, gotta head back to Gwen's house afterwards."

Big T looked around and said, "You think it's wise to work out in the park?" as he pointed at a flyer that was discarded on the ground. I walked over to pick it up and stared at the crumpled paper.

A minute later, Robert was shouting, "Earth to Kirin, what is it?"

Numbly, I showed him exactly what I was looking at, thinking that reality was quick to remind us all the truth.

Doc asked, "Kirin, can I take a look at that?" I handed him the flyer.

"Wow, can't believe this day would come," said Doc in surprise as he flashed the paper to the rest of the group. It was a flyer reminding people of the impending bill banning guns. It did not matter who you were or what side you had taken, the powers that be were going to make this happen.

Ken thought about it and replied, "We should be okay. Besides, everyone thinks we're doing patty cake drills."

Robert added, "Yeah, Ken's right. Besides, those new patrols never come around here."

Danny said, "Why are you headed out, Kirin? I wanted to work out with you."

I replied, "The other guys will be here, but I can't stay ... sorry."

Danny finished another bite and said, "I don't know what it is, Kirin, but the last several months, I've never seen someone improve as much as you have. I'm not sure how, because you only come to class once a week."

When I didn't respond, Danny looked at the rest of the group. "Can I get a show of hands if I'm not the only one who thinks this?"

I looked around as one by one all of my friends raised their hands in agreement. Tobias took his time after everyone else did, and was the last to follow.

Robert asked, "Yeah, what gives? You're the youngest in the art, show up the least amount, and now you're picking up stuff like gang busters."

Doc joked, "At this rate, you can replace Tobias and be the most bestest."

I laughed and said, "Hey, that's my catch phrase."

Doc said, "Sorry, it's already patent pending."

Tobias stared at Doc as I finished eating another bite.

Ken asked, "So, what's the secret, Kirin?"

Big T said, "It's because she's a girl. Sifu always said girls pick it up quicker."

I looked at Big T and shook my head. "That's not it, Big T."

Big T said, "You're right; otherwise, Robert would've picked it up quicker."

"You dick," said Robert as he threw a napkin at Big T, laughing.

Everyone was looking at me, waiting for an answer. "Well, there's probably several answers to that question, but I think the most important one is my lack of distractions. Guys, I've talked to you about my past. When I was little, I had nothing.

I was only exposed to cell phones, TV, and the Internet when I came to the States at age eight. You could say, I kinda find the beauty in the boredom."

Danny said, "I don't get it. How does not having all that help you in Wing Chun?"

I said, "This is just observation, but in America, little kids are given tons of things to distract them from an early age. You guys are built on the idea of multitasking. Why do one thing, when you can kill several things at the same time, right?"

Doc said, "Go on, Kirin. This is interesting."

"How do I say this? People lack focus. They get bored easier. I, on the other hand, can work on a single exercise that Sifu's shown me, for weeks and months. Everybody wants to juggle so many things; fusion is the trend. So, the way I see it, trying to master something is a dead art. All I do is juggle a single thing. While the typical guy would get bored, I find new ways to look at the same subject."

"Oh, kinda like how Tobias gets bored of girls," said Ken.

Tobias just stared at Ken.

"Damn my ADHD," said Danny.

"You dumb ass, you don't have ADHD," said Robert.

Danny was busy texting on his phone and said, "What did you say, Robert?"

I laughed and pointed at Danny. "See? That's what I mean."

Tobias said, "So, you're catching on quickly because you're a boring person? Okay, we get it."

Everyone laughed, and I giggled and said, "You jerk, Tobias."

Danny added, "Okay, so you have better focus than the average Joe, but how about training wise?"

I thought about it some more and added, "You could say, by doing the same thing many times, you start to see it in a new light ... and I know most people would say that's not the case. For example, I've watched the same movie with my Dad at least fifty times, and each time, I pick up something new about it, something I didn't catch before, even though I've seen it a ton."

Robert interrupted, "Well, now you just sound like a freak.... Who does that?"

I said, "Let me get to the point. Because I stick to the basics, I started noticing things I took for granted when Sifu first taught me. I asked Sifu some details on the stance, and after spending some time with him, I realized not only was I interpreting it incorrectly, but my training and focus were concentrated on the wrong thing."

Doc asked, "How so?"

I looked around and said, "It wasn't the idea of just do it. Looking at it that way is old school thinking and misses the big picture. I had to dig deeper and go further than that. So it got me thinking, it's not how much I know, but what I know and how well I can do it. Everyone else knows more than me, but I simply have focused on the core basics."

Robert asked, "Which core?"

I replied, "The stuff we learned in the first couple of weeks of ever attending class–stance, punch, Siu Lim Tao, and turning."

The guys were definitely hanging on my every word as I continued to speak.

"Now, you guys all know that going to class once a week isn't by choice. It's hard for me to sneak out since my parents don't know. But, I realized that wasn't an excuse to suck. Sifu said something that got me thinking. Before that, I was practicing by number count, thinking if I did fifteen or thirty minutes of punching, that I was really practicing hard. But like all things Sifu says, it usually sticks, and he said it's not the quantity of punches that I do but the quality. I asked him what he meant by that, and he said you have to know the what, how, and why in everything that you do."

Danny said, "Say that again?"

"You know, the what, how, and why," I said.

When no one spoke, I explained, "Sifu gave me an example. It's one thing to drive a car, but most people don't understand beyond stepping on the gas pedal. Let me think ... how did Sifu phrase it? Yeah, kinda like this ... the art is broken into mind, body, and spirit.

"The mind oversees everything and understands why you do things. The body is the physical, overseeing what you do, and the spirit is knowing how to do it. Without knowing all phases of each one evenly, you won't be able to make it work properly. Ah yeah, and then Sifu said with a smile: balance."

Everyone looked at me with puzzled expressions.

I replied, "What?"

They exchanged glances, and Tobias said, "I've never heard Sifu say that. Have you guys?"

From the head shaking that followed, it appeared I was the only one who had ever heard that before.

I said, "You guys mentioned the value of asking questions, so I took that to heart. You said you have to ask, so I simply have been asking more questions."

Danny said, "So much focus on what you're doing, that's mentally taxing. I have a hard time remembering what I did five minutes ago."

"Dang, guys, I promised Gwen I'd be over soon. I gotta go," I said.

I waved goodbye and began walking away. From a distance, I could still hear them talking.

Tobias said, "Guys, show of hands if you think she's gonna be a beast in the art."

I peeked over my shoulder after over hearing Tobias, and saw everyone had raised their hands.

Sifu's Journey Entry #9–We Can Help Each Other

Early Fall 2030

It was a dreary fall afternoon. The weekend was going to begin with cold winds and more rain. However, this did not stop Sifu from his daily exercise of walking around his neighborhood. He took the same path as he normally did for his walks, but little did he know that today was going to be a bit more exciting. From a distance, he could hear some shouting, and he knew something was off. Curiosity got the better of him as he went to investigate.

As he rounded the alley corner, he saw a man surrounded by four teenagers. One of the teenagers was holding a knife and threatening the lone gentleman, "I know you got some credits, you homeless freak."

The other teenagers laughed, but looked around in concern and said, "Man, hurry up! The police might come."

"Nah, we got nothing to worry about. The cops never come in this area," said the teen with the knife.

Sifu recognized from a distance who was being harassed; it was Lance. Lance's voice trembled as he said, "Look, I barely got enough credits to eat a meal. Please don't take any from me."

One of the teenagers looked at his leg. "Dude, let's take his credits and his fake leg ... I bet that's worth a lot more money on the open market."

Sifu had seen enough and casually approached everyone. He said out loud, "It's a beautiful day. Don't you think?" Sifu's comment caught everyone off guard, as Lance and the four teens quickly looked in his direction.

The head teen spoke, "Listen, man, stay out of this. This isn't any of your business."

Lance added, "Sifu, stay out of this. I'm okay."

Sifu responded with certainty, "I know you're okay. In fact, I'm sure these fine gentlemen would agree that you're safe."

The teen looked toward Sifu and pointed his knife at him. "You don't want none of this, old man."

Sifu smiled. "You know, I was just thinking that the other day when looking in the mirror: I am looking old."

The teen was surprised by his remark, taking the focus away from Lance.

Sifu asked, "Seriously, how old do you think I look?"

Shaking his head, the teen waved his knife in front of Sifu. "This is no joke, old man."

"I know it's not. All four of you are fortunate that you are still young. When you get older, it's terrible. I have to say, when you get much older, the one thing that always annoyed me was white hair. Did you know you get white hair even in your nostrils?"

The teens exchanged confused glances as Sifu continued discussing his old age.

"Are you crazy or something?" said the lead teen.

"Actually, I'm not. I'm just enjoying the beautiful fall weather like all of you," said Sifu.

"What the hell you talking about, old man? It's been miserable weather for the last several days."

"Old man, you know we're robbing this guy, don't you?" said the teen.

Sifu acted surprised. "Oh, I don't think you really plan on doing that."

"What the hell do you mean?" said the teen.

"First, this fine gentleman you speak of has a name and it is Lance. Second, Lance is a little down on his luck; it would be like squeezing blood from of a turnip. Finally, I didn't think you guys would rob somebody with a butter knife. Besides, you four gentlemen don't look like robbers to me, but just growing teen boys who are hungry," said Sifu.

"Shut up, old man," said the teen as he waved the knife in front of Sifu. "You still think this is a butter—"

In mid-sentence, Sifu paked his arm as the knife flew up and Sifu grabbed it. The teens and Lance looked at Sifu in surprise.

Sifu held the knife and smiled as he said, "Okay, let me tell you what I want to do. I want to treat all you guys out to eat because you all look hungry. If you four guys join me, I'll give back your knife."

The teens looked bewildered at his gesture as one tapped the leader and said, "Dude, screw this. Let's get out of here." All four of them turned around quickly and ran in the other direction.

Sifu yelled, "I'll be back here next week about the same time, if you want to take me up on the offer."

Lance shook his head. "I don't know how you did it, but that was amazing."

Sifu said, "I didn't do anything. I just talked to them."

"Back in my day, four guys would've been no problem," said Lance as he looked down sadly at his leg.

Sifu said, "It can be, but at an even higher level."

Lance looked at Sifu and asked, "How?"

"I don't believe it is by chance that we continue to run into one another, Lance. I think the universe is telling us that we can help one another."

Lance didn't speak, simply listening to Sifu.

Sifu extended his hand. "Come with me; it's time to reinvent yourself."

Lance hesitated, "Sifu, why are you being so kind? I have nothing to offer in return."

Sifu chuckled. "A former special forces with nothing to offer? I highly doubt that.... Come on, let's get you cleaned up and put some food in your tummy." Lance shook his head and smiled, eventually taking Sifu up on his offer.

Sifu said, "By the way, do you like ramen?"

> *"If you use violence to solve things, the cycle will continue." —Sifu*

CHAPTER 10
One Step Ahead

Tuesday October 12, 2032

Sifu and Lance were in the back of the restaurant getting ready for a late evening. A large crowd had gathered that night and were already waiting for them to prepare the soups for their consumption.

Lance took a piece of the noodle that was being prepared and tasted it.

Slurp.

Lance said, "Sifu, taste this for a second. Tell me if you think this is ready."

Sifu came over and took a noodle from the pot and tasted it for himself. *Slurp.* Then he said, "Lance, give it two more minutes."

"Sure thing, Sifu."

A couple of minutes passed before Sifu tasted another noodle. "Ah, that's it ... perfect."

Stirring the contents of the pot, Sifu said, "Lance, try this and compare the textures of the noodle."

Lance came over, grabbed a piece, and then compared the texture in his mind. Lance said, "I got it. You're right. The texture is better with this."

Knock. Knock. Knock.

Both Lance and Sifu looked at each other briefly and then turned to the back door.

Sifu said, "Wonder who that could be? Cover for me, Lance." Lance nodded his head and continued to concentrate on his cooking, but his attention was now split.

Sifu opened the door and saw a gaunt stranger waiting in the back of his alley. "Ah, Billy."

Billy was a teenager who Sifu had helped often at the soup kitchen. He stood in the alley and seemed nervous as he constantly checked his surroundings.

Sifu asked, "What's wrong, Billy?"

Billy answered, "Can't talk long, Sifu. I got some information for you."

The conversation was quick between Sifu and Billy, and Sifu listened to every word that was spoken.

Sifu said, "Thanks for the heads up."

Billy smiled and said, "Any time."

Sifu grabbed some credits from his wallet and said, "Take this, Billy."

Billy waved it off, "No, no, Sifu ... you've helped me so often."

Sifu asked, "You're sure there's nothing that you want?"

Billy looked around again and said, "Can I have some soup to go?"

Sifu chuckled and said, "You know you can have both."

With another smiled, Billy said, "I'll take extra soup in place of the credits."

"Okay, okay ... I get the hint. Can you come back in thirty minutes, and I'll have some ready just for you?"

A big grin came over Billy's face as he said, "Can't wait ... I'll be back in thirty." Seconds later, he was gone.

Sifu immediately pulled out his phone and checked the time. "10:10 pm ... it's a little late, but he should still be up."

Sifu dialed and waited until the line connected. "Hey Mike, it's—"

Mike answered, "Hey, Sifu, is there anything wrong?"

Sifu replied, "Hope I'm not calling too late."

"No, I'm awake Sifu. What's up?"

Sifu answered, "I need a little favor. Do you think you can be here in fifteen minutes? I'll fill you in on the details when you get here."

"Yeah, that's not a problem, Sifu. I'll be down there."

Sifu said, "Thanks again, Mike."

Mike replied, "See you soon, Sifu...."

Sifu walked back into the kitchen and filled Lance in on the current situation.

With a look of surprise, Lance replied, "Wow ... this should be an interesting night."

Sifu laughed. "Can you make sure we have more than enough soup?"

Lance said, "Sure thing, are you gonna talk to everyone out front?"

Sifu smiled. "Of course, I'm a social butterfly."

The two laughed and went on their way. Lance was almost in tears as he muttered, "Social butterfly."

11:14 pm, One Hour Later

Lance was busy preparing soups as Sifu was in the front chatting with the guests. Compliments were being spread through the energetic crowd, and happiness was in the air.

Sifu came up to his most regular customer, Newton. He was there almost every night. Sifu thought, *Does this guy work?*

Newton said to Sifu, "Tonight's soup was the most bestest ever, Sifu."

Sifu patted him on the back and said, "I'm glad you like it. By the way, Newton, your grammar is horrible."

Newton laughed and continued enjoying the ramen.

Suddenly Fawn walked into the front door and said, "Party's over, bitches."

Everyone stared at Fawn for a brief moment as silence filled the air, and then quickly continued on with their soups and conversation. Fawn stood there, surprised by their lack of attention to his entrance. Feeling snubbed, he pounded the ground with his cane several times.

Stomp. Stomp. Stomp.

Fawn said, "Officers, if you will."

Suddenly an officer came from behind Fawn and held up a piece of paper and his badge.

"I'm Officer Callahan. This is a warrant, and we're here to conduct a legal search of this premises."

As he stated that, a storm of police officers came from behind, swarming the entire room. The group of patrons were unaffected and continued with their business.

Officer Callahan said, "Search everything and everywhere. I want three guys to check the back kitchen area."

Sifu approached the officer and said, "Can I help you, officer?"

Officer Callahan said, "Yes, you can get out of our way and let us do our business." He then rudely pressed the warrant against Sifu's chest but felt himself bounce back as if he just touched a wall. Callahan looked at Sifu in surprise. Sifu grabbed his glasses as he began trying to read the warrant

Suddenly Phil came in as one of the officers and said to Sifu, "Sorry about this, Sifu."

Sifu patted Phil on the arm and said, "Nothing to be sorry about."

Then Sifu cleared his throat and said, "Officer Callahan, if I can trouble you for a second, I'm not quite sure what all these fancy legal words mean?"

Officer Callahan said, "I'm sorry, but maybe if you had a lawyer, he could explain the finer details of what's going on." He turned his back on Sifu and continued to direct the officers through Sifu's place.

Scratching his chin, Sifu said, "Oh, a lawyer, thank you so much for that suggestion."

Sifu looked around the restaurant and said, "Uh, Mike, can you come here for a second and help me with this?"

The crowd in the restaurant turned silent as everyone then whipped out their cell phones and began recording. This got Officer Callahan's attention as he turned around to face Sifu.

Mike grabbed one last sip of his soup and cleaned his mouth with a napkin. He stood and walked toward Sifu. Mike grabbed the warrant from Sifu and began reading it.

Officer Callahan was looking at Sifu, who said with a smile, "It must be my lucky night, Officer Callahan, because Mike here happens to be my attorney." Sifu pointed at Mike.

Mike continued to read the document and then spoke, "Officer Callahan, I think your men have gone into my client's establishment far enough. If you don't want them as well as yourself to be suspended, I suggest you cease and desist what you're doing immediately."

Sifu watched as Mike started explaining to Officer Callahan who was in violation of the law. Several minutes passed as Officer Callahan's facial expression changed.

Officer Callahan then went up to Sifu and said, "I'm sorry, sir, for taking up your time. My men and I will be leaving."

Sifu patted Officer Callahan on the shoulder, "Officer, there is no need to apologize.... I'm sure you were just doing your job."

Sifu then waved his hand and said, "Lance ... if you will."

Several of Sifu's guests got up and started putting some tables together. Others went into the back room and started helping Lance carry out some soup.

Sifu said, "Officers, it would be my honor if you would be kind enough to have some extra soup I made...."

Officer Callahan looked at the other men and then smelled the air. "Well, I guess it couldn't hurt. It does smell incredibly good." He removed his hat and motioned to the other officers to sit down.

Fawn got into Officer Callahan's face. "What are you doing?"

Officer Callahan responded, "I'm gonna eat."

Fawn shouted back, "What about the warrant?"

Officer Callahan explained, "I'm sorry, but maybe if you had a lawyer, he could explain the finer details of what's going on." Just like that, he brushed Fawn aside and joined them for some ramen.

Everyone started cheering and clapping as the officers grabbed their seats and began eating the soup. Lance gave Sifu a quick wink as Sifu said, "Enjoy, enjoy...."

Phil came up behind Sifu and said, "I don't know how you do it."

Fawn was furious as he was smashing his cane on the ground, but it was drowned out by the rest of the crowd.

Sifu went up to Fawn and said, "Mr. Fawn, there's an extra seat and some freshly made ramen for you. You are more than welcome to join the rest of us." Sifu held a bowl right in front of Fawn.

Fawn lifted his nose to Sifu. "Hmm, peasant food ... I'll have no part of this." Fawn started walking away and then came back to Sifu and grabbed the bowl of ramen. He stormed out of the door, as people watched and laughed.

The officers continued eating the soup in amazement.

Officer Callahan said, "Holy smoke, this is phenomenal.... This without a doubt is the greatest soup I have ever had."

Sifu smiled as one customer said, "Hey, let me take a picture of all of you."

The officers called Sifu over to the table, and Sifu waved Lance in as well. The officers all grinned as Sifu smiled and created a heart with his hands. The customer with the camera said, "Okay, everyone say ... Most bestest."

Everyone in the entire restaurant shouted, "Most bestest!" *Click.*

Several Days Later, October 15, 7:18 pm

Hunter said, "So, the training is going well?"

Adjusting the phone at her ear, Kirin said, "Yes, I'm so sorry I have to cut the conversation short, Hunter, but Sifu's here."

Hunter replied, "I should know better than to call at this time. I just wanted to hear your voice."

Kirin said, "I'll make it up to you. Do you have free time to talk tomorrow?"

Hunter said, "I'll always make free time for you, Kirin."

Kirin blushed, glad he couldn't see that over the phone. "Okay, I'll talk to you tomorrow. Night, night."

Kirin hung up and then spoke to Sifu, "Sorry, Sifu, I didn't mean to interrupt our training."

Sifu said, "No, no ... I was young once. There's always time to spend for young love."

Kirin shied away from the comment and said, "I wonder why Tobias is late?"

Sifu replied, "Let's get to work. I still have to go to the restaurant tonight."

Kirin said, "Thanks for coming over to my place to train, Sifu. You know how difficult it is to leave the loft without a ton of people following me."

Sifu smiled and said, "Whatever makes it easier."

With a curious look on her face, Kirin said, "Sifu, what I don't get is how you sneak up here every time without anyone detecting you."

Sifu laughed. "No one ever pays attention to the Asian guy. They probably think I'm here to fix your Internet."

They laughed briefly before Sifu changed his tone, "Okay, Kirin, we must work further on your form. After watching your last match, I'd say you were lucky to win."

Kirin replied, "Thirty-five seconds was too slow, Sifu?"

Sifu raised his eyebrow and didn't say a word.

Kirin hung her head and said, "Sorry, Sifu, I know, I know ... control the ego."

Sifu cleared his throat and said, "Let's look at the first form deeper. You're using it at such a basic level."

Kirin thought for a second. "You know, Sifu, it just kills people that we spend so much time on forms when people think we should be sparring to get ready for the tournament."

Sifu humbly said, "People are people, Kirin, and you must remember when you have the skill, you can easily see both sides."

Kirin confessed, "It's difficult at times for me to remember that, Sifu."

"It is not difficult, Kirin. It is the ego that clouds your vision. That is why you must have that compassion and understanding. Don't forget to refine the heart. Remember why you spend time working on making the moves natural. I do not want to waste time sparring. You know that leads to play fighting."

Kirin responded, "I know, Sifu. Develop the skill to kill."

Sifu said, "Let's get deeper into the first form."

Kirin scratched her head and said, "How so?"

Sifu asked, "Tell me what you know about the tan sau?"

Kirin paused for a couple of seconds, gathering her thoughts. "Okay," she said, taking a deep breath, "Like all things, you have to touch and then apply the tan sau to make it work. Never use the tan sau to close the gap because there is no control, and finally tan sau is merely a transitional movement."

Sifu nodded. "Good, good ... now time to graduate from first grade."

Kirin frowned in disappointment, thinking she had gone much further than his current grading system.

Sifu tried to explain, "You're limiting your way of thinking, Kirin. You look at a technique as a singular motion. What you have to do is look at what you are developing from that motion.

Thus, right now if I asked you to show me all the things you can do with tan sau, you can probably show me one or two things at best. Do you know why that is?"

Kirin shook her head. "I don't know, Sifu. Why?"

Sifu responded, "Because you have become a slave to the technique. With that mentality, you limit the ability to express and create with your own imagination. If that was the case, if I gave you an egg, all you could make from it would be a fried egg. A great chef could take that very same egg and create so much more."

Kirin did not say a word, but merely contemplated what Sifu just said.

Sifu said, "Every motion that you develop in the first form serves a purpose, the limits of which are based solely on the individual's creativity. Any technique has four functions; it can be used as an attack, block, shi na (joint lock), and takedown."

Kirin had a look of disbelief. "What? How come you never mentioned that before?"

Sifu laughed. "How come you never asked me?"

Kirin bit her lip in embarrassment. Then she said, "Can you give me an example?"

Sifu said, "Sure." They engaged hands and began to chi sao. Seconds later, a quick attack by Sifu had Kirin on the ground. Sifu helped her back up as she looked stunned from the technique.

Kirin said, "What the heck was that?"

Sifu smiled. "Tan sau."

"I never knew tan sau could be used like that."

Sifu started doing the motion of tan sau again to Kirin so she could see the correlation of how that joint lock came about.

Kirin responded, "Oh my god, that is tan sau.... I can't believe that."

Kirin paused, watching Sifu's hands with a frown. "Why add joint locks and takedowns, Sifu? Shouldn't I just attack the center and knock him out?"

Sifu nodded. "Yes, that is true, but the purpose of joint locks and takedowns is when the line isn't clear for you to hit the center, use the alternatives to set yourself up to get to the center on your next move."

Suddenly Kirin received a text. "One second, Sifu, let me see who it is."

Looking at the screen, she said, "It's Tobias. He'll be here in fifteen minutes. He's been delayed because of work."

Sifu worked with Kirin for the next fifteen minutes, making sure she had the main understanding in how to train and practice it properly.

Sifu said, "Unfortunately, I'll have to be leaving when Tobias arrives. Make sure you practice what I showed you with him for the next hour or so."

"I will, Sifu."

Sifu said, "Remember, all these functions should come out naturally. You cannot plan a joint lock or a takedown. Let yourself go with the will of the force and retain the target to the center."

Kirin gave Sifu a hug. "Thanks again, Sifu."

Sifu said, "Practice...." Just like that, Sifu made a quick goodbye and left through the front door.

A few seconds passed before Kirin heard her buzzer.

Sounding unsure, Kirin said, "Tobias, is that you?"

Tobias answered, "Kirin, it's me. Let me up before all these crazies mob me."

A minute later, Kirin heard a knock on the door.

Tobias said, "Sorry I'm late. Boss kept me later than I expected."

Kirin said, "No need to apologize ... did you say bye to Sifu on the way up?"

Tobias answered, "I didn't run into Sifu. When did he leave?"

Kirin answered with a perplexed look, "He just left like less than a minute ago.... You didn't run into him?

Tobias shook his head. "No, seriously nothing."

Kirin thought, *Hmm, how does he do that?*

Kirin and Tobias practiced for an hour, working on the drills Sifu had given her.

Tobias said, "All right, I'm done for the night. I'm starving."

Kirin nodded her head and agreed.

She put her hand on her belly as it rumbled. Kirin said, "Well, what do you want to do, go out and eat?"

Tobias didn't answer Kirin. He walked by the window and opened the shade. Immediately the crowd from outside started jeering and cheering, asking for Kirin. He lowered the shade and said, "You got another idea?"

Kirin suggested, "We can order out?"

Tobias thought for a second. "The only thing that delivers around here is pizza. You in the mood for pizza?"

They shook their heads at the same time and simultaneously said, "No!"

Tobias said, "What do you have in your fridge? Maybe we can cook something."

Kirin strolled over to the fridge and frowned upon opening it. "Uh, not sure I can Iron Chef this, but I got a tomato, some onions, garlic, and a jar of kimchi." Then she saw one more item that was still sealed in the back. It was some salsa that she bought for her little brother who often stopped by. It was Kyle's favorite. She reached back to look at it–she had never paid attention to the label before, but it caught her eye. It read "All Profits To Charity," which she found extremely unusual.

Tobias yelled for her, and she snapped out of her trance. He looked at Kirin oddly. "I thought you told me you can cook?"

Kirin did not answer Tobias right away. Instead, she walked to the window and pulled the shade. Again, the crowd erupted, and she closed it immediately. Kirin looked at Tobias and said, "Kinda hard going grocery shopping."

Tobias nodded as she made her point. He continued snooping around. "Do you keep any canned foods in your cabinet?" Kirin pointed over toward several of them. As Tobias looked through her nearly empty cabinet, he finally spotted something.

"Bingo!" he said. "Okay, Kirin, go bring me the tomato, onion, garlic ... and I'm hoping you have some rice?"

Tobias quickly found a chopping board and a knife and started getting to work. He said, "Kirin, make some rice while I start preparing this."

Kirin asked, "What did you find in my cabinet?"

Tobias smiled with confidence. "A can of corned beef."

Kirin made a yuck face, as she wrinkled her nose and stuck out her tongue. "What can you do with that?"

"I got this, trust me," said Tobias.

Kirin watched as Tobias was slicing and dicing like a pro. She was amazed at what she was seeing.

"Holy crap, you can cook?" she said.

"Yes, I can cook.... I worked in my dad's restaurant during my teen years," said Tobias.

After prepping the food for a few more minutes, Tobias said, "Didn't you ever wonder why I smelled like grease all the time?"

Kirin smiled. "I just thought you didn't like to shower."

Tobias tossed a piece of tomato at Kirin, as they both laughed.

Bacon saw the piece fall to the floor and ran over. After further investigation with a sniff and a lick, he left it alone and went right back to his bed.

Kirin asked, "Can you teach me how to cut like that?"

Tobias waved her over and demonstrated to Kirin how he was dicing the onion so fast and so fine. He said, "Now you try it."

Kirin attempted to do the same thing, but it was not ending with the same results.

Kirin frowned and said, "I thought Wing Chun skills were supposed to help you with everything that you do?"

"Here, let me help," said Tobias.

Tobias got behind Kirin and placed his hand gently on her hand with the knife. With his other hand, he reached around her and placed it over the onion.

He then whispered into her ear, "Promise me you won't cut my fingers off."

Kirin smiled as Tobias was guiding her to cut the onion properly.

Tobias encouraged her, saying, "That's it. Go slow first and get the right rhythm.... There you go.... You're a natural."

Kirin was concentrating on her chopping when Tobias got a whiff of her hair. He murmured, "Damn ... your hair smells good."

Kirin got distracted by his comment and accidentally nicked Tobias's finger.

"Oh my god!" she said. "Are you all right?"

Tobias looked at his finger and said, "It's fine; it's fine. It's just a little cut. I'll just wash it up."

Kirin said, "This is your fault."

Tobias looked confused. "Uh, you're the one who cut me, remember?"

Kirin replied, "You don't make a comment about a girl's hair while she's holding an edged weapon."

Tobias looked up and thought about it for a second. "Okay, maybe you're right about the bad timing ... but you still did cut me."

Kirin approached Tobias and looked at his hand. "Here, let me take care of that." Kirin washed Tobias's hand and put some medicine on it. Then she grabbed a bandage and wrapped it up.

"There you go, big baby. It should be better now," said Kirin.

"Thanks."

Thirty minutes passed as Kirin watched Tobias prepare a meal. She was surprised by him yet again—this was a side of him she'd never seen.

"Okay, it's ready. Set the table," said Tobias.

Kirin set the table as Bacon positioned himself underneath. Tobias grabbed the bowls and poured his stew in with the rice.

Kirin smelled the air. "Wow, that really smells good."

Kirin tasted his corned beef stew. "Mmm, this is so simple yet really good. This makes my belly smile."

"I told you it would be good," said Tobias.

"I can't believe this all came from canned corned beef," said Kirin.

The two friends ate and talked the night away. They fell into a companionable rhythm of talking earnestly and teasing each other.

Tobias laughed at Kirin's last comment and then said, "Damn, what time is it?"

Kirin checked her phone. "Umm ... almost 10:00 pm."

Tobias looked upset. "Crap, I gotta take off.... I promised my bro to babysit for him in the morning."

Surprised, Kirin said, "You babysit?"

Tobias said, "Don't look too impressed. It's basically me playing video games with his two kids for several hours."

Tobias grabbed his stuff and headed out of Kirin's front door.

Kirin said, "I know it was practice, but I had fun tonight."

Tobias was putting on his jacket and was halfway out of Kirin's door.

Kirin asked, "Are we practicing again tomorrow?"

Tobias replied, "Wouldn't miss it, but what time are you thinking?"

Kirin replied, "Is afternoon better for you or the evening?"

Tobias thought for a second and then said, "Yeah, why don't we do early evening, like fiveish? I have to head to the burbs in the morning like I said and babysit for my brother. He can sometimes run a little late."

Kirin said, "You're headed back to your place.... You can save another twenty minutes if you just left from here."

Tobias didn't have a response for that and just stood silently. Kirin moved closer to him and said softly, "Why don't you just stay the night?"

Unsure what was happening, Tobias said, "Uh ... okay." He then came back into Kirin's loft and took his jacket off. Kirin poked her head out of the doorway to see if anyone was in the hall, before closing the door.

12:03 am

Ring. Ring. Ring.

Kirin was sound asleep in her bed. In a daze, she stumbled to find her phone by the night stand. *This better be important,* she thought as she finally answered her phone.

Half-asleep, Kirin said in a groggy voice, "Hello?"

A frantic voice on the other side of the phone said, "Kirin, it's your mom."

Kirin's eyes popped open as she sat up. "Mom, Mom ... what's wrong? Hello?"

Suddenly a voice she recognized spoke on the phone, "Everyone has something to lose, don't they, Kirin? You should've taken the fall."

Kirin shouted, "Hello? Hello?" Kirin jumped out of her bed and headed to the living room, where she screamed at Tobias, "Wake up!"

Tobias stumbled as he tried to get up from Kirin's couch. "What's going on? What's wrong?"

Kirin was shouting frantically, "My mom just called, and she's not alone. Someone took the phone from her."

Tobias tried to clear his head. "What do you mean? Isn't she at home?"

Feeling frenzied, Kirin replied, "She's at home. She has to be with Dad and Kyle."

Tobias said, "Call her back up and see what's happening."

Kirin's hand shook as she dialed. She listened to the phone ring endlessly before going to her voicemail.

Kirin said, "Mom, give me a call back immediately."

Still unclear, Tobias said, "I don't get what's going on, Kirin."

In a panic, Kirin explained, "I had a run-in with a mobster about two weeks ago. He said that he wanted me to take a dive, and I didn't. I swear it was his voice on the other line."

Tobias, now fully awake, pieced things together. He said, "Call the police and have them head over to your mom's. Get dressed. It'll take us fifteen minutes by bike to get over to your parents' place."

Kirin dialed frantically in tears and spoke to the operator, telling them to send the police to her parents' location.

Tobias grabbed his stuff and said, "Hurry, Kirin! Just toss on anything." Kirin grabbed a pair of jeans and was ready to go. They rushed downstairs to Tobias's bike.

Tobias said, "Here, you wear the helmet. Let's go."

Kirin held on to Tobias tightly as he disregarded every light to get to the Rises' house. Tobias was speaking to Kirin, "Are you sure it was the same guy?"

Kirin sobbed, "I'm positive. He said the same thing to me in the coffee shop when he left."

Tobias kicked into high gear and sped even faster. "Son of a bitch."

Tobias said, "Try calling again!"

Kirin dialed and said, "Nothing, it's right to voicemail."

Tobias shouted in the wind, "Call your dad's number and Kyle's as well."

Kirin was trying her best not to drop her phone as she got the same results from both attempts.

Kirin cried, "Nothing, Tobias, nothing!"

As quickly as Tobias weaved through the streets of Chicago, it felt like an eternity to get to her house.

Finally Tobias said, "About two minutes away, Kirin."

Kirin knew Tobias was going as fast as possible, but she still screamed, "Hurry, Tobias, please!"

From a distance, Kirin could see her street, but it was different.

"Oh no," she said.

From a hundred yards away, she saw tons of red and blue lights flashing from the circle of squad cars.

"Faster, Tobias!"

Tobias screeched to a halt and pulled as close as he could to Kirin's house. There, she could see at least a dozen squad cars along with many police officers gathered around. To make matters worse, several news crews had gathered in front of her parents' home. Kirin did not wait for Tobias and jumped off the bike once he stopped. She tossed Tobias's helmet to the ground.

Tobias shouted, "Kirin, wait!"

Kirin ran as fast as she could till she reached the outer perimeter that was formed by the officers.

In a panic, Kirin shouted, "What's happened? You have to let me in!"

The officer said, "Ma'am, you can't go in there. It's not safe. Please stay behind the perimeter."

Kirin yelled, "That's my parents' home! I'm the one who called 911. You have to let me in."

Tobias finally caught up to Kirin and said, "What's going on?"

In tears, Kirin said, "They won't let me go in."

Images flashed through her head; everything bad she could have dreamed up ran rampant with her imagination.

Suddenly through all the chaos and confusion, someone shouted, "Hey, it's Kirin Rise!" Reporters everywhere scrambled to find her. Finally one of them recognized Kirin from a distance and motioned to her camera crew. "This is a news story. Let's interview her." Like starving locusts, they all surrounded Kirin with cameras and bombarded her with questions as lights blinded her. The other officers moved in and tried to control the already chaotic situation.

Even with all this confusion, Kirin had a single goal. "Officer, you have to let me through. I have to know if they're safe."

The officer said, "Hey, listen, as soon as I hear something—"

While he was in mid-sentence, Kirin just took off and ran toward the house. She got as close as fifteen feet from the entrance before several officers grabbed her as she struggled.

The news crew went crazy, filming all this and taking pictures. Tobias tried to go through as well, but several officers warned him against such action.

Kirin screamed, "Let me through! Mom! Dad!" She was in pure panic mode as she felt like she was reliving her past.

Suddenly the doors opened, and she stopped struggling and stood still. All eyes were locked on to the first thing that came out of her parents' house.

Finally a man with his hands cuffed and his head lowered came out the front door followed by an officer. Kirin watched, wondering what was going on.

Kirin said, "Let me go," but the two officers held her by her arm as they all watched the events unfold.

Then the same thing happened as another man was led out of the house in handcuffs. One by one, twelve men were escorted out of the house and taken by the police officers.

The area continued to glow in the middle of the night, as more camera crews and then the neighbors gathered around the Rises' house to witness this event. In tears, Kirin said, "Please, I'm begging you. I need to know what happened to my family." An officer several feet in front of Kirin heard her plea and turned around.

Phil came up to the other officers and said, "Let her go. I'll take her."

Kirin had emotionally lost it and did not recognize Phil right away. She jumped when he touched her and screamed, trying to pull away. Phil turned her to face him and stared into her eyes as he said soothingly, "Kirin, it's me, Phil ... Kirin."

Moments later, Kirin finally recognized him. She sobbed, "Phil, what's going on? Please let me in."

Phil said, "Just stand next to me, Kirin. I'm not quite sure what's going on."

Finally, they stood side by side waiting to see who would come out the front door. Kirin grabbed Phil's arm and held it tightly. Then amongst all the chaos and confusion, a paramedic stepped backwards through the door, lifting a stretcher with someone lying on it.

Kirin looked with concern and then said, "Oh no."

A few seconds passed before both paramedics were able to lift the stretcher out of the door. Kirin's stomach lurched as she studied the face frantically.

Kirin said in surprise, stuttering, "It's ... Jab ... Jabbiano."

Phil looked at her and said, "Do you know him?"

Cameras zoomed in to capture images of the man in pain who was handcuffed to the stretcher. Several police officers surrounded him as they brought him to the ambulance.

Phil grabbed his radio and spoke, "Just wait, Kirin. What's going on?"

A voice answered, "Phil, we got two guys on the side of the house who are bound and gagged." Phil was distracted as Kirin seized the opportunity and took off.

Phil yelled, "Kirin, no!"

Kirin moved quickly as she entered her house. Police officers were still moving around inside. Her first sight was disturbing: the house was a mess and spattered with blood.

Kirin screamed, "Mom! Dad!" But, her voice was drowned by all the commotion.

A few officers looked at her and said, "Hey, you can't be in here."

Kirin ignored them and raced up the stairs.

Phil got to the entrance and said, "No, Kirin, just wait." She ignored him, and Phil waved down his fellow officers, indicating he was going to deal with it.

Kirin dashed toward her parents' room and stopped as several officers blocked her path. Phil finally caught up to her.

Phil yelled, "Kirin, stop it! Please just wait."

Kirin screamed, "Let me through! I don't care."

Phil looked at the other two officers who were blocking the room entrance. They nodded it was okay, and Kirin barged through. When she saw her parents on the bed, she froze and started crying with tears running down her face uncontrollably.

The detective looked at her and stopped what he was doing. Kirin darted to the bed and hugged her mom and dad where they were sitting. Kyle, who had been talking to the detective, came from behind and hugged Kirin.

"Oh my god, you're okay ... you're okay," Kirin sobbed as tears streamed down her cheeks.

Phil stood by the bedroom doorway and just watched the flood of emotions. The detective cleared his throat and spoke, "Uhm, ma'am, I need to finish my interview."

Phil walked in and motioned to the detective, who stepped over to speak to Phil for a brief minute.

Phil said, "Give them a couple of minutes. They'll be able to tell you what you need with a clearer head."

Phil and the detective walked out of the room to give the family a moment of privacy.

Kirin sobbed, "Mom, Dad, Kyle, you're all okay?"

"Yes, baby," Kirin's mom said, hugging her tightly.

Kirin's dad and Kyle let go, letting mother and daughter have their moment.

Kyle handed Kirin and his mom some tissue, and they tried to dry away their tears. Kirin asked, "What happened? Tell me what happened."

Kirin's dad looked like he was in disbelief. "I don't even know where to begin. We were all sound asleep, and when I woke up, several masked individuals duct taped your mother and I. I swear it happened in a blink because by the time I opened my mouth, I couldn't move or speak.

Kyle added, "Same thing happened to me, but as soon as I was tied up, they dragged me out of the room."

Kirin listened and saw how upset her dad was. He began to cry as he said, "I thought we were all gonna die." Kirin hugged her dad, trying to comfort him. He stopped and took a deep breath, taking a moment to gather himself.

"I couldn't speak, but I heard some guy tell your mom to call for you," said Kirin's dad. She began crying as Kyle hugged her and their dad continued to speak.

"The next several minutes are kinda a blur. After he hung up the phone, I think he said, "Get them ready.""

Kirin asked softly, "What happened, Dad?"

"I honestly don't know. I can only recall bits and pieces," said Kirin's dad.

Kyle jumped in and said, "They talked about the house losing power, and when that happened, there was a ton of yelling going on."

Kirin frowned. "I don't understand. There was no storm, but I think it was kinda windy."

Kirin's mom said, "I don't think so, but they were just shouting to check downstairs, check downstairs ... over and over again. There was something going on."

Dad said, "I had no idea what was going on, and then we finally heard some guy scream downstairs. I don't know ... a few seconds, a couple of minutes ... we couldn't communicate to one another since they gagged my mouth."

Kirin was more confused than ever about what happened.

Kirin's mom glanced at her dad and could tell he was having trouble speaking. Mom said, "Then I was really afraid because that's the first time I've ever heard gunfire. It came in a barrage, one after another, and then everything was eerily silent until it came again."

Dad added, "The guy who spoke was barking orders to guard the door, and then it was dead silent for a while."

Kyle leaned over and said, "It was dead silent, like they said, but then someone knocked on the door. I can only speak for myself, but I think that was the most tense part. It was like everyone was waiting for something to happen."

I looked at all of them and asked, "And...?"

Dad shook his head. "The next thing I knew, I heard a huge crash as several people were screaming at each other.... What did he keep saying? Yeah, that's it. Don't shoot! Don't shoot! Yeah someone was shouting that." Kirin's dad got up and walked toward the door, which was cracked in half on the floor. He was examining it and asked, "Who the heck destroyed the door?"

Kirin stared at the door briefly and wondered for a moment, *Who or what could've done this?*

Mom said, "Then afterwards, I just heard this scream of pain.... It seemed like it was coming from every direction. I cringed every time I heard a man scream. That moment felt so intense ... it was like death entered, and I honestly thought we were all going to die."

Kirin could see that this was upsetting the entire family, so she said, "Guys, that's enough.... You've told me enough. All that matters is that you guys are safe. That's all that matters."

Dad looked her in the eyes and said, "I don't know what happened then. I'm not sure what else to tell you. But whatever your Mom felt, I felt it also. But just as intense as it was for that time being, it quickly turned quiet. And I don't know how to say this, and it may sound weird, but it was almost peaceful."

Kirin looked confused and wondered how that was possible.

"Moments later a voice I did not recognize–but one that I'll never forget–spoke to me."

Kirin asked, "What did he say?"

Kirin's dad said, "He said, 'Stay calm. You're safe.' I remember once I heard him speak, I felt a sense of comfort. I don't know why, since we were all tied up, but I did feel safe. For some reason I trusted him...."

Both Kirin's mom and Kyle agreed with Dad's explanation. Kirin's mom said, "It's true. I felt that, too. I'm not sure why, but I did."

Kirin asked, "Then what, Dad?"

"He whispered softly only to me," her dad murmured.

"He asked me to shake my head if I could hear him, so I did. Then he told me the police were already on their way. He said they should be here within a few minutes. Then he said,

'I'm going to untie only your hands. I want you to count for a minute; then afterwards, remove your gag and blindfold.' He asked me if I understood, so I nodded again. Then the stranger said, 'I will leave the knife by you so you can untie the rest of your family. Do not leave the room.'"

His face twisted with emotion and his words became muffled as he started to cry. "He apologized to me."

Kirin asked, "Why?"

Kirin's dad replied, "He ... he said he was sorry he couldn't save the dog. Then he left. I did exactly as he told me and freed everyone else as the lights came back on."

Kirin sobbed, "Not Butterscotch."

Kirin cried on her mom's lap as the family tried to deal with what just had happened. Several minutes passed as they tried to comfort one another.

Still trembling from the events, Kirin picked up her cell phone and texted the rest of her brothers who were away.

Knock. Knock.

The detective came back into the room and said, "I hate to interrupt, but would you guys mind if I asked you some more questions?"

Kirin looked at her mom and dad. "Are you guys okay to handle this?"

All three of them nodded.

Kirin looked to her mom and said, "Mom, I'll just be nearby, okay?"

Her mom kissed her one more time and said, "I'll be okay."

Kirin said, "Phil, come with me."

Kirin ran down the stairs, and Phil followed her. As she stepped out of the house, a flood of reporters started shouting out her name from beyond the perimeter.

Kirin ignored them as she turned to Phil and said, "Phil, can you let Tobias through?"

Phil motioned to the other officers that Tobias could come within the perimeter.

Phil asked, "Is there anything else you need?"

Kirin said, "No, Phil, thank you. I owe you one."

Phil looked at her funny and said, "I'm pretty sure you owe me two." As Phil was about to head back upstairs, he said, "Kirin, make sure you guys don't touch a thing."

Tobias got up to the front door and entered the house. There, Kirin spent the next several minutes explaining to him what had happened.

At last, Kirin said, "Who do you think could've saved my parents and my brother?" Both Tobias and Kirin thought for several seconds and then looked at each other. "Sifu?"

Frowning slightly, Tobias said, "It can't be Sifu. Can it?"

Kirin asked, "Why?"

Tobias said, "Because if it was him, none of those guys would be alive."

Kirin thought about that and said, "You do have a point."

Kirin said, "Tobias, call Sifu's restaurant."

Tobias pulled out his phone and dialed. "Uh, technically, it's not a restaurant."

Kirin glared at him. "Now is not the time to argue semantics. Just call."

Ring. Ring. Ring.

Suddenly a voice popped up. "Lance speaking, can I help you?"

Tobias replied, "Lance, it's Tobias. Can I ask you something?"

Lance said, "Sure, make it quick, though. I'm busy."

Staring at Kirin, Tobias asked, "Lance, is Sifu there?"

Lance replied, "Yup, he's here."

Tobias asked, "Has he been there all night?"

Lance replied, "Yeah, all night … it's been pretty packed, more so than usual."

Listening in on the conversation, Kirin punched Tobias on the shoulder. "Ask Lance if you could speak with Sifu," she whispered.

Tobias grinned and whispered to Kirin, "Good idea."

Tobias said, "Lance, do you mind if I talk to Sifu for just a second?"

Lance said, "Sure, he's right here."

On the other side of the phone, Sifu said, "Hey, Tobias, what's up?"

Caught off guard, Tobias replied, "Oh, Sifu, uh ... I just wanted to know if there's any more soup left if Kirin and I happen to stop by."

Sifu took several seconds and said, "I could save you guys two bowls."

Kirin shook her head and motioned to Tobias to hang up.

Tobias said, "Uh, Kirin just said she's not feeling well. Maybe another time."

Sifu said, "Okay, no problem. I gotta go."

Tobias hung up the phone and stared at Kirin.

Several Days Later

On Sunday morning, Thorne sat at the table across from Fawn. Thorne rubbed his eyes, exhausted from the long, trying weekend.

Thorne spoke in the air, "Linda, please bring me my coffee."

Linda responded, "It'll be at least several minutes, Mr. Thorne. The special delivery of your coffee is late."

Thorne thought, *For a Sunday, this sure as hell feels like a Monday.* Aloud, he said, "That's fine, Linda. Just bring it to me once it arrives."

Linda replies back, "Of course, sir."

Thorne looked over to Fawn, who was busy on his pad. "How bad are the numbers, Fawn?"

Not looking up, Fawn said, "At the start, before she announced she was gonna forfeit her match, we were breaking record numbers in ratings. But once word got out, boss, it sank like a rock."

Thorne asked, "Other than the obvious that she wasn't fighting, what happened?"

Fawn replied, "Numbers show people were more concerned with what happened to her and her family. They tuned in to the news, instead of the fights."

Thorne asked, "How bad a hit does our analyst think we're gonna take from this?"

Fawn replied, "They won't know the real numbers for several days, but our stock is expected to drop upon opening bell Monday morning."

Thorne responded, "Fawn, I thought we had a tight leash on these mobsters, especially Jabbiano."

Fawn responded, "We do, and Justice made sure he wouldn't forget our last encounter."

Thorne shook his head. "Then how did this happen?" He smashed his hand on his table, upset with the weekend's affairs.

Fawn nervously answered, "We just found out that he created a dummy corporation, which kept his main funds secret from our detection until now. He had been betting heavily against Kirin all this time and had been losing millions. The last match was against his very own fighter. He went all in. After Kirin kicked his fighter's ass, it practically wiped him out."

Thorne was upset with this news. "The millions that fool lost will look like nothing compared to how much this company will stand to lose since he decided to go rogue."

Thorne ground his teeth when Fawn didn't reply. Finally, Thorne asked, "Well, what state is she in?"

Fawn responded, "I've sent emails, phone calls, and had some of our representatives try to contact her face to face, but she's refused all of our actions."

Thorne responded, "Damn bitch!"

Fawn replied, "Sir, what did you expect? She thinks we're tied into what happened."

Thorne laughed. "The irony of it ... for once, we're actually not involved in this matter." Thorne raised his hands and stared up at the ceiling.

With a sigh, Thorne stood up and said, "She's got two weeks to recover from this till her next match."

Fawn said, "I hate to be the bearer of bad news, but there's a possibility she may not fight any more. From all accounts, this has really shaken her up."

Thorne said, "What's her current record?"

Fawn replied, "Well, after forfeiting her match yesterday, she's seven and one, sir."

"Give me the worst case scenario."

Fawn answered, "You mean if she doesn't come back?"

Thorne shouted, "No, I refuse to allow that to happen! What I meant is, if she forfeits her remaining four matches, her record would be seven and five, right?"

"Yes, sir," said Fawn.

"Seven and five should be enough to qualify her for the DOME, right?"

"It should be enough for her to squeak by. Keep in mind she got a good amount of style points from all of her seven previous matches," said Fawn.

Thorne started seeing some possibilities. "You're right about that, Fawn. We have to prepare now and make sure even if she doesn't get back into the league fights, we draw her into the DOME somehow."

Fawn remained silent. Nothing on his face revealed any hint of his thoughts, just as Thorne liked it.

Thorne said, "Fawn, I want you to go for now, but send Justice in."

Moments passed as Justice entered into Thorne's office. He did not speak a word.

Thorne watched the city, keeping his back toward Justice as he said, "I need for you to pay a visit...."

Later That Evening

Kirin was at her parents' home watching TV when the screen flickered and a voice said, "We interrupt this programming for a special news announcement." Kirin watched in silence as the reporter continued, "We have just gotten word that famous mobster Frank Jabbiano who is currently in custody and has been staying at North-Eastern Hospital was found just moments ago, dead! It appears he has killed himself...."

Kirin exchanged shocked glances with her parents as they watched the news unfold.

> *"Life can be unpredictable and change in the blink of an eye. That is why one needs to learn the difference between want, need, and appreciate. If you spend more time appreciating what you have, you'll come to realize, the things that you want, you don't really need." –Sifu*

Short Stories #10–Kirin's P.O.V.

The Chance of Winning–1 year 349 days

It was a jam-packed class. About twelve people were there for a Saturday morning Wing Chun workout. While most schools would consider that a low showing, it was unusual for our school to post double digits in attendance. We had been drilling punches for the entire class, trying to get the motions to flow smoothly. Tobias was working with the beginners, while a handful of us concentrated on the eight punch drill, and the rest dealt with blocking the punch.

I overheard Sifu giving instructions regarding the punch block drill. "Remember when working with your partner and trying to execute the technique, aim to the target. Do you understand?"

I raised my hand and asked, "Sifu, can you come over here and watch how I do it?"

Sifu allowed me to demonstrate several times as I randomly choose several blocks while Doc continued to punch at me.

Sifu said, "Not bad, but you weren't aiming at the target."

I frowned. "I thought I was aiming at Doc's center."

Sifu said, "Do it again."

I looked at Doc and asked him to punch again while I performed my blocks. Suddenly, Sifu said, "Stop right there."

I had just blocked his punch with my tan sau and held the position. Sifu looked at Doc and moved his hand to the side. As that happened, my tan sau drifted and followed his punch toward the side, which was away from his center line.

Sifu said, "Do you see that, Kirin? If your aim was the target, your hand would not chase his punch. Remember, always deal with the main source."

I was bummed. I thought I had been doing it correctly. Sifu patted me on the back and said, "More practice."

Class was interrupted as a man in a seemingly expensive suit came walking in. At first, I thought it was a challenge match, since we were one of the few schools that hadn't been shut down. The class had gotten so accustomed to strangers entering the school that he was somewhat ignored.

The man shouted, "Who's the owner of this school?"

Sifu raised his hands and greeted the gentleman. The men exchanged friendly greetings as Sifu directed to him to the back office.

As Sifu followed the man, he said, "Tobias, check on everyone and continue to practice." Tobias confirmed and waved everyone to ignore the happenings and concentrate on what they were doing.

When a few stared at the men passing by, Tobias said, "Everyone, continue practicing."

I could tell the core from the school was wondering what was going on.

I asked Doc, "Do you know who that is?"

Doc nodded and said, "Yeah, I do. Word on the street is that the schools they haven't been able to knock out of business, they've been offering hefty sums and buying them out."

Ken, Ryan, and Robert were listening and were as taken aback as I was.

Tobias swung around and said, "Guys, what's with the chit chat? You're supposed to be practicing."

I replied, "We can't, Tobias. Doc just told us who that guy was that Sifu's talking to."

I could tell from Tobias's face that he already knew the man in the back room.

I asked, "There's more, isn't there, Tobias?"

Tobias hesitated and looked around, though he spoke only with us.

Tobias said, "Look, guys, I shouldn't be telling you this, but Simo lost her job a month ago."

I replied, "I didn't know that."

Tobias shook his head. "It's not something Sifu would say."

Robert asked, "How did you know about it?"

Tobias said, "I was last to leave class several weeks ago, and I saw Simo come in crying. Sifu took her to the back room, and when he came out, I asked him what was wrong."

Ken said, "He told you she lost her job."

Tobias confirmed, "You know Sifu doesn't lie, so when I asked him, he told me what had happened."

As I looked around, I saw we all wore matching worried expressions. Almost as one, we glanced at the back room.

Ken said, "Man, you'd think Sifu would have a hundred students with his skill and knowledge."

Ryan said, "Tell me about it, and he charges way less then those UFMF schools."

Danny stepped in and said, "Sorry, I was listening to the entire conversation. I know this sounds bad, but we're all being selfish."

Everyone stared at Danny.

Danny said, "Don't get me wrong. I don't want Sifu to sell the school either, but he's got three mouths to feed. And, let's face it, he could be making a ton of cash if he joined the UFMF franchises. They advertise heavily once you join, and he'd finally be able to pack in the school on a regular basis."

Ryan said sadly, "And don't forget how bad the economy is now. It'll be tough for Simo to find another job."

Big T said, "I wouldn't hold it against Sifu if he sold out. I can't say I wouldn't do the same thing."

Danny replied, "Big T, you'd sell out for a sandwich."

Big T replied, "A six-inch or a foot-long sandwich?"

I snickered at Big T's joke but was more concerned about Sifu's status. "How's Sifu gonna take care of everyone? He can't possibly make that much money from the school."

Tobias said, "Well, it hurts that Simo lost her job, but Sifu does have his other job."

We all looked at one another and stared at Tobias till he gave us an answer.

Ken said, "Sifu has a second job?"

Tobias said, "Yeah, he works night shift. He does some kind of tech support."

I was surprised and said, "Really? I never knew that."

Robert said, "I thought they outsourced all those kinds of jobs."

Tobias replied, "As far as I know, he's been working at the same place for years. Didn't you guys know that?"

Ken said, "I never knew that. How come you never mentioned it before?"

Tobias said, "You never asked."

His joke fell flat as we heard some noise in the back office.

Tobias said, "Everyone, get back to practice."

We all scrambled back to our positions and continued the drill.

Sifu was smiling and talking to the gentleman as he walked him to the front door. I was trying my best to practice, but I ended up blatantly staring at what was unfolding. I saw him pat the man on the back and shake his hand. I thought, *Oh no ... he wouldn't sell, would he?*

Sifu said, "Thank you for coming."

When I saw the other man's smile, I felt my heart sink. I knew I was being selfish, but I loved how the school was run. Doc tapped my arm and said, "Kirin, stop it. Come back here and practice."

The gentleman left, and Sifu walked back into the room. Sifu said, "Okay, sorry about that. Do you guys have any questions on the drill?"

The class stood silently and did not respond, but I was shaking, ready to erupt and ask him what was going to happen.

And then it happened.

I just couldn't help myself. I shouted, "Sifu, you can't sell the school! I know it's selfish of me to ask, but please don't sell it."

I felt the daggers of everyone staring at me. I bit my lip, realizing what I had just done.

Sifu laughed. "Kirin ... you should know me better than that. What have I always told you about teaching the art?"

I didn't answer as I thought, *I don't know. I don't recall you telling me anything about it.*

Tobias stepped in and said, "Uhm, Sifu has always said never teach the art for money."

Sifu smiled. "Thank you, Tobias."

Ryan said, "I was banking on teaching Wing Chun as my future profession."

Sifu laughed. "You can still teach Wing Chun and charge people for it, Ryan, but you're gonna be eating from those ten-cent ramen packets."

Ryan frowned and muttered, "Dammit, I might need a plan B."

Sifu said, "Ah, speaking of plan B...."

Sifu pulled out a lottery ticket. "Simo's been playing this every week, and I have a feeling my luck will change."

> *"When you sellout, the gain is so little compared to what you lose—your integrity." –Sifu*

The Buzz Bars—2 years 193 days

The music was blasting, making it extremely difficult to hold a conversation without shouting at the top of your lungs. The place was packed to capacity for such an event. I was never a fan of loud and crowded spaces, but I wanted to support Sage for his video game tournament. Sage had made it to the finale, which was going to begin in about ten minutes.

I asked Gwen, "Where's Sage?"

Gwen said, "He's getting interviewed by the local TV stations." Gwen pointed toward his direction.

I said, "I never realized how big these events are."

Gwen replied, "This is nothing. This is only local. The regional and national events are huge."

Buzz bars were your local teenager hangout spots. In the world of hi-tech gadgetry, in order for information to continue to flow, one needed power. So, buzz bars opened up across the country as charging stations where teens could gather. They were a teenager's dream: a place to hang out, get something to eat, and wirelessly charge everything that you needed at a small price. Buzz bars were this century's malls.

Gwen saw my unease. "Relax, Kirin, these places aren't so bad."

I looked around and tried to sit comfortably. "I know. I'm just not a fan of the people around here." Feeling somewhat self-conscious, I combed my hair over my face.

Gwen said, "How so?"

I replied, "Gwen, most of these people here are bangers."

Gwen looked around to confirm and said, "Yeah, I know, but it should be safe in here."

The tournament centered around one of the most popular games in the country. *King of the Kage* was a virtual fighting game. It seemed everything always revolved around fighting– the UFMF had its claws into everything. They wanted to make sure they were grooming everyone from an early age to get involved in their event one way or another.

While I wasn't an early fan of the game when I first saw Sage play it, I had to admit, *King of the Kage* was a cool idea. A virtual helmet created an imaginary world for you and your opponent to battle on, while scanners mimicked your every motion and simulated it in the game. Sensors registered through the helmet gave you the sensation of getting hit, without really getting hit.

Gwen observed. "You're not much of a gamer, are you, Kirin?"

I asked her, "Does solitaire count?"

She started laughing. "No ... you should try it. With all your Saturday Gung Fu classes, I'm sure you'd pick up on the game quickly."

I nodded my head, but deep down I didn't understand investing so much time at virtual fighting, when I could practice it in real life and get real skill. The sad fact was that since I first played the game of chi sao, I couldn't find anything that was more mentally and physically stimulating.

Sage finally came over and said, "Isn't this great?"

I smiled at him. "This is awesome. Go kick some butt."

Sage looked surprised, and said, "Uh … cool, thanks, Kirin."

Both Gwen and I cheered him on as they started prepping him for the start of the battle.

The owner of the bar said, "This fight is sponsored by the UFMF, which encourages you all to look for a career in fighting."

I rolled my eyes at the blatant advertising.

He continued, "Are you all ready for the most electrifying match of the night? I can't hear you!"

The room shook with the growing excitement, and Gwen and I clapped along like lemmings.

The owner said, "In this corner, with an overall record for this year of thirty-three and four, we have Sage, the Demonic Demon, and his opponent, with a record of thirty-one and six, Thomas the Silencer! Now I've explained to both of you that this is the best three out of five. Winner gets to go to the regionals. I want a fair fight and good sportsmanship. Now, go shake hands."

For the next twenty minutes, we watched Sage and Thomas in a heated battle. A giant screen featured their every move, as insane combos were being chained, one after another. The crowd went wild as Sage pulled off a killer move in the very end and won. I was so happy for him.

The owner said, "The winner of *King of the Kage*, Sage!"

Sage was ecstatic, as he jumped up and down to celebrate.

I said, "Congrats, Sage! You were incredible."

Gwen hugged him and said, "Yeah, for once, I gotta agree. Right now, you're cool."

Sage blushed and held his trophy up as the crowd cheered again. After about an hour of celebrating, we decided to head home and call it a night.

Sage said, "Guys, let's walk home. The weather's so awesome, and I'm feeling like a million bucks!"

Gwen and I looked at each other and nodded. "Okay, *King of the Kage!*"

Sage said smugly, "I like the sound of that."

Gwen punched Sage in the arm. "Don't let it go to your head."

Several minutes passed, and we had another five minutes before we reached our neighborhood.

"So, Sage, when is the regional tournament?" I asked.

"Oh, it's a good two weeks away. Plenty of time for me to practice," he said.

"Hey, *King of the Kage!*" a voice shouted from behind. We all turned to find the source.

I recognized that it was Sage's opponent from the tournament, with two of his friends accompanying him.

Sage waved naively at him and said, "Hey, what's up, Thomas? Good game." He extended his hand out to shake, but Thomas did not reciprocate.

Thomas responded, "Shut up."

As they headed closer, I thought, *I have a bad feeling about this.*

Thomas said angrily, "Listen, jerk, you took away my chance at regionals."

Sage said, "Hey, it was a good match, but I won fair and square."

"I hate to disappoint you, but you won't be able to make it to regionals."

Sage looked confused. "What do you mean?"

Thomas said, "The rules say, if the winner can't make it to regionals, the runner up in the tournament can go."

"Why wouldn't I go?"

Thomas looked at his friends and chuckled. "Oh, it's because you're gonna have an accident." His friends started to laugh.

Sage looked back at us, clearly confused.

Thomas said, "You see, my friends and I are gonna beat you to a pulp."

Thomas's friend said, "We're gonna kick your ass in real life, Poindexter." Thomas turned his back slightly as if he were gonna walk away.

I screamed, "Sage, watch out!"

But it was too late. He threw a sucker punch, as Sage flew back to the ground.

Thomas said, "Virtual fighting is fun, but nothing's more entertaining than kicking real ass!"

Sage was on the ground terrified, gathering his senses–he was no fighter. When he reached up and felt the blood coming out of his nose, he started shaking in panic.

Thomas pointed and laughed. "Look at the *King of the Kage*.

They were distracted just enough as I said quietly, "Gwen, get ready."

Gwen looked up. "For what?"

I smiled and pushed Gwen from behind, sending her wheelchair straight toward all three guys.

"Kirin!" screamed Gwen.

All three guys were caught off guard as Gwen ran into them, making her the center of attention.

Perfect, I thought.

I moved in quickly right behind Gwen. I planned on picking them apart one at a time.

I kept telling myself, *The leader gets it worst. The leader gets it worst.* I charged in and timed it perfectly. As Gwen's wheelchair ran into Thomas, he leaned forward and came down. I punched him straight in the face as he flew backwards.

Both his friends were in shock, and I made sure they knew how Thomas felt.

Pak punch the guy on the right; lop chop the guy on the left. I was in a rush because this was the first time that I had ever put my Wing Chun to the test. Just like Sifu said: go in straight and show no fear. All three were caught by surprise.

Thomas was getting back up, as I hopped over Gwen to meet him. He stood there still stunned from the punch as I kicked him right in the nuts. He dropped to the ground, and the rush of emotions were kicking in. I never wanted that helpless feeling ever again. I grabbed him by the back of his shirt as he struggled to get up.

I shouted, "Now apologize to Sage."

Gasping in pain, Thomas said, "I'm sorry.... I'm sorry."

I looked him directly in the eye. "If you ever threaten my friend Sage again...."

He cowered and said, "I promise, I won't.... I won't."

"Get out of here and take your friends with you," I said.

Thomas struggled to move as he and his friends ran away into the night.

I extended my hand to Sage.

Sage looked at me. "Thanks, Kirin. Thanks for saving my butt."

"You don't have to thank me." I looked at him, watching as blood continued to drip down his nose.

"Here's some tissue; just keep pinching it," I told Sage.

Gwen had her arms crossed over her chest, looking upset.

"What's wrong, Gwen?" I said.

Gwen looked at me with disbelief. "What's wrong? Seriously, you're asking me what's wrong? You just used me as human bait. Your best friend," she said angrily.

"Oh, come on now, you're exaggerating. Bait is when you know something is gonna die. I would say, I used you more for distraction. Besides, it's total Wing Chun strategy, and technically you were in the safest position," I replied.

Gwen looked confused and said, "How is that the safest position?"

"Think about it, the closer you are to danger the safer you are from harm," I replied.

"I don't get it," as Gwen shook her head in frustration.

Sage said, "Are you quoting...."

"Uh, not now Sage," I said. "You see, let me give you an example—"

"I don't care! That's it, I'm not talking to you till you apologize," said Gwen.

"Come on, Gwen. I'm sorry," I giggled slightly.

"This is how you repay me for saving your butt back in grade school," pouted Gwen. She started moving ahead of us, still upset at what had happened.

I tended to Sage's wound, deciding to deal with Gwen's feelings later. Sage smiled and tried to cover his laughter.

Family Lunch–1 year 34 days

Robert was complaining as he normally does. "I'm telling you, we should pick a different location to eat." He walked behind the pack like a little kid sulking.

Ryan got behind Ken and placed his hand on his shoulder. "It's only fair that it's Ken's turn to pick the place to eat."

Ken said, "Guys, trust me on this," in his best car-salesman voice.

Robert rolled his eyes. "Like your last restaurant that served peanut butter and jelly?"

Ken looked at Robert. "Seriously, you didn't think that was the best peanut butter and jelly you've ever had?"

Robert said, "Dude it's peanut butter and jelly, for Christ's sakes. Only in America will you find people who would pay for peanut butter and jelly and somehow justify it. Oh and by the way Ken, I refuse to ever eat at the cereal joint you mentioned, even if it is your turn."

The guys were busy goofing off like they normally do, as I felt the drain from the lack of sleep.

Big T turned around, noticing that I stood behind him, covered in his shadow.

Big T asked, "What's wrong, lil sista? You look tired."

"I haven't been getting a good night's sleep lately, Big T," I tried to say as I yawned. Suddenly I realized I forgot something.

"Crap!" I started patting myself down, hoping I was wrong.

Doc turned around and asked, "What's wrong, Kirin?"

"I left my phone at the school. Go ahead, and I'll catch up," I replied. I began running back as the rest of the guys went ahead of me.

Ten minutes later, I stood in the front of Sifu's school and knocked on the door, hoping he was still there. I heard a voice from a distance yell, "Coming, coming...."

Relieved, I called, "Hey, Sifu, can I come in? I left my cell phone in the school."

Sifu smiled and said, "Come in, Kirin."

I walked in and saw that Simo and the kids were there. She had a picnic blanket laid out on the floor and was preparing a meal for everyone.

Hana saw me and said, "Hey, Kirin, did you come by to join us for lunch?"

I answered, "Oh no, Hana, I don't want to disturb you. I'm just here for my phone. I was gonna go to lunch with the rest of the guys."

Hana asked Simo, "Mom, can Kirin join us for lunch?"

Simo said, "Kirin, we have more than enough food. Come join us, please."

Hanging out with Sifu and his family is better than eating at another one of Ken's favorite places, I thought.

"Okay, let me just text the guys I'm not gonna join them," I said with a smile.

Sifu sat down and told me to relax and do the same. Hana was busy helping her mom as the two boys became impatient.

Sifu said sternly, "Akira, Hideo, sit still. Lunch is almost ready." The boys seemed to ignore their father's request and continued to goof around. It was rare for me to see this, but Sifu seemed frustrated.

Hana came by and said to her father, "Dad, do your magic trick. That always settles them down."

Sifu looked at Hana and replied, "Ah, yes, that's a good idea." Sifu got up and went to the back office. Moments later, he popped back into the room holding something in his hands. I wasn't quite sure what it was right away, but the two boys immediately became obedient and sat perfectly still. In unison, both Hideo and Akira said to each other, "Quiet, Dad's gonna do magic."

Sifu sat down and unveiled a deck of cards. He rolled up his sleeves to reveal that there was nothing there. For the next several minutes, the boys and I were mesmerized as he would take several cards from the deck and make them disappear and reappear out of thin air. I watch intently, but I could not see from even a close distance how he was doing it. I looked at Sifu and said, "Wow, that was incredible. I never knew that you did magic?"

Sifu said humbly, "Only the cards, that's the only trick I know."

"If that's the only trick you know, that's incredible," I said.

"It is?" replied Sifu.

Hideo said, "Dad, do your best trick."

Akira clapped his hands excitedly. "Yes, Dad, please, please!"

Sifu smiled and showed an empty hand again as a deck of cards appeared out of nowhere. He then began bouncing the cards off the floor one by one. I shook my head, again unsure how we was doing it. The boys continued to clap in excitement. I had never even realized cards could bounce.

Then Akira said, "The clock, Dad, the clock," as he pointed toward it. Sifu looked at the clock, which was a good twenty feet away from where we all sat. He stood up and began throwing the cards one after the other. He hit the clock with dead accuracy every time.

I leaned over to Sifu and said, "You never cease to amaze me."

Akira looked at me and said, "You should see him cut carrots with the card!" I wasn't sure if Akira was joking or not, so I gave him a strange look.

Sifu smiled and said, "Oh, I think the food's ready."

Hana came by and began putting bowls of soup in front of everyone. "Lunch is served! Everyone, get ready."

Simo said, "It tastes a lot better fresh, but I had to bring it from home."

I asked Simo, "Did you make it yourself?"

Sifu jumped in, "Oh, you've never had Simo's famous ramen, have you? It's delicious."

I got excited when Sifu was selling it as famous and delicious. Then I smelled it and said, "Wow, it *smells* delicious."

Sifu said, "Simo's dad is a famous ramen chef in Japan. He has his own shop that people flock to. Isn't that right, honey?"

Simo smiled appreciatively at the comment. "Yes, that's true…. Dad showed me how to make the noodles. He had me practicing it all the time."

Simo then said in Japanese, "Tabe te, kudasai."

Hana kindly translated for her mom, whispering to me, "Kirin, that means, 'please eat'." I looked at the twins who were usually so rambunctious, but they sat still, ready to eat their mom's food.

Finally, I held the soup in my hands and felt the heat. I knew the broth told the truth as that was the first thing I tasted. I took a quick sip, savoring the moment, before I said, "Oh my gosh, this is absolutely incredible."

Slurp.

"Excuse me," I said.

Hana laughed. "Kirin, in Japan, it's customary to slurp your noodles."

"Oh, I didn't know that." I smiled and slurped again, enjoying the soup.

Sifu and Simo both smiled during the fairly quiet conversation with tons of slurping. Fifteen minutes passed as we all enjoyed Simo's soup; it was hard to believe that food could be so memorable. Once the twins were no longer occupied by it, they began to revert to their playful state. Simo knew the cure and said, "Hon, I'm gonna take the kids to the park. Do you mind if you clean up?"

Sifu smiled and said, "I'll clean up. I'll meet you there in a bit."

I said, "Sifu, I'll help you clean up. That's the least I can do."

Hana said, "Don't take long, okay, Daddy?"

"I won't, pumpkin," said Sifu.

Hana came by and said, "I'll see you next time, okay, Kirin." Then she hugged me and whispered into my ear, "Make sure you get enough sleep, Kirin."

I gave her half a smile and nodded. I thought, *She's as observant as Sifu.*

Sifu kissed Simo and the kids goodbye as they left through the door.

I began helping with the clean up as Sifu said, "Hana looks up to you, Kirin. You know that?"

"I like Hana a lot. It's weird, but we bonded the moment we first met."

Sifu laughed. "Matching energies, Kirin ... that's because you two are exactly alike. I swear you're the older version of Hana."

I smiled at the thought and said, "If that's the case, how come the older version of Hana has worse Wing Chun?"

Sifu and I both laughed at the joke, or so I thought it was.

I said, "Here, let me finish the rest of the clean up, Sifu."

Sifu said, "Don't worry about that; besides, I wanted to talk to you."

I gave Sifu a curious look and asked him, "What is it, Sifu?"

Sifu didn't hesitate. "I know something's troubling you, Kirin."

"It's nothing, Sifu," I looked away and did my best to lie to him.

Sifu didn't say a word at first, but then.... "Kirin, I don't need to ask to see someone who has suffered a great loss."

I turned around quickly with watery eyes. "You can tell that?"

Sifu nodded.

I said, "It's the nightmares, Sifu. I get them almost every night, and I can't seem to let it go." I stared at the ground, but as the images began to appear in my head as I closed my eyes, trying to force them out.

Sifu touched my shoulder and spoke softly. "I know, Kirin.... I know this is difficult for you to understand at this age or ... the truth is, any age. Often times when people go through something so tragic, we look for a reason to understand or somehow justify how things could've happened."

I stared at Sifu, wanting to tell him more. The pain of the loss was great, but the most haunting factor was that I didn't do anything to stop it. People had told me that I was a child, that there was nothing that I could've done, but I couldn't accept that, nor did I believe it.

Sifu said, "I'd like to tell you in time that it'll get better. But, that's not always the case. That sometimes that wound will remain fresh with you forever. So, what I'm trying to tell you is that you'll have to learn how to detach and control your focus."

I looked at him and said, "I don't understand what that means, Sifu.... Does that mean I shouldn't care?"

Sifu said, "Detachment isn't about not caring, Kirin. It's ... how do you say ... learning to let go."

I looked at him with frustration and sadness. "I just can't make sense of why all this had to happen. Don't get me wrong, Sifu. It's not a case of me saying, why me? The truth is, what pains me is ... I see the suffering everyday, and I have no answer for it, and I continue to ask myself...." I paused. I couldn't complete what I wanted to say as I looked away. I waited in silence for a moment before I said softly, "I don't know what to do, Sifu. I know that the last year of training has done more for me than anything else ... but I still feel so lost."

Sifu looked at me with thoughtful eyes. "You know the art is made of the physical, mental, and spiritual. Normally, I don't speak of the spiritual side so often. That's because most people are afraid when I discuss it."

I looked at him. "Why, Sifu?"

"Because when they hear spirituality, they think I'm talking religion, when it has nothing to do with that," said Sifu.

Sifu exhaled deeply and patted me on the shoulder. He said, "Kirin, everything I know, everything I learned is from Wing Chun. It has and will always serve me well. Trust in it, and it will do the same for you. I tell you this ... people think martial arts is all about fighting, but it is so much more. Martial arts has taught me everything.

"You see, people need answers, and we look to greater powers to make sense of it, to justify in our minds that there's some rhyme and reason. In a way, it's to deal with the pain. For me, the way I see it, there is no beginning or end, for when that happens, the universe as we know it would be over."

I asked, "Can you explain, Sifu? I'm don't quite understand."

"Kirin, I look at the balance of things, and I see that everyone is equal. So, if you take two people born at the same time, one suffers and the other one lives in the lap of luxury; imagine if the universe only allowed one shot at this.... To me, I don't see how that would be fair; it doesn't make sense. It lacks the overall balance."

I stared at him silently, still searching for peace.

Sifu looked at me and then squeezed my arm. "It's difficult to see in the beginning, but there is a bigger picture. We think only in terms of flesh and blood, but the way I see it, we are ...

energy–an energy that is part of the universe around us. Eventually when we figure that out, we become part of it." Sifu paused and said, "Hmm ... I think I'm talking about something that might be beyond your understanding."

I thought about Sifu's words and tried desperately to make sense of it.

Sifu said, "For now, let's try to deal with those nightmares you're having ... okay?"

I nodded my head.

"Do you trust me, Kirin?"

I didn't reply, but I answered him with only my eyes.

"I think you need to learn how to control your focus. You need to learn how to quiet the mind, Kirin. Let me explain to you the process first, and then I'm gonna show you how to do it, okay?

"There are four stages of mental development: empty the mind, quiet it, sinking, and softness. The truth is, I've already been showing you how to do it."

I stared at him with a confused look.

"You said the training has helped you.... That statement alone tells me that you've been practicing the first form on your own."

I nodded my head to confirm as he really caught my attention.

"Now, it doesn't necessarily have to be practicing the first form. It could be something like meditating, or anything that allows you to focus on one thing. It could be a repetitive action, like mopping the floor for thirty minutes and just focusing on that alone. You see, to empty the mind, you need a single thought, the simplest thought. You have to kick out all the things that are racing in your head, and have that singular focus.... Do you understand?"

I said, "I do. That makes sense, Sifu."

Sifu whispered and said, "Once you have emptied the mind, you'll notice that it becomes quiet. Just like it is now in the school. Since the kids left, it's really quiet. Imagine if I left you ... and you were in the school by yourself, what sound would you hear, if any?"

I thought for a second, *I could never imagine you leaving, Sifu.*

Sifu continued, "Thus, the empty room leads to a quiet mind, a steadiness and balance that we all seek. The quiet mind allows you to do things, to see things, and heightens your level of awareness. Am I making sense to you so far?"

"You are, Sifu," I replied.

"Good, once the mind is quiet, you have the ability to sink. Sinking is the ability to control your emotions, so that you don't react like a wild animal. Now don't misunderstand this; you'll still get mad, sad, upset, and have all the natural reactions to the world around you. But, the difference is, you'll be able to sink or pull back and control your emotions.

"Finally, after sinking is softness. The mind and body are linked as one; a tight mind leads to a rigid body. But with the ability to empty the mind, it becomes soft, and by that I mean that thought doesn't distract the mind from moving naturally. So the body in turn doesn't become tight.

"Now you're wondering how this can possibly help you," said Sifu.

"Yes," I simply said.

"I want you to breathe with me, Kirin. It's as simple as that: breathe with me. Let's count up to ten," said Sifu.

"Okay."

"When I count, don't concentrate on anything other than your own breath. Focus on one thing; focus on the sound of your own breath, and take your time inhaling and exhaling," said Sifu. "It's not a race, but learn to listen to your own breath."

For the next minute, we did something so natural in human nature: breathing. I didn't understand the point of this little exercise, but I trusted Sifu and did as he instructed. It was an effort in the beginning to just focus on my own breath. But by the fourth breath, I was feeling exactly what Sifu was talking about. While I thought I could hear him count, it eventually got lost in the focus of my breathing. I thought, *In and out, nice and slow.* After my tenth breath, I exhaled and opened my eyes. I stared at Sifu with a smile. I wasn't sure why, but I felt a lot better.

Sifu said, "How do you feel?"

"I don't know why or how exactly to describe it ... but yet ... I feel different. I feel a lot better," I said.

"Did you hear the traffic outside or the clock ticking on the wall? Or, did you even hear me continue to count?" he asked.

"I heard nothing ... nothing at all, just dead silence," I replied.

"A single thought can calm the mind. You must learn to continue to train your mind, Kirin." Sifu smiled.

His words were always comforting, even from the first day I met him. I said nothing, smiled, and gave him a hug. "Thanks, Sifu," I said.

> *"While there is always and answer, sometimes it's best to leave it unknown." —Sifu*

Sifu's Journey Entry #10–Getting the Recipe Right

Fall 2030

Lance put his spoon down and then grabbed a napkin. He took his time savoring the moment as he wiped his beard clean, smiling at Sifu. He said, "Mmm, that's really good."

Sifu looked somewhat disappointed at Lance's response. "Hmm, we need to work on this some more. So far, everyone who has tasted it has said the same thing, that the soup is really good."

Lance looked puzzled. "Isn't that a good thing, Sifu?"

Sifu replied, "Life is short, Lance. We don't want to spend our lives just being average."

Lance thought about Sifu's comment and then shook his head. "Well, this is far from average, don't you think, Sifu?"

Sifu moved toward the stove and turned it off. He thought, *I remember when it was incredible.* A moment later, he replied to Lance, "That's enough work today on the soup. For now, we need to get you to work on your stance."

Lance hesitated for a second and said, "Sifu, don't get me wrong, I appreciate everything you've done for me ... you've gone above and beyond what any human being should do for a stranger, but I don't see how working on my stance is gonna help me further."

Sifu turned toward Lance and said sternly, "I ask you to take a leap of faith."

Lance responded, "I owe you that at least."

Sifu asked Lance, "What did I say to you in that alley several weeks ago?"

Lance thought for a second and said, "You said I needed to reinvent myself."

Sifu nodded and said, "Good, you remember. Making great soup doesn't start with the soup or the recipe, but it begins with us."

Lance nodded, and Sifu said, "Watch me step by step first and listen to everything I have to say about the stance." Lance watched Sifu intently and then had Sifu repeat it several more times.

Sifu pointed to an area that was clear for Lance to give it a go. "Now it's your turn to try."

Lance stood there apprehensively with his feet together. Lance said, "I'm afraid to try it, Sifu. You know about my leg." Lance glance down at his prosthetic leg. He then said, "Since I lost my leg, I have not been the same. I feel like I've lost my connection.... I don't feel whole."

Sifu was always so calm when he spoke, but this time he said sternly to Lance, "The leg is nothing. As a child, you stood even before you could because of your will, as you fought to take your very first step. I asked you to take a leap of faith, but that was not in me. Trust yourself; trust in you."

Lance believed in Sifu's words and ability, but upon looking down at his leg, doubt began to creep in. "I don't know."

Sifu said, "Enough with excuses, Lance. You're special forces.... Now do it!"

Lance looked up and stared Sifu eye to eye. Then he opened up his YGKYM stance just like Sifu had told him to.

Sifu said, "Remember awareness and maintenance of your center."

Lance struggled to understand what that meant as the frustration on his face grew. Sifu came close to him and made a slight adjustment here and there to his stance. He said, "Feel the tension, Lance, and tuck in the hip."

Lance replied, "I think I feel it."

Sifu looked over his stance and said, "Hold your position and relax your body. Give me a deep breath and release it."

Lance let out a deep breath as his entire body sank and relaxed. He did as Sifu had told him but still was unsure why Sifu stressed the stance.

"Now, Lance, don't focus on the force coming at your chest. I want you just to trust what you feel and let the force run through your body." Sifu took his finger and begin pressing against his chest.

Sifu said, "Let the force come through. Maintain your vertical and feel it."

At first Lance wasn't so sure what to expect, but his facial expression began to slowly change. As Sifu increased the force, he stood in place and felt his structure hold. He looked at Sifu and said, "What ... what the hell is that?"

Sifu maintained the pressure on Lance's chest, as his stance held.

Lance looked baffled and said, "What the heck is that? I can ... I can feel all of me!"

Sifu continued the same pressure as the force went through Lance's body. He could feel it through his feet and into the ground. It didn't matter that he had a fake leg; Lance could feel everything.

As Sifu dropped his hand, Lance straightened out of the stance and began scratching his head. "Sorry, Sifu, for my foul language, but what the f– was that all about?"

Sifu smiled, "That, my friend, is body unity. That is your body connected even with your artificial leg functioning as one."

Lance said, "Oh my god, it's the craziest sensation. Even when I had both legs, I had no idea what it meant to be whole. I've never felt anything like this before."

Sifu laughed. "Funny, I've heard that before." He saw the same wonder on Lance's face that he'd seen in many students who experienced the stance for the first time. Sifu said, "Shall we continue?"

Lance didn't say a word as he stood in place and began opening the stance.

"To rise, to fall, and repeat this multiple times within your life time, is what living is all about." –Sifu

CHAPTER 11
The Choice

December 5, 2032

In the background of a room, the TV was broadcasting the UFMF's main channel. There, a panel of experts were discussing the end of the regular season and previewing the upcoming main event of the DOME. Linkwater, Connor, and Stabler were in a heated debate about the upcoming fights.

Linkwater said, "From day one, Connor, I knew this was not gonna be like any other season, and so far that's proven to be the case."

Connor turned to Linkwater and replied, "While the regular season is at an end, many questions still remain."

Linkwater jumped in, "You would think the biggest news was having the first fighter, Diesel 'The Wall' Williams achieve something that no fighter has, going twelve and O during the regular season. Instead, that story still comes in at a distant second, as everyone is wondering about the status of Kirin Rise."

Connor said, "I agree. Kirin Rise had a seven and O record before forfeiting her last five matches. The question remains: is she going to enter the DOME?" He paused for a moment and added, "You could say that's the twenty-five million dollar question of the day."

Linkwater added, "It's a tough call, as her supporters are mixed. I'm sure everyone is empathetic to the ordeal she went through several months ago with her parents, but fans can be impatient."

Connor said, "Her rise to the top was astronomical. She became the people's fighter. Now she's all but disappeared from the spotlight, and her status is unknown."

Linkwater added, "I'm willing to bet she doesn't even know what she wants to do."

Stabler entered in on the conversation, "Let's face it ... many questions remain. All of which, need I remind you, have to be answered by the deadline this Wednesday." Stabler looked at both of his cohosts and then stared into the camera. "If she decides to enter, would she be ready to go? How is her

368

state of mind since the incident with her family? Has she been training?"

Linkwater said snidely, "Well, we have all seen her training, so I don't believe that's really an issue."

The sound of all three gentlemen chuckling could be heard from the TV.

Kirin only heard pieces of the conversation. To her, it was all the same. Even with her dominating start, the doubters continued to grow, but that was the least of her concerns. Kirin sat by her window in her parents' house, where she had been staying for the last several months. In her mind, she was the only one capable of protecting them, and she did not want to leave them alone for a second. Looking outside, she breathed a deep sigh, as she found herself lost again.

Kirin recalled something Sifu said to her when she first decided to fight. He told her that a sacrifice would be necessary in her endeavors. Kirin felt that the risk was greater than the cause as she almost lost her family, something she was not willing to do. Since that night, she had been struggling for weeks. The nightmares, which she had been able to control for the last several years, had come back. The horror of her past remained alive.

The future posed no answers as she pondered some more.

Kirin looked down at Bacon. "I'm sorry, boy." She rubbed Bacon with her feet. "I miss Butterscotch as much as you do." Bacon looked up at Kirin and whimpered. Kirin's eyes became watery as his sadness reminded her of the reality.

Kirin cried herself to sleep, lying down by her bay window with Bacon by her side. A few hours passed before a gentle knock came at her door.

Knock. Knock.

Slowly her mom opened the door and peeked in. "Kirin, honey?"

"Nooo!" screamed Kirin as she woke herself up.

Kirin did not realize it was a dream and looked around in a daze. Her mom came by and held her. "Kirin, it's okay. It's just a dream. It's okay, baby."

Kirin hugged her mom tightly and said, "No, it's not okay, Mom. I'm so sorry.... I'm so sorry."

Kirin's mom said, "Kirin, you know we don't blame you for anything that's happened. We've been through this. You have to let it go."

Kirin cried, "I can't, Mom. I was so selfish, and didn't think out my actions. I didn't realize all the people I would get involved. Now, I find myself torn."

Kirin's mom kissed her on the head. "I have to be honest with you, Kirin. While I don't want you to fight, I also know that what you've done has brought hope and change to many people. I can't tell you what to do, baby, but whatever it is, your father and I will always support you."

Kirin looked over her mother's shoulder and saw all the unopened gifts she had received over the last several months. There had been a huge outpouring of support from Kirin's fans.

She looked at her mom and said, "So many people are depending on me, but my actions almost made me lose you guys."

Kirin's mom tried to comfort her. "We're safe, sweety."

Kirin looked her in the eye. "Mom, I can't be here all the time, and your safety is something I'm not willing to sacrifice."

Kirin held her mom and did not speak. Then her mom said, "Trust me, everything will be okay."

The Next Day

Kirin found peace at her favorite spot as she sat quietly by the park bench. She disguised herself with sunglasses and a hoodie, to avoid the crowds and the media. It had been awhile since she felt normal—well, almost normal. Deep down, she knew those days were a thing of the past.

At the planetarium, it was a beautiful winter day, and the weather was warm for December. People were outside trying to take advantage of the forgiving temperature. As she looked around, everything seemed normal. Couples were holding hands chatting together, joggers and bicyclists were getting their exercise, and families mingled, sharing moments.

Strangely enough, no safety tactical defense could be found, patrolling the area. At first glance, the world seemed right, as if there were no troubles or cares.

For a moment, Kirin thought, *Maybe things aren't as bad as they seem.*

Several minutes passed as she continued to people watch. Kirin knew a decision was imminent, but continued to procrastinate the inevitable.

Two days away, she thought.

Suddenly a tiny voice caught her off guard, "Ms. Rise?"

Surprised and afraid of revealing herself, she cowered and looked slowly toward the source of the voice.

"I'm sorry to bother you, Ms. Rise. I won't give away who you are," said a little girl.

Kirin was still cautious as she looked around to see if anyone had taken notice.

"I promise," the little girl reassured her.

Comforted by the voice, Kirin smiled at her. At first she was taken aback. She was a cute little girl, dressed in raggedy clothes, probably about eight or nine years old.

With some concern, Kirin asked, "Are you by yourself?"

Slightly confused, the little girl answered, "I'm by myself right now, but I'm usually with my mommy."

Kirin said, "You shouldn't be by yourself, you know."

With a cute frown on her face, she said, "I'm sorry, Ms. Rise."

Kirin patted her on the head and said, "Tell you what ... call me, Kirin, okay?"

The little girl smiled briefly and looked away.

Kirin said, "Do you live around here?"

The little girl looked embarrassed and said, "We kinda live wherever my mommy decides to stay that day."

Kirin quickly put two and two together and realized she was homeless. She wasn't sure how to respond, so she said, "I'm sure things will get better. Can I help you with anything?" At first, the little girl hesitated, with one hand behind her back. Then she bit her lip and handed over a doll. Kirin accepted it and realized it was a doll the UFMF had been marketing of her.

Kirin said, "It's a doll of me. Why are you giving it away?" Kirin knew how popular—and expensive—these were.

The little girl did not answer right away, as she looked sad. She said, "My mom surprised me several months ago and was able to get one for me." Kirin wondered what she had to do to be able to get hold of it.

Then she looked up at Kirin and said, "I want you to have it."

Startled by her remark, Kirin asked, "But, why?"

The little girl said, "Ms. Rise ... I, uh, mean Kirin, the doll is a symbol of hope. I believed you when you said that, if you try hard enough, eventually good things will happen. I saw you saying that on a TV interview."

Kirin said, "It's true; it will."

The little girl said, "My mommy said not to have high hopes in other people because they will always let you down. That's why Daddy left us and why we have no place to stay anymore."

Kirin was saddened by the statement. She said, "I want you to keep the doll. I want you to still believe."

The little girl pushed it back from her hands and said, "I haven't seen you fight in months. Everyone on the street says that you've quit."

Kirin replied, "It's not as simple as that."

The little girl with a sad face looked up and said, "You're not gonna fight in the DOME, are you?"

Kirin looked down with uncertainty and said, "I, uh ... I'm not sure." Kirin placed her hand on the little girl's shoulder as they both stood silently. She felt as helpless as the little girl with no answer to comfort her.

"Maria!" yelled a woman from the distance.

The little girl turned around and called, "Mommy, I'm over here."

Kirin looked up to see a young woman, probably only in her mid-twenties, approach the little girl.

The woman looked upset and said, "Maria, what did I say about talking to strangers?"

Maria said, "I'm sorry, Mommy." The woman grabbed the little girl and started pulling her away from Kirin.

Kirin watched as the little girl walked away. In her hand, she held the doll and squeezed it hard as she started to cry. She felt the weight of the people suddenly upon her.

Two Days Later

Fawn was sitting in his chair across from Thorne's table. He was nervous, and he tapped his foot on the ground and continued to squirm around. It unnerved those around him.

On the other end of the table, Thorne was the complete opposite: he looked to be the essence of serenity. He was reading his pad until his eyes shifted to stare directly at Fawn.

That action alone spoke louder than words as Fawn apologized. "Sorry, boss! I don't know how you can stay so calm," he said in a jittery voice. Fawn often wondered how Thorne kept his cool even in the most heated situations—it was one of the many traits he admired about his boss.

Thorne took a sip of his morning coffee and then spoke, "Fawn, people are emotional creatures, in reality no different from an animal.... If you pull the right strings, they move precisely how you want them to, just like a trained dog."

"You're so confident, boss." Fawn tried his best to calm his own nerves, but continued to fidget around.

"Always remember: it's the unknown that creates the fear. Be several steps ahead of your opponent, and you'll never have to worry about the outcome." He said it with such reassurance that it helped Fawn finally settle down.

Thorne stood up from his desk and peered over the edge of his window. His hand shook for a moment, but he eventually got control of it. Then, he began to admire the view and asked, "How many hours till the official deadline for declaring?"

Fawn checked his watch. "There's still another three hours, boss."

Thorne said, "Did you pay the actors already?"

Fawn said, "Yes, boss, I made sure we got the best actors for the job and promised them double if it worked."

Thorne asked, "You were able to find the actors to my exact specifications?" Thorne's head titled slightly, waiting for an answer.

"Oh yes, boss, see for yourself." Fawn showed a picture of the little girl, clearly proud of his own work.

Thorne turned around and looked at the picture. She was exactly how he had imagined her to be. He handed it back to Fawn and said, "Perfect, there's no doubt this will work."

Fawn nervously replied, "Boss, I'm sure this will work, since your plans always do, but let's say Kirin comes back ... uh, there's a strong possibility she could win the entire thing."

"I've got everything covered, Fawn ... everything," said Thorne confidently as he pulled out a small object from his pocket and stared at it.

Several minutes passed as neither said a word. Fawn's nerves began to get the best of him again, while Thorne continued to look outside, each with his own way of dealing with the wait. Fawn said, "It's been two days since Kirin spoke to the little girl, boss. Is she gonna wait till the last minute?"

Thorne said, "Timing is a difficult process, Fawn, that one can't predict with total accuracy. It's like trying to pick the exact bottom when to buy a stock. Most people waste so much time trying to achieve that level of perfection that they often miss the right opportunity. However ... I can guarantee you this," he stared directly at Fawn, "she will be coming back." Fawn nodded at Thorne, moved by his commanding voice. Fawn was sure that Thorne had the power to mentally will things into happening.

Just then, Linda spoke, startling Fawn from his seat. Thorne remained emotionless and waited to see what she had to say. Through the intercom, she said, "Sir, turn on your TVs now!" Her voice had a sense of urgency, alerting them that something important just happened. Fawn thought that the timing of this was somewhat ironic.

Thorne looked devilishly at Fawn and replied, "Thanks, Linda." Fawn eagerly awaited the news, hoping that this would finally answer the question that had been plaguing him for days. He leaned forward with his good ear.

"TVs on," Thorne spoke into the air. Several of the large-screen TVs that were located throughout the office simultaneously powered on. It did not matter where Fawn looked since the size and the multitude of options to view from were unlimited.

"Breaking news: Kirin Rise will be appearing in just a minute to speak to the entire press regarding her status in the upcoming UFMF event." On the screen was a podium surrounded by over thirty microphones from all different networks covering the event.

Thorne and Fawn were glued to the TV set as they waited for events to unfold. Fawn began shaking again, wondering what was going to happen, as he took a big gulp and held his breath.

A minute later Kirin came strolling toward the podium, wearing her usual red hoodie. It was difficult to read anything from her facial expression. The TV captured the sound of reporters jostling to get into position, as hundreds of clicks and flashes began showering her as she stood by the podium. Kirin stared straight into the camera, as a hush spread over the crowd—and likely everyone watching on TV. Her lips began to move slowly, as she said causally, "I'm in." With that, she turned around and began to walk away. The screams of reporters bombarded her with questions, wanting to know more, but their cries fell upon deaf ears as she faded away.

Fawn let out a deep sigh. He was relieved that everything had worked out. He turned immediately to look at Thorne, who wore a confident grin on his face.

Thorne said, "As expected."

Later That Day

A knock came on Sifu's apartment door.

"One-second," Sifu called as he hurried to see who it was.

He opened the door to find Kirin standing there with a somber look on her face.

Sifu did not speak a word.

Kirin said, "Does it ever bother you that you are always right?"

Sifu thought about it for a second and said, "I would be extremely bothered if I was wrong."

Kirin shook her head and said, "Sifu, I have less than two weeks to prepare for the DOME. Will you help me get ready?"

Sifu opened the door and welcomed her in. Kirin got halfway through and saw Tobias sitting on the couch.

She turned back to look at Sifu and said, "You do this on purpose to torture me?"

Sifu shrugged his shoulders.

Kirin looked at Tobias and said, "Random luck you stopped by?"

Tobias smiled. "Of course not ... more like a random call out of the blue to come to his place just now."

Both Tobias and Kirin rolled their eyes, knowing an explanation was not coming soon. It was Sifu performing the unexplainable.

Sifu clapped his hands, causing both of them to jerk their heads. He said, "Let's train."

Several hours passed as training continued between the two.

"Maybe you should take a break?" said Sifu.

Kirin said, "I'm good to go."

Tobias looked at Kirin and said, "Uh, let's take a little break, okay?"

"Fine, you wimp," said Kirin.

Tobias laughed and threw a bottle of water at Kirin.

"Well, how do you think I'm looking, Sifu?" asked Kirin.

"Same as always, not bad," replied Sifu.

"Sifu, do you think that, in my lifetime, I'll do anything that might be good?"

Sifu responded, "When that happens, Kirin, you'll be the first to know."

Kirin sighed. "Sifu, I'm not questioning your teaching style, and there's no doubt I would never have gotten this far without your help, but I guess I always wonder ... how is it that I'm doing the polar opposite of what every fighter is doing to train for this tournament and yet it's working?"

"There's still so much I need to teach you, but for now, I'm giving you only what's necessary so you can win this tournament," said Sifu. "The last thing I want is you to be thinking too much. I want you to move out there naturally without thought."

Kirin listened obediently and nodded her head.

Sifu looked at Kirin seriously. "The key is playing our game. All those UFMF fighters are playing a game. The difference is the approach to how we play our game. I don't want you to spar because that hinders your overall game. I'm teaching you the skill to kill, not the ability to play around with people. Once you do that, then you'll be in trouble."

Kirin asked, "I understand, Sifu, so what's our focus over the next week?"

"We are gonna work on one thing, and that's closing the gap," said Sifu.

Kirin said, "I believe I've been staying true to hitting the line straight when I've closed the gap, Sifu."

"For the most part, Kirin, you have, but on some occasions I could see your center leaning off the line," stated Sifu.

"Why is it so important that I don't step to the side?"

"Our game is that domination of the line, as if you and your opponent are on a tight rope. Once you fade to the side, you're no longer aiming at the target. You don't want to be the one to step off that tight rope first and initiate an attack from the side. Hit him straight, hit him hard, and focus everything at his target!" said Sifu.

Kirin nodded somewhat uncertainly, and Sifu stressed, "Remember, make the opponent move. Don't move for him."

"Why is that, Sifu?"

Sifu said, "That's because you're nobody's bitch."

Kirin laughed, for it was rare for Sifu to swear. In fact, Kirin tried to recall if Sifu had ever sworn before, but he was dead serious.

"When you close that gap, give them nothing to counter, but once they make that move, take their center and do what we do best," said Sifu.

Kirin smiled and said, "Let's do a drill. Are you ready, Tobias, or do you need a latte and another ten minutes of rest?"

"Sifu, you sure I can't hit her to make the drill more realistic?"

Sifu laughed. "Okay, let's work on this drill for now."

The Day of the DOME

The last two weeks passed quickly, as the entire country put everything on hold for the biggest event of the year. Everywhere you looked, the UFMF heavily advertised. Not a second passed by that was not related to the DOME. Rich or poor, it did not matter. Everyone was talking about what to expect from the upcoming fights. Debates at the water cooler and family meals ran heated. Little kids pretended to be their favorite fighters. Expectations were set high.

Media was at an all-time frenzy covering the top sixteen fighters who qualified for the DOME. Every fighter was required to accommodate the press. However, jealousy formed, as Kirin took the majority of the attention.

The growth of the UFMF had been exponential this season, unmatched by previous years. The source was Kirin, who was both a blessing and curse. There was no question that her presence generated global attention. However, the foundation that led to their dominance in the States was being tested by her outspoken opinion on the laws that the UFMF had lobbied for. On the outside, the UFMF's global growth was all but assured after this season. However, structures that rise quickly tend to be weaker and fall. Was the foundation that led them to the top being destroyed from the inside out?

Stabler and Krenzel were broadcasting the main event to hundreds of millions while in front of a frenzied crowd of two hundred and fifty thousand.

At a motion from the camera man, Stabler began to speak, and the crowd erupted. He smiled to the camera and looked behind. Then, like a seasoned professional, he used the moment to his advantage.

Stabler shook his head and muttered, "Insane."

Basking in the moment, Krenzel absorbed the energy and then turned to Stabler. "This is my fifth year doing this, and

Stabler, you've been fortunate enough to be here from the very start. This is unbelievable."

Stabler said, "This is the tenth year of the DOME, and each year it continues to grow dramatically. Still, this is like nothing I have ever seen before."

Inside the Locker Room

Tobias watched Kirin pacing back and forth. His eyes felt strained as she repeated the same pattern for several minutes. He had trained diligently with Kirin for the last week and a half and wondered why the nerves were kicking in. Curious, he asked, "Why are you nervous?"

Kirin turned around, stopping dead in her tracks. She glanced at Tobias first and then pointed to the TV screen. Tobias peeked over Kirin's shoulder, but saw nothing except the crowd being broadcasted. He sneered at Kirin and said, "You're more worried about all those people watching than the fights?"

Kirin frowned at Tobias, and said, "Fighting is simply hit the center and hit it hard. It's kinda unnerving to have a billion plus people watching your every move.'"

Tobias said in jest, "I thought you would be used to it by now, Ms. Celebrity."

Kirin folded her arms and made an annoyed sound that most guys would consider cute, "Hmh!" It was her way of pouting and letting Tobias know that he wasn't being much help at all.

Realizing he might have put himself in the doghouse with her, he quickly changed the subject. Tobias stared at his watch and asked Kirin, "How much longer till your first match?" He leaned further back in his seat, looking bored with the wait.

That did the trick, as Kirin quickly forgot what she was pouting about and calculated an answer for Tobias. "It'll be a good hour to an hour and a half." Then she realized the length of time they had to endure and sulked at the fact.

Kirin stared at the screen as one of the fighters made his entrance into the ring. She admired the effort in putting together such a huge procession and shared her thoughts quickly with

Tobias, "You know, Tobias, it would be kinda cool to have a huge, elaborate entrance like everyone else, don't you think?"

Tobias recalled Kirin mentioning this before, but pretended to act surprised. He blurted out, "You, with a huge group? You've always had that solo mentality. Besides, not sure what we can conjure up with a budget of only fifty credits."

Kirin looked back toward the screen and murmured, "I'm just saying." She realized he was right and such an elaborate entrance would be a waste of funds.

Tobias teased, "So, hanging with me and playing Sifu's old eighties music for an entrance isn't good enough for you?"

Kirin swung around, fearing she had made him feel bad. "That's not what I meant."

Tobias merely laughed as he looked at Kirin. She jumped next to him and punched him hard on the arm. He cowered and laughed. "I hope you hit harder than that in the match."

"Oh, you want me to hit harder?" asked Kirin, as she lifted her fist, threatening that the next punch would really hurt.

Tobias chuckled and quickly said, "I'm kidding! I'm kidding.... I know you can hit hard." They were giggling as a way to kill some time, but their moment of laughter was interrupted by the sudden sound of knocking at the door.

Knock. Knock. Knock.

Both of them looked at the door, but Kirin was the only one wondering who that could be. Kirin pulled away from Tobias and said, "Do you know who it is?"

Tobias pretended to be unaware and said, "Why don't you open it and see for yourself?" He sat back as Kirin moved toward the door.

Kirin called out, "Who is it?" but did not get a response. She grabbed the handle and slowly pulled it open, cheating to see who it was through the little crack. Her heart skipped a beat. She leaped backwards with both her hands covering her mouth.

"Oh my god!" exclaimed Kirin. She asked, "What are you doing here?" as she giggled with excitement.

"Hey, lil sista," said Big T in his smooth voice. He smiled as his hulking body passed through the doorway. Kirin was taken aback, but then became even more overwhelmed as the entire gang appeared: Ken, Danny, Robert, Ryan, Doc, and, of course, Big T.

Kirin ran toward Big T and leaped into his arms. It looked like a bear hugging a little rabbit. She was so excited, and all her friends appreciated her reaction. It was one of those rare, genuine moments that you wish to be part of.

"The biggest fight of the year and you representing–how could we not be here for you?" said Robert. Kirin smiled, looking somewhat stunned that Robert had a compliment come out of his mouth. She wondered if that was really him or an impostor.

Then Ryan said, "Do we get a hug also?"

Big T gently put her down, and she greeted each one of her old friends with a hug and a smile. She said, "I'm so happy you guys are all here, but ... but...." She looked back and forth, surprised and confused how all this could be happening.

Doc decided to answer her questions and said, "Thank the leader. He gave us a call to be here as your marching entourage." He bowed as his arms stretched out in the direction of Tobias.

She was genuinely surprised as she said, "Tobias?" Doc nodded his head to confirm. She smiled, ran to Tobias, and gave him a quick peck on the cheek followed by a hug.

Tobias joked, "This is much better than you punching me."

Kirin said, "How'd you know?" as she gazed into Tobias's eyes.

Tobias replied, "You know, hanging out with Sifu, you pick up a thing or two. Besides, didn't you say you wanted to march out with a huge entourage?"

Kirin squeezed harder and whispered into his ear, "Thank you. I guess you do listen ... sometimes."

She was busy chatting when her focus got interrupted yet again. A voice from behind the door said, "Don't your closest friends count?"

Kirin let go of Tobias and stood waiting to see who else would walk through the door. Gwen, Sage, and Hunter emerged from the shadows. Kirin greeted them with enthusiasm, hugging Gwen and giving Sage a friendly kiss on his cheek. Kirin liked that Sage and Gwen were holding hands. "My two best friends in the world! Aren't you guys busy with school?"

Gwen and Sage looked at each other, like couples do, and smiled. Sage said, "We wouldn't dare miss our best friend's fight for anything." Gwen nodded in agreement and held Kirin's hand tightly.

Kirin was so happy as she turned her eyes to Hunter standing behind them. He seemed shy as he waited for his turn to greet her.

"You came," she said in a sweet and tender voice. Hunter stood there watching her with a smile and then began to approach. Kirin moved closer as the two tightly embraced one another. Kirin whispered, "I'm so glad you're here."

Hunter whispered back, "I'll always be here for you." Kirin blushed and hugged him tightly as everyone watched.

Finally, Hunter said, "There's one last person still."

Kirin wondered who could it be. Everyone was there that she wanted to be in her march. The entire room turned to see who was behind Hunter as he slowly stepped to the side to reveal ... Sifu. He stood there, in his stance, with his hands behind his back. His gentle demeanor was a refreshing sight.

Kirin's face fell, a look of concern consuming her features. She immediately stepped back and shook her head. "No, no ... you promised you would not be linked with me. You don't need to be here and risk any more, Sifu."

Sifu smiled and tried to put her fears at ease. "For far too long, I've stayed in the shadows. If you are going to win this tournament, you are going to need my help."

Kirin was speechless as she stood silently while everyone watched. She knew that Sifu was right, but she was concerned about him.

"Trust me," Sifu said with such confidence that Kirin felt reassured that things would be okay.

Kirin slowly nodded as she approached Sifu and gave him a hug. She whispered lightly, "I always will." She wiped away the tears of happiness at having everyone together.

Gwen clapped, interrupting the Hallmark moment, as she cleared her throat and got Kirin's attention. She had a smile on her face, hinting that there was more to come. "I have a surprise for you."

Kirin squinted and looked at her, wondering what she was up to. Her best friend had that devilish look. Gwen made a gesture to look behind her, and Kirin watched as several men came in to drop off multiple packages. The room was soon filled with five big boxes, and Gwen shouted out instructions to begin opening them, but to make sure Kirin was the first to look inside. Kirin was excited, just like a kid opening a gift for Xmas—she had no idea what could be inside. Her eyes sparkled as she first saw the object. She lifted it up, revealing a garment for all to see. She began examining it and asked Gwen, "Can I try it on?"

Gwen nodded. "Of course. But most importantly, do you like it?"

Kirin placed the robe on and began modeling it, spinning around and letting the outfit flow in the air. The colors were vibrant as the red edges captured and highlighted the robe. Gwen began to explain, "So, I know you've been wearing your signature red hoodie for your entrance, but I thought for the finale you needed something special."

Kirin admired the robe as Gwen continued to explain. "I looked at the traditional Korean dress, the Hanbok, and thought that the overall design was cool, but needed a more modernized look. So ... I got creative and made a few changes here and there, and I hope you like it."

While Kirin had never been much of a girlie girl, she felt like a woman as she appreciated the style and effort Gwen had put into designing her a new robe. "Do I like it? I love it! You've outdone yourself, Gwen," exclaimed Kirin, as she ran over to hug her best friend.

Gwen gasped for air and said, "Everyone should have a uniform with their name on it."

Robert pulled robes out of the box and began handing them out. "Holy shit, this is pretty bad ass."

Gwen said, "Now I modified the Hanbok between the sexes. Basically, there's only me and Kirin and the rest of you guys. However, I spiced it up for you guys and gave you a bit of a rougher edge. The last thing I want is for the guys to bitch at me."

Kirin watched as Robert put on a hooded uniform similar to the one she was wearing. The rest of her friends began putting on their outfits as well, and it was clear everyone was smitten over Gwen's design and fashion skills.

"Gwen, you made all these? Wasn't this expensive?" asked Kirin.

Gwen smiled. "I made it, but it was Sifu's idea and his bank account."

Kirin turned toward Sifu. "Sifu, this is too much. I should pay you back."

Sifu waved her off. "You can pay me back by winning this entire thing. Don't give it another thought."

Kirin had always wondered how, in a world that revolved around money, how Sifu was able be the exception.

Once the gang was all dressed in their uniforms, Tobias said, "Damn, Gwen, you really did a good job."

Gwen smiled, "Thanks, Tobias. Less than two weeks to get everyone fitted and get this all ready was insane. But if there's one thing I like more than hacking computers, it's designing clothes with a challenge."

Kirin was excited and said, "Hey, we gotta get a group shot, okay?"

Gwen said, "Kirin, before we do that, you need to look at the very last box. Check out the banner we made!" There was one box left that needed to be opened. Kirin opened it and started unfolding the banner. "Oh my god, are we going to fly this when I come out?"

Gwen nodded. "Yup."

Kirin's smile could no longer be contained as she shouted, "I love it!"

As everyone straightened their robes, Kirin set up the camera and put her friends into position. She looked through the view finder to line up the shot.

Kirin said, "Tobias, can't you look normal for one pose?"

Tobias answered, "What have I always said? If you don't look like a superhero or a supermodel when you pose, you're doing it wrong." Everyone laughed. The group settled in for the final shot, and Kirin pushed the button to start the timer's countdown.

3, 2, 1 ... *Click.*

At the End of the Day 1

The cameras turned to Stabler as he began to wrap up the broadcast. He said, "The first day of the DOME did not disappoint, as a few underdogs surprised the pack. Tomorrow we'll be gearing up for the afternoon semifinal followed by the evening finale. I cannot wait to see how this plays out."

Krenzel said, "As impressed as I am to see Kirin back from her layoff, to me, the domination of the fighting of Diesel 'The Wall' Williams seems almost super human."

Stabler nodded. "Yeah, there is no denying that. Don't get me wrong; as much as I like what Kirin's done in the fights, there's something about The Wall that just makes you want to run and hide."

Krenzel said, "Okay, Stabler, with all this frenzy, Eliza, our in the DOME foot reporter, was able to get a few words with The Wall. Eliza, let's hear from the favorite."

A slight delay occurred as Eliza had a difficult time hearing her cue as the sound of the audience was overwhelming. She finally said, "Diesel, as my colleagues were saying, you almost seem super human in this tournament. Any thoughts on how you feel you're doing so far?"

Diesel said, "First, Eliza, I thank God for giving me the opportunity to showcase my talents. Super human comes from one thing: hard work and the man from above!"

Eliza said, "While there's several possibilities of who's gonna make it to the finale, right now it looks like you and Kirin have a date with destiny."

"I don't believe in destiny. I believe in God's will."

Eliza nodded and replied, "Any thoughts on your possible opponents, especially Kirin Rise?" She covered her other ear and brought the microphone even closer for Diesel to speak into.

Diesel grabbed the microphone from Eliza and was very animated. "I understand that the people think that Kirin Rise is the people's fighter; she fights for their cause. But, unlike Kirin, I fight for a higher power ... God!"

Eliza started to speak, but Diesel, all heated up, barreled on, "God has spoken to me and has told me to do whatever I need to do to win this tournament ... and since this is God's will and I am but his humble soldier willing to do his bidding, I guarantee that I'm going to win it. I am, in fact, God's warrior."

With that, Diesel handed the microphone back to Eliza and began to walk away. The crowds began to swarm over him, as security did their best to maintain the distance.

Eliza spoke, "Well, you heard it here first; The Wall has guaranteed victory."

Suddenly Diesel came back, startling Eliza as he grabbed the mic to say, "By the way, Eliza, you're looking mighty fine."

Eliza was taken aback and stammered, "Well, I don't want to be the one to argue against God ... uh, thanks, Diesel." Diesel smiled into the camera, made the symbol of the cross with his hands, and finally walked away.

Krenzel said, "Is it just me, or does it make you shiver when The Wall speaks?"

Stabler in all seriousness said, "I'm shivering, and it's not because it's cold."

Eliza commented, "That makes three of us."

Krenzel smiled. "We'll be back after a word from our sponsors."

"Never forget that you set the standard for what is acceptable." –Sifu

SECTION 1

Short Stories #11–2/3rds Kirin's P.O.V.

<u>Halloween–1 year 210 days</u>

When I first came to the States, the idea of strangers giving candy was foreign to me, but I quickly caught on to tradition and soon Halloween became my favorite holiday. My brothers, even Kyle who was younger than me, told me that I was past the "cool age," but it didn't matter. I planned on doing this for as long as I could.

The game plan was always the same: meet up with Gwen and Sage and load up on the loot, even beyond the suggested curfew time. I was halfway to Sage's house when I saw him from a distance. I couldn't help myself as I burst into laughter.

Sage was still busy fidgeting with his costume as he asked me, "What's so funny?" I covered my mouth and just pointed toward him from head to toe.

"You're laughing at me? Uh, what the hell are you dressed up as?" asked Sage.

Proudly, I replied, "Sushi ... cool, huh?" I spun in place, modeling my outfit.

"You mean as in raw fish?"

"Technically, sushi is all about the rice, not the raw fish," I said.

"Dork!" He grimaced at my costume.

"Wait, you're complaining about my costume? Look at you!" I began to giggle again.

"I'm dressed up as a nerd," he said, adjusting his glasses and pulling up his waist-high pants.

"And this is different from your everyday outfits?" I replied cautiously.

"Of course! I'm wearing my ankle-high pants with suspenders. I added tape in the middle of my glasses, and I got my pocket pencil holder in my shirt ... snazzy," he replied.

I kept my karma clean by not saying anything else about his outfit. "Let's head out to Gwen." We began our brisk walk and got involved in useless talk about nothing. Other kids were passing us by, and we exchanged glances to check out each other's costumes.

Sage suddenly asked, "Hey ... did you catch the news about the meteor that passed by the earth's atmosphere?"

"I know, totally creepy. I heard that was the closest one yet, and that fragments hit several areas on the planet–some just a few miles from here," I said.

"Come on; let's hurry and get to Gwen's," said Sage as he walked in a bowlegged manner.

"Let me guess: you're also staying in character?" as I looked at him and rolled my eyes. He nodded.

I wondered if I could do the same, but a sushi doesn't do anything.

Glancing around, I realized we were still about five minutes away from Gwen's house. The sun set sooner than I expected as we came to the neighborhood cemetery. It was a small area which I was told had been there for the last century. Cemeteries always gave me the creeps, but everything from the iron-rusted gates that forged the outside entrance to the giant willow tree that was naked after all the leaves fell created an eerie feeling.

"Man, I know it's Halloween, but this place has always creeped me out," I said to Sage as I stared at the tombstones from a distance.

"Ditto," agreed Sage as we both felt unnerved just walking by. Suddenly, we heard a scream within the cemetery.

"What the hell was that?" asked Sage as he quickly jerked around to see where it came from.

"It's probably some teenagers playing a practical joke," I said, hoping that I was right. However, I trusted my gut and felt something was off.

"Maybe we should take a look ... just in case it's not," I said as curiosity got the better of me.

"Fine, but I'm walking behind you," replied Sage.

"Hey, you're breaking character," I said in jest.

Sage replied, "I don't think I am. If I were being brave, I'd be walking in front?"

I nodded my head as he made a valid point.

As we walked closer toward to the source of the scream, we began hearing more sounds of terror surrounding us. My heart began to race as Sage grabbed my arm. I stood in place wondering why, exactly, we were going toward the screams.

"Kirin, this is kinda freaking me out," said Sage, his voice trembling.

"I'm getting that same vibe, Sage," I said with some concern and a little discomfort as he clung tightly to my arm. We waited, wondering what to do next, the tension building. Then a group of teens ran past us. I heard them screaming at us to run. One of them shouted, "Zombies! It's freaking zombies."

"This has to be a joke," said Sage as he loosened his grip on me. We heard more screaming and then saw one of our friends, Rico, running toward us. Either he was acting brilliantly or he was in absolute terror.

I said, "Hey, it's, Rico. He'll know what's going on."

He ran toward us with a look of fear in his eyes. As he turned to look behind him, he tripped and fell. He struggled to get back up, but several individuals jumped on him and began tearing him apart.

"What the...?" said Sage. "What the hell is happening!"

We watched in horror as Rico screamed and blood spurted everywhere. The last thing I remembered seeing was his arm being ripped apart from his body.

I yelled in terror, "That can't be fake! Run, Sage!"

We began running, unsure where we were headed. "Sage, how can this be happening?" I said, as I struggled to talk while running. Sage was huffing and puffing, running as fast as I had ever seen him.

"Sage?" I stopped for a second to get my breath once I thought we were out of harm's way. "You're the genius. What do you think is happening?"

He leaned over, bracing his hands on his knees as he gasped for breath. I continued to scan around while we both caught our breath. Lifting his head, he looked around and said, "I don't know.... Maybe it's some Chinese bird flu that spread or...." he paused, and I could see the wheels in his head churning for an answer.

"What, Sage, what?" I asked, looking all around to make sure we were safe.

He looked at me and responded, "The meteor?"

We stood there for a moment and thought it was a logical answer to a seemingly impossible situation. More screams around the neighborhood occurred, and kids who were trick or treating were running randomly in panic.

Trembling, Sage said, "What should we do? Where should we go?"

"Let's go get Gwen. She's a block away," I said. Sage nodded, and we ran toward Gwen's house. We pounded on the door, screaming her name, but no one answered.

"Let's head to the back," I said.

Sage and I walked away from the door, and then–BANG! The door exploded, shattering in pieces, as a body flew through it. We both screamed in terror and fell to the ground, now more confused and panicked than ever.

"What the frick!" shouted Sage.

We looked up at the entrance and saw Gwen in a schoolgirl outfit holding a shotgun. She stood before us with her feet planted shoulder-width apart, the barrel of the gun still smoking.

"Oh my god, it's Gwen," I said.

"Holy crap, why is she walking?" said Sage.

Gwen asked, "Are you guys okay?" as she ran toward us.

390

We didn't know how to respond at first, but I finally asked, "Gwen you're walking?"

Sage said, "How is this possible?"

Gwen frowned and said, "There's a zombie apocalypse happening, undead are destroying our neighborhood as we speak, and you're most surprised that I can walk. Seriously?"

Sage and I looked at each other, realizing she had a point. "All right, screw it. Where should go? Let's brainstorm some ideas."

Before we could respond, Sage snapped his fingers. "I got an idea: we hit the Apple store."

Gwen rolled her eyes. "Why are we gonna go there, genius?"

Sage replied, "I figure this is the perfect time to loot."

I said sarcastically, "So, you've decided to pick a location made entirely of glass. Are you on drugs?"

Gwen added, "This is the end of the world, Sage, not the Cubs finally winning a championship, you dumb ass. Besides, the Internet and power won't be readily available to run that stuff."

Sage said, "See? She was thinking it, too."

I said angrily, "Come on, guys, be serious. This is no joking matter."

Gwen suggested, "Costco?"

Sage asked, "Why there?"

Gwen answered, "Oh, I don't know ... unlimited supplies and limited entries."

Sage replied, "I don't have a membership card."

Gwen and I stared at Sage till he could feel it. I said, "Uh ... Anyway. Gwen's got a good idea, but let's put that at second."

Gwen asked, "Why?"

I replied, "'Cause we're headed to Sifu's."

Sage frowned, "Why Sifu?"

I said, "He's only five minutes away, he's got an arsenal of weapons at his school, and you want the guy who's spent all his life mastering killing at a moment like this."

Sage and Gwen exchanged a glance and said, "Agreed."

Sage yelled, "Jinx."

I looked at both of them and yelled, "Guys, this is not the time."

The neighborhood was in chaos, just like one saw in the movies, but definitely worse. Looting was happening, cars were set on fire, and people were screaming and running from every imaginable direction. We were two blocks away when two guys dressed up in costume ran into us.

They said, "What are you kids doing out here? This place is too dangerous."

Sage said, "We're headed somewhere safe."

The one guy looked at Gwen and said, "Is that your shotgun?"

She replied, "It's my dad's."

One of the guys shifted his eyes toward the other and said, "We should stick together. The bigger the group, the safer we will be. Safety in numbers and all that."

I hesitated. Something was off; I could feel it in my gut.

Sage said, "That's a good idea. You guys come with us. We know a place with tons of weapons."

They smiled at one another and said, "Lead the way. We have no weapons at all. We could use some."

A few minutes later, we finally got to Sifu's place and pounded on the door.

"Sifu, it's me, Kirin ... Sifu!" I screamed, praying that he was there.

The door swung open, and I sighed in relief as Sifu shouted, "Hurry up! Get in ... hurry."

We rushed inside, and Sifu slammed the door behind us. In his hands were his favorite butterfly swords.

"Thank god you're okay, Sifu," I said as I gave him a quick hug.

"Are you kids okay?" asked Sifu as he looked at us.

Gwen and Sage nodded their heads, still in shock.

Sifu asked, "Who are these two fine gentlemen with you? Why don't you introduce them to me?"

I turned around to introduce them to Sifu and said, "I never got your names before. My name is Kirin, and you are...?"

As they extended their arms to greet me, all I saw were two quick flashes before my eyes. Suddenly blood squirted all over my face.

Slash! Stab.

"Ahhhh!" Gwen screamed at the top of her lungs.

"Holy crap!" yelled Sage.

Blood was everywhere as their bodies dropped to the floor. We all looked at Sifu, who had just killed the two strangers on the spot.

I turned around in horror, saying, "What the hell, Sifu? Why'd you do that?" I began shaking in shock.

Without a single ounce of emotion, Sifu began cleaning his blades. He said, "Kirin, check them both. They have weapons on them."

I shook my head. "Sifu, they came with us because they were looking for weapons as well. They don't have anything. We were all going to team together."

More concerned about his blades, Sifu said, "Just check, please."

I was hesitant to touch them, but I pushed down my revulsion and found guns behind both of their backs. Sage found two knives hidden by their ankles.

Gwen said, "Oh my god ... they said they had no weapons."

Sifu went to lock the door and said, "They were both gang members. You could see it from the marking on their hands. That's why I asked you to introduce them to me. I'm also willing to bet that they were going to kill you guys for Gwen's shotgun."

I shook my head. "How'd you know this?"

Sifu said, "In self-defense, never hesitate. It's either yes or no. You can't tell me, Kirin, that you did not feel a disturbing presence when you first met them." I looked at Sifu and swallowed hard. This was all so overwhelming.... The room began to spin as I tried to process the way the world had abruptly changed. I just screamed.

"Aaahh!"

In My Bedroom

I found myself sitting up screaming, still in a daze. Breathing heavily, I realized I was in my room. I looked around and breathed a sigh of relief. "Oh my god, it was just a dream." I jumped again, startled at the sound in the hallway.

"Kirin, Kirin, what's wrong?" said my mom, running into my room.

"I guess I was dreaming that zombies were attacking me," I said.

My mom shook her head. "I told you not to watch those scary movies with your brothers. I'm going to have a talk with them, first thing in the morning."

> *"When trained properly, that gut feeling is never wrong. We often just choose not to listen." –Sifu*

The Price to Pay–1 year 293 days

"Dang it!" I stumbled over.

"Ten more seconds to go. Keep your eyes closed," said Sifu as he looked at a classroom of goofs struggling to stand on one leg.

"Come on; it's only fifteen seconds with your eyes closed."

A quick glance told me I wasn't the only one struggling with this exercise. One by one, everyone was stumbling over. Even Tobias was having a hard time.

"Five seconds to go," said Sifu.

I looked at Ryan, who said, "Remind me to skip leg development class."

I giggled as I tried to lift my leg again.

"Okay, that's one minute," said Sifu.

The entire class grumbled.

Robert said, "Oh my god, that sucks."

Doc agreed, "Yeah, I don't know what it is about leg exercise that just gives me an ass cramp."

Ryan said, "Oh my god, I think I am burning calories during class. What's wrong with this picture?"

Ken laughed. "Just because it's called the lazy man's art doesn't mean there's no movement, you know?"

Sifu listened to everybody whine and said, "That looked God awful."

Tobias said, "Sifu, is that why you never became a motivational speaker?"

Everyone–including Sifu–laughed at Tobias's comment.

I decided to ask a question. "Sifu, I know the single leg exercise is for balance, but what's with the last fifteen seconds doing it with closed eyes?"

Sifu said, "You are all still young, but when you get older, the mind needs to be stimulated. So, when you lift your leg with your eyes closed, it's extremely difficult to do. The mind is then mentally challenged."

Doc asked, "Is this preventative?"

Sifu nodded. "Yes, you don't want any of the mental ills that people suffer when they get older. The whole point of me teaching you Wing Chun is so that you can do it and remember it."

Danny said, "When you're an adult and doing work, doesn't that involve the mental?"

Sifu said, "More often than not, it doesn't. Because once you pick a career, unless it involves a lot of creativity, you end up doing repetitive tasks. It's much different when you are young. You're constantly getting bombarded with new information at school, whether you like it or not."

This was definitely a new subject that Sifu never discussed before, so I paid closer attention. "Thanks, Sifu, I never knew that," I said.

Sifu smiled and said, "It's good you asked; otherwise, I wouldn't remember to tell you guys."

Robert laughed and said, "Hey, Sifu, I thought the whole point was that it helped your memory." Everyone chuckled.

Sifu grinned. "I know it and remember it all, but it's your job to get the information from me. When I perform an action, I just do it. There's no more thought on how I do it."

We pondered his words for a moment, and then Sifu called out, "Tobias, spend another ten minutes going over the kicks with everyone."

During those ten minutes, students continued to tumble around the room. More grumbling was being echoed by everyone. Sifu came back, "Okay, now that you're all warmed up, let's switch from legs to hands. Warm up and chi sao, and work on the basic attack, palm strike countered by Jut Sau."

Sifu always gave a little tip in the beginning, something to look for when performing the drill.

That day, Sifu said, "Okay, keep in mind the thing I care about the least in this drill is if the palm strike gets through. That means the hit is irrelevant to me. Everything else up to the hit plays a more significant role."

"Yes, Sifu," we all answered.

Big T asked, "Sifu, can you demonstrate how to properly do this?"

Sifu nodded his head and called upon Tobias. We watched as Sifu and Tobias began the drill. Watching Sifu's motion, he was so smooth. Normally, I would say it was perfect, but Sifu would say there is no such thing. Instead, perfection in his mind was how natural you can make it. Sifu would roll and randomly execute the palm strike. He performed it several times as we watched and tried to observe everything.

"Simple, isn't it?" said Sifu.

Ken raised his hand and asked, "Tobias, are you trying to block Sifu?"

Tobias looked at Ken and said, "Uh duh, yes."

Ken said, "No seriously, Sifu, can you attack him again and Tobias try everything you got to block it?"

Sifu said, "Okay, let's do it."

Sifu and Tobias began to chi sao, and every time Sifu would do a palm strike, it would easily go through.

I had to ask, "I don't get it. You're moving in slow motion, and Tobias can't block you? Am I the only one seeing this?"

Tobias added, "Seriously, I know it's coming, it's going dirt slow, and no matter what I do, I just can't stop him."

Robert shook his head. "What the heck!"

Ken asked, "How are you doing that?"

Robert raised his hands. "How is the palm just going through?"

Sifu said, "I just do it, naturally."

I thought about it. "We aren't asking the right questions. What was it that Sifu said before? Ah, that's it: ask a simple question; get a simple answer."

Everyone looked frustrated, and Sifu stood there, waiting.

I got it. I need to ask him a deeper question. This man does it automatically, so I need to work in reverse to figure out how to get to that stage, I thought.

I asked, "Okay, I have a question: when doing the attack, is the pressure on both hands fifty-fifty?"

Sifu looked at me with a grin. "It is not fifty-fifty."

Everyone looked around, thinking about that answer.

Danny said, "I thought it had to be fifty-fifty to drill into the opponent?

Sifu replied, "It's fifty-fifty in that I know how to hold my base evenly, but when I want to attack, that attack hand has to be free and clear from any obstruction."

I added, "So, it's like how I walk. I don't drag my feet, but the pressure changes just enough so I can move it."

Sifu nodded. "Bingo."

Frowning, I said, "Dang, that's common sense.... How come I didn't see that before?"

"Now what you've asked goes deeper than you can imagine, but for now let's keep things simple. Wing Chun is the only art that utilizes two hands, and the reason I say that is because we fight square. I want to control the force, so I have to have one over the amount. Imagine both hands being fifty-fifty; I still maintain the balance when I apply the attack. So that you can visualize it, imagine that, in my control hand, the fok sau is fifty-one while my palm strike is forty-nine. Thus, fok sau is one over to control that point, and the palm strike is one under to be free to hit. Makes sense, doesn't it?

"Simple theory, deep in detail, difficult to execute ... but once perfected, it becomes unstoppable," said Sifu.

"Remind me to keep that quote," said Sifu, as his own words caught his attention.

Tobias said, "I never knew that."

Sifu said, "You never asked."

I smiled on the inside and thought, *I think I kinda figured out how to learn from Sifu.*

"So, that's it? That's how you do it?" I asked.

Sifu smiled. "That's one way of doing it. Okay, grab a new partner and practice.... Nice questions, Kirin."

Robert and Ryan both gave me a pat on the back.

Ken said, "Yeah, that was a really good question. That helped me a lot."

Another thirty minutes went by as we continued to switch partners and practice a single attack. I had to admit that, even with the new information, it still didn't help. The idea was simple, but doing it was another thing.

Sifu said, "Okay, one minute break time, everyone."

Robert said, "This is fricking hard as hell."

Ryan nodded, "I agree. Getting that control with that much precision is not a simple task at all."

Big T said, "Yeah, I swear I got a headache from thinking so much."

Danny sighed. "I don't know what's going on. It feels like I'm pressing to the point."

Even Tobias was having a hard time. "I can get it through," he said, "but it doesn't feel like how Sifu does it. I can feel myself muscling it almost eighty-five percent of the time."

Ken replied, "I think it was better when I was dumber."

Doc mused, "I think it's frustrating because the theory is simple, but the execution is a bitch."

Big T simply added, "Yeah."

I didn't say a word, but they were all right. I thought, *This is really difficult.*

After grabbing a drink of water, Sifu returned to our group. Robert replied, "Sifu, I hate to speak for everyone, but this is really hard."

Sifu replied, "Let me check my empathy wallet.... Yup, just like last time, it's empty."

Sifu looked disappointed and said, "Enough of the whining! I know all of you are young, but just think for a second what you're doing when you train here. You are looking at a skill that a handful of people possess in this entire world, yet you want this given to you like something on the value menu at your local fast food joint."

I felt guilty about complaining as everyone else started hanging their heads down.

Sifu continued, "Life is balanced. It's fair. Any time you can't do something, before you complain how hard it is, ask yourself: what have I done to earn it?"

It was rare for Sifu to give speeches, but it seemed like he wanted to hit home with this lesson.

Sifu said, "I know it's difficult today to maintain focus. In today's world, everything is given at the press of a button. Just because you pull up information from a search engine doesn't mean you learned it. Remember that, okay?"

We shifted our eyes around the room guiltily.

Sifu added, "When people see me do things, it looks so simple. But they never think about how much time and effort was devoted to get to that point. That's because most people focus on the end result and not the process. If you can understand what that means, the world will change for you."

None of us had any response, and as Sifu began to walk away, he said, "Continue to practice."

> *"The day you quit whining that something is difficult is the day you realize how little effort you've put into it." –Sifu*

Things to Come–2 years 1 day

In a dark and shaded corner of a restaurant, an unsightly being continued to gorge upon his meal. "Hurry up! Bring me more food. Do you want me to starve?" said Mr. Jabbiano.

"I'm coming, sir." The waiter carrying the food rushed to his table and set the dishes appropriately.

"Here you go, sir. Sorry for the wait," said the waiter nervously. Mr. Jabbiano did not care for the apology as he immediately stuffed his face in an unruly manner. His actions were of a starving man, but his looks said otherwise.

"Next time, boy, I'll have your head," said Mr. Jabbiano.

"Sir, my apologies, but I can only bring out the food when the chef's done cooking it," said the waiter with a huge gulp.

Mr. Jabbiano swallowed his bite and made a slight motion to his two henchmen who were standing beside him. Like dogs given an order, they moved toward the waiter and began pummeling him.

"I'm sorry! I'm sorry!" he screamed, apologizing just so they would stop the beating.

They did not hesitate at his cries, continuing to beat on him. Meanwhile, Mr. Jabbiano ate his food, oblivious to the cries of pain. For the next minute, they tortured the waiter in public, stripping him of any dignity or value.

Suddenly a voice spoke from a distance. "Your men are quite effective and handsome, but their method is quite sloppy." The stranger sashayed his way into restaurant.

Mr. Jabbiano looked up and began wiping his mouth. He tossed his grease-stained napkin to the side.

"Who dares disturb my meal?" said Mr. Jabbiano.

With a flirtatious wave, Fawn said, "The one and only!" as he finally came into full view.

"Mr. Fawn, I'm glad you could take time from your busy schedule to join me for lunch," said Jabbiano, as he struggled to speak in his strained clothing.

"The pleasure is all mine," said Fawn, smiling devilishly at Jabbiano.

"Come, come, grab a seat." Jabbiano gestured for a chair. Immediately, one henchman dragged the bloody waiter from the spot, while the other pulled out a seat for Fawn. Fawn looked over the area and dusted his chair before sitting. A new waiter came and poured a drink for Fawn.

"This is a quaint little restaurant. It's like Olive Garden, but homier," said Fawn as he tucked his handkerchief back into his pocket.

Mr. Jabbiano looked at Fawn and then took a sip of his wine. He said, "This is my great-great-grandfather's restaurant. He earned this through the blood and sweat ... of others. Fawn, you must have a huge set of balls to come into my house and insult me?"

Fawn looked up to the ceiling and said, "Hmm, a big set of balls ... dare to dream." He closed his eyes and appeared to be doing just that.

Mr. Jabbiano said, "God rest his soul," as he made a sign of the cross. "In his day, you come into a man's house and insult him, he would've shot you on the spot."

Fawn said, "If you're gonna shoot me, I suggest you do it now because we're less than two weeks before the law passes, and those days of having a gun will be a thing of the past."

Jabbiano said, "You're assuming the bad guys are gonna abide by this."

Fawn replied, "When you're the boss of all the bad guys ... I'm willing to bet you're all going to follow."

Mr. Jabbiano made another gesture, and his henchmen moved toward Fawn. One of them pulled out a gun and pointed it at Fawn's head.

Fawn stared directly into the barrel, cross-eyed. "My, such a long and powerful gun. I wonder if it matches what's in your pants." The henchman looked confused by the comment and cocked his gun.

Fawn took his time and sipped a drink. He snapped his fingers, and ten of his men stormed inside the restaurant and surrounded him. The henchman with the gun switched his attention to Fawn's men but couldn't decide who to aim at.

Fawn said, "Manpower: it's the wave of the future. The economy is so terrible that it's created cheap labor. Technically, that single bullet is more expensive than one of my bodyguards."

Mr. Jabbiano was listening to Fawn while staring directly at him.

Fawn said, "You should play some chess. One doesn't sacrifice the queen to kill a pawn. Besides, you could pull that trigger, but then there's another twenty-five waiting in the wing."

Mr. Jabbiano finally understood how Fawn would play things out.

Fawn continued, "The thing about guns ... it's so quick. I would think most people would prefer dying a quick death, don't you think? But, there's more of a sense of accomplishment when you break a man with your own two hands." Fawn mimicked a snapping motion. "It requires so much more skill, as opposed to pulling a trigger and squeezing it. It's so much more personal." Fawn paused and admired the words he had spoken.

Jabbiano stared at Fawn, intrigued by his comments. "I doubt you've ever broken a man with your own two hands."

Fawn nodded. "You're right. I wasn't blessed by the gods physically. But I found my own niche, you could say."

Jabbiano laughed and stared down Fawn.

"By the way, the things I told them to do to you and your men if anything happened to me ... makes me kind of queasy ... even for me. I'm picturing what really would have happened had the three bears found Goldilocks in their house." Fawn smiled coyly and enjoyed his drink.

Jabbiano motioned to his henchman to put away the gun. Jabbiano smiled, chuckled, and said, "I have to hand it to you guys: you have done us one better. Corporations have taken crime to a whole new level. When you can do what we do and make it legal ... it's pure genius."

Fawn said, "Laws simply support whoever has the deepest pockets. Let's face it: no one has more than the corporations do, not even the governments. The deeper, the better; the formula of money making the world go round hasn't changed since the beginning of time."

After seeing the manpower that was being displayed, Mr. Jabbiano realized that the numbers were not in his favor.

"Enough blood has been spilled for today, don't you think, Mr. Fawn?" said Jabbiano, trying to save face. He motioned for both his henchmen to step back toward his side.

Fawn waved his hands, and ten of his men stepped back. "Choice—or should I say freedom of choice—is an illusion. It's an old salesman's technique of giving you two options: Would you prefer A or B? Only deep down, you don't really want either one. It's no longer choice when it's picking the lesser of two evils. So, I'm sure that's what you're feeling right now, Mr. Jabbiano," said Fawn.

Jabbiano squirmed uncomfortably in his chair as Fawn stared him down.

"See ... the question in your mind is: will you be the last of the organized gangs to fall under the umbrella of the UFMF or simply die?" said Fawn.

Mr. Jabbiano looked up at Fawn with resentment, but realized someone was playing his own game better than he could.

"I'm assuming the other mob bosses are performing the same duties you're requesting?" said Jabbiano, who still sounded out of breath.

"Like the good employees they are, but the difference is they are being rewarded handsomely," said Fawn.

"So, what do you need me to do?" said Jabbiano.

Fawn said, "Research says that, in two years, we should have everything franchised. Right now, we are projected ahead of schedule. I believe fifty-three percent conformity amongst the schools joining the UFMF, since the challenge matches have passed."

Jabbiano waited in silence until Fawn added, "This is your neighborhood, and you know it inside and out. We need for you to make sure we hit our goal. The other bosses are doing the same. Do you think you can handle that?"

Jabbiano said, "I believe I can help you there," as he took a sip of wine.

Fawn stared at Jabbiano and asked, "You seem to have a question. What, pray tell, is dwelling in your big cabeza?"

Jabbiano sat back up and adjusted his collar. "Why? Why eliminate all the martial arts schools?"

Fawn changed his tone as a seriousness came over his face. "My boss has a bigger goal, a new way he envisions the future. In order to create this, you must eliminate the past. The old way of thinking can no longer exist."

Jabbiano said, "You are one sick bastard, Fawn, and that I can respect."

Fawn smiled. "Enough about the dream, we need to ensure that we get there. Word on the street says there are a handful of schools that might be difficult to shut down."

"Everyone has a price," said Jabbiano.

Fawn replied, "What about those idealists?"

"Hey, these are dangerous times; things happen. Who am I to play God and predict the future? If it's not crime, then perhaps a random accident occurs. Besides, people are so desensitized from the news. Who would care?"

Fawn smiled. "Ooh, I love the unknown, the suspense. It's like cuddling up with a good book by the fireplace."

"Uh, yeah ... sure," said Jabbiano. With more confidence, he added, "One way or another, you will hit your goal. You said on the phone you had a second thing brewing."

Fawn clapped his hands in delight. "Oh, thanks for reminding me. Yes, we've been experimenting with a new drug. It's still in its early phases, but we'd like you to do the R&D behind this little project."

Fawn handed Jabbiano a little red pill.

Jabbiano studied it as he said, "So, what's it do? Give you a high, put you to sleep, or make your dick hard?"

Fawn shook his hand and said, "I like the latter, but no, no, no ... none of that. We're in the business of fighting, creating that ... oh, super fighter/soldier. Ask yourself: what makes a fighter dominant?"

"A good hook?"

Fawn said, "No, no, the bigger picture. You see, human beings fear the worst, the pain. All the pleasure offered can't overcome the fear of pain. Thus, as a fighter, if you don't feel it or it doesn't affect you...."

Jabbiano leaned forward and finished Fawn's sentence, "You'll be unstoppable."

Fawn smiled. "Exactly."

Jabbiano looked at the red pill with greater interest, as he held it up to the light. "Not that I care, but what are the side effects?"

Fawn replied, "Some dizziness, vomiting, and a handful of minor stuff."

"It sounds ready to go. Why the extra effort?" said Jabbiano.

Fawn thought about it and leaned over to whisper to Jabbiano, "The side effects seem minor enough, but what we're hoping for in stage one is one-hundred percent undetectability if tested."

"I'd be a fool not to ask, but it seems stage two is even better?" said Jabbiano.

With an evil grin, Fawn said, "Oh, stage two is a gold mine."

> *"If you look at the evil and good that is around us, I'm thoroughly convinced that heaven and hell isn't something that happens after you die. Instead, we already are living in it." –Sifu*

Sifu's Journey Entry #11—Favor Returned

Early Winter 2030

For the last several months, the line between student and teacher had been blurred. Sifu and Lance had been trading knowledge. Once mere acquaintances, their friendship had grown and blossomed to mutual respect for each other's craft.

Both men were in the basement, which had been finally transformed to the original vision—or so it would seem, for at the very least it wasn't the junk pile which it closely resembled just a few months earlier. It was Lance's turn to play the role of the teacher as Sifu was the student absorbing what he could from Lance's military background.

"You know, I'm the one who's supposed to be teaching you," Lance said in jest.

Sifu was coy and answered, "I'm listening." He was a good listener, as his appreciation to detail tested whether the instructor really knew what he was doing.

Lance, on the other hand, continued to be amazed as he shook his head at Sifu. "I know you are. I'm just taken aback at how much of the Wing Chun you taught me is tied into my own special forces training. No wonder you're picking up the stuff I'm teaching you like it's second nature."

Sifu made everything look so easy, even things he had never dealt with before. He said, "Wing Chun is life itself.... It's universal. Anything and everything you do involves Wing Chun. Besides, training is training. Understand the foundation, and everything falls into place." He caught himself and smiled ruefully as he realized he was supposed to be the student.

"Excuse me, I got carried away. Now, what were you saying about stealth?" asked Sifu.

"You said you wanted to learn what I know, so the topic for today is all about the stalk," said Lance.

"If I fail that, do I get a restraining order?" Sifu joked.

Lance looked at him strangely and said seriously, "No, in real combat, if you get seen, you get shot and killed."

"Oh," said Sifu. His joking manner finally turned serious.

Lance cleared his throat and began going into detail, "Anyway, the stalk is a training game that I had to go through. As a student, I had to be one thousand meters out to within one hundred and fifty meters of the instructor, avoiding detection by the instructors as well as the walkers."

"That sounds pretty cool. What are walkers?" asked Sifu.

"To make it more challenging, they would have two soldiers combing the area. If the instructor spotted you or the walkers after firing a shot, you were done," said Lance. He added, "Now what do you remember about the stuff I've taught regarding stealth?"

Sifu thought for a second. "Be aware of what's around you, especially on the ground. You said when you sneak up on somebody, a mere ant hill looks like a mountain to you. Thus, you have to think several steps ahead because once you select a position you have to ask yourself, will this cover me? If I'm spotted, what are my options to escape?"

Lance patted Sifu on the shoulder. "That's good, really good. Come to think of it, that's not different from the lines of attack and blocking that you've taught me in Wing Chun." Lance paused for a second and contemplated. He asked, "You sure I'm teaching you anything?"

Sifu smiled and patted Lance on the shoulder. "Of course, in the last few months, I've learned a lot from you as well."

Lance appreciated the compliment and said, "Okay then, if that's the case ... let's continue. I thought today we'd take a break from some of the physical activity and work on something fun."

"Fun?" asked Sifu, intrigued. He wondered what could possibly be more fun than learning stealth.

Keeping Sifu at bay filled with anticipation, Lance slowly revealed his plans for the day. Dragging his speech to make the words grander, he said, "Today, I'm gonna teach you how to ... paint your face."

Sifu wasn't expecting that as an answer and said, "Is my mascara running again?" He smiled at his own joke, which was a good thing, since finding reasons to laugh had been difficult the last several years.

"Funny," laughed Lance, "but no, I'm one hundred percent serious that this is something you definitely need to learn, if you want to know how to be fully invisible."

Sifu asked, "Can't I just put on a hood like the ninjas did?"

Lance replied, "Try wearing a hood in one hundred degree temperatures all day, and tell me how long you think you would last before you ripped it off your head."

"Hmm, you have a point," said Sifu as he had the look of disappointment. Sifu grew up in the 80's when Ninjas were the craze. "Oh well," he muttered.

Lance stared at Sifu and said, "Besides, you asked me to teach you everything ... so, yes, this is something you need to know."

"Let's get started," said Lance. "In the movies when you see the army guys paint their faces, they make it fancy. The key thing is to knock down the shine. You want to hit the high points with the darker colors and the low points with your lighter colors. The key is to trick the eye, and not draw attention to yourself."

For the next fifteen minutes, Lance continued to give hands-on instruction on how to properly apply camouflage. Every little detail, from pattern to color, was explained.

Sifu said, "I never thought putting on makeup would be this much fun."

"Why fear the unknown, embrace it. It's life pinching you to make sure you're living." –Sifu

CHAPTER 12
The Final Fight

That Evening

Kirin was in the living room of the hotel performing the first form, Siu Lim Tao. All fighters were required to stay at the accommodations that the UFMF provided, a trademark of their control, though they marketed it under the "for your protection" policy. It was roughly 8:30 pm after a long first day of battling in the DOME. Crowds were still gathered outside, enjoying this weekend's festivities, while the remaining fighters were preparing for the next day's battle.

Sifu was in the room with Kirin, but his attention was elsewhere. Strangely enough, it was aimed at the television.

Kirin glanced over at Sifu and asked, "Sifu, how long have I been doing the form?"

He glanced at the time and barked, "Kirin, it's only been thirty minutes. I said at least one hour." He returned his attention to the TV as Kirin, frustrated by the answer, mustered up some air and blew three strands of hair away from her face.

Several seconds later, like a kid bored doing her homework, she asked, "Sifu, I've been fighting all day. Isn't it a better strategy if I just got some rest for tomorrow?" Proud of her inventive response, she waited to see how Sifu would counter.

His attention never wavering from the TV, Sifu grabbed some chips from the side table and said, "Oh, stop your whining. You had two fights that took you less than one minute each. How tired could you possibly be?"

Unable to refute Sifu's argument, Kirin vented with a "Hmh."

Several minutes passed as she finally got to the right side of the first section. Kirin was concentrating on making sure her tan sau was directly in her center and that the elbow was leading the motion. She went slowly to feel for any muscle tension and finally managed to focus on a single thought. Her focus was easily distracted by the sounds of crunching from a distance.

Crunch. Crunch.

Kirin could hear Sifu eating as she turned in his direction. Kirin said, "You know it doesn't help that you're watching TV and eating while I'm working on first form."

Sifu looked at Kirin and said, "You're doing first form, not a hundred push ups," and he left it at that. Kirin thought for a second and again had no answer.

A minute passed as a devilish look came about Kirin's face. She blurted out, "Well, as my Sifu, shouldn't you be watching to see if I'm doing it correctly?" Kirin grinned from ear to ear, sure she'd finally thought of something clever enough that even Sifu couldn't object.

Sifu responded, "The point of you doing Siu Lim Tao right now is to work on your concentration of a single thought ... which, by the way, with all your talking, you're not doing too good a job." He went back to watching more TV and took a large bite out of a chip. The sound echoed back to Kirin and made her cringe.

I hate that he has an answer for everything, thought Kirin as she continued with her form. Thirty minutes passed without her speaking another word. Instead, she did as Sifu had instructed and concentrated on the task at hand. Finally at the end of the form, she punched with her left hand, circled her fist, and stepped foot to foot from left to right. Then she closed out the last motion of the form and took one last, deep breath, before letting it all out. Kirin grabbed a towel and wiped the sweat from her head. Her body felt warm as she strolled toward Sifu to see what he was doing.

"Okay, Sifu, I'm done," said Kirin. Sifu did not respond; instead, he continued to watch TV and ignore Kirin.

Kirin wondered what was so important on TV that Sifu would ignore her. She asked, "Sifu, why are you watching TV? You never watch TV."

"I'm not watching TV. I'm studying film on your opponent, Diesel Williams," replied Sifu. At first Kirin nodded, but upon further examination, she frowned in confusion. "Sifu, why? All year you told me to concentrate on only myself, and now you're studying film on my opponent?"

Sifu said, "TV pause," and turned around to face Kirin. He had a look of concern when he uttered, "It's true you should concentrate on yourself, but I've watched his last two matches that he had today. Then I checked out his previous matches from the entire season."

Kirin asked, "What is it, Sifu?"

Sifu shook his head. "There is something wrong with how he's fighting. Something's off." Kirin looked at Sifu, hoping he could explain further.

Sifu gestured toward the TV and said, "TV, play back part 1:15 in slow motion. Now, pay close attention to this, Kirin." The TV rewound to the exact spot and played. There on the screen, Diesel took a punch to the face as both Sifu and Kirin watched.

Kirin asked, "He got tagged, Sifu. What's the big deal?"

Sifu pointed to the screen. "That was a solid hit, and he barely flinched from it. Not even a slight reaction." Sifu stared at the screen where Diesel took the hit, and then heard Kirin's stomach grumble.

"Hmm, we should do something about that," said Sifu. Kirin grabbed her stomach and looked at him.

Knock. Knock.

Kirin looked at the door, curious about the timing.

"Did you order room service?" asked Kirin.

"Did you want a burger?" replied Sifu.

Kirin responded, "No!"

Sifu smiled. "Good thing I ordered you something better." Sifu got up and headed toward the door. He opened it to reveal a teenage boy holding a plastic bag.

"Ah, Sifu, I got your order," said the delivery boy.

"Right on time ... is everything here?" asked Sifu.

"Yeah, I double-checked; it's all there. Even the damn security to the hotel checked it," said the delivery boy, laughing. Sifu grabbed the bag and gave him several credits for tip.

The delivery boy's face cheered up as he looked at the credits. "Wow ... thanks, Sifu, much appreciated," he said as he began tallying up the amount.

Sifu patted him on the back and said, "Jahl muck-guess-eum-nee-da."

Kirin looked at Sifu funny. "Uh, when did you learn to speak Korean?"

Sifu laughed. "I only speak Korean food. Here ... see what's for dinner." He handed the bag over to Kirin.

She started unpacking Sifu's bag as her face brightened up as well. "All my favorites! Sifu, you shouldn't have," said Kirin.

"Come on; let's eat.... Then afterwards you do need to get some rest," said Sifu.

30 Minutes Later

Outside Kirin's hotel door, two individuals accidentally ran into each other. Each had a surprised looked and an annoyed reaction upon discovering who his counterpart was. Hunter looked at Tobias and said, "What the heck are you doing here, late-night training?"

Caught off guard, Tobias said, "Yeah, I wanted to go over some stuff with Kirin."

Hunter looked at his clock. "At 10:15 pm? Some last-minute tips? Admit it; you're here to talk to Kirin."

"Well, what are you doing here, looking to reminisce about your high school days?" said Tobias.

Hunter looked away and said, "Uh, I just had something I wanted to talk to Kirin about."

Anger and jealousy began to grow between them, each suspicious of the other's reason for being there. The two began arguing outside of Kirin's door, both finally venting what had been held back for so long.

Hunter said, "If she didn't care about me, then why would she kiss me?"

Upset, Tobias blurted, "You mean that friend kiss by the planetarium? Please, that's the same kiss she gives to Bacon."

Hunter's eyes narrowed as he hissed, "That's a lot closer to her than you've ever come, other then your chi sao drills."

Tobias replied, "Really? Raise your hand if Kirin ever asked you to spend the night." Tobias raised his hand and titled his head.

Hunter was surprised and saddened by that fact. He was curious when this had happened and asked, "Did she really ask you ... to spend the night?"

Tobias's triumphant look faded as he said, "Uh ... I, uh, spent the night at her place, but I slept on the couch."

Hunter was briefly relieved to find out the truth from Tobias, but seconds later the arguing between the two continued.

The door opened as both Tobias and Hunter stopped mid-sentence during their spirited discussion. As they both turned to look, Sifu came through the door.

"Good night, Kirin!" said Sifu as he shut the door behind him.

Sifu looked at both of them and shook his head. Hunter and Tobias exchanged a glance, but neither one said a word. Sifu let out a huge sigh and watched them both. It was an awkward several seconds as only Sifu had a clue what was going on. He said, "Young men have such terrible timing. If you don't mind, let me look at both of your hands."

Tobias and Hunter found the request odd, but did as Sifu had asked. Sifu spent several seconds examining both of their hands, as he nodded and grunted.

"Hmm, interesting. Very, very interesting," said Sifu. "It's funny how somehow you both justified in your minds that this would be the best time to confess your love."

Sifu chuckled and shook his head. Both Tobias and Hunter were embarrassed and looked downward, knowing that Sifu had pegged their reason for being there.

Sifu placed a hand on each of their shoulders and said, "If you both really care for her, then I suggest you set aside your feelings for one more night, and let her focus on tomorrow's fight. The last thing Kirin needs is emotional distraction, don't you think?" Sifu did not say another word. He walked away from the two standing by Kirin's door, letting his last comment hit hard.

Tobias looked at Hunter and saw they both agreed this was not the best time.

Hunter said, "Did we just get mind f–ed?"

Tobias replied, "Sifu refers to it as indisputable common sense."

Hunter said, "My god, that sucks ... so that's what Kirin's been talking about all this time?"

"Tell me about it; he does that to me all the time."

Hunter asked, "He also reads palms?"

"Yeah, yeah, he does." Tobias face looked stressed as he said, "I've always been hesitant to let him read mine."

"Why's that?" replied Hunter.

"'Because he's always right."

In hearing distance, Sifu stood unnoticed by the two gentlemen talking together. He said, "I'm headed down to the bar. I could use some company." He coughed several times like a B-level actor, signaling he wanted some response from both of them.

Tobias looked at Hunter and said, "Do you want to get a drink?"

Hunter said, "Sure, first one's on me. What about Sifu?"

"He doesn't drink," replied Tobias.

"So, I guess this is what it means to go with the force?" asked Hunter.

Tobias shook his head, "Nah, this is what it's like to have a Sifu who knows way too much." Tobias extended his hand and said, "For Kirin ... truce for now?"

Hunter hesitated for a second and then thought about Kirin. He extended his hand to Tobias. "Truce ... for now." They shook hands and began walking toward Sifu.

Meanwhile, in Another Section of the Hotel

In the penthouse suite of the hotel, loud music was blaring from wall to wall, causing it to shake. Alcohol was overflowing, and illegal substances were being used casually. The suite was packed with several scantily clad women running throughout the rooms, giggling for no reason at all.

In the mist of all this, sitting in the bubbling hot tub, Diesel was enjoying himself in excess the night before his biggest match. There were at least three women with him in the tub who were taking care of his needs as he savored the taste of his cigar and let out several puffs into the air. The doorbell rang, and one of Diesel's yes men ran to Diesel and asked, "Hey, Diesel, someone's at the door?"

Diesel shouted, "Then go get it, fool! Do I look like I'm the butler?" He scurried along, following Diesel's order. A minute passed before Fawn entered into Diesel's domain with a gentleman standing behind him. As always, Fawn was dressed in style, matching the wealth of his surroundings.

Fawn said, "My, this is quite ... uh, entertaining," as he looked around, somewhat repulsed at the sight. He waved his hand in the air, clearing out the smoke.

Having a hard time hearing Fawn, Diesel shouted, "Someone, turn off the goddamn music!" Moments later, the room became quiet other than the sound of bubbles and women giggling. Diesel took another puff from his cigar, savoring the moment, and said, "I'm glad you could stop by for the fun ... Fawn." He gestured for Fawn to speak.

Fawn smiled. "Oh no, while it's all so tempting, I thought we could go over a little bit of business for tomorrow." He placed his hand over his chest and with an embarrassed look on his face said, "Where are my manners? By the way, this kind gentleman behind me is Dr. Smith."

"What's up, doc?" Diesel took one final puff. He put his cigar down by the edge of the tub and lowered his sunglasses to get a better look at his guest. He nodded at Fawn, agreeing that it was time for work. Diesel didn't want the good times to end, but realized that this was his guarantee for making sure moments like this would continue in the future. He looked at the women who were admiring him and said, "Bitches ... leave."

His comment saddened them as one by one they got out of the tub. The last one gave him a special kiss to remember her by, as their tongues locked for several seconds. She slowly got out of the tub, and he glanced at her behind, appreciating her many talents.

Fawn coughed from all the smoke and waved his hands feverishly, trying to rid the area of it. Fawn said sarcastically, "I won't take too long. You must be tired ... only three?"

Diesel shook his head, looking for empathy. "Please understand, it's been a long day. I need to conserve my strength for tomorrow."

Fawn replied, "Right, right ... of course, Mr. Williams."

Diesel got out of the tub and stood in full glory in front of Fawn, leaving nothing to the imagination. Fawn looked down, and his eyes widened as he stuttered, "Hmm, no wonder they say once you go black ... uh, it leaves an echo."

Diesel snickered at his comment and then said, "I like you, Fawn. You always crack me up." He turned away for a moment and shouted, "Jerome, go get me a damn robe, will ya!"

Fawn asked, "Where would you like to do this?"

Diesel pointed in another direction. "Let's head over to the living room."

Diesel stood like a king while his subjects helped dry him off and placed a robe on him. There, they began their long walk down a hallway that seemed to stretch for a mile. Money was laid out for this penthouse inch by inch, yet those who dwelled in it were somewhat questionable in their entitlement. Jerome led them all to the living room, where he opened the double doors on a huge, luxurious space. In the center was a table and sofas for them to do their business, and the windows glowed with the light from the surrounding buildings.

Diesel turned toward Jerome and said, "Make sure nobody disturbs us!" Jerome acknowledge the order and closed the door behind him to give the three their privacy.

Diesel and Fawn sat down. "Let's get down to business."

Fawn snapped his fingers. "Dr. Smith here is gonna take a blood sample and ask you some questions."

Dr. Smith asked Diesel to extend his arm as he began to draw blood. Diesel's arm was finely sculpted out of pure muscle, so it was not difficult to find the vein from which to draw blood. He began to ask several questions of Diesel. Ten minutes passed as the examination went smoothly.

Dr. Smith turned to Fawn and said, "He looks a hundred percent, no side effects at all."

Fawn clapped in excitement. "Good, good ... is the tox-screen negative?"

Looking confident, Dr. Smith nodded. "Not even the smallest trace could be found on Mr. Williams."

Diesel gloated, "See, I told, you, Fawn. There was nothing to be worried about."

Fawn sarcastically replied, "Must be God's doing!"

Diesel looked above and made a cross symbol. "Damn straight."

Jerome entered the room and said, "Hey, Diesel, your wife is on the line."

Diesel waved him in and said, "Give me a second, will ya, fellas?"

Taking the phone, Diesel said, "Hey, baby, yeah ... I miss you, too. Nah, can't talk right now, busy with business and training. Yeah, I love you, too. Bye."

Hanging up the phone, Diesel said, "Sorry about that, gentlemen."

Fawn said, "Well, Mr. Williams, it seems like you're clear."

Diesel smiled. "So, do you have my insurance policy for tomorrow?"

Fawn pulled out a tiny red pill and said, "Take this first thing in the morning."

Diesel held the pill, admiring it. "I asked God for help this morning–and lo and behold, he sends me his message in a little red pill."

Diesel pocketed the pill and asked, "Are we done here, Fawn?"

He snapped his fingers, and a beautiful woman came running from the other room to sit on his lap.

Fawn joked, "Is God okay with this?"

Diesel replied, "If we confess our sins, he is faithful and just to forgive us our sins, and to cleanse us from all unrighteousness. John one, verse nine."

Fawn smiled and said, "Right, right ... nice backup plan. Uh, we should be going now." Fawn and Dr. Smith were escorted out of Diesel's room.

Diesel smoked one more puff from his cigar and said, "Pleasure doing business with you, gentlemen."

The Next Afternoon, Following the Third Round of Fights

The semifinals continued to build up the anticipation. Kirin and Diesel were set to meet one another in the final showdown.

418

Kirin left her locker room and headed up to her hotel room. She had several hours to prepare for the main event, and she wanted to get away from all the commotion and ruckus. Peace and quite were valuable commodities to her.

Kirin said, "Sifu, I'm gonna grab a bite to eat in my room. Do you want to join me?"

Sifu replied, "No, I'm okay," as he grabbed his belly and added, "Gotta watch my figure."

Kirin asked, "What are you gonna do?"

Sifu said, "I'll be downstairs by the lobby just relaxing."

Kirin looked at Sifu, knowing all too well what his favorite hobby was. "People watching?"

Sifu pointed to his nose and nodded. "People watching, much more entertaining than reality TV and it's free."

Kirin laughed and said, "I'll see you in a few," as she gave a quick wave goodbye.

From a distance, she could see the elevator, with no crowds or reporters, which motivated her to sprint toward it. Being a bit superstitious, she deemed this to be luck and hoped it would continue. The bellman kindly opened the elevator for her as she walked in and waited. The bellman looked back and whispered, "By the way, Ms. Rise, nice fight," as he nervously got back to his position.

A couple seconds passed before he turned again toward her and asked, "I hate to bother you, Ms. Rise, but can I ask a request from you?"

The last several months had many strange requests, but he appeared to be a nice guy, so Kirin replied, "Uh ... yeah, sure, what is it?" At first, she was thinking the usual photo or autograph, but he surprised Kirin with his answer.

"I was just wondering if I could just, uhm ... shake your hand." He looked down immediately, embarrassed by the request.

"Sure, why not?" said Kirin. There seemed to be no harm in that. The bellman grasped her hand firmly, shaking it several times as his smile grew from ear to ear.

"Thank you. Thank you so much, Ms. Rise." He began to stutter in excitement. "I've never touched the hand of greatness." He said it with such sincerity and honesty that it made Kirin blush. She was unsure how to respond to such a huge compliment. Afterwards, he got back to position, but was staring at the hand that shook hers.

She saw this and thought, *Hmm, a wee bit creepy.* She hoped the doors would close quicker.

Just then, a voice shouted, "Hold the elevator!" Kirin frowned as luck was not on her side. She'd have to share it.

The bellman did as he was instructed and said, "Here you go, Mr. Thorne." Immediately Kirin's stomach turned, and she bit her lip and looked downward.

Thorne entered the elevator, but Kirin refused to make any eye contact with him. He looked at her as he punched in the number to his designated floor. The doors closed as it slowly started changing numbers. A few seconds passed, and the elevator music did not help speed up the process. Kirin could feel the awkwardness of the moment and hoped it would all end soon. Ironically, she was now hoping someone else would come on the elevator as well.

Thorne broke the silence by clearing his throat and said, "Congratulations, Kirin, I have to admit I didn't think you'd survive all the way to the finale."

Kirin winced as her body tightened all over. She realized now she had to say something. After waiting a bit, she glanced over to Thorne and replied, "I have to be honest; I didn't think I'd get so much pleasure in making you eat your own words."

Thorne felt the dig but did not give Kirin any satisfaction by reacting to it. Tension filled the elevator, and the numbers flashing by seemed to gauge the level of discomfort that Kirin was feeling. *This is taking forever,* she thought, feeling her heart racing.

Thorne quoted to Kirin, "No one ever remembers the battles, only who won the war." Kirin let those words pass, but just his presence was beginning to make her blood boil. The elevator finally stopped, and Kirin began to walk out.

Thorne got in one last dig, "Running away so soon, Kirin?"

She stopped in her tracks and turned around, looking at Thorne directly. She said confidently, "After tonight's match, I'll give the world something they will never forget."

Thorne smiled at her response, liking the challenge, almost as if she were playing right into his hands.

Kirin looked him in the eye and firmly stated, "With all that money you spent on education and your fancy degrees, you never learned an ounce of humility. Tonight, I'm gonna do you a favor and give that lesson to you for free."

Thorne stood there staring at Kirin as neither one of them blinked. The elevators doors began to close, and Thorne said, "Oh, by the way, Kirin, say hi to your Sifu for me." His final words were timed perfectly to the elevator doors closing. Taken aback, Kirin felt her adrenaline pumping.

One Hour before the Main Event

The DOME was known for its brutality, and yesterday reminded everyone why this was not for the faint of heart. Two fighters did not recover from their injuries. One passed away during the night at the hospital, while another was killed during the match. This was the price to pay for fame and fortune. This was what society had grown accustomed to and had accepted as the norm. Oppression breeds hate and destroys the structure of humanity.

The final match consisted of five rounds lasting three minutes each. The rules were simple: go in and survive. The fighter could win by decision, forfeit, submission, knockout, or worse.

There was no outer cage but a circular ring that was twenty-four feet in diameter. The edge of the ring had a drop off that was padded. Hits or throws that led to ring outs were given massive bonus points in style. However, the fighter that was knocked out of the ring received massive point deductions.

A panel of experts were gathered to go over the main fight. Krenzel and Stabler, the main announcers for the event, were seated, getting ready. Assistants were helping with the makeup and making sure their equipment was working. Linkwater and

Connor were asked to join since they were announcers for the majority of Kirin's fights. The remaining panel was made up of Grandmaster Chang along with Dryden Rodriguez.

Stabler started the conversation as the cameras began to role. He said enthusiastically, "We are a mere hour away from the main event, and we have assembled an incredibly talented crew to give you the most in-depth analysis of this fight." He looked toward his crew and began introducing them, "Before we begin, we are fortunate enough to have three-time defending champion Dryden Rodriguez join us."

Dryden responded, "Thanks for having me here."

Krenzel asked, "Champ, before we get your analysis about this fight, we'd like to know what your status is for next year. How's the rehab going?"

Dryden responded, "Thanks for asking, Krenzel. I've been working extremely hard to get back into fighting shape. The rehab is ahead of schedule, and, yes, there is no doubt I'll be ready for the 2033 calendar season."

Stabler said, "As you've seen first hand, this season has been unbelievable. It's a story that could have only been written in Hollywood, yet here we are partaking in history ... your thoughts, champ?"

Dryden replied, "It's been difficult, staying by the sideline watching everything unfold. I wanted to be a part of all this excitement. To tell you the truth, watching this season inspired me to train harder than ever. I never want to take an opportunity like this for granted."

Stabler added, "I'm sure the millions of fans are looking forward to your return. Thanks for being here, champ. After a word from our sponsors, let's dive into the analysis of the fight and each fighter." Several commercials played, each one costing a ridiculous amount for every second aired. Finally, an assistant waved to Stabler that they were back on air.

Stabler ranted, "Gentlemen, let's get started, six-foot-one, two-hundred and twenty pounds of pure muscle, the first UFMF fighter to go twelve and O, ever! Diesel 'The Wall' Williams ... your thoughts, Krenzel?"

"What else can I say that you can't see with the naked eye? He is a beast; he's intimidating. He's highly skilled both as a striker and a grappler. When you look at him, you ask yourself: what is his weakness? Personally I can't come up with one. You don't go twelve and O by luck."

Rodriguez added, "When I fought him last year and beat him, he was about to hit his stride. Watching him fight this year, I can tell he's peaked at the exact right time. The match last year was honestly the toughest match I had ever gone through in my career in the UFMF."

Linkwater jumped into the conversation, "For me, the one thing that sticks out is that he can take a hit. There's a reason he's called The Wall—because that's what it feels like if you happen to connect. Most fighters today can deliver a good punch, but you gotta be able to receive as good as you get. He trains properly, and he knows that he can take a hit, something his challenger has yet to answer."

Grand Master Chang, "What can I say that hasn't already been said? He possesses all the key qualities you need in fighting: speed, power, muscle. He is the epitome of the perfect weapon."

Connor said, "The intimidation factor has to be it. I believe the majority of his opponents believe they can't beat him once they walk into the ring. Physically, he's got you beat, like Grandmaster Chang said, but mentally he's attacking you even before you step into the ring."

For the next ten minutes, the panel covered every statistic on The Wall. On paper, he looked unbeatable, and nothing but praise was thrown his way. One would have to be a fool to bet against him.

Stabler said, "All right, gentlemen, we're here to analyze both fighters. Without a doubt, the dark horse from the very start is Kirin Rise. Your thoughts, please, in any order."

Linkwater was first to give his two cents. "I've watched her for the entire year and seen every one of her fights. The truth is, I'm still not sure what I'm looking at. I keep wondering: how is she winning? I personally don't get it. At the same time, to be fair, one could make an argument that she could have easily been twelve and O, just like The Wall."

Stabler pointed to Rodriguez and asked, "As a fighter, I'm really curious what you've seen from her."

Rodriguez answered. "I'll be honest; I don't quite understand everything she's doing, especially how she's trained for this tournament. Let's face it: she is relentless. Once she closes the gap, she overwhelms you with attacks that are extremely difficult to block. My initial impression, just like the majority out there, was that these hits didn't pack a punch. But every fight she's been in, including what we've seen at the DOME, end in devastating hits. This is truly gonna be a test for her, but at the same time, she's proven everyone, especially the doubters, haters, and myself, wrong."

Krenzel said, "I'd like to touch on the unknowns. There's still so many questions remaining regarding Kirin Rise, but here are things I'm sure of. She's five-foot-three, a hundred and five pounds. If The Wall sneezes on her, it'll break her. Not rocket science, just pure logic. Her style of fighting may have caught everyone off guard, but I believe if anyone is capable of figuring her out, it would be The Wall. Finally, what I don't get is ... if she hits people down a straight line, why not cut her from an angle and flank her?"

Grandmaster Chang wanted to get in on the action. "I can sum up Kirin Rise with one single word: pure luck!"

Stabler said, "Grandmaster Chang, that's, uh ... two words."

"Uhm, yeah ... I meant, just luck." Grandmaster Chang tried to cover up his mistake. "Anyway, I know what everyone is thinking—she's like a cat with nine lives—but this match between her and Diesel is where it runs out."

Stabler finally said, "Thanks, Grandmaster Chang for your incredible, uh, insight." He coughed. "Everything on paper says there is no way she can win: her size, her sex, his skill. Logic dictates that she would have to do the impossible. Even if she were to fight the perfect fight, I can't see her winning. Even if they were to fight one hundred times, each time, without hesitation, I would pick The Wall. I have to agree with Grandmaster Chang that this fairy tale story won't have a happy ending."

The panel continued to pick apart Kirin, ending with a vote.

Stabler said, "Ten minutes away from the start of the introduction, your pick?"

Krenzel adamantly said, "Diesel," with no hint of hesitation.

Linkwater nodded. "Bet the farm, Diesel," he said as he and the camera turned to the next panel member.

Rodriguez thought a moment. "I have to be honest ... I'm torn, but I'll go with what my gut says, and that's Diesel."

Connor went for the dramatics as he took his time to look at each of the panel members. He paused to garnish more attention and said, "Hands down, Diesel."

Grandmaster Chang said, "Diesel, one hit, this will be over quick."

Stabler looked at everyone and then turned to the camera. "It would be tempting to pick the underdog and prove everyone wrong, but there's no way I can go against the panel of experts, the masses around us, and the universe. Diesel will take this fight."

The sound indicating that they were moments away from the start of the match caught Stabler's attention. He added, "There you have it, folks. Our expert panel has picked Diesel 'The Wall' Williams as the favorite. We'll be back for the introduction and the start of the match after these messages."

10 Minutes before the Match in Kirin's Dressing Room

Kirin found herself alone staring at the mirror in her dressing room. She was fully dressed in her new wardrobe that Gwen had designed. It felt surreal, almost like the Chum Night when everything first started. A knock on the door caught her attention as a voice spoke. "Can I come in?" asked Sifu.

"Sure, Sifu," she said softly, just loud enough for Sifu to hear.

Sifu poked his head in and said, "The guy just told me ten minutes before they announce you."

Kirin asked, "Are the guys all lined up?"

Sifu nodded. "Yup, they're just waiting for you to get ready."

Sifu could tell something was troubling Kirin as he entered the room. He approached her as she continued to stare into the mirror.

Kirin said, "Okay."

He walked toward Kirin and put his hand on her shoulder. "You okay?" he said as only Sifu could, with his voice of comfort.

Kirin did not look at Sifu and spoke, "I think every emotion one can go through I'm experiencing at this very moment."

Sifu smiled and said, "It is only natural."

Kirin chuckled and said, "Natural ... well, that's a good thing, I guess." Her eyes never strayed from the mirror, almost as if she were looking for something.

Sifu called her name, but Kirin interrupted him and said, "I look outside, and for every one person that believes in me, there's another thousand, give or take, who doubt. No matter how many fights I win, no matter how decisive the victory, it's like I'm speaking a foreign language to the masses."

"Patience, Kirin, patience ... you're asking people to see at your level, when they just can't. Belief starts with doubt; you've already got them questioning the system. That's how change begins," said Sifu.

When Kirin remained silent, Sifu added, "You have done more than any one person can expect or imagine. Remember, that single drop of water that lands in a still lake will spread further than one can dream of. But as the drop, it is difficult to see how far it stretches."

Kirin jerked toward Sifu and said, "Your teaching could do much more than all my fighting."

Sifu said, "No, you're wrong, Kirin. My job was to teach you.... Your job is to inspire the world."

Kirin laughed. "It's funny; most people would be concerned about winning or losing. Here I am, questioning whether my actions really make any difference, wondering ... is this all worth it? What if, in the end, no one believes?"

Sifu looked at Kirin and said, "All that matters is that you believe."

Kirin looked intently at Sifu.

Sifu said, "Win the fight, and you'll have a voice that the masses cannot deny and the undivided attention of the world." Kirin stood silent, absorbing what Sifu had said as she took a deep breath.

Sifu added, "There is one final lesson I wanted to go over before the match."

Kirin looked puzzled as she said, "Ten minutes before the match, and you're gonna give me a tip now?" She turned and faced Sifu squarely as he put both hands on her shoulders.

Sifu laughed at her comment, but quickly switched to a serious voice. "All the training I have given you, the skill to kill, it means absolutely nothing without the will. Your desire to go further, dig deeper, push beyond what you think you're capable of doing, will be called upon for this fight. Don't forget that!"

Kirin looked at Sifu and swore, "I won't forget."

Sifu leaned over and whispered into Kirin's ear, "By the end of this fight, you will be put in a position of power. You must decide for yourself which path to take."

Kirin looked at Sifu and smiled. "Let's show the world."

The Introduction

Diesel was waiting in the middle of the ring with his entourage. He was decorated like a king–and getting paid like one, judging from the advertising that was on his wardrobe. He danced around and joked with his manager as he waited for his opponent to be introduced.

Everyone was at the edge of their seats as the entire stadium went dark. The spotlight focused on the southern entrance where the audience could see a glimpse of Gwen. A flag was attached to her wheelchair, but it flopped down, unable to be made out. Gwen covered her eyes with her hand, shading them from the blinding light. The music started blaring, the signal everyone had been waiting for to begin the long march toward the ring.

Gwen led the processions, with Sage and Hunter following immediately behind her. Kirin's Wing Chun brothers formed a two by three line: Ken and Robert, Ryan and Doc, Danny and

Big T. All of them were wearing a uniform similar to the one Kirin was wearing. Just before Kirin, Sifu and Tobias stood side by side. Kirin waited for everyone to move, holding her place as the last one in line. As they made their way to the ring, the flag began to fly with a little help from Big T, who stretched it out fully for everyone to read.

It read, "The Illusion of Choice." The crowd stared, the short phrase capturing the attention and imagination of all. What did that mean?

Kirin entered into the stadium. This was her fourth and final time going into the DOME, but she was left speechless, in awe of the fandom. Her robe shifted with each step, and she felt every eye on her. Kirin still had the single sponsorship etched in the back, showing the symbol and name of the Salvation Army.

Flashes from cameras were exploding from every direction. She could see thousands of fans dressed up exactly like her, cosplaying. Signs were everywhere, both positive and negative, proposing marriage, telling her she'd lose, cheering her on to kick ass. The hundreds of news reporters from around the world were covering every step she took. As she neared the ring, she could see countless celebrities in the front row, clapping for her entrance. She shook her head and thought, *All this for a fight.*

The Fight

Minutes passed as the formalities were completed quickly. Anticipation filled the air—everyone was eager to see how the entire season would play out. The referee looked at both fighters to see if they were ready. Then he made a hand gesture and shouted, "Begin!" A bell rang. The moment everyone had waited for was at hand.

As in all her matches, Kirin stood in the middle of the ring with no guard. The switch had been turned on in an instant. This was no fight for Kirin; this was a duel to the death. She stared directly into the eyes of Diesel. No fear, no hesitation, no doubt.

Neither made an initial motion as the crowd's cheers shook the entire arena. They worked themselves into a frenzy of anticipation that threatened the very structure of the stadium.

Diesel flashed a smile and then brought his hands up, forming a guard. With a cockiness about him, he waved her in with his hand, inviting her, taunting her. He dared her to close the gap like she had done with every fighter she'd faced.

Kirin accepted the invitation and muttered the words she always said before the fight, "Target, center, own it." With that, she charged in, completely focused with one goal in mind. With no guard hands up, she dashed across the gap. As she sprinted in, Diesel began shifting his center to throw a kick.

In an instant, Kirin got what she was waiting for: a counter to his movement, and she moved in ready to deliver an attack.

She was there in an instant. Even before Diesel could fully unload his kick, her punch shot forward, forming a triangle guard as she connected to his center. He sailed back, the impact propelling him away from Kirin, but she snagged his arm and jerked him back in to deliver another solid blow to the face. The impact was devastating as Diesel's head snapped back in an unnatural manner—but Kirin was far from done. The flow always came in three. She planted a final pak punch hit to his face.

Wham!

It happened so quickly that the crowd struggled to process what they saw. Kirin unleashed a flurry of attacks that landed squarely upon Diesel, and he collapsed backwards and fell to the ground like a rag doll.

The crowd roared. Regardless of who they were supporting, they had witnessed greatness. The underdog appeared to have done the impossible. The referee ran in to see how Diesel was doing.

Kirin smiled as she turned toward the crowd with both her hands in the air. She had done what no one else could have conceived. Even she was in shock over what had just happened.

Silence reigned in the announcer booth until Stabler recovered. His voice was breathless, revealing he felt the crowd's disbelief. "When the impossible happens, what do you say?"

Krenzel tapped Stabler on the shoulder and said, "It's not over ... not yet." Both Stabler and Krenzel looked toward Diesel as Kirin was still celebrating her victory.

With her back turned, Kirin heard a voice shout from behind her, "Those were nice hits, little girl, but I hope those weren't your best shots."

Kirin heard the rustle of the mat as Diesel stood up. He rubbed his chin and stretched himself, seeming to return to normal.

Tobias turned to Sifu and said, "What the f–! There's no way humanly possible he could've survived those hits." Sifu did not respond, as he watched what would transpire.

A chill raced down Kirin's spine as she slowly turned around, recognizing the source of the voice. She was more surprised than anyone else to see Diesel standing there as if nothing had happened. He looked at Kirin with an evil smile and cracked his neck both ways.

Diesel stated, "Celebrating a wee bit early, aren't we?"

Ding. Ding. Ding.

The bell rang, signaling the end of round one, which had more twists and turns than a roller coaster. No one had expected what they had just witnessed. Kirin walked to her corner in a daze. Tobias pulled out a seat for her to rest as he and Sifu both tended to her.

Tobias asked Kirin, "Are you okay?"

Breathlessly, Kirin said, "Yeah, yeah ... I'm okay, just in a little bit of a shock." She was reliving the first round in her head.

She turned to Sifu and asked, "Sifu, I got solid hits on him, didn't I?"

Sifu nodded and with a look of concern said, "Aye, those were definitely solid hits."

Tobias looked at both of them and asked, "What's the plan?"

Kirin said, "Same as always, down the center."

Sifu whispered into Kirin's ear, "Stay within your game." As Kirin felt the words creep into her ear, she could see Diesel from afar eyeing her every move.

Round two began as all eyes were wondering what, if any, more surprises were in store. The referee shouted, "Begin!"

Kirin thought, *This time, when I hit, make it count even more.* Diesel charged in, and Kirin rushed to meet him. As often as they had seen Kirin charge, people were still in awe that someone of her stature would have the gall to run toward a runaway bus. But, the previous round made Kirin even more determined.

Diesel unleashed a cross punch toward Kirin, which she quickly tan sau'd off the line. Before he could finish his motion, she changed the block to a pak punch to land the initial blow. Again, she landed a three-hit combo on Diesel.

Hit. Hit. Hit.

This time, Diesel stumbled back, but did not fall over. Instead, he looked at Kirin and shouted, "Bring it!" He flexed his muscles, taunting her, and charged in hard.

He took several swipes at Kirin, but she was able to dodge and block them. Kirin countered each hit Diesel threw, her mind racing. Why weren't her hits damaging him? Were they not connecting? Kirin stuck to her plan, but her patience was wearing thin. Again, she thought, *That hit was solid; he should be going down.*

For the last minute of the round, they went back and forth, as Diesel was beginning to block more of Kirin's attacks. She was forcing her way in, trying to deliver that killer blow.

Suddenly...

Sifu shouted, "Kirin, no!" but his voice was drowned out by the thousands at hand.

It was too late. Kirin was frustrated and made a critical error. She invested one hundred percent in her last attack, which missed. Diesel seized the opportunity and delivered a devastating hit. Fortunately, she caught only a portion of the attack, but she had taken her very first hit.

Kirin flew backwards and fell to the ground. The crowd was in shock.

Stabler shouted, "This is the first time we've seen Kirin take a hit. Now it's time to answer everyone's question: can she get up?"

Krenzel added, "It wasn't a clean hit by Diesel. I think that's the only reason she survived, Stabler."

Size matters, and even a small hit from a man of his size could do considerable damage. Kirin got up and shook it off as Diesel smiled and clapped. "Impressive."

The bell rang as Kirin headed back to her corner. Tobias was concerned as he looked Kirin over. "Shit, her eye is closing up," he muttered as he began to place some Vaseline on her face.

Kirin joked, "I'm Asian. How much more could it possibly close up?"

Tobias said angrily, "Quit joking around, Kirin. This is serious," as he continued to exam her to see if she was okay.

Sifu said, "Any pain in the eye or blurriness?"

Kirin shook her head. "No, he grazed me at best. I'm okay. I'm more concerned with hitting him. My strikes they don't seem to be affecting him at all."

Tobias grew thoughtful as he finished his examination and then said, "Kirin, this reminds me of our gang fight several years ago, the one group we had a hard time against."

Kirin thought for a moment and recalled what Tobias was talking about. She said, "Yeah, you're right–I remember that now. It does seem just like it–but kinda different, 'cause this guy seems like he's ten times worse. I'm hitting him with everything I got, and he's still taking it."

Sifu gave Kirin some water and said, "Watch your defense. Make sure you make him stick. Don't over commit."

Kirin said, "Okay, okay!" Doubt was starting to creep into her mind. How was he taking these hits? How was it possible he couldn't feel the pain? As Sifu continued to give her some tips, Kirin was lost in thought.

As the bell rang for the beginning of the third round, Diesel charged in again, but this time Kirin placed her guard hands up.

Sifu shouted, "Don't spar!" as he slammed his fist. Tobias watched as Kirin went against Sifu's advice.

This time, Diesel was on the offensive as Kirin was blocking relentlessly. If not for her sticky hands ability, she would have eaten those attacks. Any normal fighter would, but she continued to go with the force, which aided her. However, in a fight, you never think defensively because there is a limit to what you can block, and eventually the numbers game wasn't in her favor. After stringing in combo after combo, a second punch connected, knocking Kirin to the ground.

Stunned from the hit, Kirin clenched her ribs and did her best to recover quickly. Diesel's hit got through, but it was not a clean shot. She was able to deflect the main force from connecting.

Stabler looked on and voiced what everyone was wondering, "Why isn't Diesel finishing her off?"

Krenzel replied, "She's down on the ground, but he's not ending it yet."

Diesel smiled at Kirin as she lay on the ground. He gritted his teeth and said, "Get up, Kirin Rise. I'm not gonna end this. I'm gonna make you suffer." She staggered up, grimacing from the pain, and immediately put her guard up.

Sifu shouted instructions again, "Stop blocking and attack! Fight, dammit, fight!" Tobias was shouting the same thing.

But it fell upon deaf ears, as Diesel charged in again and unleashed hate upon her. Block after block, she continued to stop the attacks, but a big hit finally got through, and Diesel pressed her hard toward the edge. Kirin went down hard. She literally flew across the ring and landed outside. The crowd gasped, knowing that falling outside the ring was both a huge bonus for Diesel and a massive deduction in points for Kirin.

Tobias turned toward Sifu and yelled, "Shit, she's gonna get killed, Sifu!"

Kirin could hear Tobias's voice in the background as she stared upward toward the ring, sprawled across the floor. She was in a daze, trying to shake off the impact of the last hit. Blood began to dribble down her nose, and her face felt numb. Suddenly everything became silent, and she closed her eyes, trying to muster up some strength. She felt it again, pain wrapped around her heart. It stabbed at her, reminding her of that time. The image became vivid again: she was there in that moment of helplessness, being carried off, screaming to her parents. She began to tear up as emotional pain clenched her chest, dwarfing the hit she'd just taken. That feeling she had promised herself she would never feel again was at hand. She told herself, *Get up, Kirin! Get up. Don't you dare quit. Get up, dammit. Don't you dare run from this.... Don't run from this, Kirin. Fight! Fight, dammit!* As the words echoed in her head, she saw the vision of her parents begin to fade away from a distance. The screams of the crowd jolted her memory, as if her parents were yelling for help. Kirin's eyes flashed open as she clenched her fists and inhaled deeply.

Diesel stood in the center of the ring absorbing the cheers of the crowd, while the referee hovered over the edge to check Kirin's status. Everyone was wondering if there was any fight left in her. Was this the end?

Stabler spoke to Krenzel as the cameras focused on their discussion. "Even if she somehow gets back into the ring, the massive point deduction will be almost impossible to overcome."

Krenzel nodded in agreement. "You're right. She's gonna have to end the fight with a KO or submission. Diesel's amassed a huge point bonus."

In the upper executive suites, Fawn waited eagerly for the conclusion. He was nervously pacing as his head jerked back and forth between the TV and the ring. He wondered, just like everyone else, if this was the end for Kirin. "Dammit, can't they get a better angle of her?" he shouted, frustrated at the network station.

Thorne watched intently, growing agitated by Fawn's nervousness. "Will you please sit down, Fawn?" he ordered.

Fawn went toward the bar to get a drink. He poured himself some relaxing liquor and said to Thorne, "You're right, boss. Again, you've got nerves of steel. There's no way she can win." His hand shook while holding his drink.

Thorne did not reply, trying to be an example of calmness. Then he stood up from his chair and looked toward the ring in disbelief.

Diesel was enjoying all the attention, as the crowd began to cheer even louder. He was full of himself, thinking that his time had come, and he had earned all admiration. But just like Kirin had celebrated too early, karma had come back to haunt him. A single hand appeared at the edge of the ring, as the cheers grew to a deafening level. He turned to look at the edge, and his facial expression said it all.

Moments later, a tiny girl crawled up. She planted both feet, energized by the support of the crowd. Kirin was showing what she was made of. There was no run in her; it was time to fight.

Stabler asked, awestruck, "How did she get back up?"

Krenzel shook his head. "I have no idea, and I thought *Diesel* could take a hit."

Diesel stood across from her and said, "James one, verses two through four: Consider it all joy, my brethren, when you encounter various trials, knowing that the testing of your faith produces endurance. And let endurance have its perfect result, that you may be perfect and complete, lacking in nothing."

Kirin looked at him and said, "F– you, Diesel!"

Diesel was insulted and was about to move in for another blow, when the bell rang just in time. Her snide comment had infuriated him, and the referee had to restrain Diesel from Kirin.

Tobias ran into the ring and helped Kirin to the corner. Kirin sat on the chair, as Tobias held her by the arms and yelled, "That's enough! You've proven you're tough. There's no beating him. Sifu, say something! Tell her to listen to me." Tobias looked to him for some support.

Kirin turned to Sifu, hoping he could figure out something. Now more than ever, she needed his wisdom as the will to fight and not run was fueling her. However, she had no answer for stopping Diesel. Both Tobias and Kirin waited anxiously for Sifu to come up with some strategy. He looked at Kirin with such intensity that she could feel it.

Sifu said in a stern voice, "Break him."

Both Tobias and Kirin flinched and shared a look of surprise. Neither one was quite sure what Sifu meant as they turned toward him for an explanation.

"What do you mean?" Kirin asked eagerly.

"Kirin, break him. Stop going for the hit and break him. He may not be feeling the pain when you hit his center, but his body still needs a structure to be able to move. Break him; destroy the very structure that's keeping him standing," said Sifu.

Sifu got in front of Kirin and looked her in the eye. He grabbed her hands and held them firmly. "This is what I was talking about earlier. He's cheating.... You've got to go beyond what you think is possible and dig deeper.... Your *will* will determine this outcome. Do you understand me, Kirin?" Sifu did not say another word, almost instilling his own will into Kirin.

Kirin looked at Sifu as if she were staring into his soul, "YES, SIFU!"

The bell to signal the next round was about to sound. The crowd was on the verge of erupting, as the tension kept building, from one round to the next. Kirin didn't say a word and began to walk away to the center of the ring, oblivious to her surroundings.

Sifu called her name for one last instruction. Kirin turned around and waited. He shouted, "Kirin ... unleash the art."

Stabler said, "We just took a quick online vote, and ninety-five percent believe that Diesel is going to kill Kirin."

Krenzel said, "I'm surprised it's only ninety-five percent. I don't know how she's gonna survive the next round," as he scratched his head, wondering who the five percent were.

The start of the fourth round was electrifying. No matter how this ended, the single thing everyone would agree on was that this was the greatest battle anyone had ever seen.

Thoughts flashed through Kirin's mind. The death of her parents fueled her; the burden of the people reminded her what needed to be done. She had to overcome. It was up to her; she wasn't helpless. She thought, *I have to do what I am destined to do!*

"Focus, Kirin, focus," she said to herself. She began breathing, in and out, in and out. She needed the single thought to give her purpose.

Diesel shouted from across the ring, "You think you're funny little girl? Well, guess what ... play time's over! I'm coming for you." His long outstretched hand pointed directly at her. Kirin could hear only her breath as the sound of Diesel as well as the thousands watching were lost to her focus.

The referee signaled to both corners, asking if they were prepared to begin. He got confirmation from both sides and waved them to fight. Kirin did not hesitate this time and charged in toward Diesel. He did the same, wanting to end this fight, conclusively. She threw out a punch that connected, but it didn't bring Diesel down. She threw another one, which Diesel blocked, but it forced him to spin. Diesel went with the force and threw a spinning back fist, but Kirin was there waiting for it. When he came around in full force, she timed it perfectly and went for the break.

Crack!

His arm snapped like a twig, but he barely flinched from the pain. The first chink in his armor finally was exposed. Surprisingly, the break merely stunned him as he looked at his arm just flailing away. Diesel staggered backward, wondering what just happened. It was a horrific sight that forced others to cringe and turn away.

Sifu shouted, "Don't stop! Go! Go, Kirin ... go!"

Kirin moved in again, but this time Diesel tried to swing with his only good arm, his right. Kirin ducked the attack and pulled him off center with a lop, bringing him halfway to the ground. She used his arm to control his position but did not go for the break. Instead, her leg was in perfect position for a sweep as she exposed his entire limb. Once he was vulnerable, Kirin did not hesitate. This time, she snapped the ankle first and then went to break his knee.

Crack. Snap.

As loud as the crowd was cheering, every bone breaking could be heard and felt by others. The crowd reacted to the break; it was both devastating and gruesome to watch. Stabler and Krenzel had seen this before, yet they were taken aback by such brutality.

He fell to the ground, but did not agonize in pain. Instead, he stared in disbelief at the bone sticking out of his leg as he got up. He hobbled onto one leg and stood there. As he tried to move toward Kirin, he stumbled over. Struggling to support his own body, he fell to the ground.

He looked up at Kirin with his hate-filled eyes, as he shouted from the top of his lungs, "F– you, bitch!"

Kirin looked at Diesel, who was in pieces, and shook her head, indicating this match was over. But Diesel was not to be denied. His physical attributes allowed him to stand up as he had one last ounce of fight within him.

As Kirin moved in for the kill, he tried his best to use his only good arm, but Kirin easily blocked it and made him pay the final price. The block flowed into a joint lock, and the crack of his bone echoed through the arena. She had rendered his other arm useless.

Diesel fell to the ground broken and unable to defend himself. The once-powerful figure lay helpless on the ring floor. The crowd shouted for her to finish off Diesel–the greatest fight in the history of the UFMF needed an ending that no one would ever forget.

"Kill him! Kill him! Kill him!"

Kirin looked around at the thousands chanting for his demise. She grabbed him by his head as the rest of his body lay limp–unable to move. She was prepared for the final break: his neck. Her heart was racing at a hundred beats a second as blood and sweat poured down her face.

Diesel was fearless. Even at this vulnerable state, he stared at Kirin directly and egged her own. He screamed, "Do it, you coward! You're afraid to finish it?"

Thoughts were racing through her head. She remembered all the times that power had been used against her and how she ran. This time, it was finally in her hands: she had the final decision, she had all the power, she had total control. She could end the wrongs with a single twist. Kirin could feel her body tense up, something she wasn't used to in applying any of her techniques.

Sifu had taught her, in a fight situation, decide yes or no. Never hesitate. There was no doubt that if Diesel were put in command of the situation, he would end her. The roaring noise of over two hundred thousand people gradually became silent, replaced by the sound of each breath, as that was all that Kirin could hear. She stared in the sea of humanity, watching the masses demand his death, but through the crowd of hate, she was able to spot a familiar face. She thought, *This seems familiar.* She shook her head, as the blurred image finally became focused. It was Sifu. As Kirin gazed at him, she could see his eyes, and she saw nothing but kindness. As they locked stares, her breath became slower and slower, until her last exhale froze in time....

Kirin looked over at Diesel, who she was holding by the head, and said, "God isn't sparing your life today–I am!"

She lowered Diesel's head gently to the ground and waved the referee in to end the match. The crowd went wild, shouting and screaming as security tightened up to make sure no one could enter the ring. Exhausted and drained, Kirin dropped to her knees, crying as both Sifu and Tobias ran in to catch her.

Stabler said, "Kirin Rise has shocked the world. She is the new UFMF undisputed DOME Champion of the world!"

The ring announcer started speaking, "Ladies and gentlemen, in a stunning upset scoring a win by forfeit, Kirin Rise is your new champion of the world!" His words resonated in total pandemonium.

Krenzel added to the comments, "Unfricking believable, I can't imagine anyone walking away from this not being surprised by the outcome. This was just beyond incredible how this fight turned out. No words can do it justice."

Stabler added, "I'm totally speechless. I'm gonna let the camera take over so you can just watch the commotion below. Wow ... just incredible!" The rest of the panel remained silent, stunned by what they had witnessed.

Sifu got on his knees and held Kirin. He said, "You did it!"

Kirin tried to smile at him, but suddenly tears began rolling down her face. She whimpered, struggling to speak, "No, Sifu ... we did it."

As Sifu held her in his embrace, he began to cry, like a father being proud of his daughter's accomplishment. They hugged each other tightly in the ring, comforting one another, while everyone celebrated around them.

Several Days Later

In a beautiful high-rise building in New York City, outside waiting in the grande lounge, Thorne sat in his chair with his team of associates: Linda, Fawn, and Justice.

Thorne asked Linda, "What's my schedule for today?"

Linda looked at him with trepidation and said, "I, uh ... cleared your entire schedule, sir. This meeting is it."

Even Thorne seemed uneasy at being kept waiting for over thirty minutes. Fawn broke the tension by speaking, "Boss, it can't be that bad ... astronomical ratings for the fight, the deal's been set to go global for next year, and UFMF stock prices are at an all-time high."

Thorne did not say a word. He knew on the outside things looked in favor of the UFMF, but Kirin's defeat of Diesel weakened them internally. The foundation had been compromised as Kirin's latest humanitarian gesture gave her an even stronger voice within the community. Most importantly, a sense of doubt may have been created over their top project with the government.

Linda wrestled with her pad, putting it to the side as she asked, "Mr. Thorne when was the last time you saw him?"

Thorne did not answer right away. Fawn jumped in and said, "I've never met him at all," as he glanced toward Linda and Justice and added, "Come to think of it, other than Mr. Thorne, this will be our first meeting with him ever!"

Thorne was lost in a thought, trying to remember the exact period. Finally, he replied, "It's been years since I've seen him face to face." As they continued waiting in the large, luxurious room, a cold, eerie feeling spread throughout. The sofas were aligned so that, even as a group, they felt distant from one another. As the silence stretched, it was filled at last by the sounds of several footsteps coming closer. All heads turned toward the source as they waited to see.

There stood three of the most gorgeous secretaries one could imagine. If not for their attire, one would've thought they were runway models. Each one rivaled the looks of Linda as they stopped to pose in unison. Justice definitely took notice, and even Fawn–for a brief moment–questioned his sexuality. The trio stood in a straight line and then, without a word spoken, created a triangle formation. Two stood behind the main one, as she took her time posing before uttering a word. She looked directly at Thorne and said, "Mr. Thorne, he's ready to see you now."

Thorne acknowledged the request as he got up from his chair and then adjusted his suit. Justice, Linda, and Fawn stood up as well, ready to accompany Thorne in the meeting.

The head secretary placed her hand up, saying, "I'm sorry; only Mr. Thorne is needed for this meeting." She gave Linda a snobbish look that didn't sit too well with her. "If you will please follow me, sir." The rest of Thorne's team exchanged glances, realizing that the situation was more serious than they thought. Thorne waved them down, doing his best to reassure them that everything would be all right. But, as he began to walk away, Linda noticed a hint of perspiration at the edge of his brow. She struggled to put a smile on her face and did not say a word. Thorne did as he was requested and began the long walk by himself.

Meanwhile, Back in Chicago

Kirin was surrounded by her friends sitting at her favorite coffee shop. Word quickly spread that she was there, and a large crowd gathered outside. Fans were hoping for a peek or a chance of an autograph and pic with her. Kirin calmly sipped her latte as the presence of a huge crowd no longer put her at unease. She put her cup down and kindly waved to the crowd as they cheered at her, thankful for her acknowledgement.

Sage said, "Thanks for treating us out to coffee, Kirin."

Gwen snickered. "Yeah, I mean, when you make twenty-five million, who can't spare three bucks?"

Hunter joked, "Uh, is there a reason I couldn't order a large?"

Kirin listened to their voices, relishing the sound and the company of her friends. She took another sip and savored the moment.

Tobias interrupted the silence and said, "Guys, don't get used to this." He shook his head, and the rest of the gang looked at Tobias, puzzled by his comments. He paused and stared at Kirin. "Uh, Kirin, did you tell them?" he asked cautiously.

With a look of serious concern on his face, Sage asked, "Oh crap, tell us what?" He held his breath, expecting the worst.

Gwen folded her hands in a prayer. "Oh my god, please don't tell me you did good. Please, please, please, God, no!"

Hunter looked at the chain reaction forming and asked cautiously, "What ... what did you ... do, Kirin?"

Kirin put down her latte, grabbed a napkin, and wiped her mouth. She made the group wait even longer, building up the suspense at hand. She said, "I ... uh, donated the entire twenty-five million to charity!" Like a bandage waiting to be pulled, she blurted it out with a single rip.

All her friends were in a state of shock. Gwen and Hunter's jaws dropped from the news, and Sage almost spit out his coffee as he looked at Kirin in disbelief. Silence fell briefly around the table.

"God damn Salvation Army!" Sage was the first to break the silence. He pounded his fist in jest as Kirin giggled at his act.

Gwen laughed at his comment, but reality finally set. "This is bad karma, Kirin. Mark my words! Bad fricking karma." Gwen looked dead serious, which caught Kirin's attention.

Kirin frowned in confusion. "How so?"

Gwen's eyes squinted just a hint as she made Kirin wait. In a seedy voice, she said, "Twenty-five million ... now the Salvation Army can buy real weapons. Is that what you want? Huh? You want them to start a war?"

Kirin crumpled a napkin and threw it at Gwen, who did a terrible job trying to block it. Gwen looked at her with a smile, still shaking her head as she added, "You think you know your friends, and then–bam, this happens."

Hunter sank back in his chair. "Looks like I'm gonna have cheap ramen once I go back to my classes."

Tobias uttered, "Thank God I didn't quit my day job."

Kirin glanced at all the sulking faces and laughed. "Look, guys, it's just too much money. There comes a point when you ask yourself: how many houses do I need? How many cars do I want?"

Gwen asked Kirin, "Do you want me to answer that with a specific number?"

Sage replied, "I wish that point would happen in my lifetime."

Kirin cleared her throat loudly, indicating she had more to say. "We all live good lives, decent ones.... I just thought it would be fair to let those who are less fortunate get a piece of the pie, don't you think?" Even in speech, Kirin used Wing Chun, as her last statement made the group contemplate the facts.

Everyone fundamentally agreed with Kirin, but at the same time, she could sense that, deep down, each one was hoping to enjoy just a little of the winnings. Her friends looked like they were fantasizing about what could've been, had she kept all the money. Kirin wasn't sure if Gwen was acting or not when she shriveled into a ball and laid her head on the table.

The somber mood was broken by a voice from a distance, "Why the long faces?"

Kirin smiled, recognizing the soothing voice. She turned around and greeted Sifu.

"Sifu, glad you were able to make it," said Kirin as her voice perked up.

With her head on the table, Gwen mumbled, "Why don't you ask Ms. Goody Two-Shoes what she did, Sifu?"

Sifu looked at Kirin and waited for her to speak.

Kirin didn't hesitate and said, "I was just telling everyone ... that I gave all the money I won to charity."

Sifu did not react like everyone else; he was emotionless and just stood in place. He paused before speaking, leaving everyone curious about what he would say. Even Gwen raised her head up slightly, peeking through the crevice of her arms.

"It's an act of kindness, and you've always stayed true to your feelings, but such actions sometimes lack balance," Sifu said.

Sage pointed at Kirin and with a hint of cockiness said, "Ah ha ... see, Sifu agrees with us. You should've kept some money."

Kirin was caught off guard by Sifu's comment and was about to speak, but then she noticed Sifu reaching into his pocket.

"I had a feeling you would probably give away your winnings, Kirin." He pulled out an envelope and gently laid it down on the table in front of Kirin.

She asked, "What is this?" though she was really wondering how Sifu knew what she had planned. Kirin just stared at, it clueless to the contents.

Sifu replied, "Go ahead and open it."

All eyes were glued to the envelope as everyone was on the edge of their seats, wondering what it could be. Kirin slowly opened the envelope and pulled out a sheet of paper that she began to read.

With each line that she read, Kirin's eyes widened. She giggled, not out of humor but with a puzzled look on her face. "Am I reading this right?" she asked, still focused on the writing at hand. The anticipation was killing everybody as the group shouted and asked her what it was. Kirin put the note down and with a blank look on her face said, "I'm not sure how this is possible, but I think ... this is a fully paid vacation for all my friends and family."

Everyone looked flabbergasted, not expecting the words that came out of Kirin's mouth. Gwen took the initiative and asked, "Not that I'm being picky, but is this a vacation, or more of a vacation like a road trip to the Dells?"

Kirin looked at Gwen and shook her head. "No, Gwen." She exhaled and took another breath. "It's a first class flight, all expenses paid, seven-day cruise to the Bahamas." She placed her hand on the envelope as she looked to see everyone's reaction.

"Shut up!" shouted Gwen as she reached out to grab the note.

As everyone started celebrating the news, Kirin looked back at Sifu and asked, "How is this possible?"

"Consider it a gift for all your hard work," said Sifu.

"I can't accept this, Sifu, and how is it you were able to pay for all this? asked Kirin with a concerned look on her face. "This had to cost a small fortune." The group was curious but also cautiously concerned that Kirin would again turn down this opportunity.

Sifu smiled and said, "Technically ... you kinda paid for all this...."

Kirin frowned at Sifu, even more confused. "I don't understand?"

Sifu said, "It's very simple. I bet on you.... I bet that you would win the entire tournament, and you did just that."

Kirin said, "You did what?" With a shocked look on her face, she scratched her head and rubbed her eyes, acting as if she were in a dream. She asked Sifu, "I thought Wing Chun people don't gamble?"

Sifu replied, "You're right. I would never gamble, but gambling is a game of chance. It's betting on the uncertain outcome. I, on the other hand, never once doubted that you would win. Remember our conversation before, Kirin? It's not a question of if, but when." A big grin appeared on Sifu's face.

Kirin sat there frozen, stunned by Sifu's explanation.

Sifu put his hand on Kirin's shoulder and said, "Anyway, I thought this would be an admirable gesture on your part to thank all of your friends and family. I'm sure you would agree that, without their support, getting through this entire year would've been a difficult task."

Kirin smiled at her friends and nodded, "Thanks, Sifu. As usual you're totally right ... but I know I couldn't have done this without you." Kirin stood up and hugged Sifu. She leaned over and whispered into his ear, "Thank you for everything, always."

Her friends were all smiles hearing the news. Excited for their future plans, they were in a jovial mood to celebrate.

Tobias got the attention of the group and said, "Guys, I know these are lattes and coffees, but I thought we should do a toast."

Hunter agreed and said, "What should we toast to?"

Sage stood up and looked at all his friends. "Ladies and gentlemen, if you don't mind ... I'm sure we'd love to see Kirin win the next UFMF DOME Fight ... and hopefully next time, keep the damn money!" Everyone giggled and laughed as Kirin smiled bashfully at the comment. Sage waved his hands requesting for their full attention as they took a moment to settle down. He had a look of seriousness as he stared at each of his friends and paused once he got to Kirin. "To my dear friend ... excuse me, correction ... to our dear friend Kirin Rise. Raise your hands and toast with me if you believe ... that everyone in the world now wants to fight ... *just like a girl.*

"Hear, hear!" The group smiled proudly and raised their cups to cheer.

THE END

"The world will move on without you, unless you give it a reason to stop." –Sifu

Short Stories #12–P.O.V.s–Tobias, Diane Rise, Sifu

<u>Undelivered–January 5, 2032–Tobias's P.O.V.</u>

"What's wrong with you, Tobias?" I felt like a zombie as I stared numbly into the mirror. The longer I looked into the mirror, the more difficult it became to see my own reflection. I splashed some water onto my face, hoping it would cure the situation.

Splash. Splash. The water felt refreshing, physically, but mentally I had been out of it all day.

"I've practically wasted this entire day sulking–and for what? I didn't do anything wrong. I was right for yelling at Kirin for entering the fight."

I looked outside my little apartment window and saw people hanging around outside in the street. The streetlights made it glow like the stars, even if it wasn't comparable to downtown's skyline view. However, there was something different about tonight. From a distance, I saw a couple walking together arm in arm; they seemed to be enjoying each other's company. I looked closer at the girl, who was looking intently at the man's face. It was hard to describe, but she was giving him that look of complete attention, as if she were mesmerized by every word coming from his mouth. I had seen that look before, but where?

I grabbed a half-empty can of beer that sat by my window ledge and decided to finish it. "Blah," I muttered as it tasted stale. I threw the can into the garbage.

In the background, I could hear the sound of my television as I stared into oblivion.

A reporter droned, "The talk of the town continues to be the mystery fighter who has captured the attention of the entire world. What everyone wants to know is: who is this mystery fighter?"

I turned toward the TV to see a picture of Kirin's fight being replayed over and over.

I shouted, "It's Kirin Rise, you dumb asses!" I laughed a little as I realized I was talking to no one.

"Volume up," I said less vibrantly, letting the TV tell me the latest news. I walked into the kitchen and opened the fridge. It was a typical bachelor fridge: beer and several pieces of fruit and some leftover stuff, which I wasn't sure was still good.

As I searched the fridge for something appealing, the latest news report caught my attention. I turned to the TV and listened. "The UFMF has signed a contract with the government which investors are expecting will massively impact tomorrow morning's opening trade. Reports are not clear as to the role the UFMF will be playing, but...."

"F–ing UFMF," I grumbled as I focused my attention on my nearly empty fridge. "Well, the choice is still the same," I said to myself as I tried to decide between nutrition or wasted calories.

"Dark side wins. Beer it is!" I grabbed another one and popped it open. With a can of beer in my hand and a sense of accomplishment from my major decision of the day, I sat down on my couch and watched more TV. Suddenly my phone rang, but I did not answer it. I made a halfhearted attempt to pick it up, but did not get it in time.

Several seconds passed as I let whoever decided to call me enter their voice message.

Then I said, "Phone, playback message."

The phone beeped, and a familiar voice said: "Hey, baby, it's Jasmine. You haven't called me in a while. Give me a call back.... I thought we could hang out tonight and hit a coffee shop or something ... and, I promise you that you'll get a little taste of mocha."

I shook my head and threw my phone across the room, where it landed on my bed.

I peered over to the corner and saw that it was 9:00 pm. *Damn, what a waste of a day,* I thought.

I sat there on my couch finishing another beer as the TV bombarded me with news of Kirin's fight. Minutes passed as the sound of the broadcast echoed in my head. Every word coming out of the reporter's mouth sounded the same, and it all came down to one repeated question: Who is she? Who is she? Who is she? Each time he asked, the name "Kirin" entered my mind like a throbbing headache.

I finished my beer and crushed the can. I threw it away but missed the garbage can completely this time. Instead, it hit a picture on my desk and knocked it over. It startled my one true friend in the world–Brutus, my fighting fish–he spun around erratically in his fish bowl.

"Dammit," I said. *I can't even do that right,* I thought.

I got up and walked over to pick up the frame I had knocked over. As I grabbed it, I looked at the picture, and saw one of the rare pics of me and Kirin hanging out. She had taken it awhile back. As I studied it, I got lost in a daze. Finally, I saw something that I had never noticed before. Kirin was giving me that look, the same look the woman on the street was giving that man.

What am I doing? I thought. A minute passed before I scrambled, searching for my phone I had thrown in my bedroom.

"Dammit, where is it!" I made a greater mess of my room before I finally pulled it from a pile of clothes.

"Ah, there it is." I quickly started to dial.

I first called Kirin directly but only got her voicemail. "Dammit, of course she's not answering. Knowing her, she probably doesn't have it on her." I shook my head, wondering where she could be.

"Who would know where she is? Who?" I muttered as I scanned through the list of her friends in my head and said,

"Gwen, definitely Gwen." I dialed Gwen's number, hoping she would know.

Ring. Ring.

"Come on, pick up.... Pick up," I said in a hurried voice.

"Hello, this is Gwen."

I said, "Gwen, it's Tobias.... Do you know where Kirin is?"

Gwen answered, "Nah, I haven't heard from her in a couple of days.... I'm actually looking for her now."

"F–!"

Gwen said, "You know, I was thinking–"

I rudely hung up on Gwen, as my need to find Kirin grew.

I grabbed my jacket and my motorcycle helmet and said, "I gotta find her."

I ran out of my apartment, talking to myself as I leaped onto my motorcycle.

"She's a creature of habit. She can only be in a few spots," I said to myself.

Okay, let's try the coffee shop first, I thought. Several minutes passed as I flew through the streets till I got to her favorite coffee shop, Red Eye. I could see from outside that several people were still there, probably having their late-night lattes and espressos.

I opened the door and walked into the coffee shop, scanning the area quickly. "Dammit, I don't see her," I said.

"Where else? Where else could she have gone?"

"Hmm, maybe she's at home. It's possible she didn't pick up 'cause she saw it was me calling." I tried to kick the negative thoughts out of my head.

Like the wind, I was a blur as I drove to her place. Ten minutes later, I parked my bike on the sidewalk and ran to her front door.

Buzz. Buzz. Buzz.

No response as I waited. I decided to look up to her loft and noticed there were no lights.

"She wouldn't be asleep this early in the night," I said. Frustrated, I got back on my bike and started driving again. I was zipping in and out of traffic through the streets of Chicago. Several minutes passed as I tried to figure out where she might be. My mind was racing, unable to pinpoint a single thought as I came upon a stoplight.

At first I was pissed that the traffic light had caught me, but that moment of silence allowed me to gather my thoughts.

"Come on, come on...." From the corner of my eye, I noticed a local flower vendor who was calling it quits for the day.

"Hey, you?" I shouted over to him.

He looked at me, somewhat happy at human interaction as he said, "Hey buddy, I still have a bunch of unsold flowers; you interested?"

I asked, "What you got left?" I tried to think what Kirin liked and remembered tulips! "Hey, any chance you have any yellow tulips?"

He checked quickly in the remainder of his stash and said, "You're in luck. I do have some."

I asked, "Any idea how many flowers represent I'm sorry?"

He thought about it for a second and said, "How about three?"

"Doesn't three flowers mean I love you?"

He replied, "It could also mean I am sorry."

I thought about it for a second and decided it made sense. "Fine, give me three."

He laughed and said, "I guess you got no choice; all I have is three."

I thought, *Then why are we having this conversation?*

He wrapped up three yellow tulips for me as I paid him. The florist said, "Thank you for your business." Just like that, I thanked him, stowed away the flowers in my bike, and took off.

Well, this does me no good if I can't find her, I thought. Weaving through the streets of Chicago, I was paying attention to not killing myself from my reckless driving and trying to figure out where Kirin could be.

"It's 9:50.... Where would I be if I were you? Where would I be?" I said; the need for an answer was killing me.

I needed to clear my mind, so I parked my bike on the side. Just like Sifu said, I needed to empty it to see the answer. Several minutes passed as I did just that, focusing on my breathing and quieting my mind. I finally felt decent again as my head cleared. I looked up at the sky and saw the stars. "Holy shit! I'm so stupid, the planetarium."

I kicked-started my bike and made like the wind as I started darting again through the streets, weaving illegally and dangerously. I did not care; I was on a mission to find her.

Finally, I got to the Chicago planetarium. "She's gotta be here. This is her favorite spot when she wants to get away," I said. I parked my motorcycle and started looking around. Suddenly, I noticed a bike along with a carrier.

"That's her. She must be taking pictures with Bacon."

I ran back to my bike and grabbed the flowers, realizing I knew exactly what to say. I had finally figured out what was bumming me this entire time: I felt bad that I had yelled at her after the fight. I was scanning the area and suddenly saw Kirin from a distance.

My heart raced, and I felt alive after feeling so numb and almost dead the entire day. I started running toward her and then stopped in my tracks.

She wasn't alone. As I approached closer, I saw that Hunter was there. I stood there silently from a distance as I watched them. They were engaged in a conversation ... and then it happened.

From life to death as my heart sank and skipped a beat. Kirin move toward Hunter and kissed him. I closed my eyes and felt foolish. Disgusted, I dropped the flowers and walked back to my bike.

<u>Seeing Eye to Eye—July 2, 2032—Diane Rise's P.O.V.</u>

Ding Dong. I heard the doorbell ring from the kitchen. "One minute!" I shouted as I dried my hands and made my way to the front door.

Butterscotch was already there, barking and jumping, reminding me that my attention was needed.

"Good girl," I said and petted her on the head.

I looked through the glass door and saw an elderly Asian gentleman standing patiently. Examining him, I was sure I did not recognize him, so I cautiously opened the door slightly and said, "Can I help you?"

The gentleman spoke in a soft and comforting voice, "Hi, Mrs. Rise, you don't know me, but I'd like to speak with you for a moment, if you will."

It didn't look like he was selling anything, so I asked, "What's this about?" as my voice carried through the narrow crevice.

The man cleared his throat and said, "It's about your daughter."

I don't know if it was the frustration that had built up for the last several months, but I reacted by slamming the door immediately. Almost as quickly, the anger faded, and I felt bad for treating him that way. I looked through the glass and saw that the gentleman was standing there, calm and unflinching. I shouted, "I'm sorry, but I'm not talking to any reporters or paparazzi. Please go and leave us alone!"

His calm voice carried through the door. "Mrs. Rise, it's a very important matter. If you would please just give me a moment of your time, I have some explaining to do."

I leaned back against the door, feeling the pain of not having spoken to Kirin since she decided to enter the tournament. I took a deep breath and shouted, "If you don't leave, I'm gonna call the police. God, I wish you people would just go away."

There was no sound for several moments as I looked to Butterscotch, who remained excited by the door. Suddenly the voice said, "Mrs. Rise, I'm neither a reporter nor a paparazzo. I'm merely ... your daughter's teacher."

Hearing that caught me off guard, *Teacher?* I thought. I didn't think Kirin was taking any classes.

It was silent for a good, uncomfortable minute. I rubbed my eyes, trying to make sense of the matter as I finally asked, "You're Kirin's teacher?"

"Yes," he replied.

I asked sternly, "Teacher of what? Kirin's not taking any classes."

"I guess you could say I'm her Gung Fu teacher," he said humbly.

I thought for a second, *Doesn't he mean Kung Fu?* I was curious to know who this man was, as I needed answers for myself. I began to turn the knob slowly, and Butterscotch hopped up, curious as well to see this person. As I opened the door even further, I held her by the collar. She no longer barked but continued to squirm in excitement.

"I'm sorry, but what was your name again?" I asked.

"My apologies, you can call me Mr. Kwan," said the gentleman.

Curiosity got the better of me, and I opened the door slightly. With Butterscotch's uncontrollable jumping, I lost my grip on her. The feisty golden retriever jumped through the door and leaped toward the gentleman. She was extremely friendly toward him as he returned the favor and petted her. "Good girl ... good girl, Butterscotch," said Mr. Kwan.

I was taken aback that this stranger knew my dog's name. "I'm sorry, but you seem to know quite a bit about me and my family."

He stopped petting the dog and signaled for her to sit. I watch as Butterscotch graciously followed his order. He said, "My apologies, Mrs. Rise, for my intrusion. I'm sure my being here is a bit of a shock to you, but like I said earlier, I'm here to talk about your daughter."

I looked at Mr. Kwan and did not say a word; instead, I waited to hear what he had to say.

"I'm sure you know that your daughter is going into her first fight in two days," said Mr. Kwan slowly and calmly, almost as if he were testing the waters. My slight change of expression told him I was well aware.

"I'm here to ask something of you." Mr. Kwan looked down toward the ground as if he were bowing. "While Kirin has not said a word to me, I can tell that you have not spoken to your daughter since she mentioned what her plans were." I looked at him, knowing he was right, as I began to tear up and cry.

Mr. Kwan then looked up and stared into my eyes. "My apologies for your pain. But, I humbly request that you speak to her before the fight. Your daughter needs to hear from you again."

My sadness turned to anger as I said sternly, "This is all I have. I'm hoping she'll put her family first and quit this nonsense.... If I speak to her now, there's no way she'll back down from the fight."

Mr. Kwan remained calm even in the heat of the moment as he said, "Mrs. Rise, as a parent, I can understand your frustration, but I can also tell you that, whether you talk to her or not, Kirin is going to fight ... regardless."

"Then why do you need me to talk to her?" I asked.

Mr. Kwan replied, "Because I would rather have her fight with a clear head tomorrow, than have this issue linger in the back of her mind."

I asked, "If you're her teacher, why would you let her do this? Why would you put her in harm's way?"

"This was not my idea. Kirin did this all on her own. When I found out about her intention to join the league, my choice was simple: either help her or not," replied Mr. Kwan.

He met my gaze levelly and said, "So, I chose to help her."

As much as I felt angered by his comment, he did make me think. He wasn't pushy like a salesman, but I couldn't argue against his logic. I was still confused, unsure of what to do. "She's gonna get killed out there. There's no way she can win."

He replied confidently without hesitation, "She won't."

I asked, "How can you say that?"

"Because I taught her. She will not lose, Mrs. Rise. I'm willing to bet on it." Mr. Kwan stared directly into my eyes.

I was having a hard time accepting all of this; it was too much to process. It troubled me, not helping my daughter.

As if sensing my uncertainty, Mr. Kwan said, "I know this is difficult to understand, and if anything does happen, I take full responsibility." His voice changed and sadness was clear on his face as he said, "Mrs. Rise, do you mind if I share something with you?" I looked at him and waited.

"When your daughter first walked into my school eight years ago, I knew right away there was something about her. At the time, I thought I was the one helping her out. I could feel her pain, her loss, even without her ever mentioning a word.

I thought if I taught her, the art could help her overcome her troubles," said Mr. Kwan.

I knew, of course, what Mr. Kwan spoke of. Kirin's struggles with her past and the nightmares of her parents constantly haunted my daughter. I remembered the pains so vividly, and it upset me that nothing we did could help her. But as I listened to him explain what he did, it was starting to make sense. Looking back, I could see how she did improve and eventually overcame it.

Mr. Kwan continued, "So ... even though I knew she was going without your permission, I accepted her as a student. She was a good student, practiced harder than anyone, almost driven by her past. She always listened to every word that came out of my mouth. She trusted me like a daughter would trust her father. And with time, I too looked upon her like my very own."

His kind words were soothing to me, but then he paused as his voice cracked. "Little did I know that, in the end, it would be her helping me."

I could see that Mr. Kwan did care about Kirin deeply.

For the next several minutes, Mr. Kwan spoke of his past, opening up as I listened with a heavy heart.

Mr. Kwan said, "I don't know why I told you that. I have never told anyone that ... but Mrs. Rise, life is short, and I believe, without a doubt, your daughter needs you now more than ever."

I didn't know what to say as I was still torn and pained by the moment. Mr. Kwan did not utter another word. He bowed to me and petted Butterscotch one last time. Then he walked away as I watched.

Skill Unleashed—October 15, 2032—Sifu's P.O.V.

"Billy, are you one hundred percent sure about this info?" Looking at his face, I could tell he spoke the truth, but I needed to hear it one more time.

Billy said in a jittery voice, "Yeah ... definitely, Sifu," as he continued to look around in a nervous manner and struggled to stand still.

"What about the cops?"

"They bought off the right ones for tonight," said Billy. Even for a young kid, he knew how the world really functioned. The fact was he never had the chance to enjoy a normal childhood.

I pulled out my phone to check on the time. Then I said with urgency, "All right, Billy, get out of here before you get spotted ... and be careful."

Billy looked at me with concern and said, "Sifu, there's one more thing. I wasn't able to fully confirm it, but my source also told me that they could be packing heat.... What are you going to do?"

I looked at him and replied, "Don't underestimate the power of the mind when it comes to bullets." I patted him on the shoulder and scooted him on his way. Billy was gone within seconds.

If the mob was willing to stoop so low to defy the corporation, then they were willing to lose everything. The gravity of the situation was dire.

Immediately I rushed back into the kitchen, where Lance was working on the night's preparations. He looked at me and could tell something was off. "What's wrong?"

I began to explain to him the situation and my plans. Knowing we were pressed for time and couldn't go into greater detail, Lance suggested, "Let's close up for tonight. I should go with you."

I shook my head and replied, "No ... you need to stay here and make it look like everything's normal. You're my alibi if this somehow comes back." I checked my clock again and added, "There's no time to argue, Lance. You have to trust me on this one," as I put my hand on his shoulder.

Lance shook his head. "I don't like this plan one bit. I know I've taught you a good amount of what I was trained for in the forces, but you're gonna hit this place blind?"

Lance was right; hitting this place blind would put me at a significant disadvantage. Suddenly, I knew how I could even the playing field a bit and said, "I know who we can call to help us." I quickly scrolled through my phone and, as luck would have it, Kirin had placed a call to her friend Gwen on it. I dialed the number, hoping that she would answer.

Ring. Ring. "Come on, Gwen, pick up the phone." I was trying to will her to be there mentally.

"Gwen speaking?" she answered as I breathed a quick sigh of relief.

"Gwen, it's me."

"Is that you, Sifu?"

"Yes, it is."

Gwen replied, "Uh, hey, Sifu, didn't expect you to be calling me."

I said, "Listen very carefully to what I'm about to say to you." I quickly explained to Gwen the urgency of the moment and told her of my plan to head to Kirin's parents' house. I asked, "Do you understand, Gwen? Can you get me a full layout of her parents' house?"

Gwen replied in a hurried voice, "Give me five minutes. I'll pull it up and send the information directly to your phone."

I stressed to Gwen, "Gwen, no one can know. Do you understand me? No one!"

In a concerned voice, Gwen said, "I understand, Sifu."

With that, I gathered my belongings and prepared to head out. At the last minute, I went to my drawer and pulled out two new decks of unopened playing cards. I tossed them in my bag, thinking, *This might come in handy.*

I needed to make sure that the crowd saw me, so I walked into the main room and greeted everyone. I explained to them that I'd be busy with inventory and hoped that they would enjoy their soup. Several minutes later, I was ready to go as I handed Lance a flash drive.

He looked at me and asked, "What's this for?"

I replied, "I recorded my voice on it. Play it every so often and interact with me, okay?" He nodded and took the drive from me.

"I gotta hurry, Lance."

Lance looked at me and said, "Sifu, you can't leave body bags."

"I know, just enough to put them down. I'll do my best."

Lance was agitated about the entire situation. "I don't like this; you'll be at a disadvantage. You taught me yes or no in this kind of situation, that Wing Chun always fights from a position of strength."

I smiled and said, "It'll make it more challenging." I pulled a key from my pocket and placed it firmly in Lance's hand.

Lance looked at it and then asked me directly. "What's this?"

I said, "Just in case karma's not on my side tonight."

Lance replied, "God speed," and with that, I gave him a handshake and a hug.

20 Minutes Later

Dressed in all black from the neck down, I did a rush job on my facial camouflage. I didn't have time to do a thorough survey of the entire perimeter of the house, so I circled once on foot, selecting the best view that I could get, which was the back of the Rises' home. I sat quietly, blending in with the darkness as well as the trees. I could see activity was already happening. Billy's time was a bit off, but he was dead on that a gang would hit Kirin's family tonight. I checked my time to see that it was five minutes before midnight. The winds were howling, which would aid in covering any sound that might carry.

I hope I'm not too late.

I had only been to the front steps of the Rises' house once. If not for Gwen, I'd be going in blind to the inside layout. She did as she promised, delivering a full schematics of their house. Lance's training came in handy, as he taught me how to memorize things quickly, allowing me to create a mental plan of attack. Normally, one prepares entry for days, but I did not have that luxury on my side.

Billy said possibly ten to twelve guys could be inside, I thought. *I'm gonna shut down the power, create some confusion, and draw them out.*

One of the bedrooms was currently lit, and shadows of figures moved about on both the top and the bottom floors. The main light was stemming from the master bedroom. I quickly ran to the side of the house and got access to the fuse box that was linked to the inside. I put into play more of Lance's training as the power went off and the house went dark. Immediately I could hear the reaction from inside.

I changed position again, staying close to the source of power, while looking to see how many guys would come. The backyard layout was to my advantage as I was in hearing distance as well. The house was pitch black, and I could hear the commotion within. The winds continued to rustle the trees and leaves outside, making it easier for me to blend my motion with the sound. My plan was simple: take out whoever came through the door and use the same entry, which I calculated to be the back door to the patio.

I waited patiently and, within a minute, two men came out running, using their phones as makeshift lights. I sat quietly trying to pick up any information I could from their discussion. Once they were in position, I would take them out swiftly. I waited a pinch just to make sure they were the only ones. I could clearly hear them bitching, as they were less than fifteen feet away from the fuse box. I listened in on their conversation.

"Hey, I think it's over here by the side of the house," said one of the henchmen as he drew nearer.

"You sure? I can't see shit out here."

"Hurry up, will you, before the boss gets pissed that we took so long."

"How do you know it's not a power outage?"

"I don't know. Frankie and Tony are checking the basement, and Johnny ordered me to check the outside," he replied.

"Hey, I found it!" said the henchman who began checking the fuse box to see if it was all right. "Larry, come over here and help shine some light," he ordered. His friend did as he was told and began flashing the light so he could see.

He said, "What the hell is going on here? This things is all screwed up."

The henchman holding the light replied, "You sure you know what you're doing?"

Both of them were preoccupied with their little task. I made sure that I stayed out of the line of sight of the guy holding the light, but I was prepared to close the gap just in case. I snuck up, timing my steps with the sound of the night. Once within striking distance, I hit Larry at the right moment and grabbed his phone. It was just enough to knock him out, but the transition wasn't perfect.

"Hey, give me some light, will ya? Quit goofing off," said the henchman working on the fuse box. A second later, I flashed the light back on the fuse. "Thank you, now to figure this crap out." I did not take him out right away, since he was the chatty type and I wanted to see if he would say anything of relevance.

"I think I see what the problem is," he continued to fidget with it. "You know, Larry, that bitch Kirin is in for a surprise. I've never seen the boss so upset losing that much money before."

As the minutes passed, it became clear that he had nothing more to offer, so I flashed the lights off again. He turned around and said, "Will you quit goofing—"

Whack. I gave a quick lop chop to the side of his neck and made sure his structure didn't support the hit. He was out cold.

That's two down, I thought as I grabbed both men and tied and muzzled them up appropriately. A quick frisk revealed that one of them was armed with a gun. I removed the clip and tossed it into the dark. It was confirmed: they were packing. How many was unknown, but I'd have to assume the worst. Moments later, both henchmen were secured tightly and hidden in the backyard bushes.

Shaking my head, I thought, *Dammit, wasting too much time on this.* Realizing that time wasn't my friend, I ran for the patio door and broke some rules of stealth by not bouncing from one object to the next and blending in with my environment. The priority was to make sure no harm came to Kirin's family, so it was a calculated risk that I thought I could afford.

Entering the patio, I found the sliding door unlocked, so I opened it cautiously. I remembered the layout of the house, and had already calculated which route to take to the stairs. The priority was to get to the bedroom at all costs. If my stealth was blown, running was not an option.

Entering the kitchen, I heard the sounds of footsteps creaking overhead. Inside the kitchen, it was silent, almost too quiet, so I left the sliding doors open as the wind penetrated the room, creating an echoey sound. A door straight ahead would lead directly to the hallway and staircase. I began walking toward it and was about to open it, when I suddenly heard voices on the other side. I quickly crouched down in the corner as the door swung open, slowly controlling my breathing.

"What the hell is taking those guys so long? Frankie, go outside and see what those goofs are up to." I recalled the conversation outside and realized these must be the two guys who went downstairs to check the basement. Deduction led to the realization that this must be Tony.

"God, those idiots even left the door open," said Tony as I was positioned directly behind them, waiting in the shadows. From behind, I hit their centers and dropped both of them to the ground. They were clean hits, and both of them fell exactly where they stood. I had no time to make it pretty and left them both in their places. I searched them as well, but neither was armed with a gun, only a knife and some brass knuckles. A second passed as I closed my eyes and felt for something. Normally, I should've gone directly through the doors into the hallway, but my gut told me otherwise. I circled toward the dining room and waited before entering their living room. As I sat there, I could tell from their motion that they were unaware that I was hunting them down.

A voice called out from the living room, "Guys, the lights are still out. What gives?"

As footsteps approached closer, I waited along the wall of the dining room right by the entrance. The room was brighter, as the starlight cast through the side windows. The doorway swung to the right; thus, the eyes would take a moment to adjust to the light, giving me my opportunity to strike. As the footsteps approached closer, I was waiting for the right timing. I used the sound of his footsteps as well as his voice to judge the distance. Just as I suspected, a slight pause once the door was opened.

"Hey, what's going on—" said the henchman. I struck in midsentence, and the body had no time to react to the hits.

His arm was a handle which was easily pulled, and as his body leaned forward toward the ground, a single punch to the back of his head knocked him out.

The henchman dropped to the ground as I caught him and tried to reduce the noise. *Hmm, a bit of overkill,* I thought as I checked for his pulse. *He'll live.* He already had his gun drawn, and the routine of emptying it and hiding continued.

More voices started circulating on the main floor, but I felt a coldness in the dining room. *What is that?* I started looking around, searching for the source of that eerie feeling. Along their long dining table, there it was.

Dammit, I thought, shaking my head as Butterscotch lay on the floor in a pool of blood. I got down on one knee to check on her, but her stillness was confirmation that she was already dead. *Gotta move quicker.* I made my way through to the living room entrance.

I did a quick count in my head, noting five men were down and two were packing heat. I moved quietly through the living room, no longer hugging the corners as I needed to get up the stairs. Halfway inside, two henchmen stopped me dead in my tracks. I lost focus for a second as I let my guard down.

One of them said, "What the f– is that?" in clear confusion. Without any hesitation, I closed the gap. His partner behind him made a motion to draw his gun, but that was not my concern. Panic filled their eyes. Whether they had a weapon or not, the target was always the center. The combination of a sudden rush along with a man's natural fear of the dark created terror. They were no trouble at all, and I sliced through both of them with my attacks, using enough precision to stop each hit from becoming a fatal blow. Unfortunately, one of the men let out a scream upon my last hit.

Shit, I thought.

Immediately I could feel the change as the energy of panic filled the house. More sound came upstairs as the pace confirmed it. The darkness made it difficult for all to see, but mentally I knew exactly where I was. I turned my head slightly and calculated that I was fifteen feet from the stairs. I heard the footsteps of another henchman creak of the base of the steps.

He pulled out a knife and said in a crackled voice, "Angelo, Larry, is that you?"

The time for stealth was over. It was time to move in quickly and get to the goal. I stared into his eyes and then into his soul, as I rushed in. My directness held him in place for a brief second as his hesitation was his undoing. He stood there frozen with his knife out in front for a brief second. He swung wildly with no purpose, allowing me to counter easily. The fear, darkness, and chaos made it difficult for him to target me. However, I did not need a clear light to see him. I could feel his intent even before the touch, and I knew exactly where the target would be after. The years of training and sacrifice had allowed me to do things others could only imagine. In a blink of an eye, he was disarmed and lying on the ground. I dashed up the stairs, laying low, and suddenly heard the cracking of bullets fire through the air. It was panic fire; they were shooting blindly into the darkness.

The sounds told me that two men were creaking down the upper hallway, making their way toward me. My positioning was terrible, as options were limited: either go back down, head toward them, or run to the other side of the bedrooms. With no time to think, I acted on instinct, going for broke and risking more. I saw both men were carrying guns as their footsteps drew within fifteen feet of my position.

I grabbed one of my decks of cards and pulled out several from the stack. *It doesn't have to hit them, just get their attention,* I thought.

As they approached the staircase, I quickly threw two pairs of cards. One of the cards hit a henchman in the face, while the other two whizzed by and did the job of distracting them. They fired immediately–and randomly.

Bang! Bang! Bang!

Perfect, I thought as I tossed the remaining deck in the air toward their faces. It rained in front of them, creating a flutter of confusion. They fired again in a panic. I counted: five, four, three, two, and I ran toward the edge of the hallway and hit them hard.

Whack, whack. Hit, hit.

Down they went, as my adrenaline was pumping and I took a moment to catch my breath. At the end of the hallway, the sound of more shuffling continued. Everything was unknown: the number of people in the room, what weapons they carried, and most importantly if Kirin's family was safe. Looking around at the two goons on the floor, I made a decision. *One of you guys are gonna help me out.* The biggest of the two helped with the sorting process as his unfortunate soul was dragged to the bedroom.

Looking at the crevice through the door, the uneven pattern of the moonlight indicated that there were three guys nearby. I checked my inventory and put my last deck of cards by my holder next to my arm.

Several deep breaths to begin the process of emptying the mind created the focus, and the silence led to the emptiness which finally gave me an answer. Staring at the door, I thought, *There are five people inside.... If my feelings are correct, there are five.*

So, I did what any reasonable guest would do and knocked on the door. Staying low and to the side, I knocked rhythmically seven times. By the end of the last knock, whoever was inside fired several rounds at the door.

Bang, bang, bang, bang.

The holes in the door let the rays of starlight pass through. The holes gave me an idea of the angle from which the shots were fired. Listening as more shuffling occurred in the room, I thought, *Time for some better bait,* as I grabbed my reluctant volunteer.

The henchman was still down and out, so I sat him up and I began to massage a point by his lip to wake him up. Within several seconds, he was dazed and confused but conscious.

I whispered to him in a coarse voice, "Thanks for helping me." With that, I kicked the door open. It shattered into halves, and I shoved him into bedroom. He screamed in panic, "What's going on?"

Natural human reaction froze them in their tracks for a second and allowed me the opportunity to enter. Springing into action behind him, I saw my feelings were right: there were five people. I whipped several cards at the thugs on the outer edge. The throws were dead accurate, and as they were struck in the face, they tried to regain their bearings. The distance was now fully to my advantage because all three of them were within kicking range. The confused henchman functioned as my straight shield as I kicked him from behind. He fell on top of his colleague who stood in front of him.

It was time to unleash savagery upon them. I wanted the screams to be haunting. My aim was not to knock them out, but to break them. Their confusion left them vulnerable as each one was being broken within seconds. They were on the floor rolling around in agony, and I felt merciful for allowing them to live. My will would not be denied, not by them, not by their weapons, as I released a force of destruction they were not prepared to see. The four henchmen were downed in seconds, and I focused my attention on the two remaining men.

A quick glance told me the disgusting blob of a man was in charge—and guarded by his last henchman, who carried a knife. I looked at the family bound on the bed, but they appeared to be safe for the moment. I thought, *Just another minute, you'll be okay ... I promise.*

The blob grabbed the last henchman and yelled, "Get him! Kill that f–!" but the henchman was shaking in fear as he looked me in the eyes. He was no longer in a position of strength as his true colors showed. As he moved closer, he suddenly dropped the knife and lifted his hands in surrender, shaking and begging, "I'm sorry.... I'm sorry."

I smiled at him to assure him that he would be all right. Timing it perfectly, as he breathed a sigh of relief, a quick hit to the side of his neck knocked him out cold. He crumpled at my feet as I slowly began walking toward the last man standing.

You can always tell a weasel when you see one—and this man was a weasel. He used his only defense, trying to talk his way out of the situation. Shaking uncontrollably, he said, "Who the f– are you?" I did not respond, nor did I need to. I wanted him to feel the fear, the terror, as I drew ever closer. The silence alone screamed louder than words.

He tried to bargain with me, "I swear I wasn't going to hurt them. It was just a scare." His voice shook, and he was sweating profusely. I thought for a second that I would be doing the world a favor by getting rid of scum like this, but I remembered paying a huge price to karma for playing judge and jury. As I moved toward him, he began to sway and collapsed right on my feet. I kneeled to check his pulse, as I thought, *Bastard, passed out. I guess the universe saved my karma.*

I got up and headed toward Kirin's family, but suddenly I stopped in my tracks. I turned around to look at the piece of garbage on the floor and decided I had some karma to burn....

Sifu's Journey Entry #12—A New Start

Day 1, Spring 2029

It had been a long day, and Sifu was on the brink of calling it quits. They had been driving around for hours now, looking at one location after another. This was the fifth and final spot. Like an itch that couldn't be scratched, something deep down told him to press on and just give this one last chance.

The realtor pulled to the side of the street and parked the car. Sifu glanced outside and saw they were here. He tried to stay neutral upon looking at the place and thought, *Don't judge a book by the cover.*

"We're here!" She smiled enthusiastically and directed Sifu to the front door. The realtor was busy searching for the key, as Sifu examined the outside. The windows were all boarded up and covered from the outside. *Run down, filthy, dilapidated....* Yeah, that was the word he was looking for to describe this eyesore, dilapidated. He cringed ever so slightly that he would soon hear the words, "Fixer upper."

Ahhh! They heard a loud scream from a distance which caused both of them to look suspiciously around. Sifu cautiously said, "Uh ... I'm sure it was nothing," as he tried to reassure the realtor that they were safe.

The realtor turned slightly pale and nervously laughed. "I'm sure it was nothing, either?" She scrambled to find the right key, wanting to open the door hastily.

Sifu did his best to lighten the mood, "Looks like a fresh can of paint would do wonders," but his voice lacked conviction.

The realtor faked a laugh and hoped he was saying it only in jest. She finally opened the door and waved Sifu to hurry along inside.

Once inside, she immediately slammed the door and locked it. Sifu stared straight ahead, into the abyss of darkness. "Hold on; let me turn on the light," said the realtor who realized that Sifu was staring at nothing. Upon illuminating the room, Sifu's first thoughts were to turn the light off. He cringed at the thought, wondering how much time and effort this would take. The place was already an eyesore, but that was the lesser of the evils when compared to the smell.

Ever the salesperson, she quickly got into form and began pitching it to Sifu. "Mr. Kwan, this is about twenty-five hundred square feet, give or take. I know at first glance you have to use your imagination, but there are two things that make this place quite unique. Due to some crazy zoning law, this specific property can be used either for residential or business. In addition, this top room has a matching basement right underneath."

Everywhere he scanned screamed, "Don't get this place!" There was no glimmer of hope to be found. No sooner had he thought that, than he saw something sparkle in the distance of this dreary room, almost like a gold piece stuffed inside a dungeon.

Sifu whispered, "Well, this is interesting," as he began walking to the only bright part of the room. Several feet later, he saw what it was. He turned around to the realtor and said, "There's a kitchen? A professional one?"

The realtor peered over to see what Sifu was looking at. "Hmm." She reached into her purse and pulled out her pad, but she did not see any information what this place was used for before. Thinking quick on her feet, she used it as a good angle to sell the place. "I'm not sure why there's a kitchen, but depending on how you look at it, this could be a good thing."

She flashed Sifu a winning smile. "Any chance you cook, Mr. Kwan?" She fervently hoped that the answer was yes.

Sifu replied, "I know how to cook, but I've never done anything professionally." He spent the next several minutes walking around the top floor, examining areas that most people would consider untouchable. Cobwebs seemed to cover every room from top to bottom, and the dust all over would be an allergy sufferer's worst nightmare. The realtor was studying his actions, gauging whether this would end up a sale. Sifu broke the silence, startling her. "You said there was a basement?"

The realtor replied, "Yes, I believe it's somewhere over here." She turned on more lights and fought through thick cobwebs as she saw a door leading to the basement. She said, "Right this way, Mr. Kwan."

Sifu looked down the pitch black steps and turned to the realtor to state, "Kinda scary."

She smiled and turned on the lights. "There, that looks a lot better." She grimaced after seeing what was down there and hoped that Sifu didn't catch her reaction.

Sifu shouted, "Is anyone down there?" He waited for a second, but fortunately no one responded. Sifu walked down the old steps till he got to the bottom floor.

Once there, Sifu said, "I thought the top floor looked bad, but this is—"

The realtor cut him off, "Sorry to interrupt. I know it needs a ton of work, but it does come at a good price, don't you think?" She flashed the overall price on her pad for Sifu to see.

Sifu ignored her words, seeming unconcerned about the price as he walked to the center of the room. There, he closed his eyes and stood eerily still in place. Several minutes passed as the silence made for an uncomfortable tension. Unsure whether she should disturb him or not, the realtor hesitantly asked, "Mr. Kwan, is everything okay?" She tapped him on the shoulder.

Sifu paused before answering and let out a slow breath. "Everything's okay; I'm just trying to feel for something."

The realtor wasn't sure what that meant, but she stood there alongside Sifu. She looked around the basement some more, staying relatively close to his presence, while Sifu continued standing in silence. The realtor again interrupted, "Mr. Kwan,

I've got other listings we can check out tomorrow that are much better than this if you like. Might I suggest we–"

Sifu held his hand up and smiled. He had felt enough and trusted in that. "I don't know why, but ... I'll take it." Relief fell over the realtor's face, as the sound of money rang silently in her head.

Just like that, the beginning of something new had started.

> *"You must constantly look around as opportunity exist all the time, not just once in a lifetime." –Sifu*